ILL WIND

A Deuce Mora Mystery, Volume 4

by

Jean Heller

This is a work of fiction.
With the exception of some Chicago landmarks and commercial
establishments, similarities to real people, places, and events are
entirely coincidental.

ILL WIND

Copyright 2020 Jean Heller

First edition February 2020

ISBN: 978-1-7327252-3-2

For America's newspapers
and the dedicated journalists
who still seek truth and justice for all.

1

The body hung against the façade of an office building, too far up the glass wall to be illuminated by streetlamps, their glow smothered in the gloom of a snowy night. The man's form emerged as a ghostly and nightmarish spectacle only when a steel-gray dawn began to shoulder aside the darkness.

The noose trenched into the neck had been fashioned in a hangman's knot of braided rope. The corpse reminded me of a grisly rag doll, swaying and twisting erratically in an early morning squall that blustered ashore off Lake Michigan and ricocheted among the high-rise towers of Chicago's Loop.

I shivered hard as I stood in Federal Plaza next to the Kluczynski Federal Office Building and the bright red Alexander Calder sculpture called "Flamingo." To me the fifty-three-foot-tall artwork looked more like a giant flower wilted under a brutal August sun. But it wasn't August; it was April. And it wasn't sunny; it was dismally overcast and continuing to spit sleet and snow. Though I was five long blocks from the shore of a raging Lake Michigan, it wasn't nearly far enough to buffer me from the wind.

My body chilled to the marrow of my bones, but my gut churned up a fiery eruption of disbelief and grief.

I hadn't gotten out of a warm bed to sightsee a famous Calder sculpture. I stood in the brutal weather because I'd gotten a rollout call from someone able to identify the dead man in the emerging dawn and recognize that he was a friend of mine.

The body had exited the federal building through a fourteenth-story window, the rope tied off somewhere inside. The frame was clear of glass, suggesting the window had been removed with a glass cutter rather than a hammer, possibly a precaution against leaving behind embedded shards that could slice through the rope and foil the hanging. The dislodged window had shattered over a wide area of the plaza 180 feet below the dead man's feet. His body had come to rest against the exterior of another window two stories down. It hit the window so hard its glass cracked in the pattern of an automobile windshield struck by a rock.

The icy wind whipped tears from my eyes, but the wind wasn't responsible for all of them. They were warm when they squeezed through my lashes. They turned cold as they mixed with snow melting on my skin and sliding to my jaw. I raised a glove and wiped them away, but they kept coming.

Images of my experience with the dead man flowed like a slide show from my memory. He had been a courageous news source, a partner in uncovering solutions to difficult mysteries, and a very good friend. Former FBI Special Agent Carl Cribben was one of the gutsiest people I had ever known.

And now he was dead, hanging by a noose, his face disfigured, his neck twisted at an impossible angle, his hands bent and claw-like. He wore only a white long-sleeved dress shirt with sleeves rolled to the elbows, gray slacks, and black laced dress shoes. I hoped he wasn't cold and wondered where that ridiculous thought came from.

Carl was not a man to commit suicide, and certainly not this way, grim and ostentatious and disrespectful of the city he loved. I knew he had been murdered.

I felt the hollow pain of loss.

And the hot bristle of rage.

2

Three days earlier...

I met Carl Cribben for lunch at the Mai Tai Sushi and Sake Bar on Wabash on one of the nicest April days to grace Chicago this year. Almost 100 years ago, T.S. Eliot published a poem called, "The Waste Land," in which the first line was, "April is the cruelest month." Eliot's masterpiece wasn't about the weather, but that first line generally fits Chicago during the first full month of spring. The weather will whipsaw between gorgeous and desperately uncomfortable in the space of a few hours.

The day I met Carl was at the gorgeous end of the spectrum. Because the forecast for the rest of the week predicted a return to the desperately uncomfortable, we decided to take advantage of the break from the cold and eat at an outside table in the sun. Despite the nice temperatures, I wore a jacket as protection against the light breeze.

Carl and his wife, Nancy, had just returned from a two-week vacation in Belize that coincided with Congress's Easter recess. Carl was nicely tanned but not burned as he might have been from lying on a beach the entire time. I wondered aloud if he'd been playing golf.

"Yes," he said, "and tennis. And deep-sea fishing. And hiking and sight-seeing."

I asked about Nancy.

"Same itinerary," he said with a big smile. "We're pretty much into the same things. Except shopping. That's her thing exclusively."

That didn't surprise me. Nancy Cribben was an accomplished athlete and always well turned out no matter what she wore.

Cribben, a Chicago native, was retired FBI. He had been in charge of the

Bureau's Las Vegas field office when he turned in his badge at age fifty-five. I met him a year later when I sought his help on a news story. He provided a huge assist as I struggled to figure out how three ghastly murder events spanning nearly sixty years could be tied together. We had been good friends since.

"Are you back in Chicago for good," I asked, "or is this a stopover to do laundry?"

He laughed, which he didn't do often. It was a good laugh that showed off good teeth and great laugh lines beside his mouth and blue-gray eyes.

"Laundry," he said. "And we're going to close up the house for a while. Nancy finally agreed to put aside her distaste for our nation's capital and come to Washington with me for the duration of my business there. I want to be close to Shiloh, too. He's not getting any younger, and I don't want to miss any more of his life."

Shiloh was Carl's handsome Labrador retriever and definitely an integral part of the Cribben household.

We sipped hot tea as we awaited the arrival of our sushi and green curry. A deep shadow crossed my friend's face.

I cocked my head in question, though I didn't give voice to my concern. My natural journalist's curiosity wanted an explanation, but Carl wasn't a man to be pushed. If something was bothering him, he would tell me if he wanted me to know.

"Why did you pick Belize?" I asked, trying to draw his attention back to the table.

He didn't answer. I waited for a bit then interrupted his reverie.

"Deuce to Carl," I said. "Are you out there?"

His eyes refocused on mine, and he looked embarrassed.

"Sorry," he said as our server set a plate of sushi on the table between us. It was meant to be a prelude to the curry, though I knew I'd be taking the curry home for dinner.

"You were off on another planet there for a bit," I said.

"Yeah. What did you ask?"

"Why did you pick Belize?"

"Oh. Nancy and I are both goofy for Mayan ruins, and they're all over

Belize. There was one cave we wanted to see in particular, called Actun Tunichil Muknal. It's fascinating."

"Actun who?"

"The translation's probably easier. The Cave of the Crystal Sepulchre. It's full of artifacts. Ceramics, stoneware, skeletons, bats, otters, and the biggest freaking spiders I've ever seen. There's also a two-mile-long river you have to swim in places. On dry land you've got to take your shoes off and walk around in socks because some careless tourists have damaged a few skeletons by stepping on them. There's one skeleton, a teen-age girl who was probably sacrificed, whose bones have calcified until they sparkle like crystals. She's known as The Crystal Maiden."

"Sounds lovely," I said, trying to sound sarcastic. "Especially the spiders part."

"Maybe you've gotta be there," he said with a shrug.

Carl laid his chopsticks on his plate and pinched the bridge of his nose. "I'm sorry I'm so distracted. I need to get back to Washington as fast as we can close up the house."

I didn't realize what I was getting into when I asked, "So without going into classified material, how's the investigation going?"

His eyes snapped to mine again, and he frowned. "That's why I have to get back to D.C. We've got a world of trouble, and it can only get worse."

* * *

I used my chopsticks to mix green wasabi horseradish into a little cup with soy sauce for dipping the sushi. I picked up two slices of rainbow roll and two slices of dragon roll and put them on my plate. I was ready to start eating. Carl sat and looked pensive.

When he finally moved to take some of the food, he talked to me without looking at me. I gave him the benefit of the doubt and decided he was trying to concentrate so he didn't drip soy sauce on his shirt.

"I don't want to drag you into this, Deuce. You're a terrific reporter and one of the most natural detectives I've ever met. The investigation itself isn't secret anymore, but the findings, subjects, and procedures are. I can't talk about them, even friend-to-friend. I hope you understand."

"Do you want to talk friend-to-friend without going into anything classified? I have a working set of sympathetic ears."

I chewed a slice of rainbow roll, one topped with yellowtail that was as fresh and creamy as any raw fish I'd ever eaten.

"If you'd rather not, I understand," I added.

"No, I don't mind talking to you in generalities. But I can't answer any questions about the substance of the investigation."

I waited and watched his eyes. He kept them on his food. He took a whole slice of dragon roll and popped it in his mouth, delaying whatever he wanted to say. When he spoke, his voice was so low I could barely hear him. There was no one sitting near enough to eavesdrop, but Carl was a cautious man by nature.

"While I was out of the country, two key witnesses died."

"Really? How?" I asked.

For some reason he looked annoyed. "They went from being alive to being not alive."

"I think I got that part."

"That part is all we know. Autopsies on both of them found no obvious causes of death. Not even a hint. Their hearts stopped. But neither had heart problems. Tox studies found nothing suspicious in their systems. There were no marks on them. No bleeding inside or out. There's no reason for them to be dead, but dead they are."

"Well, you were out of the country, so you're not a suspect."

I was trying to lighten the mood, but from the look on Carl's face, I made it worse.

I tried another tack.

"The obvious questions I would ask, if I were going to ask you any questions, which I'm not, are how much time separated their deaths, did they die in proximity to one another, did they know one another, and who might have had reason to kill them? Also, what roles would they have played in your investigation had they lived?"

Carl flashed a wry smile. "I'm glad you're not going to ask. I can answer a few of your 'unasked questions.' The two thugs died a little more than three weeks and a fair number of miles apart. They did know each other, but I don't know how well. I can't tell you who had a reason to kill them because that's classified. But you're a smart lady. You might be able to figure it out. They were about to flip on the top leaders of one of Chicago's biggest Mob operations. In Chapter Four of your Junior G-Man Handbook, it tells you this is a clue that makes murder an obvious possibility."

"What are you asking me to do?"

Carl shook his head and sat back in his chair. "Nothing, really. It might help us in solving the murders to know what could have killed them without leaving a trace. Knowing how they were killed could lead us to an M.O. that could lead us to the people who did the deed. Our forensics people have no clue. Unless you're an expert on exotic means of murder, I don't expect you to come up with answers, either, though you do tend to pull rabbits out of hats at times. I just needed to unload my frustration on somebody."

I said, "With no entry wounds from a knife, no gunshot wounds, no burns from electric shocks, poison is about the only option left. But you said..."

"No traces of common poisons or other toxic substances in their blood."

"Common poisons?" I asked. "Maybe the toxicologists should widen the search to the uncommon. If the killers are trying to throw you off track, maybe they used venom from a snake found only in the Antarctic."

Carl shook his head in exasperation. "There are no snakes in the Antarctic."

"That you know of," I said. "I know I'm sounding flip, but I was making a serious point. There must be thousands of toxins in the world we wouldn't expect to show up in the bodies of murder victims in Chicago."

"We've already widened the search twice with the help of a couple of zoo biologists from California," Carl said. "Still got nothing."

"Have you ruled out suicide?" I asked. "Maybe the Mob found out they were flipping and was closing in on them. Maybe they chose to go out on their own terms."

"There aren't that many ways to commit suicide, Deuce. You put a gun to your head, a knife to your chest, you sit in your car with the motor running in a closed garage, you step in front of a bus, you jump off a bridge, you leap into the river and inhale it, or you drink drain cleaner. All of those methods leave traces, some more obvious than others but all readily apparent. At the risk of repeating myself, we got nuthin'."

"Well, if anything else comes up you can discuss with me, I hope you will. One thing tends to lead to another."

We spent the rest of lunch talking about the Cribbens' vacation in Belize. Crystalized skeletons and giant spiders aside, it sounded like a place I should put on my bucket list.

After lunch we walked together toward the lot where my car was parked. It was on Carl's way to an "L" station a few blocks north.

We stopped at Wabash and Congress, and I took Carl's arm. I broached a subject I didn't really want to raise. "Are you in danger?"

He gave me a slight shrug. "Who knows?"

"Can you walk away?"

"Quitting isn't my style any more than it's yours."

The light changed and we started across the street.

He asked, "On a happier note, I hope, how's Mark?"

"Way out of town, unfortunately."

My partner was in California teaching a series of arson seminars. He wouldn't be back until mid-May.

"Bummer. Tell him I'm sorry I missed him this trip. Well, I'd better get going. Packing awaits."

I hadn't taken my hand from Carl's arm.

"Can I give you a ride to the train?"

"Thanks, but it's only a few blocks. Maybe the walk will help clear the fog out of my brain and provide a sudden useful insight."

He paused, then turned to face me and enveloped me in a big hug. I returned it. When we broke, he slid his hands down to my waist then backed away.

"Take it easy, kid," he said. "I'll call the next time I'm in town."

I replied, "Give my love to Nancy. And Shiloh."

He waved as he walked away.

It was the last time I saw him alive.

3

The present...

It had been four bleak days since Carl Cribben died. I'd not had the opportunity to get up to Rogers Park, the neighborhood at the extreme north end of the city where Carl and Nancy lived, to pay my respects to the family. I had called, but one of their sons said Nancy was near a breakdown and didn't want to see anyone but her children and her brother. There would be a wake for Carl today. Apparently, Nancy resisted attending. But since it would be held at her home, she didn't have much choice.

"Mom refuses to leave the house," Josh Cribben said, his voice cracking. "She refuses to accept reality. She keeps thinking Dad is going to walk in the door. She sits out by the pool and cries all day and roams the house and cries all night. Even Shiloh can't help her. He knows something's wrong. He just lies next to Dad's chair and broods."

That was the end of it. It made my heart hurt.

Now I was sitting in the reception area for the offices of the United States Attorney for the Northern District of Illinois waiting for my old federal prosecutor friend, Jerry Alvarez. We planned to drive together to the wake. Jerry had given me a tip a while back on what he thought might make a decent human-interest story. When I finally got around to checking it out, it led me into a labyrinth of treachery, deceit, and murder. It was while reporting that story that I first met Carl.

I hadn't seen Jerry for a while, so I was shocked when he walked toward me. Jerry had stopped growing vertically at five-foot-five, but he had continued growing horizontally and couldn't seem to stop the weight gains. Now he appeared to have dropped at least fifty pounds. He was lighter on his feet, and his color was great. I smiled for what felt like the first time in a week.

"Wow," was all I could think of to say for a moment. He took my hands and craned his neck toward my face. I bent down and kissed him on the cheek. I'm six feet tall. Kissing a man seven inches shorter is an awkward maneuver.

I waved my hand across his chest. "Tell me this was on purpose. You're not sick or anything, are you?"

Jerry smiled broadly. "Nope. I have a new love in my life. *Tengo un nuevo amor en mi vida.* She motivates me. And I'm going to ask her to marry me. *Casarte conmingo.*"

Jerry was second-generation Mexican-American, and he spoke his family's native language flawlessly. He spoke English flawlessly, too, which embarrassed me. I noted once that I could stuff my knowledge of Spanish into a taco shell without it spilling over. I didn't consider this a good thing since Chicago has a large Mexican community, and it would have been nice to be able to converse with some of our readers in their native language.

Jerry had developed a habit of saying something in English and then translating it to Spanish. Perhaps it stemmed from growing up in a bi-lingual household where the children spoke English, the parents spoke some of each, and the grandparents spoke only Spanish.

Jerry was fifty-seven now, maybe late to start a family, but not out of the question.

"I want to hear all about her," I said. "But let's talk while we drive. I'm double parked downstairs, and I'm hoping the press shield on the visor will keep the meter thugs at bay. By the way, congrats again on the promotion."

About two weeks earlier Jerry had been named an assistant U.S. attorney. His specialty would be white-collar crime and racketeering. I'd called to congratulate him, but he was in court, so I sent him an email. This was the first time I'd had a chance to congratulate him in person.

When we got downstairs there were no nastygrams under my wipers, and we set off. I worked my way over to East Randolph Street at the top of Grant Park and entered Lake Shore Drive northbound.

"So, tell me about her, Jerry," I said when I'd settled into traffic.

"Her name is Sara Asturias, like the province of Spain. She's a translator. She's fifteen years younger than I am, divorced, two children, one in college, another about to be."

"Ouch. Two at once. She marrying you for your money?"

Jerry chuffed and went quiet. He turned and gazed out at the expanse of Lake Michigan, in inland freshwater sea scoured out by glaciers and today sparkling turquoise under a cold, bright spring sun.

"Let's talk about something else," he said. "It doesn't feel right, given where we're going, to be discussing how happy I am."

I glanced at him in surprise. "Carl would be happy for you."

"It doesn't feel right. *No se siente bien.*"

We both fell quiet. My emotions whipsawed between happiness for Jerry and painful sorrow for Carl. I finally let my heart choose where it wanted to go, and it chose Carl.

"Why is this a wake and not a funeral?" I asked.

"A lot of Roman Catholics have both," he said. "It might be a while before there's a funeral." He didn't offer to elaborate. So, I pressed.

"Why is that?"

"The ME hasn't been able to determine the cause of death and won't release the body until he's made a final determination. Or gives up and admits it will forever be a mystery. Whichever way it goes, it looks like it might take a while."

"Just like Carl's two witnesses, who died while he and Nancy were on vacation," I said. "There's speculation that Carl committed suicide. I guess that's to be expected."

Jerry turned to look at me. "That explanation satisfy you?"

I had to admit it didn't. "Carl never seemed like a suicide candidate. I understand he could have hidden his guilt or depression or whatever. But he was more likely to fight than to give up on life. I had lunch with him a couple of days before he died. He was mostly upbeat because he'd finally prevailed on Nancy to move to Washington with him. He was worried about one aspect of the investigation, but he wouldn't tell me much about it."

"The two witnesses?"

I knew Jerry was still looking at me, so I just nodded.

"That's the context that makes me doubt suicide," I said. "If the two guys flipping on the Mob died mysteriously and without obvious cause, I have to at least consider the same thing happened to Carl. Dying wasn't his idea."

"Did he express any concerns to you?"

I told Jerry everything Carl told me. Then I asked, "What do you know about the events that led up to Carl's death?"

"You're beginning to sound like a cop, you know that?"

"Could be worse," I said. "I could sound like a used car salesman on late-night TV."

"Your wardrobe isn't stupid enough."

"So what do you know?"

"Actually, the U.S. Attorney's office isn't involved in this case—yet—and won't be unless somebody develops evidence of a federal crime. Right now we have three bodies and no idea how any of them died. But we suspect homicide, so we're sitting in on the investigation. Observing only at this point."

"Isn't the murder of a federal investigator a federal crime?"

"It would be if the medical examiner rules that Carl was murdered and if there's strong evidence his death was connected to his investigation. But Tony Donato hasn't given us a cause of death yet."

"I repeat, can you tell me what you know?"

"As long as it doesn't go any farther than the interior of your car."

"Promise."

"You already know everything I know about the deaths of the button men, which is pretty much nothing. Somebody was gonna get crushed when the two of 'em flipped, and whoever that is had plenty of motive for murder. But motive is only a third of the trilogy. We still need means and opportunity. And a suspect would be nice."

"Wouldn't the suspect or suspects be identified in Carl's investigative files?"

"There are plenty of names in the files, but without proof of a crime, none of them are suspects. You can't have a suspect without an evidentiary link to a provable crime. We're going through the files now, and we're running in circles.

I thought about that for a moment. Then I suggested that somebody talk to the other investigators on Carl's team. Surely, they could help.

"They could," Jerry said. "But they won't until we show them cause, which would be proof of foul play. They're protecting the integrity of their investigation, which is probably the same thing I'd do in their shoes."

"What about Carl?"

"Well, I'm sure he didn't commit suicide. First, like you said, it's not like him. Second, there's no suicide note. Most suicides leave notes, but nobody's found one in any of the places Carl might have left it, including his pockets. Given how close Carl and Nancy were, it's hard to believe he wouldn't have left some last words for her. If this was a murder, the who and the how are only part of the mystery. There's one even larger. *Un gran misterioso.* The door of the office where this happened was locked. From the inside. There was no other way in or out but that one door. And, of course, the window."

I glanced over at him. "So the killers did their thing and used a key to lock the door when they left."

"Not according to the woman who occupied the office. She said she had added two locks to the original one. One of them was a chain, and the other was a heavy-duty deadbolt. Building security had a master that fit the original lock. But she insists she had the only key to the new deadbolt. And yet that's the only one of the three locks that was secure when the first responders got to the scene."

I felt confused. "Run that by me again."

"Forget the original deadbolt and the chain lock," Jerry said. "Focus on the new deadbolt. To lock or unlock it from the inside, you simply used a knob to turn the bolt into or out of the frame. Once retracted, the door remained unlocked until it was locked again. To relock it from the inside, as I said, you have to turn the knob again. *But* to lock or unlock it from the outside you need a key."

"And the tenant is sure she never gave a copy of the key to anyone, including security, and didn't lose it or have it stolen?"

"Very sure. She showed it to the responding detectives."

"You're telling me the killer, who could not have had a copy of that key, nonetheless locked the door from the outside when he or she left."

"Yes. I'm also telling you that doesn't seem possible."

"Could the killer have let himself down from the window with a rope?"

"There was no second rope. How did he tie the rope off inside the office, scale down the outside of the building, and then untie the rope and take it with him? But in case there's a way, the forensics crew is checking the window frame for rope fibers or anything else that might have been left behind."

"A classic locked room mystery. They happen sometimes in fiction, and the explanation is always ridiculous. This isn't fiction. You have my attention."

"I figured."

I ran through recollections of all the door locks I'd ever used. I couldn't think of a single one that you could lock from the inside while you were standing on the outside.

"Whose office was it?"

"No one with the slightest connection to any of this. I think she works for the USDA. Counting pigs in Indiana, or something."

He looked over at me again. "There's one other thing you should know, Deuce. It pretty much cements the conclusion that Carl didn't kill himself."

His voice sounded ominous.

"What?" I asked.

"When Carl went out that window, he was already dead."

4

"What do you mean you can't talk to me about this, Tony?" I demanded. "I'm not here as a reporter. Carl Cribben was my friend."

Anthony Donato, the Cook County medical examiner, looked dubious and troubled. It was the day after the memorial for Carl, a full-out Irish wake that had none of the aspects that make an Irish wake a memorable, cathartic event. What should have been a respectful, and even a jocular remembrance of a friend, a family member, was solemn to the point of depressing. The prayers and tears came wrapped in disbelief and anger. The family priest was there, but no one introduced us. Everyone in attendance seemed immobilized by grief.

I had joined the receiving line with Jerry and Ron Colter, the head of the Chicago division of the FBI. Colter and I had met under terrible circumstances, and I found him initially to be arrogant, devious, and cold. After our last adventure together, which almost killed us both, we had become friends. He was the one who rousted me from bed the morning Carl died. He stood in front of me in the receiving line.

Nancy was sitting in a lone chair in the middle of her living room. Family members hovered nearby. Nobody introduced me to them, either. There was no casket. Her late husband still occupied a steel drawer in Tony Donato's morgue.

Ron took her hands and spoke quietly to her. Tears began running down her cheeks.

"What am I going to do, Ron?" she asked in misery.

He got down on one knee. "Lean on me," he said. "I'm here. All Carl's friends at the Bureau are here. Whatever you need."

"I need my husband."

"I know. I'm so sorry, Nancy."

Her face didn't contort in a fit of crying, but the tears continued washing over her cheeks. She used a handkerchief to try to wipe them away before they dripped onto the black skirt of her dress, but she couldn't catch them all. I wondered if the human body could produce tears indefinitely. I hoped for Nancy's sake the answer was no.

I talked with her briefly. She looked at me as if she wasn't sure where she'd seen me before though we had met and socialized several times. She wore no makeup. She looked unkempt, a total departure from her norm, and I wished for her that the wake would end soon. When Jerry and I left we both felt distraught at the circumstances that laid such a path of destruction through a loving family.

And now the ME, a man who had always trusted me, was giving me a cold shoulder.

"Look, Tony, I know you haven't figured out yet who and what killed Carl, but I also know that you've determined Carl was already dead when he went out the window. Doesn't that sort of suggest murder?"

His head snapped up. "Who told you that? That he was dead before he was hanged?"

"Does it matter? Is it true?"

"Deuce, don't put yourself through this. You're grieving like a reporter. Try grieving like a friend."

"How do you know, Tony? That Carl was dead when he went out the window?"

He sighed and shrugged. "The ligature marks. There was no bruising around them. In order to have bruising you have to have blood moving through the body. Dead hearts don't pump blood, and it takes only about ten minutes for all the blood to drain from the head and neck of a body in an upright position. So Carl must have been dead, maybe propped up in a chair, for at least ten minutes before he went out the window. About the length of time it would take someone to cut the glass from the window frame."

"I know you're doing a tox screen."

Tony nodded. "Multiple tox screens. So far, all we have is a lot of nothing."

"What's your speculation?"

"We don't speculate, Deuce. We investigate. We're testing for some of the deadliest poisons on earth. Batrachotoxin, for one, a very fast killer found on the skin of a few species of frogs, none indigenous to the United States, thankfully. There's one little guy in Columbia small enough to sit on the tip of your finger, but I wouldn't allow it. He has enough deadly toxin on his skin to kill a couple dozen people or several elephants."

"How would that stuff get to Chicago? Smugglers?"

"Sure. We're also looking at nerve agents, like the VX that killed Kim Jong-un's half-brother. Funguses, bacteria, viruses, they're all in the running. Most of them—actually all of them we've got on our list—leave some traces that wouldn't show up in a normal tox panel because we wouldn't be looking for them. Now we are. Looking, but not finding."

"So, what killed him?"

Tony shook his head again.

"Not a damned thing we've found. And not a damned thing I can imagine."

5

I sat slumped at my desk later that day, trying at once to wrap my head around three mysterious deaths and fleshing out a column for the next day. I wanted to write about Carl, but I couldn't. I had given Jerry and Tony my word that I wouldn't violate their confidences.

My newspaper, the Chicago *Journal*, carried a lengthy account of Carl's life and death. It shaped up to be a rather spectacular story. Two of our police reporters wrote it and quoted police officials as saying the case was being investigated as a homicide, though they emphasized there wasn't yet a final conclusion. The hint of foul play in the death of a former high-ranking federal agent, especially given his involvement in a lengthy, ongoing examination of organized crime, drew a lot of media attention from all over the country.

I had asked to be left out of any role in the coverage. My editor agreed. He understood that I was too involved emotionally to be impartial. When our reporters weren't getting anything useful from the FBI and sought my assistance, I declined. I had no desire to serve as an intermediary. That didn't make me any new friends among the younger reporters looking for a scoop. They'd get over it.

I began a column about a Chicago City Council member—though in my city we call them aldermen—from the upper northwest side. She got caught with her hand deep in a cookie jar and had the lid slammed on her fingers. It was no surprise that authorities found corruption in the dealings of yet another Chicago pol, especially this one. What I found stunning was how completely she turned her back on the matter, blaming everyone in her life except herself, and refusing to stand down from office even for the duration of the probe into her finances. This trouble had been developing for her for years. Her daddy was a rich and famous hedge fund operator who had lined the pockets of many of the powerful in our city, and she hid behind him and his connections most of the time. This time I didn't see how she was going to wiggle out of it.

"How you doin'?"

I hadn't seen my editor, Eric Ryland, approaching my desk, and I was so deep into my own head that his voice made me jump.

"Didn't mean to startle you," he said. "I need to know if you're up to writing a column for tomorrow. You can take a day off if you want."

I shook my head. "I'm good. I'm writing now." I told him about the subject matter.

"I like it," he said. "I don't have to remind you, but I will anyway, she hasn't been convicted of anything yet, and it's not our place to act as judge and jury."

"You mean I can't write that's she's an amoral bitch, a thief, and a liar who deserves about ten years at Logan?"

Logan Correctional was a women's prison in Lincoln, Illinois about two and a half hours southwest of Chicago on the highway to the state capital in Springfield. I thought the location of a prison between Chicago and Springfield to be both prescient and appropriate. The cities were the two greatest sources of crime in the state. Having the prison between them was convenient and saved on travel expense tabs picked up by taxpayers.

"Probably not," Eric said sarcastically. "Maybe I'd better edit this one myself."

He watched me for a bit then asked, "You sure you're okay?"

"No," I said, sounding snappish. "I'm not okay. I'm angry and frustrated and sad. Did you really think I'd be okay?"

"All right then. I'll be leaving now." He turned and walked away, checking around us to see if anyone had overheard the exchange.

* * *

When I finished the column, I called Chicago Police Sgt. Pete Rizzo, who served as the department's chief spokesman. Pete was a good guy who had been forced into a desk job after a gang member ran him down during a traffic stop of another gang member. Pete's body would never fully recover, and his choice became a desk job or a disability retirement. He took the desk job, and he was good at it.

"Hey, Deuce," he said when he picked up. "What have you planned to ruin my day?"

"I have a tricky request, Pete, one I know you will treat with the grace, style, and sarcasm you always bring to my simple reporter's requests. Unless it's one of those times when you hang up on me."

"I never hang up on you, though occasionally I've been known to drop the receiver—accidentally of course—and have it fall into the phone's cradle."

"Is this going to be one of those times?"

"Let's hope not, for both our sakes. On the other hand, why should I expect today to be different from all other days?"

"You shouldn't," I said honestly. "I'm wondering if there's any chance I can see the office in the federal building where Carl Cribben died."

"Jesus, Deuce, no," he said. "It's a crime scene. Not even the person who occupies that office can get in. She's probably working from home for the duration."

"She works for the U.S. Agriculture Department, right?"

"I think so."

"Do you know her name?"

"Not off the top of my head. Why?"

"I might want to talk to her at some point."

Pete sighed the sigh of an exasperated man. "She's been interviewed by the police and the FBI. It's my understanding she has absolutely nothing to do with this."

"Still,..." I said.

"I'll see if I can get her information without leaving a trail that leads back to me."

I nodded to no one in particular. "Also, is there a way you can find out the make and model of the lock on her office door, the one that was locked when your guys first responded to the call?"

"Now you're trying to cost me my job. Again."

"You say that every time we talk."

"Because every time you call, I feel forced retirement closing in."

"So you'll become CEO of your own private investigations firm and make a ton of money. Will you even remember to thank me?"

"No, and I won't feel obligated to take your calls anymore, either."

"I love you, too, Pete. Talk soon."

I hung up before he could mount a comeback.

6

I pressed myself into the deep cushions of my sofa and tucked my favorite old quilt tighter around me. The gas fireplace worked hard to erase the chill from my living room, but in an old house that had settled over the decades, tight windows were a luxury of the past. I'd been thinking about having all the windows replaced, but I got three estimates for the cost of the job, and each of them made me think it made more sense to stay cold.

Maybe next year.

I felt warmer for a little while, while I was on the phone with Mark. He'd called a little after 9 p.m. to see how I was doing and what, if anything, was new in the investigation of Carl Cribben's death. I told him what I knew, which wasn't much additional insight since our previous conversation.

"How're you feeling?" he asked.

I said, "Like I want to rip somebody's head off. And I'm very, very lonely."

"Why don't you get on a plane and come out here for a while," he suggested. "I think I can help with the lonely part. They've put me in a nice apartment. It's not big, but with only Murphy and me living here it feels empty."

"You're busy, Mark. We wouldn't have much time together."

"I'll make time."

"I wish. But I can't leave now."

"Are you working on Carl's story?"

"No, I'm too angry and depressed to stay impartial."

"Probably better you leave it to somebody else. But if you're not working on that story, why can't you come visit?"

I didn't have a good answer. I didn't want to tell him that even though others were covering Carl's death, I didn't want to get too far away from developments. So I didn't say anything, and he dropped the subject.

We chatted for another twenty minutes and ended the call. My house felt empty. If I felt lonely and sad earlier, the feelings redoubled now.

My cats, Caesar and Cleo, had nested deep in the quilt and slept through my conversation with Mark. Now Cleo deigned to disturb herself. She stood up, stretched, peered into my eyes, and crawled up on my chest where she pushed her head into my face, kneaded at my shoulder for a minute, then nestled down to purr and sleep. It was her way of telling me someone in the house loved me.

I stared into the fire feeling incomparably sorry for myself. The phone rang again.

Unknown caller.

I sent it to voice mail. I was in no mood to talk to anyone who wasn't Mark, and he wouldn't be calling again tonight. Certainly not from a phone that wasn't in my contacts list.

It rang again.

I sent it to voice mail again.

The third time I frowned at the screen and answered.

"What?" If it was a human solicitor, I was prepared to cut off his junk and feed it to my cats. Virtually speaking.

The caller didn't introduce himself. He didn't need to. I recognized the voice.

"You busy right now?"

"Yes. I'm perfecting the art of lying on my sofa, feeling sorry for myself, and staring into the fireplace at the same time. It's an exercise in attention management."

"Can you meet me in about an hour?"

"What? Why? It's almost ten o'clock now."

"I need to talk to you, and I need to do it in a place that will be deserted and dark."

"Wow, that sounds like fun. A little weird for a first date though."

"Deuce."

"Where and when?"

He told me, which surprised me even more.

* * *

The place was a parking garage near the corner of Halsted and North Avenue in Lincoln Park. It was part of a Bank of America complex. I knew it well because it was behind my favorite kitchen store, Sur La Table, and across the street from an Apple store. It also sat just south of a block of Halsted filled with great theaters and restaurants, most of which I frequented often. A most dangerous neighborhood for my budget. At this late hour, though, all my temptations were closed or closing, so my checkbook was safe.

My caller had told me to come to the area of the garage that accessed the bank drive-through lanes. At this time of night they would be deserted. Other areas of the garage might still house the cars of theater-goers having a late, post-curtain supper.

The only vehicle in the bank area was a white Subaru Outback. I pulled up next to it.

The driver looked over at me as if to let me see his face and confirm his identity. Since he didn't make a move to come to me, I got out of my car and into the passenger seat of his. He stared straight ahead for a moment then asked a question I never expected.

"Is there a story behind your name?"

"Mora?"

He glanced at me with impatience. "Deuce."

"Is that why I'm sitting in a dark parking garage with the district director of the FBI, so we can discuss my name? At eleven-ten at night? Really?"

Ron Colter dropped his head. "I'm building up to the reason I called. Indulge me."

I repeated the explanation I gave each of the hundreds of times I'd been asked before. I was the second born of fraternal twins. My parents named my brother Gary, but they hadn't decided what to name me. My father started calling me Deuce. A hospital staffer heard him, took him seriously, and put the name on my birth certificate.

I added, "I get even by calling my brother, Uno."

"Then you should be, Due, uno being Italian for 'one,' and due being Italian for 'two.'"

"'Uno' is also Spanish for 'one.'"

"But you're at least part Italian. Hence, you should be 'Due.'"

"People might mistake me for one of Donald Duck's nephews."

He fell silent, and I'd had enough idle chat about cartoon characters.

I asked, "How are you feeling?"

He and I had been burned not long before in the process of taking down an arsonist. My injuries were minor and healed, leaving only a small scar on the inside of my left wrist. Ron had been burned on both arms, his upper chest, and the lower part of his neck. Some of his burns had required grafts.

"I'm doing fine," he said. "Still in physical therapy to get back as much flexibility as possible, but it's all good."

I had run out of things to talk about, so I demanded bluntly, "Why are we here?"

"I want to ask you to do something that you probably will want to do but which might violate your ethical rules as a journalist."

I felt myself frown. "That doesn't sound good."

"It has to do with Carl's death."

I felt myself cringe. "Why don't you tell me what it is before I say no."

"I hope you don't say no."

I hoped I would have that option. But if it had to do with Carl's death, it would be hard to turn my back on it.

I waited him out with my eyes glued to his face in the gloom of the garage. My mind drifted to Bob Woodward and his Deep Throat meetings in a much larger parking facility in the dark of night in Washington, D.C. discussing the Watergate presidential scandal of the 70s. I wasn't born then, but every reporter knew the story, saw the movie, and read the books. It was a major part of our craft's history and culture. I'd had my fill of major stories in the recent past and wasn't psyched for another. Still, I would hear out what Ron was leading up to—if he got to the point before I reached retirement age.

"There's someone I'd like you to interview without making it seem like an interview," he said. "It will take finesse and a big dose of empathy."

"So, who?"

"Her name is Emily Goodsill."

"Am I supposed to know her?"

"No. Not yet, anyway. She's from Walnut, Iowa, population around 800. It's west of Des Moines about two-thirds of the way from here to Nebraska. It's just south of I-80. In the summer you probably can't see it for the corn."

"You want me to go there?"

"No, Miss Goodsill is here, but I'm not sure for how long."

I snapped at him. "Stop gaming me, Ron. Get to the point."

"Wow, you're sure in a crappy mood."

"You don't know the half of it. Why did you call me out in the middle of the night?"

"When Emily Goodsill graduated from high school, she went off to community college. It was all her parents could afford. Her father was barely hanging onto his family farm, struggling to make it go by allowing an electrical co-op to build wind turbines in his cornfields. Her mother worked in an antique store in Walnut, a town I'm told is known for its fine Midwest antiquing. When Emily finished community college, she got a job at the Pottawattamie County ag extension office and enrolled in an online college where she earned a bachelor's degree in agriculture economics."

I now knew more about Emily Goodsill than I knew about most of my friends.

I asked, "Is there a point to this?"

"Ease up, Deuce. I'm coming to it. Emily was recruited by the USDA, the U.S. Agriculture Department, for a job managing farm subsidy programs in this region, and she came to the big city."

"I didn't know we had farm subsidies in Chicago," I said. "I didn't know we had farms in Chicago." An adrenaline rush stopped me, and my mind flashed back to a conversation I had with Jerry Alvarez while driving to Carl's wake. "It was her office?"

"Yep."

This was the woman I asked Pete Rizzo to identify for me. Now he was off the hook.

"And why," I asked, "do you want me to interview her? Isn't that your job?"

"It is, and we've tried. She's terrified of something she won't talk about. The two best agents I have tried to open her up. Nothing. We called in the best shrink we have in the country. She's known for her ability to get reluctant witnesses to remember things and talk about them. She had almost no luck at all with Emily Goodsill. That's why I'd like you to try. I've watched before how you handled reluctant witnesses—that street kid, Charles, and the witness from Missouri, Beth Daley. You have more empathy than anyone I've ever known."

I stared at my hands in my lap for a moment then said, "This feels like a pretty desperate long shot to me."

"It is," he said. "And it's made all the more desperate because you have to promise not to publish anything she tells you. You'd be endangering her life and possibly the investigation into Carl's death."

I blew out a deep breath. "Boy, you don't ask much."

We both fell silent for a moment. I had a question. I had nothing but questions.

"What makes you think she'll talk to me when she wouldn't talk to your pros?"

He shrugged. "I'm an optimist. I think the fact that you're *not* FBI gives you an edge. Some people have the impression that if they talk to the FBI and make even a small mistake they'll wind up in prison."

"They could be right."

"We don't consider a mistake to be a criminal act. Deliberately lying, yes. But not a momentary memory lapse."

"Have you asked her?"

"Not yet."

I turned in my seat to look Ron straight on. "You know it's almost unheard of for the FBI to involve a reporter in an investigation. Law enforcement and journalism usually have adversarial roles. Does Washington know you're asking me to do this?"

"No."

"Could you get into trouble?"

"Not unless you rat me out."

"And you trust me not to do that?"

"I do."

"It's intriguing, but I can't make a decision like this on my own. Reporters can't run around acting as agents for law enforcement. This is a decision well above my pay grade."

"Get a decision fast, Deuce. This woman is terrified. She might run back home to Walnut. Or she might run off somewhere we'll never find her again."

Z

I arrived at my desk in the *Journal's* newsroom shortly before 7:30 the next morning. Even at that I had to fuss around the house for a while to eat up time so I didn't raise any eyebrows over my early arrival, not that there were many eyebrows around at that hour.

It was after 1 a.m. when I got home from my clandestine meeting with Colter. When you expect to have trouble sleeping it becomes a self-fulfilling prophecy. I kept staring at the ceiling wondering how the hell I would approach Emily Goodsill, of the Walnut, Iowa Goodsills, on the unlikely chance she agreed to see me. What could I possibly say to her to get her to open up that professionals from the FBI overlooked? I'd had no Eureka moments on that score by 5 a.m., so I got out of bed and went about preparing for the new day.

I made it as far as the lobby of the *Journal* building when a security guard motioned me over to the big desk flanked by body scanners, facial recognition equipment, and metal detectors. These days, with armed crazies screaming that the media were the "enemies of the people," there was no such thing as being too careful. After a bomb was mailed to CNN a few months back, the *Journal* even installed scanners in the mail room.

"How're you doing this morning, Bobby?" I said to the guard about to go off duty.

"Surprised to see you this early, Deuce," he replied. "Something big goin' down?"

"The biggest thing that's happened to me was losing a night's sleep. If I get tired later, you suppose I could crawl under your desk and take a nap? Doing it in the newsroom would be too conspicuous."

"Well, I'll be gone in half an hour, but I'm sure Jamal and Steve would be amenable."

"Why'd you call me over?" I asked.

"Oh," Bobby said as if just remembering something important. "A man came in, wanted to talk to you. That was about 7 a.m. Let's see." He began rummaging for his log sheet. "Yeah, 6:58. Gave me this business card. Says his name's Steven Pace, and he's from the *Washington Chronicle* in D.C."

"I never heard of him," I said. "Did he say what he wanted?"

"No, ma'am. I told him you don't usually get in before nine-thirty or ten, depending on what's goin' on, and he'd have to come back later. He didn't seem to mind. He said he'd go get some breakfast and read the papers while he waited."

"I expect to be at my desk all morning if he shows up," I said. "Thanks."

I stopped in the second-floor cafeteria where I knew there would be fresh coffee and something packed with carbohydrates to eat. I never ate donuts, but the croissants were passable. I carried my breakfast to my desk where I sipped and munched while going through my personal stack of morning papers. I read my competitors in Chicago and the *New York Times* online, and a copy of the *Wall Street Journal* I borrowed from the business department. I would return it before any of them showed up. By the time I finished, it was nearly ten, and the newsroom was bustling as much as any newsroom can in this era of huge budget and staff cuts.

My mind drifted back to Emily Goodsill, but I shook her off and opened my computer, went to Google, and searched for Steven Pace of the *Washington Chronicle*. There was a lot of material from 1993 and 1994 when he apparently broke the biggest story of his career, an investigation of the cause of a horrific airliner crash at Dulles International Airport outside Washington. Aside from the huge number of people who died, the tale of Flight 1117 had additional tragic aspects that I was just getting into when the front desk called to say Pace had reappeared and was waiting in the lobby.

"Can he hear you?" I asked Jamal, the guard.

"No, Ma'am. He's standing over on the other side of the lobby, looking at the famous front pages on the walls."

"How does he look? Sane or dangerous?"

Jamal chuckled. "His card says he's a reporter from Washington, D.C."

"Anybody can make a card, Jamal," I said.

"Well, he looks a little worse for wear. But his demeanor is pleasant and low-key. He's not pushy. I'd say he's in his late fifties. Maybe sixty. Looks pretty fit. Talk to him down here where Steve and I can keep an eye on you."

"Thanks. I'll be down in five."

* * *

I saw Steven Pace as soon as I got off the elevator. At least I saw his back. He was wearing one of the uniforms of newspaper reporters: khaki slacks, a blue blazer, and cordovan loafers. He had a full head of graying hair that was slightly long, so it ran along the top of his collar. I couldn't see anything more. I glanced at Jamal and tilted my head once toward the visitor. Jamal nodded.

"Mr. Pace?" I said as I approached him.

He turned and smiled. "Steve, please. And you're Deuce Mora?"

We shook hands. His grip was dry and firm but not vice-like. He was an attractive man who looked to be aging well. He was a couple of inches shorter than me. The features that caught and held my attention were Pace's eyes. While the lower part of his face smiled, something in his eyes radiated enduring pain, like a man haunted.

"What can I do for you?" I asked.

"Is there some place I could buy you a coffee and have a conversation?"

"There's a cafeteria on the second floor."

He cleared his throat. "I'd rather do it away from the office."

My suspicions ticked up. "Why?"

"It's not a matter I want to be overheard discussing."

The connection between Washington and Carl Cribben clicked in my mind. I couldn't be certain that's what Pace wanted to talk about, but that's where my hunch took me.

"There's a Peet's coffee shop over on Michigan Avenue, if you don't mind walking a couple of blocks. It shouldn't be overly crowded at this hour."

I realized my messenger bag was back upstairs under my desk. But I had my wallet and my phone, so I was good to go.

We didn't talk about anything serious in the eleven minutes it took to get to Peet's, mostly the vast array of Democrats running for the White House in 2020. He wondered if they would so splinter the party that the incumbent president would get his coveted second term. I said I thought a finite supply of campaign cash would begin knocking some Dems out of the running by winter.

"People have lots of different reasons to run for president," I said. "Most of them have nothing to do with being elected."

Peet's was busier than I expected, but mostly with takeout customers. Steve and I got coffees and a table away from four folks with their noses buried in their computers. For several minutes our discussion continued where we'd left it. When I began to think he was avoiding the subject that brought him to me, I nudged him back in that direction.

"So, what did you want to talk about?"

"Your friend Carl Cribben."

My coffee cup stopped halfway to my lips, and then I set it back on the table.

"What?"

Pace flinched, as if he had read the incredulity in my voice and on my face.

I pressed. "What is it you want to know? And why?"

"I've been trying for maybe nine months to get a handle on his organized crime investigation, but I've gotten nowhere. Cribben wouldn't talk to me, and his staff is as tight-lipped as Robert Mueller's was. I know some of the lawyers working for Cribben. They trust me. But even they won't return my calls."

Now I took a pull at the coffee. I needed a few seconds to collect my thoughts.

"There's nothing I can tell you," I said. "I'm not working on the story."

"Which one? The investigation or his death?"

"Either."

He pushed his cup away and sat back in his chair, a combined gesture that suggested Steve Pace didn't quite believe me.

"The two of you were friends," he said. "You worked on two major stories together."

"One."

"The murder cluster and the trafficking story."

"He wasn't really a part of the trafficking story," I said. I left out the part where Carl had pulled together and tied up all the threads of the mystery for me after the action was over. I had sworn not to discuss it, and I could go to prison if I violated that promise.

Pace raised an eyebrow. "That's not what I heard."

"You need better sources."

"I thought maybe we could work together on this…"

"I'm not working on anything related to Carl."

"But you might be if we pooled our sources and resources."

"Look, Steve, the answer is no because I have nothing to share. If I had anything to share the answer would still be no. I'm sorry, but I think this discussion is over. Thanks for the coffee. Have a good flight back to Washington."

"I'm not leaving."

"Your choice. But I am." I pushed my chair back and stood, holding out my hand. "It was nice meeting you. Good luck."

I turned and walked out. I knew deep in my gut I would see Steve Pace again.

8

During my walk back to the office I decided the first thing I needed to do was let my supervisor know about Ron Colter's proposition the night before and Steve Pace's proposition this morning. I was getting propositioned more often than streetwalkers in Little Village.

In these days of shrinking revenue, it's not unheard of for two newspapers, perhaps once archrivals, to work together on a major investigative story. But I'd never heard of it happening between two major players like the Chicago *Journal* and the Washington *Chronicle*. I didn't favor a team effort with any other reporters from any other papers.

I wasn't certain why I felt so much anxiety about Pace's proposal. Since I wasn't working any aspect of the Cribben story, I had nothing to share even if Eric Ryland green-lighted the crazy idea.

I should have had a measure of anxiety over Colter's request that I interview Emily Goodsill. Even if I could get Emily to talk to me, I couldn't publish anything she said. And I sure as hell couldn't share the interview with Pace.

Those combined developments would surely ruin Eric's day and push him to find a way to ruin mine.

I was right. Sort of.

I told him about Steve Pace first. As I let the story unspool, the color in Eric's face began to rise. It reminded me of magma in a volcano. If it exploded, the damage would burn down the newsroom, figuratively speaking. When I finished, Eric reached for his phone.

Alarms went off in my head. "Who are you calling?"

"I want to talk to the editor of the *Chronicle*, tell him to keep his staff away from my newsroom. The least he could have done was give me a courtesy call."

"Hold off a while, Eric," I asked. "I told Pace it isn't going to happen."

"In which case why do you want me to wait, and for what?"

"Let's see if he goes away. My byline hasn't been on any of the stories about Carl's death. I told Pace I wasn't involved in coverage. If he's paying attention, he should believe me. Maybe that's enough."

He put the receiver back in its cradle. "Okay, but you let me know if you hear from Pace again, and I'll raise some bloody hell in Washington."

If Eric was annoyed at that moment, the news about Ron Colter's request turned him apoplectic. He actually tried to talk but could only sputter. When he regained control, he fixed me with his what-the-hell-do-you-think-you're-doing look.

"If you want to work for the FBI please resign from the paper first." His tone was measured, but the temperature in the room dropped about twenty degrees. "Colter had no right to ask you to do that, and I forbid it. You can't serve two masters, Deuce."

I was nodding, hoping to placate him and raised my hands in a mock surrender.

"Eric, I told him the answer would be no, but I didn't have a right to make that decision without checking with you." I paused. He remained quiet. "Then I had an idea."

"I'll bet this is good," he said.

I ignored the sarcasm. "I hope so. What if I could get him to amend his request?"

"I'm listening."

"I'll interview Emily, assuming she'll sit down with me, which is doubtful since a boatload of FBI agents had no luck. If I fare better, I'll turn her information over to Ron…" Eric started to object again, and I put up my hand to stop him. "…with the proviso that when the investigation is coming to a conclusion or is solved or abandoned, if Emily's story is at all pertinent, we get to publish it exclusively. Then it becomes a deferred exclusive, and not doing favors for the FBI at the expense of the public's right to know."

Eric remained silent, his eyes still fixed on me.

"That's pretty thin reasoning," he said. "There was a time when you didn't trust Colter enough to imagine him keeping his word."

"We've come to terms," I said. "I know you probably have to go to Joe with this, but Ron is waiting for an answer, and I'd like to give it to him today."

Joseph Henry III was the publisher and part owner of the *Journal*. I was certain his newspaper background would bring him down on the side of telling Colter to go to blazes.

Then Eric surprised me. "I don't have to go to Joe or any other damned person on the sixth floor. I can make this decision myself. Go back to Colter. Give him your counter-offer and see what he says. Then bring his answer back to me, and I'll give you my final response. If he agrees to your plan, I think I'd be inclined to take a risk and go with it."

And so it was that later that afternoon I was sitting at my desk, fooling around with a column idea, waiting to hear back from Colter about Emily's reaction to the idea of talking to a columnist. A small part of me hoped she'd say no. And she did.

I tried to hide the relief in my voice as I heard the news from Colter.

He said, "You know I've been thinking that I could give you Emily's address and you could go to her apartment and work your magic on her to get her to change her mind."

The suggestion annoyed me. "That's called ambush journalism, Ron. We try very hard not do that. She told you she didn't want to talk to me. Why should I try to bully her into changing her mind?"

"I'm not suggesting you bully her," he replied. "Just try gently to reverse her decision. If she slams the door in your face, you can take it for a no."

I began wondering if there were any jobs that might suit me at my neighborhood Whole Foods.

I felt trapped. It was all my own doing. Stupid, stupid move. I should have told Colter no in the beginning and presented the foregone conclusion to Eric. Now I had to let Eric make the choice. What if he decided I should try it?

I caught him as he was leaving for the day and told him about my conversation with Colter. Much to my chagrin, he responded, "I'd be okay with you trying the direct approach, as long as you don't hound her. If she says no to you, back off."

And with that, I'd gone and stepped in it again.

2

I rang the bell at Emily Goodsill's front door at 10:30 the next morning. I got no answer. Maybe she was out shopping at the Whole Foods like the one where I hoped to find future employment in the produce department. Or the deli.

I decided to sit in my car and wait for at least ten minutes before I did what I really wanted to do, which was to abandon the mission and flee back to Chicago. The commitment to wait ten minutes was eleven minutes longer than I wanted to donate to this stakeout. The only factor that kept me locked in place was the ill-conceived notion that I was doing it for Carl Cribben.

Goodsill lived in Cicero, within Cook County but just beyond Chicago's western line. If I had to describe her apartment complex I could say it most resembled a well-kept Motel 6. It stood two stories with outdoor steps and walkways and doors to each unit opening off those walkways. It appeared to have been painted recently, a rather intense adobe color. The stairs, walkways and railings were wrought iron devoid, so far as I could see, of any rust. The doorways were painted a variety of colors that repeated five times on each level. Emily Goodsill lived behind a blue.

The narrow space between the building and the asphalt parking lot didn't leave much room for landscaping, but the plants I could see appeared to be well-kept. Each apartment unit had one assigned parking spot in a row directly fronting the building and a second spot on the far side of the lot near the street. Visitor spots filled the closed end of the lot with a few over-flow spaces next to the management office. Almost all the spaces, however marked, were empty at mid-morning. Two other cars were parked in visitor spots, an aging blue Ford Focus and a fairly recent model silver Honda Civic. A white Toyota Corolla was parked next to the management office. I assumed it belonged to the manager.

You had to be perceptive like that to make it in this world as a reporter.

One other vehicle, a white panel truck with its cab windows darkened by privacy film and with no markings on the doors or the cargo box, occupied a visitor spot about as remote as it could get and still be in the apartment parking area. It was as if the driver was trying to avoid notice. But I noticed.

I parked in another visitor spot, close enough to be able to see into the cab without being so close that my spying became easily evident. It was hard to make out much detail through the darkened windows, but I could tell it was a man sitting behind the wheel, and he wore a Chicago White Sox cap pulled low over his face. I could make out the white team logo against the black cap. He appeared to be holding an electronic tablet in front of him, pressed against the steering wheel, and appeared to be poking at the keyboard. He could have been playing Angry Birds for all I knew. Every minute or so he turned his head to look at me. He had no reason to, and this made me suspicious. It also made me understand that my effort to remain inconspicuous had failed miserably.

He was watching me. I noticed, and he knew that I noticed. I was watching him. He noticed, and I knew that he noticed. We sat there, each noticing the other, neither of us trying to disguise our curiosity.

Perhaps I was wrong to be suspicious. Perhaps he was a workman waiting for someone to come home so he could gain access to a unit that needed repairs. Perhaps he thought the same of me. I tried to recall if he had been parked there when I went up to the second floor and knocked on Emily's door, unit 211. Who knew? Why should I care? But I did, because he might have been waiting for Emily, too. If he turned out to be a killer who murdered without leaving a trace, Emily certainly could be in danger.

Or he might have left her dead inside already, the distinctive odor of decay not yet reaching beyond that blue door.

Then again, probably not. If the panel truck driver had killed Emily, he wouldn't be hanging around waiting for someone to discover her body.

I called Ron Colter to ask if he knew anything about an idling white panel truck at Goodsill's apartment complex. Maybe it was a mobile FBI surveillance unit. He said it was not. He made an unnecessarily sarcastic remark about my overly distrustful instincts.

I told him I was going to walk around the lot and get the truck's license number.

"No, you're not," Colter ordered. "If the driver is a killer, he'll take you out in a cocaine heartbeat. You stay in your car and away from the truck."

I protested. "I'll be careful."

"Deuce, no. Please. If it's a bad guy the plates are probably stolen, anyhow. You're asking for trouble for no good reason."

I had to admit that made sense.

"Well, I can't wait here all day," I said. "Maybe Emily leased a temporary office and won't be home until tonight."

"Then go back tonight," he said.

Seventy-three minutes passed, and I remained sitting in Emily's parking lot. I was watching, but I wasn't seeing. Only one thing changed. A woman young enough to have been in college pulled into the close-in space for a first-floor unit and entered it carrying two paper bags from Whole Foods. I wondered how a college student could afford Whole Foods but not a better apartment. The way she tossed the bags around said they weren't heavy. Perhaps they didn't have Whole Foods products inside. Perhaps she was transporting sweaty clothes from a visit to her gym in those bags because her meager budget didn't allow for a real athletic bag. She disappeared inside without even looking around the parking lot and the grounds. A few minutes later the white truck abruptly drove away, the driver turning his face so I couldn't get a good look.

I decided to leave, too. Before I did, I drove around the parking lot jotting down plate numbers from the Focus and the Civic, as well as the Hyundai Sonata driven by the Whole Foods bag lady. For good measure, I took the same info from the Corolla that I assumed belonged to the building manager. All had Illinois tags but the Focus, which was registered in Iowa, Emily Goodsill's home. Iowa is the next state west of Illinois, and it wasn't unusual to find vehicles with Iowa plates in Chicago.

The troubling question was, if the Focus was Emily's car, and the Focus was parked at Emily's home in Emily's spot, where was Emily?

10

The clock on the oak-paneled wall ticked to 7:57 p.m. when the first two officials who would attend the private meeting walked through the door. The room was in the domain of Chicago Mayor Marsha Mendes, just beginning her second term with an acceptable if not spectacular record of achievement and popularity.

She had chosen this location over her office for the meeting because too many people had access to her office, and in the era of eavesdropping, computer hacking, and document theft, she could never be certain that what happened in her office stayed in her office. Her security staff swept the private conference room for bugs once a week, and so far it remained clean. The last sweep had been completed an hour earlier, and a member of her security staff had been standing at the locked door since the sweep ended. Mendes forbid participants in conference room meetings to bring their laptops or cell phones into the room with them. They were kept secure in a box outside the door. So strict were her precautions that participants were wand-searched for digital voice recorders.

Such was life in the Age of Paranoia.

Mendes was first through the door, since she and her security chief were the sole holders of keys. Not even her chief of staff could get in without her.

Right on her heels was Illinois Governor Tyler Walston, a philanthropist, entrepreneur, and well-known plastic surgeon. Walston also was the surprise winner of the last statewide election. His opponent, Frank Chapin, should have won; he went into the final month of the campaign with a nine-point advantage in the polls. But the eleventh-hour disclosure that Chapin, a successful commercial builder, had ripped off Illinois taxpayers to the tune of $37 million scuttled his bid and likely would send him to prison for a good long stretch. The election was *only five months into the history books, and already the man had been indicted on more than twenty counts of embezzlement, conspiracy, extortion, mail fraud, and tax evasion. The Fab Five of white-collar crime.*

Mendes took the chair at the head of the table. Walston sat to her right. They made halting small talk until the rest of the participants drifted in. Walston fidgeted. He always fidgeted. Not the greatest trait in a plastic surgeon. Mendes thought that even now he remained overwhelmed by his election win. He seemed to wear a perpetual expression of shock and bewilderment. Mendes was certain he had plans to use the governor's office to propel himself to a presidential bid, and she prayed almost nightly that he wouldn't succeed.

Next to arrive was Dr. John Fasso, an alderman representing Chicago's 28th ward. Fasso had been chosen vice mayor by his fellow City Council members the previous year after his predecessor dropped dead during a heated debate in chambers. Fasso and Mendes had been primary opponents in the mayoral election, a race which Mendes won by 1,011 votes. Fasso and Mendes had a strained but civil relationship.

Right behind Fasso was Cabot "Cab" Hill, superintendent of the Chicago Police Department. Mendes recruited Hill from the Philadelphia PD to become Chicago's top cop because she felt the city needed a fresh outlook in that post. So far Hill was proving to be a solid choice. He insisted, though, that people call him "Cab." He said Cabot Hill sounded too much like an upper-class white neighborhood in the suburbs.

These four would be joined by Ron Colter, head of the Chicago division of the FBI, and by Jerry Alvarez, deputy U.S. attorney for the Northern District of Illinois.

* * *

Bottles of water and small note pads with pens were laid out at six places at the table. That there were no more provided a clear sign than no staff or visitors would attend.

Mendes took immediate charge. Her conference room. Her gavel.

She addressed Colter first.

She asked, "Any word on how any of the victims died, Cribben or the two Mob hit men? How recently have you talked to the ME?"

Colter was shaking his head. "I talked to Donato this afternoon. He's got nothing."

Tyler Walston, the governor, addressed Mendes, "Victims, Marsha? Really? Carl Cribben maybe. But I have difficulty seeing two professional killers as victims."

Colter replied, "If they didn't kill themselves, and there's no evidence they did, and if they didn't die of natural causes, and there's no evidence they did, then they were murdered, Governor, and they're victims."

"Oh, for Christ's sake, Ron," Walston said. "Who cares? Chicago doesn't exactly have a shortage of hired killers. Why can't we move on?"

"Because," said Alvarez, "they were key witnesses in a federal investigation, run by Cribben. It's been crippled by their deaths, not to mention Carl's."

"Murder isn't a federal crime," Walston insisted, his remarks directed at the mayor. "Why isn't the state's attorney here instead of the feds?"

"There is no murder case yet," Alvarez replied, "and there won't be unless and until the ME finds that the deaths were homicides."

Mendes had little tolerance for petty squabbling. "Let's get back on point, shall we?" She turned to Colter. "When does Donato think the tox results will come in?"

"He has no idea," Colter said. "Tox is always a long process because it has to be so precise, and every time a tox panel comes back negative, his office creates a new one for pathologists to screen. Donato has ordered each test run twice, to be sure there are no mistakes. I think the lab might run out of blood and tissue samples before they run out of toxins to search for."

"Shit," Mendes whispered. "And if they all come back negative?"

"Then," Colter said with a shrug, "he'll have to list the causes of death as 'unknown.'"

Hill jumped in. "As the top cop around here, I won't accept 'unknown causes.' We're talkin' three possible Mob hits. There have to be causes of death. And if there are causes there will be effects. I'm worried we might be lookin' at mob warfare on the streets, and then my cops start dyin'. The two hitmen have big backup. They were part of the Tricoletto family."

"That's right," said Vice Mayor John Fasso. "I know 'Tony 'Toes' some. He lives in my district. He keeps a low profile as a legit businessman. I can't see him throwin' into a mob war. His life's too cushy to risk it. And he's gettin' too old. He's what? Eighty-two? Eighty-three? Besides, that shit ended decades ago, at least where the Mafia's concerned."

"But the button men were Tony's guys," Hill insisted. "He's not gonna take it lyin' down. He might've already made a move to retaliate. Late this afternoon Fire and Rescue pulled a decomp outta the river. ID made the body as a capo for the Callisi family. So the war might have started already."

"I thought the Callisis and the Tricolettos had a truce," said Fasso. "They haven't butted heads in twenty years, as far as we know."

"You know as well as I do those things can blow up overnight," Mendes said. "Any chance we know how the guy in the river died, or is he a mystery, too?"

"No mystery," Hill replied. "He took a double-tap to the back of the head."

"Ballistics?" Mendes asked.

"Give us time," Hill said. "We just fished him outta the drink ninety minutes ago. If he's in Tony's morgue yet, he only just got there."

"The morgue's getting overcrowded," the governor observed.

"If this is the start of a war," the mayor said, "it would be a big help to learn the causes of the first three deaths. That could point us at somebody with the skill to kill without leaving any clues. I doubt that skill is exactly common."

"It's something," Colter replied, "we haven't thought of yet."

* * *

The room was quiet for almost a full minute. Colter had something on his mind, and it was making him sufficiently angry that he needed to calm himself before he opened his mouth. He let go a sigh.

"I'm concerned that all the talk here is about the dead assassins and their ties to the Mob. I lost a dear friend, and the country lost a hero when Carl Cribben drew his last breath. Finding who murdered him, if he was murdered, is my number one priority. Congress can worry about their damned organized crime investigation. My priorities are elsewhere."

"No," the mayor said, "your priorities are with the safety of this city."

"*That's the police superintendent's job,*" Colter said.

Jerry Alvarez spoke up.

"*If there was any evidence,*" Alvarez said, "*that the two button men were killed to stop them flipping on the Tricoletto family and queer a congressional investigation, then this whole mess would be a federal matter. The FBI would be fully involved, as would the U.S. attorney's office. At the moment, as far as we know, Carl Cribben is the only subject with direct federal ties. The FBI wants to learn who and what killed him. But until somebody can prove murder, there's no case for the U.S. attorney's office yet.*"

"*The two dead Mob guys had federal ties,*" Mendes said. "*They were federal witnesses.*"

"*But,*" Alvarez replied, "*we don't know that's why they were killed, or even if they were killed. That's why I sit in on these meetings, so if we determine they were murdered to keep them quiet, I'm here to get the U.S. attorney's office up to speed immediately.*"

"*Meantime,*" Colter said, "*our focus is on Cribben.*"

"*I understand your feelings for Carl,*" Mendes said. "*But this is my city, and I'm telling you to work around the clock with the others at this table to stop a blood bath on my streets.*"

"*Madam Mayor,*" Colter began, barely able to keep the rage from his voice, "*the last time I looked, I report first to the director of the FBI, and beyond her to the Attorney General of the United States. I will do what I can, but I will not take orders from you.*"

11

It was on my drive back to the office that I began to feel an inkling of enthusiasm for the next step in whatever it was I was doing. At the moment, I would define it as a *Don Quixote* quest. I hoped it didn't morph, as some of my other investigative efforts had, into a crusade and then an odyssey. As much as I wanted to clear up the reasons for Carl Cribben's death, I didn't have the rest of my life to devote to it.

But I couldn't quit now. I had some basic leads in my notebook—the license plates and the makes and models of four cars. On the surface, the data was nothing to celebrate. It could lead to progress—or to a front-end collision with an innocent windmill. But I had one of those feelings reporters learn not to ignore. I was ready for the joust.

Back in the newsroom I asked one of our researchers to run the plates on all the cars. I still felt disappointed that I hadn't gotten the plate on the white panel truck. Even if its plate turned out to be stolen, it would mark the vehicle as something to be watched.

I had a feeling I would get another chance.

It didn't take long for the search results to ping into my computer. The results surprised me. The Focus with the Iowa plate belonged to someone named Everett Smithson of Walnut, Iowa, Emily Goodsill's hometown but not Emily Goodsill.

The Honda Civic with Illinois plates did belong to Emily Goodsill, however. It was registered to her at the address of her Cicero apartment. I didn't find it especially surprising that Emily would have registered her car in Illinois. Illinois law required that a vehicle be registered to the owner's

51

legal address. But I found it remarkably curious that a car registered in her hometown of Walnut, Iowa, but not in Emily's name, should be parked at her apartment complex, too.

I asked the researcher to find out what he could about the man, Everett Smithson. He was, it turned out, the owner of Smithson Farms of Atlantic, Iowa. I checked on Atlantic. It sat a little under fifteen road miles east-southeast of Walnut and was a larger town. It had a municipal airport, a golf course, a Coca-Cola bottling plant, and a Walmart Supercenter, for heaven's sake. Look out, Chicago.

Everett Smithson lived in Walnut, so I presumed he commuted to work at the Smithson Farms home office. From my internet search I learned that Smithson Farms was a small conglomerate of three farms, two of which belonged to Smithson and one of which belonged to Rose Barnard Goodsill.

All that could have a logical explanation. Perhaps Rose Barnard Goodsill had been divorced or widowed and eventually hooked up with Everett Smithson. Even if they had married, Rose could have kept her former name and Emily, perhaps an adult by then, would likely have chosen to keep her name, as well.

But that didn't explain why Everett Smithson's car was in Chicago at the moment. Had Emily called him for help? And if so, why?

I needed to go back to Cicero and knock on the blue door again.

* * *

I finished a column and fought the start of the outgoing rush hour on I-55. This interstate was the most direct route southwest 300 miles to the busy port city of St. Louis on the banks of the Mississippi River. But direct did not translate to fast. At three in the morning drivers could make decent time. But for most of every twenty-four hours the road maintained a heavy clog of big-truck traffic. Add Chicago commuter traffic in the mornings and afternoons, and the trip to anywhere along I-55 tripled—more when the highway was under repair, as it was now, as it seemed always to be. Fortunately, I was only going as far as Cicero, nine miles from my office in The Loop. Still, the trip took nearly ninety minutes, an average speed of ten miles an hour. Most commuters got used to it. I never would.

When I pulled into the lot of Emily's apartment building a little after 5 p.m. there were quite a few more cars than there had been on my earlier visit. But it wasn't the number of cars that drew my immediate attention. It was a man I judged to be in his late fifties or early sixties striding across the asphalt as if he had a serious objective in mind. He was headed straight for the Focus with the Iowa plates.

He stood a few inches under six feet and walked with a slight slouch. His loose-fitting blue jeans looked to have about five years of permanent grime lodged among the threads of the denim. His belt looped around his back and dove under an ample belly that stretched the fabric of a t-shirt that might have been green at some point. It was hard to guess at the original color now for the dirt and yellowed sweat stains. His skin, whipped into deep lines by over-exposure to the sun and the persistent winds of the Plains, gave him an aura of exhaustion. His graying hair had gone thin. If this was Everett Smithson, he appeared to have jumped off a tractor and run from Iowa to Chicago.

As he neared his car, he took off his wire-rimmed glasses and swiped a forearm across his forehead. The weather remained chilly, but Mr. Smithson had somehow worked up a pretty good sweat.

I pulled up beside him and thumbed down my window.

"Excuse me," I said, trying to sound non-threatening. "Are you Everett Smithson?"

He didn't exactly look like a deer in the headlights, but I had definitely startled him. If he was trying to choose between flight or fight, the way his eyes hardened and his face set made me pretty sure his brain was telling him to throw a punch. Even though he probably had twenty-five years on me, he looked strong enough to fight a wild boar. Locked in as I was behind my seatbelt, I had nowhere to go.

I had to neutralize the situation quickly.

"Sir, I'm not a threat to you or anyone else," I said, sounding as genuine as I could. "I'm a newspaper columnist from Chicago, and I'm here looking for someone to help her."

His eyes narrowed again, but I thought I saw his body relax marginally.

"Are you Mr. Smithson?"

His mouth opened slightly. I saw a lot of tobacco-stained teeth.

"Who are you, and what do you want?"

"I'm looking for Emily Goodsill," I said. "I hope she's not in trouble, but I think she might be. My name is Deuce Mora. I work for the Chicago *Journal.*"

He stood stock still, as if waiting for me to say more. So I did.

"I got Ms. Goodsill's address from the FBI. I presumed the Ford Focus was hers because of the Iowa plates and the fact that the car came from a dealer not far from Walnut. But looking at DMV records, I found out the Focus belongs to Everett Smithson, and it's the Honda Civic that belongs to Emily. I've been trying to catch her at home. Her car's been here, but she isn't answering her door. Have you seen her?"

"None-a your business," the man replied.

"Do you know if she's okay?"

"So far's I know."

"Is she in her apartment?"

"That's none-a your business, neither."

"Even if her life's in danger?"

"I ain't sayin' it is, but if that's a fact, you bein' here ain't helpin' none."

I felt exasperated. Everett Smithson wasn't going to be easy.

"Okay, Mr. Smithson, I'll let you go," I told him. "Thanks for stopping."

"I ain't said I am Everett Smithson," he snapped back at me. "And I ain't goin' nowhere until you turn your vehicle around and clear outta here. If you don't do it right this minute, I'll reach in and pull you outta there and roll this piece-a junk out into traffic. You can take one-a them Uber things back wherever you come from."

I could have argued that such actions could make him vulnerable to charges of assault, kidnapping, and grand theft auto, not to mention that he'd slandered my aging but reliable Explorer. None of it seemed worth the aggravation. I glanced up at Emily's front window and saw a light on. I thought I might have seen a woman peeking through the curtains, too. So, for the sake of ending this confrontation, I would assume for the moment that Emily was alive and well, and it was safe for me to go on my way.

I didn't plan to go very far.

12

I drove out of Emily's lot intending to drive around the block and give Everett Smithson a chance to leave. My ruse took longer than planned because the first right turn I made was into a dead-end street. I had to find a place to turn around and reverse course. The next right turn and two more after that brought me back abreast of the entry to the apartment complex. I could see from the street that the Ford Focus was gone. I presumed that Everett Smithson had departed with it. My plan had worked, so far.

Rather than pull into the lot again where Emily would be able to spot and identify my Explorer, I parked at the curb behind some scraggily bushes. I killed the lights and cut the engine. The street was poorly lighted. The combination of the darkness and the bushes would give me cover. It was my intention to watch the place for a few minutes to make sure Smithson didn't come back and the white panel truck didn't show up. If everything stayed clear, I would circle the edge of the parking lot on foot until I was beneath the walkway that fronted Emily's apartment. I could get up the stairs and be at Emily's door before she realized I was there. At least that was the plan.

I'd been so intent on watching Emily's apartment that I failed to notice the black SUV pass me on the street. It's headlights in my side mirror might have gotten my attention, except his lights were off. Maybe twenty seconds later, as I pieced it together later, flickering light in the mirror did get my attention. As I turned my head I saw a man dressed in dark clothes leap at my window and try to open my door. I had locked it.

"Deuce," he screamed at me. "Open the door. Get out. Hurry."

It was Steve Pace.

"Come on, Deuce. Come on," he kept yelling.

I saw why. The flickering light was fire, and it was coming from under the rear of my Explorer, licking at the tire under the gas cap cover.

I stabbed at the seat belt clasp. It took me two tries to get it open.

I opened the door, and Steve started pulling me out.

"Go! Go! Go!" he yelled.

I grabbed for my bag on the passenger seat. Now Steve was pulling me so hard I almost dropped it.

We sprinted across the street and had just reached the far curb when the Explorer went up in a fireball. The force of the blast blew us across the grass, across the sidewalk, and into the side of a building. We both went down, stunned but not seriously hurt.

Within a minute, people were pouring out of their homes to watch the spectacle. Several brought us blankets and bottles of water. Distant sirens told us that police and fire units were on their way.

* * *

Twenty minutes later Steve and I were sitting on ambulance gurneys, wrapped in rough gray blankets to keep us warm while EMTs checked us out. I knew Steve had saved my life, but I had no idea how. What was he doing in Cicero?

I couldn't ask because two police detectives were monopolizing his time. While the police questioned Steve, two EMTs were shining lights in my eyes, taking my blood pressure, and asking me if I had any pain. I could feel a couple of bruises forming, but I was otherwise fine. They asked if I wanted to go to a hospital to be checked out farther, and I said no. What I really wanted to do was listen to what Steve was telling the police.

They asked him what he saw.

"What first caught my attention," he said, "was a big black SUV driving north on the street with no lights. I thought maybe the driver had just forgotten to turn the lights on. But most people use settings that turn lights on and off automatically. He went by Deuce's car and all the way to the corner very slowly. He stopped at the crosswalk for maybe thirty seconds, then turned on his headlights, made a right, and roared away."

"Did you happen to get the license number?" One detective asked.

"No," Steve replied. "I couldn't see it. Like I said, the car lights were off, so there was nothing to illuminate the license plate or the name of the car. By the time the driver switched on the lights, he was already going around the corner."

"Then what?"

"That's when I looked back at the Explorer and saw the fire. Deuce wasn't making any effort to get out, so I ran over to alert her."

That's when I chimed in.

"What were you doing here, Steve? Following me?"

"Guilty as charged," he replied.

"Well, you should be ashamed of yourself. But I, for one, am very grateful."

I turned to the detective. "I didn't see the fire until Steve started pounding on my door, yelling at me to get out. If the delay had been longer, it wouldn't have ended well."

While the first responders were packing up their gear, I took a few moments to mourn my faithful Explorer. Nobody would ever disparage it again. It was still sitting at the curb, iced over with white fire-suppressant foam from a Cicero Fire Department truck.

The tires had burned to the rims. The windows had exploded. What was left of the interior and the chassis had been fried well done.

If not for Steve Pace, I would have fried, too.

I closed my eyes and focused on breathing, overjoyed that it was still possible.

13

As I walked with Steve Pace to his car, my phone rang. Caller ID said it was Mark. I wondered if he just happened to take this moment to call me, or if someone had alerted him to the fire. It was the fire. And the alert was delivered by Eric Ryland, my editor.

It took me a few minutes to convince Mark I was okay, and still he wasn't happy.

"You might hate me, Deuce, but I told Eric I thought you needed security protection."

Mark was right; I wasn't happy.

"Don't you think that's my decision?" I said.

"Only if you make the right one. Besides, Eric says he's already working on it."

I replied, "Just for that, I'm not going to let you drive the new car, whatever it is."

"Don't rush the decision on what to get," Mark said. "If you're going to drive the new one as long as you drove the Explorer, you want something that will hold up."

"I think a car decision is something I can also handle for myself," I said. As much as I missed Mark, I didn't want to talk any longer. I promised to call when I got home.

While I'd been on the phone with Mark, Ron Colter had called and left a voice mail.

"Glad you're okay," he said. "I hope to see you tonight." I could only assume Eric had notified him, too. I had no idea what he meant about seeing me tonight.

As Steve walked me up my front steps, we found Eric Ryland sitting in one of the rocking chairs on the porch.

I felt Steve stiffen beside me and realized he didn't know who this stranger was. I introduced them.

"I guess," Eric said, "that I wouldn't be wrong if I presumed that you followed Deuce to Cicero tonight."

"No, you'd be correct," Pace admitted.

"Thank you," I said. "For saving my life. You're a nosy bastard, but you won't hear me complain again. Too bad nobody could save the Explorer. I was pretty fond of it."

"It was fully involved by the time the fire department got there," Steve said. "There was nothing to be done but make sure the fire didn't spread."

"You guys want to come in?" I asked. "I don't know about you, but I'd like a drink."

Both agreed. I'm not sure either man really wanted a drink. More likely they were after information from one another. I hoped Eric wouldn't agree to any notions that our two newspapers cooperate on the Cribben story.

He didn't. He had one drink and got up to go. Collaboration never came up. But protection did. Eric said he was working on setting it up. I just glared at him.

"You going to be all right?" he asked.

"Fine," I said. "Thank you."

"I'm leaving in a few minutes, too," Pace said. "I wanted to discuss something with Deuce before I go—not related to Carl Cribben or the Mob."

It turned out Pace wanted to be helpful.

"Until you get a payout from your insurance company," he said, "you're going to need transportation. Why don't I pick you up in the morning and we'll go new-car shopping? I can be your chauffer until you get squared away."

"I should be able to get a rental car," I said, "as soon as my insurance agent takes a look at what's left of the Explorer. Thanks for the offer, but I'll be fine."

"Several problems with that," he replied with a note of smugness. "How are you going to get *to* the rental car, and after you buy new wheels, who's going to take you to the dealer to pick it up after you *turn in* the loaner?"

"Uber?" I said.

"Why spend the money? Save it for the new ride."

I hated to admit it, but Steve was probably right.

When he got up to leave, he reached into his coat and fished out a slip of paper.

"I almost forgot," he said. "When we got blown down by the explosion, this fell out of your pocket. I grabbed it before the wind could carry it off. I thought it might be important."

He handed the note to me. It was folded. I opened it. It contained a name and a phone number. That's all. I didn't recognize either.

I shook my head. "This fell out of *my* pocket?"

"Yep. Your left jacket pocket. You don't know who it is?"

"No. I never saw the name or the phone number or the note before."

"Well, hang onto it. If it's important, you'll probably remember when you're feeling better how it got into your jacket and what it means. If not, then you can toss it."

When he'd gone, I wondered if he was really such a nice, accommodating guy, or if this was all a ploy to get into my good graces and perhaps invite him into the Cribben investigation. I figured the best I could hope for was a combination of the two.

* * *

I settled in to make a call to Mark. Before I dialed him, I slipped the mysterious note into my wallet behind a couple of $20 bills. I'd mull it over later, when I'd be in better shape to think straight.

Mark and I talked for the better part of an hour. Again he expressed concerns for my safety, and I told him Eric was working on a security detail. Until the protection was in place, Mark suggested I keep Steve Pace around as backup. I promised to think about it and wasn't too proud to admit it wasn't a bad idea.

Mark asked, "Is he good-looking."

I grinned and took the bait. "Well, yeah, I guess. Yes, he is."

"Should I worry?"

"About?"

"Him making a move on you?"

"Are you worried about him making a move on me, or me making?..."

"Deuce!"

I laughed. "He's turning sixty-five years old in three months," I said. "If you don't believe me, Google him."

"Maybe you like older men."

"I like all men," I said. "I only sleep with one—when he's around."

We ended the good-natured sparring and talked some about cars. I leaned toward another Explorer, but I had liked the Subaru Outback Ron Colter was driving the night of our clandestine meeting in the bank drive-through. I liked test driving new cars, so I would give myself a chance to try out any that appealed to me.

We were chatting about his experiences in California when my front doorbell rang. It was nearly 7 p.m. and almost dark, and I wasn't expecting anyone. Mark insisted on staying on the phone until I found out who was out there.

I turned on the porch light and looked through the door's glass panel.

"It's good, Honey," I said. "The FBI has arrived."

We ended the call, and I opened the door.

Ron Colter stood there with a woman who looked a few years younger than me. I didn't know her, but I could make a pretty good guess. She had the nervous look of someone from Iowa farm country who would rather be back home in the middle of a corn field than in the middle of a murder mystery in the big city.

I knew I wouldn't be going to bed any time soon.

14

Colter apologized for showing up unannounced. "I seized an opportunity," he said. The cliché made me cringe, but I thought I got his meaning. When he introduced the woman as Emily Goodsill, I invited them in.

Colter started to step through the door, but Emily appeared not to notice. She glanced up and down my street, perhaps expecting to spot trouble coming to bite her. I followed her eyes and saw nothing out of the ordinary.

"Why don't you both come in?" I suggested again.

Colter declined the offer of a drink. Emily asked for a glass of water. I joined her. While I was in the kitchen I slipped one of my little voice-activated digital recorders from my bag and turned it on. It's the size of a thumb drive. Most people didn't even notice it.

"Are you okay?" she asked me when I returned. "After the explosion, I mean."

"Some bumps and bruises," I said. "Nothing serious." I saw something resembling regret in her eyes. It prompted my next question. "Did you see what happened?"

She dropped her head and nodded. I put the recorder on the lamp table beside me.

"It was horrible," she said in a near whisper. "That's why, when Agent Colter asked me to come talk to you, I agreed. It was like the least I could do."

That puzzled me. "What do you mean, the least you?..."

"I saw you the first time you came to my apartment," she said, "when you and the guy in the white truck were sitting in the parking lot. My stepfather was inside with me, and he told me not to answer the door. If I had've, if I'd talked to you then, you might not've got almost blown up later on."

I thought, yeah, and the driver of the panel truck might have kicked in your apartment door and killed all three of us. But I didn't speak the words. They creeped me out. They would terrify Emily.

I didn't know where or how to start asking questions, an uncomfortable dilemma for a reporter. My instinct was to ease in, but if I took too long to get to the point, Emily might tire or decide she'd said enough. Colter must have seen my discomfort, and he knew Emily better than I did. So he began the conversation.

"Let's start at the beginning," he said. "Emily, you still work for the USDA, right?"

She nodded.

"Is your office still in the federal building in Chicago?"

"I don't really know," she said. "My supervisor told me I could work from home until I can go back to the office. But I don't think I ever want to go back there."

Colter turned to me. "We haven't released the space yet," he said. "It's still a crime scene and will be at least until we determine whether Carl's death was or wasn't a crime."

I understood and said so.

"Tell us what happened the last time you were in that office." Colter was leading her very professionally right where we wanted her to take us. Unless she balked. Which she very nearly did.

Emily turned to me. "Could I have some more water, please?"

I hadn't noticed that her glass was empty. She didn't say anything until I came back with a refill and took my seat.

"I don't know anything about that night," she said. "I don't want to know anything. Whoever killed that poor man might come for me next."

I felt more comfortable jumping in.

"Can you describe that whole night?"

"Like I told Agent Colter, I don't know much to tell," Emily said. "I was working late, like I have to pretty often these days. Right now we've got a lot of work to do what with so many farmers bein' flooded out by all the big rains. The Ohio, the Missouri, the Mississippi Rivers and most-a their tributaries are way over flood stage, and it's killin' the farmers out there. I've been trying to get a lotta work done so we can help 'em faster."

"Were you still working when your office was broken into?"

"No. I don't even know what time that was. I signed outta the building at 10:21 p.m. Everything looked fine to me."

Colter asked, "How do you remember the time so precisely?"

Emily shrugged. "I just do. When I work late I try to leave by ten. I don't feel safe if I'm on the streets alone much later than that. I was late getting away. That's probably how I remember what time it was."

She paused, then started again. "I remember the security guy who's usually at the front desk was away somewhere. I left the building and then had to come back. I didn't remember if I'd locked my office door, so I ran back upstairs to check."

"Had you?" I asked.

She nodded. "Yes. All three locks."

"How much later was this than the first time you left?"

"No more'n a couple minutes. I didn't even bother signing in and out again."

"Was the security guard back when you left the second time?"

"No. I have no idea where he went. I didn't know anything 'til the cops came pounding on my apartment door a little after six the next mornin'."

Colter reached into his jacket pocket and pulled out a plain white letter-sized envelope. He handed it over to Emily, who seemed reluctant to take it.

"What is it?" she asked.

"Photos," Colter said. "Please look at them. Tell me if you recognize anyone."

She handled the envelope as if it might burn her fingers.

"I'm not going to look if they're all bloody and gory."

"They aren't," Colter assured her. "Take your time."

So Emily did. There were six photos, a lineup array of sorts. Emily ran through them slowly, studying hard. I watched her face as she deliberated. She very carefully placed each photo she examined on the bottom of the stack, so when she was finished, the photos were in the same order as when Colter handed them to her.

Once I thought I saw the flash of a question in her eyes. Not much, and not for long. Maybe it meant nothing. Maybe it was a memory of something—or someone. As fast as the expression appeared it was gone. Probably nothing.

She shook he head. "I don't know any of them," she said. She handed the photos and the envelope back to Colter. I asked if I could see them, and Colter handed them to me. I had counted two photos that Emily examined after the one that prompted her puzzled expression. That meant she had been looking at the third photo from the bottom of the stack at the time.

I didn't know the man in that photo, either. I was surprised when I turned it over. Written on the back was: "Anthony J. Tricoletto Jr. 8/17/18."

I glanced at Colter.

"Surveillance photo," he said. "A godfather in waiting."

I turned back to Emily, who was regarding me with curiosity.

"What kind of security does that building have?" I asked.

"There's supposed to be a security guard in the lobby all night. But he's only one man. It worried me a little that somebody could overpower him. But I didn't dwell on it because I never really expected it to happen. If somebody did get past him, I figured they wouldn't come after me. There's nothin' in an ag subsidy office worth stealin'."

Colter broached a new subject. "Yet you put additional locks on your door."

Emily looked at him, then me, then down at her hands in her lap. Then she raised one hand to a stray lock of her light brown hair that had fallen into her face. She curled it around her finger several times before pushing it back behind her ear.

"Yeah, I did," she said. "But I paid for 'em myself. Nobody knew about 'em, not even my supervisor."

"Why did you do that?" I asked.

She shrugged. "Just bein' extra careful. A woman alone can't be too careful. Especially alone in a big city. I worked late fairly often."

I asked if she knew what kinds of locks they were.

"Well, there's one lock that came with the office, and I don't know what that is. Maybe a Yale. I had a locksmith add one of those chain things for some more security."

"And," Colter said, "you had a third lock."

"Yeah," Emily replied. "It was a Medical, or something like that."

"A Medeco," Colter said. "You can't buy a better deadbolt. It's pretty much pick-proof, and no locksmith will duplicate the key without seeing the ID and getting the signature of the owner. How many keys did you have for that lock?"

"Just the one," she replied. "They're real expensive, and I didn't want to give one to anybody else, anyway, and take a chance on it gettin' lost or stolen."

I needed clarification. "How would you get in your office if you lost it?"

"I wouldn't. I'd've been locked out until I could go back to the locksmith, prove my identity, and get him to cut a new one."

"So," I said, "since you were gone, there's no way whoever broke in could have unlocked your door when they came, or stranger still, locked the door when they left?"

"No way I know of. I had the only key, and I still have it." To prove the point she reached into her backpack and came out with a keyring. I spotted the Medeco immediately. With its big, square head and outsized footprint, it looked like no other keys on the ring. I reached for it.

"Hold on," Colter said. "Emily, since you won't be allowed back in your office for a while, you won't need that key. I'm going to have to take it for a day or two."

"Not the whole ring?" Emily asked as Colter pulled on latex gloves.

"No," he said. "Just the Medeco."

He took it from her and used his gloved hands to remove it from the ring. He dropped the Medeco into a small manila evidence envelope and handed the remaining keys back to Emily. She returned them to her backpack.

I asked Colter, "Was the Medeco locked when you got to Emily's office?"

He nodded. "When the police arrived, yes. It was the only one of the three that was locked. The original had been opened with a key. Maybe the killers took it from the night security guy. The chain lock was ripped out of the door frame. The Medeco was still locked. The cops had to take the door off the hinges and break the frame to get in." He looked away from Emily to me. "Tony Donato had some trouble estimating the time of Carl's death because his body was out in the cold for several hours, at least. Extrapolating from the outside temperature and the victim's liver temperature, he estimated the time of death was between one and two in the morning, well after Emily says she left the building."

I turned to Emily to verify something. "You were gone from the building by 10:30 p.m. or so, right?" She nodded. "And you had double checked to make sure all three locks were engaged when you went home?" She nodded again. "And you had all your keys with you, including the Medeco?"

"I already told you that."

"Had anyone ever borrowed your keyring? Did you ever walk away from it for even a few minutes? Did you ever misplace it then find it again?"

She shook her head through all the questions.

"You're sure?"

"Absolutely."

"Then how did they get into and out of your office?"

"I don't know," Emily said, her voice exasperated and cracking. "Maybe, like you said, they stole the security guard's master to open the original lock. The chain lock was busted, yanked right out of the door frame. I don't have a clue how they opened the Medeco—or relocked it when they left."

I glanced at Colter. It was clear he had no answer.

Neither did I.

15

Emily appeared to be getting tired.

I didn't have to wonder about myself. I was tired and sore, and the longer I sat up the more my body tightened up. I must have tensed every muscle as I fought to get out of the Explorer. The muscles reacted the way they do at the gym when I try to lift too much weight or do too many reps. They fill with lactic acid and bite back. The initial discomfort intensifies before it begins to dissipate, and my current discomfort required some serious consideration of Tylenol and topical CBD balm.

But there was still too much to ask Emily to stop now. I would keep going as long as she was willing to keep going.

I nodded. "So what do you plan to do now?"

"I'm gonna quit my job here and go back to Walnut, Iowa," she said. "Maybe I can get a new job with the Pottawattamie County ag extension office. I used to work there, and they liked me. I'm a lot more experienced now."

"You think the people who broke into your office know you, know where you live in Iowa, where your family is?"

Emily wiped tears from her face. "Somebody knows. I think they've been inside my mom's house."

"What makes you say that?" Colter asked.

More tears slid from Emily's eyes. "That's why my stepfather, Ev Smithson, was here." She turned toward me. "The man you met in my parking lot. He wanted to warn me that somebody's been breaking into my mother's house. They don't take anything. They just move stuff around so she'll know

69

somebody's been there. She's terrified. He thinks it'll be easier to protect us all if we're together in Walnut. I know I've got to get out of Chicago. I'll never go back to my office, even when the FBI is done with it. Knowing what happened there, I could never go back, not even to get my stuff."

"Your stepfather left you here alone?"

"It was only supposed to be for one night. I was gonna gather up what I could stuff in my car and follow him the next day."

"If you stay in Chicago," Colter said, "we can give you protection. I'm taking you to a safe house when we leave here. You'll have armed guards."

"Protect me is what the guard in the building was supposed to do," she replied. "What if I'd still been there when those people broke in? I might-a been hangin' out the window along with your friend."

"I don't know," Colter said.

Emily asked if she could use my bathroom before they left. I told her where it was. While she was gone, Colter told me about the body pulled from the river.

"A lieutenant from the Callisi family," he said. "Some city officials think this might turn into an old-fashioned Mob war in the streets."

I was chewing on something else. "Why did they choose Emily's office?" I wondered. "They could have chosen any other office in the building and had a lot easier time getting in and out. Emily probably had the only Medeco on the property."

"It makes sense if they were trying to build credible circumstantial evidence that Carl committed suicide."

I could only shake my head. "What does the building's security guard have to say?"

"There's lots of questions I'd love to ask him," Colter said. "Nobody can find him. We have no idea where he, or his body, might be."

* * *

When Emily returned from the bathroom, she paused at my front door to apologize again for my near-death experience. I assured her again that she bore no responsibility for the incident, and I was fine.

"My boyfriend's been telling me for years I needed to get a new ride," I added. "Well, now I don't have any excuse."

When I was alone after Colter left to drive Emily to the safe house I stretched out on the sofa and tried to meditate my body into a state of relaxation and peace. But my mind kept scrambling back to the mystery at hand.

We had five dead, or possibly dead, people. Two button men from the Tricoletto mob family, one from the Callisi family, Carl Cribben, and the missing security guard from the federal building.

The two Tricoletto snitches died from causes no one could identify. No health problems. No wounds. No poisons in the stomach contents, urine, body tissue, or blood streams. One found in his back yard next to his pool. The other in his car. Friends and family members professed no idea why or how they died.

Carl Cribben. Hanged but not hanged. Again, no health problems of consequence. No wounds. No poisons. No known psychological or emotional problems. And so on. The dead Callisi capo might or might not be a part of this. And the security guard? Who knew? Maybe he'd been killed and his body hauled away. A forensics examination of the security station in the lobby turned up nothing of any value. His body hadn't turned up. And his wife said she hadn't heard from him since he left for work the night he disappeared. Perhaps he'd fled after being threatened.

In none of those cases, except the man in the river with two bullets in his head, was there evidence of homicide. Carl's case was iffy, too. The lack of bruising around the noose and the absence of petechial hemorrhaging in the eyes strongly suggested he died before the hanging.

So why, under those circumstances, was the medical examiner reluctant to rule death by homicide? Okay, Tony Donato was making no assumptions. He was waiting for all the tox results to come back. That was an acceptable and responsible explanation.

Meanwhile, the mystery deepened. I hoped Emily wouldn't be its next victim.

16

The next morning Steve drove me to a Ford dealership, a Subaru dealership, and an Acura dealership. The new Explorers were prettier than my old one, but not as comfortable. I liked everything about the Subaru Outback I test drove, as well as the Acura. But I didn't want to pay the money the Acura cost. It slid off my options list. We had talked about looking at Toyotas and maybe some GMC models, but the first three dealership visits wore me out. So Steve suggested lunch instead.

We went back to my neighborhood and ate at the bar at Bacchanalia, my favorite neighborhood Italian restaurant in the city. I'd never seen anyone finish one of Bacch's huge pepper-and-egg sandwiches, but Steve did it while I had a small caprese salad of fresh tomatoes, fresh mozzarella, fresh basil, and drizzles of olive oil and red wine vinegar. I also had a side of penne pasta in vodka sauce. Either dish would have been sufficient for lunch under normal circumstances, but I was starving because I'd slept in and skipped breakfast.

I didn't feel up to any more car shopping, and I had a column to write, so I asked Steve to drop me at a body shop over by the McCormick Place convention and expo complex where my insurance company had a rental SUV waiting. It turned out to be a Jeep Compass, and I drove it only part way to the office when I concluded it would not be on my short list of possible new rides. It wasn't a bad vehicle; I just found it very uncomfortable.

Eric Ryland told me my column had already been scrapped for the next day because he assumed I wouldn't feel up to it. When I thought about it, he was right.

I decided to visit the locksmith who sold the Medeco lock to Emily.

During the interview at my house Ron Colter had asked for the name of the store, and I jotted it down even though my voice recorder would have registered it.

Emily had complained that she could find only one Medeco dealer in all of Chicago and had to take time off from work to drive way up on the North Side to get there. I suspected the high price kept Medeco out of a lot of locksmiths' inventories. Emily said with installation the lock cost close to $400, and each key cost $25.

I found a space a few doors from the store and paid the parking fee for one hour with the app on my phone. I pushed through the door into a space where it appeared there were enough devices to lock up the entire city. A burly man, perhaps in his forties and sporting a beard that more resembled a tangled bird's nest, asked if he could help me.

I handed him my card and disclosed that I was investigating circumstances surrounding a possible murder.

"And your investigation brought you here?" he asked, handing me a card of his own. It said his name was Howard Hickok. "Am I in some sort of trouble? I've had a few speeding tickets in my life, but I've never been accused of murder."

"My investigation brought me here, yes, though nobody suspects that you were involved." He didn't look reassured. "Did you ever hear of a 'locked-room' mystery?"

"Yeah, I think. Remind me what it is."

"Somebody is murdered in a room where there's only maybe one door and one window that could be used as a way in or out," I said. "When police arrive, they find both escape routes locked from the inside. The only person who could have locked the door and the window is dead. But the death definitely wasn't a suicide. How could this happen?"

"This murder you're investigating, it's a locked-room mystery?"

"It is.

"And what you're askin' is, how this could be done?"

"It is."

"Pretty simple, I think," he said. "The killer stole the victim's keys and locked the door behind him when he left. Or he stole the keys earlier and had a copy made. Or maybe it was a friend or lover who had a copy the victim gave him… or her. Or maybe the victim wasn't dead yet when the killers left, and he… or she… managed to lock the door before shuffling off, though I don't know why the victim would do that." He cocked his head and looked at me sort of sideways. "You writin' a novel?"

"I should," I said. "But I'm not. This is real, Mr. Hickok. And none of your explanations is a possible solution to the mystery. None of those things happened."

He heaved a sigh. "Well, why don't you tell me what *did* happen, and I'll try to figure it out for you."

So I did. At first, he seemed distracted, shuffling things around on his counter while I was talking. When I got to the part that revealed the lock in question was a Medeco that he installed, his eyes riveted on me.

"What was the client's name?"

"Emily Goodsill. The lock was for her office door in the federal building."

He nodded for a moment, then looked back at me sharply. "Ms. Goodsill, she isn't the one who got killed, I hope."

"No," I replied. "She's fine."

"Oh, good. Nice lady. A little shy, but very pleasant. I remember the job. I was reluctant to do it, the office not being her property and all. But she seemed desperate, like she thought she was in immediate danger. She swore she had permission from the building management to install the lock, and she told me she'd get it in writing if I wanted it. I did want it. My mistake was not putting off installation until I got the written approval. She never sent it. Am I gonna be in any trouble over this?"

"Legal trouble? I doubt it. The government might insist you come back and remove the lock and repair the holes you put in the door assembly, but I don't imagine it will be any worse than that."

"I put a chain lock in for her, too."

"Yeah. The guys who kicked in the door broke the chain and messed up the door frame pretty good in the process. You might have to fix that, too."

His mind had gone elsewhere. "How'd they do that? You can't kick in a Medeco. I remember that install. The door frame was concrete filled. You don't often see that. It costs big money to build that way. But it will with-stand anything short of a nuke."

"That's what I'm here to find out."

"If it had been the chain the killer locked when he left, I might be able to help you. I've heard of a tool that lets somebody reach through a door, grab the end of chain, and hook it back into the slide. The door appears to have been locked from the inside. I'm not sure the device is legal since its only purpose would be to disguise a break-in."

"It wasn't the chain," I said. "The chain was broken. It was the Medeco."

He put up a finger. "Hold on a second." He turned around to some metal cabinets behind him and rummaged through one, coming out with a manila file folder.

"Here we go," he said. "This is her folder." He showed me the copy he'd made of Emily's driver's license, her signature on the paperwork, the receipt for the locks and the installations, and the paperwork that proved she had asked him to make only one key. There was no paperwork indicating she had ever ordered additional keys.

"And you wouldn't have made an extra key, just for yourself in case of emergency?"

Hickok shook his head vigorously. "Never. Not without a signed request from the owners of the lock."

He thought a moment. "Have you found the key?"

"Yes. Emily still had it on her key chain, at least 'til the FBI borrowed it to check for fingerprints. I don't know how that came out."

"Oh, I was thinkin' if there was any space under the door the killer might-a taken the key outside in the hall, locked the door, then slid the key underneath, back into the office. But then you'd-a found it on the floor just inside the door."

"No, Emily said the key was never out of her possession."

Hickok looked confounded, then his eyes went wide.

He asked, "Did the killer ever see her key? I don't mean like picking it up. I mean like it was maybe lyin' on her desk, and he got a good look."

I shrugged. "Maybe. I don't think anybody asked her that. What are you getting at?"

"I'm wonderin' if somebody memorized the cut of the key."

"What? I don't think that's possible."

"I have to fess up here," he said. "I can do it. There are a few other locksmiths I know of who can do it. But very few. You hafta have an eidetic memory."

"Like a photographic memory?"

"They're not exactly the same, but that's the idea. There was one time I got called out by the police because the driver of an armored truck makin' a delivery to a bank tossed his keys on the dashboard, got out of the truck, locked the door, and slammed it shut. It's amazing the stupid things people do."

"What did you do?" I asked.

"Luckily, the keys were splayed out so the vehicle key was fully visible." He held his hand up with his fingers spread wide. "I climbed up on the front bumper and then onto the hood and stared at the key for maybe thirty seconds. Then I went to my van and cut a copy from memory. Worked on the very first try, though sometimes it takes two or three tries to get it right."

"Is that possible with a Medeco?" I asked.

"Yes. For somebody with an eidetic memory, the hardest part would be getting a Medeco blank to use. He'd either have to have a source or steal it. But possible? Sure."

In the detecting business, young grasshopper, we call this "a clue."

17

I still had time on the parking meter, so I sat in the Jeep with the late morning sun warming the interior and called Ron Colter. He was in a meeting, so I left a message saying I'd solved part of the puzzle and needed to talk to him right away.

He returned my call twenty minutes later as I was driving to the office. I didn't have my phone connected to the Bluetooth service in the rental, so I put the phone on speaker and propped it in one of the console cup holders. I told Ron in detail what I'd learned from the locksmith.

"I never heard of such a thing," he said.

"Me, neither," I said. "I mean I've heard of eidetic memory, but never in this context. I took a few minutes to research it. There's some controversy as to whether it's a real thing, but it's not a new concept. A lot of people think Mozart had an eidetic memory. At fourteen he once heard a lovely piece of music, went home, and wrote it down correctly, note for note. Nikola Tesla supposedly had the ability, and Kim Peek."

"Who's Kim Peek?"

"Was. He's dead now. He was a savant, a mega-savant, some people said. The movie *Rain Man* was based on him. Dustin Hoffman played the part."

"Yeah, good for him. Look, I don't have time for a history lesson, or a film class. Where do you think this gets us?"

I told Colter about Howard Hickok's case of the locked armored car.

"Did you ask Emily if she ever saw anyone staring at her keyring? Apparently an eidetic would only have to look at a key for half a minute or so to commit the cut to memory. If you haven't asked her, could you?"

I heard Colter sigh. "That would explain some things," he said. "Now all we have to do is identify a Mafia soldier with an eidetic memory and a key-duplicating machine. Can't be too many of those around."

"I wouldn't be surprised if people who know that button man also know about his special talent," I said. "He's probably used it before to boost his career. He likely brags about the skill. The other thing I learned about people with eidetic memories is they often have terrible social skills. They don't play well with others."

"A perfect profile for a Mafia killer," Colter said. "Don't carry this any farther. Let my folks take over from here. We've got better sources than even you do. I'll keep you in the loop. I promise."

"Okay," I said. "Good luck."

"And, Deuce, thanks. I've been summoned to a meeting with the mayor this afternoon. She's really turning the screws on us to resolve this. Until you called, I had nothing to tell her."

18

I called Tony Donato, the medical examiner, and asked if he had a few minutes.

"We're really jammed up here, Deuce," he said. "I don't have any new information. Nothing positive back from tox yet."

"I just have a question, Tony. And I think I solved one of the dilemmas we've been wrestling with in Carl's case."

"Okay, come on over. I can give you ten minutes."

I told Tony about the theory I'd heard from Howard Hickok, the locksmith. He raised his eyebrows in surprise when he figured out where the story was going.

When I finished, I asked, "Is that a feasible theory?"

"Could be," he said. "There're a lot of conflicting ideas about eidetic memory. Some medical investigators don't believe it exists at all. Some think it might exist among some young children but not adults. Some think if it exists in adults, they're usually autistic and anti-social. And some think we're mistaking the theory of eidetic memory with people who simply have very keen powers of observation and very good short-term memories."

"What do you think?"

"To be honest, I don't think anything. It's not my field, and I have plenty to worry about without adding stuff that won't come across my desk, or my autopsy tables. My suggestion is that you do what Ron Colter asked you to do and leave this to his people. Somebody's already tried to do you harm once, Deuce. Don't invite another attempt by walking around mob joints asking if anyone knows killers with eidetic memories and key-cutting machines. That's too crazy a risk, even for you."

"I'm just curious," I admitted. "It's a fascinating subject. I'd like to know more."

"Then Google it from the safety of your office."

"Already done."

"Then leave it alone." He shifted in his chair. "You said you had a question."

"Yeah." I pulled out my notebook. "So far as you know, is there any deadly animal on earth with venom that would disappear from a human body before a toxicologist could find and identify it?"

He got up and poured a cup of coffee from his office machine. He held up the mug, asking me if I wanted a cup. I remembered the low bar for the quality of coffee in the morgue and shook my head.

"This isn't the sludge from the break room," he said. "It's good."

I gave in. "Okay, as long as you can guarantee my survival."

"If it kills you," he said, "at least I'll know the cause of death."

It was good, and I complimented him on it.

"So," he said, "your question. I know what you're driving at. But toxicology isn't my field, either, which is why we send those tests to experts. Off the top of my head, I don't know a venom like that. If the culprit is something exotic, we might not even have tests for it, and we'll never find it. There is a standard list of things checked in every tox screen. With Carl and the two button men we've expanded the list exponentially, which is one reason the tests are taking so long. But if the answer's not on our list, the tox panel won't identify it. It's maddening, but it is what it is."

I nodded in understanding. I was certain my face reflected my disappointment.

"How about non-animal poisons? Man-made stuff that would fit what we're looking for? Any thoughts on who I should ask about those?"

Tony thought for a moment. "I might," he said. "Let me make a call."

* * *

He picked up his office phone then set it down in favor of his private smart phone. No sense leaving an official trail of services rendered to a journalist.

"Hi, Grace, it's Tony Donato," he said when his call was answered. "Is Dr. Naderi in?"

He paused a moment then said, "Sure." He turned to me. "He's finishing with something. This guy's good. If anybody can answer your question, he can."

"Hey, Ben," he said into the phone. "I'm fine, thanks." They exchanged pleasantries about their families and complaints about their work loads. Tony finally got to the point.

"Say, do you know who Deuce Mora is, the columnist for the *Journal?*... Right. Well, she's sitting here in my office and has a question I can't answer, and I think maybe you can. Assuming the question has an answer. Could I send her over?"

"I'm not sure. Why don't I put her on the phone?" Tony turned to me. "This is Dr. Benjamin Naderi. He's the director of pharmacy at Rush Medical Center."

I took the phone. Naderi was very pleasant, but when he asked me what my question was, I told him it would be simpler if I explained in person. We made an appointment for the next morning.

I thanked Tony and got up to leave.

"You will let me know," Tony said, "if he comes up with an answer?"

"Yep," I said. "As long as you keep me supplied with good coffee."

19

My appointment with Dr. Naderi was at noon, which gave me time to finish a column before I left the office. I told Eric Ryland what I'd learned the previous day and where I was going today. I told him I hoped to be back in a couple of hours if he had any questions about the piece I'd just turned in.

Eric was noticeably impressed, something unusual for a man whose default attitude was skeptical and brusque.

"I wish we could print some of this stuff. Have you asked Colter if he's willing to let us go with anything?"

"I've thought about it. But most of what I've learned doesn't really move the investigation forward. I don't want to press until it's something really worthwhile."

"If the eidetic memory angle works out," he said, "it would make a hell of a good sidebar to the main story. The way the human brain works is endlessly fascinating."

"Yeah," I agreed. "I almost let myself get sidetracked on the subject."

"Go," he said. "Don't get sidetracked again."

And there it was, the Eric Ryland I knew and endured had returned.

* * *

Benjamin Naderi's office was in the Rush University Medical Center Hospital, a relatively new building that looked like no hospital I'd ever seen. The lower floors were all offices and labs, but the top half was a pile of patient rooms situated in wings that shot out from a central core at angles pointing northeast, northwest, southeast, and southwest, like a giant compass. I'd heard a lot of people call it ugly. Others said it reminded them of a butterfly. It had some tremendous advantages. Every patient room was private, with a sleep sofa if a relative wanted to stay overnight. Each room got a lot of light through huge windows with clear views of the city. The hospital was the centerpiece of a sprawling urban campus of medical offices, labs, a world-renowned orthopedic center, highly regarded medical and nursing schools, a rehab facility, and a partridge in a pear tree. It all overlooked I-290, a main corridor between Chicago and its western suburbs.

When I was shown into Naderi's office at the front of the hospital pharmacy, two men awaited me. One appeared to be Middle Eastern, maybe Egyptian. The other was a younger black man. Behind them, behind several levels of glass security, there looked to be enough huge white jugs full of pills and sealed carafes full of potions to medicate every resident of Illinois, Wisconsin, Indiana, and Ohio for at least five years.

I said as much to the directors of pharmacy.

"They're not all full, you know," Naderi answered with a sly smile.

"Ever run out?" I asked.

"We try not to," he said. "We have secret stashes inside the Bean in case of emergency." He was referring to a giant sculpture in the northwest corner of Grant Park, a half dozen blocks east and a few blocks north of where we were. And he was joking.

Naderi gave me a warm smile and rose to shake my hand. He introduced the other man as Richard Malone, his deputy. I shook his hand, too, and sat down.

"I'm a fan of yours," Naderi said. "I agree with your point of view on most things, and when I don't agree, you give me something to think about. I didn't realize you were so tall."

I gave him my stock response: "It's hard to judge my height from a head shot at the top of my columns," I said.

"So what can we do for you?" Naderi asked. "Tony Donato sounded very mysterious on the phone."

"It's not so mysterious as it is complicated," I said. "It will take me a few minutes to bring you up to date, so bear with me. And you have to assure me you will hold what I tell you in as much confidence as you would patient information."

Both nodded, and I launched into the story. Neither moved during my recitation, which lasted nearly ten minutes. I'm not sure they blinked. I had captured their interest.

Then I got to the point of my conversation with Tony the day before about animal venoms that might disappear from a body quickly and leave no trace.

"Tony had no idea if such a thing existed," I said. "I don't think the animal kingdom creates poisons that disappear quickly to cover up murder."

"I don't think the human kingdom does, either," Malone said. "Though these days, I can't be positive of that."

I held up my right index finger as a signal for them to pause. "But what if," I asked, "it's something that was created for a good purpose that has been turned on its head by people who want to kill other people and hide their actions."

"I know what you're getting at," Naderi said. "But I can't immediately think of anything that fits your description." He turned to his deputy. "Do you, Rich?"

"It has to kill fast," Malone said, "and disappear fast, right?"

I nodded.

Malone shook his head. "I can't think of anything..." Then his eyebrows shot up and he looked at Naderi. "Sux?" he said.

Naderi thought about it a few seconds. "That fits what Deuce is looking for. But the average person could never lay his hands on any."

"Wait," I said. "These aren't average people. They're Mafia killers."

Naderi shrugged, admitting, "Well, that's a point. Though I've never heard of sux being used as an agent of murder. Good lord."

I asked, "Are you saying 'sucks,' s-u-c-k-s?"

They both laughed. "No," Naderi said, "but I guess that description would be apt if it kills you. We're saying s-u-x. It's medical shorthand for succinylcholine. Its full scientific name is 'suxamethonium chloride', hence the shorthand, 'sux.' It's a depolarizing muscle relaxant." He shook his head briefly and raised a hand, as if he realized he was getting too technical for me. "It works by preventing muscles from contracting. It's a paralyzing agent."

The thought horrified me. "Why," I asked, "would you use something like that?"

"I wouldn't," Naderi said. "I'm not a medical doctor. But it's often called for in the ER or the ICU if a patient is resisting intubation. In lay terms that's having a respirator tube shoved down your throat to breathe for you. Sux produces short-term paralysis. Under its influence you can't move, and you can't breathe. The effect generally lasts a few minutes, long enough to get the respirator set up and breathing for the patient. If medical personnel need to use intubation, it's an emergency, and they've got to get the tube in place fast before the patient suffocates or dies from whatever got him in life-threatening trouble in the first place. You can't waste time fighting a patient or he'll die before you can save him."

"That's the advantage sux gives us," Malone said. "If it's administered intravenously, it takes only seconds to kick in, so it's ideal in an emergency situation."

I asked, "If the syringe is wielded by someone untrained in the art of shoving a needle into a vein, could he shove it into a muscle?"

"Yes," Naderi said. "It can be administered intramuscular, but it will be a little longer taking effect and could require a larger dose."

"And once it wears off," I asked, "wouldn't it leave traces?"

"No," the senior doctor said. "It's destroyed by blood plasma very quickly. It wouldn't last long enough to do a tox screen, even if the screen was done right away."

"So," I asked, "if it wears off that fast, how do you kill somebody with it?"

"Fast is a relative term," Naderi said. "If the effect lasts ten minutes and there's no breathing assist, the patient will likely be dead. An overdose extends the time of paralysis. Resuscitation is possible, even in an OD scenario, as long as there's someone around who wants the patient to live and has the skills to make that happen. If the object is to kill, you let the sux take its course."

"I just thought of something," Malone said. "While sux in the bloodstream breaks down and disappears, that wouldn't be the case if it got on the victim's skin. If a drop or two backwashed—escaped while the needle was being inserted—the sux could survive a long time. Tell Tony Donato to look for a puncture mark. It will be fairly large because sux syringes have wider-than-normal needles for faster delivery of the drug. If he finds a mark like that, he should swab around it and test for sux."

"He told me he already looked for needle marks."

"Tell him to look again."

"Wow," I said, "this is scary stuff."

"If you think it's scary for you," Malone said, "think of how a patient feels. Sux is part of an anesthesia protocol, but it's not an anesthesia. Used without anesthesia it wouldn't put the patient out. He'd be conscious through the whole ordeal of suddenly not being able to move or breathe, until he loses consciousness from oxygen deprivation and dies."

"Sux has been around for what, over 100 years," Naderi said. "If there had been an unusual mortality rate from its use, it would have been pulled from the market a long time ago. It's so dangerous it's safe, if you know what I mean."

"Is it generally kept locked up in a hospital?"

Naderi nodded. "On refrigeration, and under lock and key."

"So how do some thugs from a Chicago Mafia family get their hands on it?"

"That," Naderi said, "is not a question for a director of pharmacy. It's a question for the police. Maybe even the FBI."

There was no question that this was critical information. But all I could think of was Carl Cribben lying on Emily Goodsill's office floor unable to move, unable to cry out, unable to breathe until he died.

I wanted to cry. Even more, I wanted to find the killer and return the favor.

20

I called Tony Donato from the street as I walked to my car.

"I already checked for needle marks," he said. "On all three vics."

"Dr. Naderi said you should check again."

"And if I find a puncture wound, for all I know it was left by a mosquito. It doesn't have to be caused by a syringe, or during the injection of a lethal dose of sux."

"No, but even though succinyl... however you say it... sux... gets neutralized inside the victims, you could find traces on the skin outside the wound where there's no blood plasma to destroy it."

Tony was getting irritated. "I fully understand the science, Deuce," he said.

I didn't let up. "And if the substance was something other than sux, maybe you'd find traces of whatever it was."

"I understand that, too. But I don't like being second-guessed."

"You're the one who set me up with Dr. Naderi," I reminded him. "He's only trying to help. What's your problem?"

"Well, for one thing, I don't have any succinylcholine lying around my morgue. None of my patients will ever need it. But I need it to make a comparison if I find a needle mark and any foreign substance on the skin. I'll call Naderi and ask him if he has a syringe or two he can spare. Meanwhile—like I have time for this—I'll start re-examining the victims for needle marks in places I didn't look the first time. I didn't wash the bodies, in case something unusual, like this, came up. If there was succinylcholine on their skin when they came in, it should still be there."

It was.

I was on the phone at the office conducting an interview for my column the next day when Tony called back. I had to let his call go to voice mail. When I listened to his message, he sounded almost breathless.

"Get over here now," he said. "Ron Colter is on his way. We got our break."

* * *

The three of us sat in Tony's office. He had given orders that he didn't want to be disturbed. We all had coffee. It was good again.

"Deuce, I don't know how you do it," Tony said. "You keep finding evidence where the rest of us miss it."

"I didn't find anything, Tony," I said. "We knew what we were looking for, a substance that kills without leaving any signs toxicology can pick up. You put me onto somebody who might have an answer, and I asked the question. Judging from your excitement I gather that Doctors Naderi and Malone gave us the right answer."

"Tell us what you found," Ron Colter instructed. He sounded impatient.

Tony pulled three manila file folders to a spot on his desk in front of him. He opened the first one and scanned it.

"Nicholas 'Nikko' Polletto, white male, forty-two according to his driver's license. Minor blockages of two blood vessels of the heart, no surprise for a man who probably spent most of his life eating high-fat Italian foods. But the blockages weren't sufficient to cause problems yet. I found a puncture wound in a place I'd never found one on my dead addict clients—between the cheeks of his buttocks, deep on the left one. A foreign substance left behind, a very small sample, tested positive for suxamethonium chloride."

"Where was his body found?" I asked.

"In his car in an alley behind an Italian restaurant at Clark and Grand in River North," Ron Colter told me. "Cops responded to a call from the restaurant after a busboy found Nikko's car blocking access to the garbage bins outside the joint's back door. Nikko was dead in the back seat. Now

I have a question. Tony, you found no sign of this sux inside Nikko's body, right?"

Tony nodded. "Right. Nothing. Presumably his blood plasma neutralized whatever dose they pumped into him."

"How long," Ron asked, "could one of these guys have lived post-injection without a respirator breathing for him?"

"That depends on the size of the doses," Tony said, "and whether they were given intravenously or into a muscle, as was the case with all three of these men. I suspect they all got massive doses to make sure they didn't recover."

"So sux is the cause of death?" Ron asked.

"There's no other possible COD, at least not until the tox screens come back. But let me finish with these files."

The second button man was Philip deGeorgio, thirty-nine, whose body was found in his back yard. His puncture wound was in the upper rear part of his right thigh, lost in the crease between the top of the thigh and the buttocks.

"And Carl?" I asked, not really wanting to know.

"Under his left arm," Tony said, "well hidden in the hair in his armpit."

We sat and drank coffee and mulled it all over for a while, trying to define where the new information left us. We now knew all three deaths were homicides, and the causes of death was succinylcholine. In and of themselves, those facts didn't take us far. They created more questions, three big ones in particular: Who were the killers, how did they get their hands on enough of the drug to kill three grown men, and how much more were they holding for additional murders?

"I think that ball's in my court," Ron Colter said, rising from his chair.

I couldn't see anywhere for me to go from here except back to my three-a-week columns for the *Journal.*

As Ron started out of Tony's office, I asked him, "How's Emily doing?"

"She's safe and working her job under armed guard at the safe house," he said. "She wants to go home to Walnut, and if she insists, we'll have to let her go. But we're trying to scare her into staying for the very real reason that she'd be much harder to protect in an old house in a small farming community pretty much out in the middle of nowhere than in a fortified building somewhere in or around Chicago."

"Anything more you want me to do with her?"

"Not for now," Ron said. "You did fine. Helped a lot."

He thanked Tony and left, and there was nothing for me to do but leave, too.

I felt like I was leaving a job half done and shirking my responsibility to Carl Cribben. Tony picked up on my bleak mood.

"If you're looking for a way to stay in the game," he said, "you might give some thought to how the killers could've gotten their hands on the sux."

"Where would it be stored?" I asked.

Tony said, "Hospital pharmacies. Emergency care clinics and surgical centers. Surgical supply houses. Places where it's produced—drug companies and their labs. Large animal vets might use it, too."

"It would be helpful if we could get all of them around here to do an inventory for us," I said. "But that might take a court order. At least a request from the FBI."

"You should talk to Ron about it," Tony said. "Most medical institutions inventory their drugs all the time. Maybe the FBI or DEA should ask if they're missing any sux."

"You think they'd admit it if they were?"

"I don't know, but I suspect they would. If they refuse, the feds wouldn't take kindly to it. Nobody wants to bring down the wrath of the feds."

"Interesting thought," I said.

Tony said, "If I think of anything else, I'll let you know."

21

The room reeked of money and cigar smoke and the uneasy scent of secrets.

The dimmed lighting wasn't much relieved by the eleven-foot arched windows that lined the east wall overlooking Lake Shore Drive and the inky expanse of Lake Michigan. Darkness had descended over the city, and light from the highway didn't reach the twenty-first floor of the chic hotel that housed the cigar salon and lounge. Reflected light from the moon, one night short of being full, was just sufficient to create eerie shadows as the few staff employed by the salon moved quietly across highly polished hardwood floors and the area rugs that cost as much as private airplanes. This was not a place the tourists knew. It was not for average men or for any women at all. It was private, exclusive, and very, very secretive.

There were no guest rooms on the twenty-first floor. The salon took up a third of the total floor space. The remainder was subdivided into twenty-one plush offices rented only to members of the exclusive club. The hotel elevators didn't stop at the twenty-first floor unless you had a digital key card to take you there. Guests were discouraged but could come if accompanied by a member and pre-approved by the board. Each had to agree to and sign a pledge to reveal nothing of what they saw or heard, and any violation would earn the member who brought the offender a $50,000 fine.

Business conducted within the nameless club, often referred to by members only as Twenty-One, was accomplished in hushed voices that would not carry between the widely spaced tables and chair clusters. It was as if walls stood between each cluster and the rest of the world, penetrated only by the occasional staff member inquiring as to the needs of the men he served. Another Martel Creation Grand Extra or a Courvoisier Initiale Extra for the Sir, perhaps? Or a

Cohiba Esplendido from the enormous walk-in humidor that served as the room's elegant centerpiece and showplace for the world's finest and most expensive cigars?

Two men sat quietly in a pair of Aidan tufted-leather wing chairs with their backs to the rest of the room talking in low voices. Their drinks sat near at hand, served in appropriate Orrefors cut crystal glasses that retailed for $90 a pair. Smoldering cigars rested in marble ashtrays on small, individual round tables made of softly finished Central American Bocate wood, highly prized for its amazing grain and generally thought to be the most expensive wood in the world. Apparently, it wasn't too expensive for this club. It had been used lavishly in accent designs in the burnished solid oak paneling that covered all the walls. Expensive tapestries hung between each Bocate inlay. It was said the tapestries were expert knockoffs of the work of Renaissance artist Raphael, but rumors persisted that some of them, at least, were the real things, recovered from the caches of stolen art amassed by the Nazis during World War II. Their purpose in the club was two-fold: the addition of beauty and the more practical job of deadening sound. They also added a good deal of pretense; at Twenty-One, pretense was a coveted style to be established and maintained through the years.

It was accepted that members did not scan the room to see who else was present. That would be considered a violation of protocols and invasion of privacy. Had anyone been able to see the faces of the two men in the back corner of the room, only one would have been immediately recognizable. The other, while of some renown, was not so much known by his face as by his deeds.

Their conversation was both quiet and cryptic.

"This last one was inexcusably sloppy," the younger of the two said. "What were your people thinking? Perhaps, more accurately, they weren't thinking. They were showing off."

"They were sending a message," the older man said, "to anyone who insists on pursuing the dangerous undertaking of turning on us."

"The first two I get," the other said. "Number three wasn't necessary, not that way."

"Yes, it was. It was meant to put the fear of God into this town. The message stated clearly that if we would remove him so flamboyantly, we'd do the same for anybody in our family or others who appear to be developing doubts about where their loyalties lie."

"*It was all supposed to look like deaths by natural causes,*" *the younger man said.* "*The latest one blew that plan out of the water.*"

"*Maybe it should have been handled differently. But the first two still look good.*"

"*But nobody's gonna believe the ruse anymore.*"

"*You don't know that. There is no evidence of a crime. They'll never identify a suspect, let alone prove murder. It was a suicide. There are no witnesses.*"

The younger man became alarmed. "*Don't talk like that. Not here. Not ever.*"

"*Nuthin' to worry about in here.*"

"*Just don't do it. Not anywhere. Not even takin' a piss in your own bathroom.*"

"*You wanna call the whole thing quits?*"

The younger man thought about it for a moment then shook his head. "*We can't. Not as long as there's still a danger that the investigation will continue.*" *He paused and then added,* "*But stay away from the reporter. That thing with trying to burn her up in her car was stupid. Really way over the top.*"

The older man said, "*We eliminate who we gotta eliminate. There's a second one nosing around, too, some guy outta D.C. He's the one pulled the woman outta her car. Now we gotta worry about him, too.*"

The younger man started to object, but his companion held up a hand to silence him.

"*Let us handle our end. We know what we're doing. We've been doin' it for generations. We will dust whoever is a necessary elimination to protect ourselves and to protect you. You keep the packages comin'.*" *He nodded toward a briefcase sitting between their chairs.* "*I presume this is mine.*"

"*Yes.*"

"*Then we'll talk again soon. Stay calm.*"

With that the older man got up, reached down and picked up the briefcase as though it were his all along, and walked toward the rear exit from the club. The two men didn't shake hands, which made the younger one happy.

As he picked up what was left of his cigar, he saw that his hand was shaking.

22

I was discouraged and distracted as I made my way through the parking garage next to the *Journal*'s office building in the South Loop. The session with Ron Colter in the medical examiner's office left me feeling as if I was living my life at the terminus of a dead-end street. I saw no way forward with the investigation into Carl's death and turning around to retrace my steps would simply lead me past dreary scenery I'd already examined to no avail.

When I left Tony Donato's office, I called Colter to ask if he planned to request a survey by all the institutions and offices in the region that keep succinylcholine on hand. Inventories might identify places from which vials of the stuff had gone missing.

"Done and done," Colter replied. "These places inventory regulated and dangerous substances frequently. Most of their inventories are recent. We're asking all of them for updates, anyway. But to be honest, if somebody stole a couple of vials of sux it was probably months ago, before the two Tricoletto guys turned up dead. The places that keep sux on hand have done inventories more recently than that. Any missing supplies would have been discovered by now. Nobody reported any."

"It had to come from somewhere," I said, stating the obvious out of frustration.

"But where?" Colter asked. "We're trying to cover all the bases, but I don't expect any big reveals."

I returned to my desk feeling even more glum and disheartened and completed a column for the next day, but my head wasn't in it. My editor noticed.

"The city's public education failings are one of the topics that always light a fire under you," Eric said, referring to the subject matter of the piece I'd just turned in. "I'm not feeling the heat today."

I nodded in agreement. "I'm not, either, Eric. Sorry."

I brought him up to date on what had happened all day.

"Get out of here," he said. "Go home. Take a bubble bath. Or go to that Italian place by your house, have a good meal, get drunk with your friends. Relax over the weekend and come back on Monday with a new attitude. You can't win 'em all, and you know it."

All this was in my head as I threaded my way down the aisles of the garage's sixth level, headed for my rental Jeep. I always felt uneasy in the garage. The anxiety dated back to the morning a sniper took a shot at me there. The bullet went through my windshield and hit a brass monkey hanging from my rearview mirror, a gift from an old boyfriend. The monkey shattered, and a piece of it came through the driver's side window and plowed a trench in my upper arm. I was lucky at that. Had the monkey not been running interference for me, the bullet would have plowed the trench inside my head. Occasionally, as I made my way to or from the elevators, I had flashbacks.

I was having one now. Several of the ceiling lights were out. It might have been a natural failure or sabotage. In either event, the dim glow cast by the remaining fluorescent tubes freaked me out.

At that moment, from deep in the gloom, someone uttered my name.

* * *

My first instinct was to dive between the two nearest vehicles and roll beneath the one that had the most ground clearance. The image that formed in my head was of a swarthy man stooping down to see under the vehicle and shooting for my head, or firing bullets into the gas tank and blowing two aisles of cars to kingdom come. I didn't much like the first image, and I'd already been through something like the second already. The only options left were to run, which didn't appeal to the fighter in me, or to use my eyes to search out the source of the voice and determine if I was dealing with friend or enemy.

I saw motion in my peripheral vision. When I turned I was staring into the eyes of Steve Pace, the Washington *Chronicle* reporter who had pulled me from my fiery SUV.

"I'm sorry," he said in a carefully modulated tone. "I was trying not to startle you."

"Your plan needs more work," I said and heard a tremble in my voice. "If you wanted to talk to me, why didn't you call or come to the office? I don't respond well to people lurking in the shadows. And if you're going to ask for any new information in the Cribben case, I'm fresh out."

"I was actually going to ask you if you knew a good place to eat. I've been in town for four days, and I still haven't had one of those great steaks Chicago's known for."

"A lot of people are more partial to its seafood these days," I said. "But I can recommend several steak places."

"I was hoping you'd go with me. I'm not planning on pressuring you for information on the story. I'm tired of eating alone. I get enough of that at home."

And, like that, I caved. I knew how Steve felt. Exactly.

"I don't suppose you'd also be up for a drink or two before the meal?" I asked.

"Oh, absolutely."

"Then hop in this poor excuse for transportation, and let's go."

It was an unusually warm evening for early May in Chicago. Thermometers had stretched into the low eighties during the day and still hovered close to eighty when the valet at Smith & Wollensky took my car as daylight began to fade. Clouds had moved in, which would help hold the temperatures up for a few hours. Steve and I decided to take the weather risk and asked for a table outside. The wait inside without a reservation on a Friday night stretched to an hour. Outside we could be seated immediately, and there were fire pits all around to insure we wouldn't freeze to death before dessert arrived. Both of us had jackets if we needed them.

While we waited for our server, we took a few minutes to look around, leaving the menus untouched on the table. We had a breathtaking view of the Chicago River right below us. Marina City Towers spiraled above us. And the newly improved and enlarged River Walk stretched out along the river-banks past shops, bars, restaurants, and coffee shops that lent their brightly lighted facades to the other city colors reflected off the slow-moving water. The Chicago River itself, now probably as clean as it had been in centuries, emitted a fresh aroma that added to the ambience.

When our waiter arrived, Steve ordered a double Hendricks martini, up with cucumber garnish to match the gin's infusion. That sounded very good. I asked for the same, but since I was driving, I specified a single. Steve mentioned to our server that we were not in any rush to get through dinner and asked for time to enjoy our drinks before we ordered.

"Absolutely," the young man said with a pleasant smile, and disappeared inside to find us our alcohol.

While we waited, we checked the menu.

"I'm buying," Steve said. "So have whatever you want." The prices, some of which ran to triple digits, didn't faze him at all. But then he was used to pretty much the same price points in the nation's capital.

As I described for him some of the remarkable development and river-front architecture visible from our table, his concentration focused entirely on what I was saying. He asked intelligent questions. His interest felt gen-uine, but then his own hometown had some pretty remarkable architecture itself.

I relaxed. I could feel the day's tension begin to dissipate—until Steve asked me a question I never expected to hear.

"How did it feel to kill a man?"

23

I couldn't answer right away because our server returned with our drinks. Mine looked like a double, rimming its glass with a clear liquid in which there were visible eddies and currents inviting me to dive in. Steve's double was served in what I can only describe as a conical swimming pool.

He held his glass up—carefully so none of the precious liquid would slosh over the rim. It was the gesture of a toast, but I was in no mood to celebrate.

"What the hell did you say?" I demanded.

Steve did a small head shrug and took a sip before setting his glass down.

"I asked, inappropriately perhaps, what it felt like to kill a man."

I would have liked to slug my drink down in one gulp, but instead I pushed it away a few inches.

"What the hell are you talking about?"

"Enjoy your drink, Deuce, and I'll explain what I asked and why I asked."

He stopped and waited, apparently expecting me to pick up my glass. I didn't.

"Okay," he said. "Before I flew out here I did some research on you. Among the many feats and great stories and prizes in your history, I also discovered reports on your encounter with operatives in an international child trafficking ring. One of them tried to abduct you with the intent to kill you, but you killed him first. With your bare hands."

It felt as if something stuck in my throat, preventing me from breathing. My untouched martini sat by my right hand. Without thinking I picked it up and took a healthy pull. It went down smoothly, and I could breathe again.

"That's my business, Steve," I said. "Most people are kind enough not to bring it up."

"I have a reason for asking," he said. "Honest, I'm not trying to dredge up unpleasantness. But something similar happened to me more than twenty-five years ago. One big difference. The man whose death is on my hands didn't do what I thought he did."

My anger dissipated, and now I wanted to know more about the man sharing the table with me.

I asked, "You want to talk about it?"

"Not really," he said. "I've gone this long without pouring my guts out. My editors never bring it up. My friends won't mention it because they know I don't want to discuss it. But I've never sat across drinks before with someone I thought might, just might, be able to give me some useful perspective."

"You should have thought about a shrink," I said.

"The *Chronicle* offered to get help for me, but I needed to move on and away from the whole affair. Eventually, everything worked out fine for everyone with the exception of the man who died. His kids have forgiven me. I can't forgive myself."

"Twenty-five years is a long time to let that kind of guilt work on your head."

"Do you still feel any queasiness about what happened to you?"

"Hell, yes. Every day of my life. But I hope to get over it before it becomes a memory that's a quarter century old. Do you want to tell me what happened to you?"

It was a long story, and a tragic one, and we were through our second drinks (the topic of conversation kept me sober) and working on appetizers when Steve finished.

I sat back for a moment and watched him. More than twenty-five years, and the story still almost brought him to tears. Or maybe it was the gin.

"So basically," I said, "you thought this man guilty of covering up a terrible crime, and when he died suddenly, you thought it might have been your relentless pursuit of the truth that killed him."

Steve didn't raise his eyes, but he nodded. "That's the nutshell version, yeah."

"Any medical evidence he was predisposed to heart attacks, strokes, aneurisms, dandruff, hangnails?"

I could see that I failed to lighten the mood.

"His doctor said he was being treated for high blood pressure and had some history of heart problems. But not so terrible that his life was in imminent danger."

"Then maybe you weren't the cause..."

"That's not the point, Deuce. The guilt I can't shake is the possibility that I put so much pressure on him that I pushed him off a ledge he wouldn't have been standing on otherwise. That the chance even exists, however slight, still keeps me awake nights."

"I think even at this late date some professional counseling would help," I said. "My friend, Mark, got me hooked up a few months ago with a psychologist who specializes in helping first responders with their PTSD aftershocks—post-traumatic stress. I resisted at first, but when I finally got around to talking to him, it did help."

"You did what was necessary to save your own life," Steve said. "I don't have any excuses. I was too eager for a story that turned out to be nothing like I had imagined."

Our main courses came. A magnificent beef filet for me and a full twenty-one-ounce bone in rib-eye for Steve. Though my piece of beef was dwarfed by his, it was still ten ounces, more by half than I would be able to enjoy in one sitting. I made a point of telling myself to leave half the meal for the take-home box, so I'd have dinner for one night over the weekend.

Steve managed to finish his half cow without even pausing to rethink it and sat eyeing the bone.

"If I was home alone, I'd pick that up in my bare hands and gnaw the heck out of it. But it's probably not appropriate here."

"Don't let me stop you," I said.

In the end, he passed on the bone, and we both passed on dessert and coffee. Steve paid the bill without flinching. I offered to leave the tip, and he declined.

We stepped up to the valet stand, and Steve took the ticket from my hand and handed it to a young man who raced off to get my rental.

It was right then we heard a woman scream.

24

The noise came from directly behind me. Steve and I whirled around and saw a woman, who had obviously had some major renovation done from her chest to the top of her forehead, holding her manicured hands to her face, looking at a man lying at her feet.

She screamed. "Joey, Joey, please don't die on me." Then she screamed again. I expected a director ten feet away to yell, "Cut!"

No such luck.

The woman seemed to be trying to find a way to drop to her knees beside the man, but her lame dress had her wrapped up so tight from knees to neck that there wasn't any range of motion to allow for kneeling or stooping. Instead, desperate to get to the ground, she allowed herself to fall. She began to drag herself closer to the man named Joey, calling his name, oblivious to the damage the pavement was perpetrating on her pricey clothing.

I looked down at Joey and realized she was better off not getting up close and personal. He was on his back, his body straining as though he was trying to find a muscle that still worked. His mouth was agape and drooling, his eyes wide in terror. Now people all around us were yelling for a doctor. A few had realized the better and quicker course was to take out their cell phones and call 9-1-1. I heard several try to describe to the operator what the problem was. The closest I heard to anything accurate came from a woman who sounded like she was forcing herself to stay calm in the face of the horror.

"He looks dead," she said, "but maybe not quite. I think he's having a seizure, or maybe convulsions. His muscles are all bunched up, and I can see terror in his eyes. I'm not sure he's breathing, though."

That sounded frighteningly familiar.

I turned a quick circle searching for someone who might be looking for Steve and me, but everyone's attention was on the man on the ground. My car pulled up. Before Steve could act, I shoved cash into the valet's hand and said to Steve, "We gotta get outta here."

"Shouldn't we stay?" he asked. "The police are going to want to talk to witnesses."

"I didn't witness anything until after the woman screamed," I said. "Did you?"

"No," he said.

"Then you can't tell the police what happened. Neither can I."

The valet stopped to tell me my fob was in a cup holder in the car.

"Do you know him?" I asked, cocking my head toward the dying man.

"I seen him around here before," the valet said. "I think his friends call him 'Joey.' Sometimes they call him 'Gimp.' Sounds like a nickname 'cause he walks with a limp. I could tell by the look on his face he didn't like to be called that."

Steve Pace was staring at me as if he had a dozen questions. I knew what they were. I also knew we didn't have time for answers.

"Like I said," I told him, "we gotta get outta here."

We jumped in the Jeep, and I peeled away, leaving the bewildered valet swiveling his head between the dead man on the pavement and the $20 bill I'd stuck into his hand.

What I missed seeing was the man who had been standing behind "Joey." He backed slowly away from the victim as he collapsed to the pavement. So focused was everyone's attention on the dying man that police did not find a single person who saw the killer remove himself from the immediate murder scene, wrap a used syringe in a latex glove, and drop both into a paper bag. He folded the bag and tucked it into his coat pocket for disposal later, away from the scene.

Then he melted like a ghost into the chaotic night.

25

I called Ron Colter's personal cell phone as soon as we were clear of the restaurant. The call went to voice mail. I called his office. Same result. I cursed and called his private phone again. Again I got no answer, so I left a message. I was cryptic, partly for the sake of speed, and partly because I wasn't certain how much I wanted to say in front of Steve.

Pace demanded, "What the hell is going on?"

"In a minute," I said.

I was southbound on Columbus Drive, where the street dips underground before emerging to run down the spine of Grant Park. I saw the Hotel Fairmont coming up on my right. I swung a hard right at the next corner, onto East Lake Street, and pulled up in front of the hotel's main entrance.

I told Steve, "Keep a sharp eye all around. Let me know if anybody approaches the car. If it's a hotel valet, tell him we don't need help, that we're waiting to pick up some friends. If it looks more threatening, tell me right away, and I'll make a run for it."

"Yeah, okay, fine," Steve said. "But not unless you tell me what's going on."

I didn't want to reveal more than I had to, but I had to tell Pace something since he was deep in this with me now. I started to speak when my phone rang. It was Colter.

"What's happening?" the FBI chief demanded. "My phones are going wild. Somebody was killed along the river a few minutes ago. I presume that's your emergency, too."

"Yeah," I said. "How'd you find out so fast?"

"One of the cops who responded to about twenty 9-1-1 calls recognized the dead guy and knew I'd be interested. Tell me what you know."

"Okay, but before I do, you should know there's a reporter from Washington, D. C. sitting beside me."

"Oh, crap," he said. "Mute the Bluetooth."

"It's a rental car. I don't have it hooked up to the phone."

"Then turn off the speaker and hold the phone to your ear."

I reached toward phone, but Steve clamped a hand over my wrist.

"I'm part of this now, whether you and the FBI like it or not," he said in a stage whisper. "I deserve to hear."

He was right.

"Well, keep watch while you're listening." I turned back to the phone. "I think maybe we witnessed the murder of a mob guy outside Smith and Wollensky. We were leaving after dinner. My first idea was that he might have been one of the thugs who killed Carl since made guys who were part of Carl's investigation are falling like flies these days. But I have no evidence at all to support that. The man's name was Joey. His nickname was 'Gimp.'"

I went through the story, short though it was.

"Did the killer make a move on you?" Ron asked.

"A move, no, not that I could tell," I said. "But since I didn't get a look at the killer, and since the whole crowd was milling around, I might not've recognized a move if I'd seen one. Nobody had eyes on us that I noticed." I glanced at Steve. He shook his head. "We just jumped in the car and left. We're sitting on Lake Street now, outside the Fairmont Hotel."

"All right, listen to me. Does the other reporter have his own car?"

"Yes. It's parked in the garage next to the *Journal* office."

"Good. Get back there and park your rental well away from his vehicle and don't use it again. Does the paper have a guard in the lobby all night?"

"Two. Both armed."

"Then get there, alert them to watch for trouble, tell them the FBI is on the way. Go upstairs to Eric's conference room. I'll meet you there as soon as I can get there. I'm sending three agents to watch the building. One will look like a member of the cleaning crew and will need to get access to be inside the lobby. The other two will look innocuous and be stationed outside, probably one in a car in front and one on the sidewalk."

"What do we do while we wait for you?"

"Not a damned thing. Just stay put."

* * *

Even though Colter hadn't told me to include my editor, I called Eric to tell him what had happened. He called in the paper's lead attorney, Jonathan Bruckner, who got on a Skype connection with Bryanna Regan, the metro editor of the *Washington Chronicle* and Steve Pace's immediate supervisor. She had called in her newspaper's attorney, Alexander Talcott, who arrived at the Washington end of the connection several minutes later. Regan and Talcott wanted to be allowed to sit in on the upcoming meeting. Nobody in the room had any objection, and I doubted that Ron Colter would, either.

I was wrong.

Regan and Talcott listened without interruption while Steve brought them up to date on what had happened thus far, to the extent that he knew. When he finished, Regan started to ask questions. Bruckner said none of us would say any more until Colter arrived, and then he would take over.

So, we sat and listened while Talcott and Bruckner kept up a steady stream of stories and experiences, none of which had anything to do with the problems immediately at hand. It was a way to pass the time until Colter arrived. The two lawyers were friends, as most big-city newspaper attorneys tended to be, due to years of wrestling with the same problems, the same governments, and the same bullheaded types of reporters who kept their wing of the legal profession busy and well-compensated.

When Colter walked in, he was noticeably annoyed that our little investigative team of two had now swelled to seven, but he had no time to argue the matter. There was business to be done, which wouldn't start until Colter had reiterated our promises that nothing could be published or in any other way made public until we all had express, written permission from the Justice Department. The editors repeated their reluctance to continue that commitment. They relented when Colter told them they could agree or watch his back as he walked out the door.

"I think this would be a matter for a court to decide," Talcott said. There was not a hint of a threat in his voice. His tone was matter-of-fact.

"You could try," Colter replied. "But make up your minds in the next ten seconds because we don't have any longer than that to waste. If you decide to make this a legal test, I have no option but to leave."

Talcott and Regan both nodded. "All right," Regan said.

Colter brought everyone up to speed quickly, and everyone seemed to be thinking about the ramifications for a few moments.

Then Eric asked, "Anything happening downstairs?"

Colter shook his head. "Your guards and my agents haven't seen anything out of the ordinary. I'm going to keep my people on duty for the rest of the night, and we'll reassess after dawn. The likelihood of trouble should go down as the sun comes up and the streets fill up with people heading to work."

I sighed. "I should remind you the sidewalk out front of the steakhouse last night was filled with people when somebody killed Joey what's-his-name."

Colter ignored my sarcasm. "Let me bring you up to date on that," he said.

In a move that could only be called suave, he pulled a top-bound spiral notebook from his jacket pocket and flipped it open. I needed to learn to do that with my notebooks. But Ron's was bound in black leather, whereas mine were covered in cheap white cardboard. Leather beat out cardboard in the suave category every time. My cool level came nowhere near his.

"The man who died at your feet and ruined what I'm sure was a perfectly wonderful steak dinner was Joseph Santoro, another Tricoletto button man," Colter said.

"What killed him?" I asked, too abruptly for Colter's liking.

He responded curtly. "Just let me get to everything, okay?" he said. "It's my story."

I smiled and nodded.

"Joey Santoro, also known as 'Gimp,' was actually more than a button man. He was a capo, the fourth level of a Cosa Nostra family. Each capo has his own crew, all sworn to the oath of silence, *omerta*, and usually required to have committed at least one murder for the family. Murder is Santoro's specialty. It took me a while to get here tonight because we had Emily Goodsill look at a photo array that included Santoro's mug. He wasn't in the previous lineup. She said she'd never seen him before, either. Still, it wouldn't surprise me if it was Santoro's crew that killed Carl and the two Tricoletto hit men about to flip on Tony Toes. If I was a member of Joey's crew, I'd be watching my back right now."

I tried again to ask my question. Colter anticipated it.

"We don't know yet what killed Santoro, Deuce," Colter said. "It's too early. He's been on Tony's table for less than an hour."

"But it's nothing obvious, like a gunshot or a knife wound?"

"No. Not that I've heard. Did either of you hear a gunshot or see a knife?" He moved a finger between Steve and me. We shook our heads.

Jonathan Bruckner cleared his throat. It was a lawyer sound. Colter recognized it and turned to the lawyer.

Bruckner asked, "How long is this going to continue before the *Journal* can report it? So far, no innocent bystanders have been hurt, but that could change if these guys run out of that drug and start using guns. I can't advise this paper to be a part of anything that might carry a legal liability, and certainly not something that would further endanger a staff member. We need to let people know there's a danger out there."

"I wish I knew, Mr. Bruckner. I don't. My suspicion would be that the killing will continue until all of the potential witnesses that Carl Cribben intended to depose have been eliminated. There is no threat to citizens on the streets at this point."

Bryanna Regan's voice came through the Skype connection. "Do you know how many names were on Cribben's list of potential witnesses?"

"We're going through his group's case notes and legal documents now," Colter said. "There are lots of file boxes full of them. It will take time."

"I'm not hearing anything Deuce and Steve didn't tell us before you arrived, Special Agent Colter," Regan continued. "So why are we here?"

I saw Colter smile.

"I'm honestly not sure why you're all here, either," he said. "I was expecting Deuce and Steve so I could debrief them on the latest murder—as witnesses, not suspects. I wasn't expecting everyone else. But as long as we are all here I will share this with you, again on condition of absolute confidence." Heads nodded. "It appears that the inventories of succinylcholine in Chicago and areas immediate adjacent have been completed, and none of the drug is reported missing. It's a drug that's been used for at least a century in many countries. The doses being used for murder here could have come from any- where in the civilized world. The U.S., Mexico, Canada, Europe, Asia." He paused for effect. "Italy, maybe."

I asked, "There's no way to narrow it down?"

"If we had one of the used syringes, yes," Colter said. "We could trace the batch code and other ID numbers and know where it was manufactured, shipped from and to whom. But without that information, it could have been made in somebody's basement, for all we know. And if that's the case, the killers could keep on making it for as long as they need it."

26

Colter wanted to question Steve and me about the murder of Joey Santoro, but he didn't want extraneous witnesses. He told Bryanna Regan and Alexander Talcott to break their Skype connection with Chicago and asked Eric and Jonathan Bruckner to leave the conference room. What ensued was a battle of wills that went nowhere.

"I'm not questioning them as suspects," Colter insisted.

"Ron, we've been through this before," Eric said with the exasperation of an impatient man who didn't like rehashing settled issues. "I don't let my reporters talk to law enforcement as suspects or witnesses without Jonathan present."

"We don't, either," Regan said. "It's hard and fast *Chronicle* policy."

"Oh, Christ," Colter said. "Okay, but the lawyers and editors will limit their involvement to listening. This will be a conversation among Deuce, Steve, and me. No one else. Is that clear?" The two lawyers reserved the right to object to any questions they deemed inappropriate.

With the cast thinned to only three speaking roles, Colter took us moment by moment through the killing, covering ground we'd already plowed. Steve and I recounted every detail we could remember about every person we could remember around the valet stand, including their words and actions. None of the faces struck familiar chords with either of us. None of the actions we related raised any suspicions. Everyone had done and said what you'd expect people in that situation to do and say.

All of us were tiring from the repetition when Colter's phone rang. He looked at the caller ID and answered.

"What've you got?" he said.

He listened, expressionless, for a minute. Then he mumbled, "Thanks," and rang off.

He said, "That was the medical examiner. The puncture wound on Santoro was in his left hip. There were traces of sux on his skin and his clothes. The killer must have slipped his hand and the syringe up under the jacket, out of sight. Nobody we interviewed saw it happen, not even the hysterical girlfriend, who's currently under sedation. We're going to question her when she's calmer. Somebody must have seen something. Might as well have been her. Santoro had two armed bodyguards, but at the moment, if they know anything, they're not talking."

"What are the chances you'll find a witness?" Steve asked.

Colter's pained expression was the only answer we needed.

* * *

The discussion proceeded for another twenty minutes or so but produced nothing new or useful. But Steve and I did get one of Colter's best lectures.

"Look, you two," he said, "even though you weren't targeted in the steakhouse killing, I'm going to try one more time to convince you to back off this story. Cab Hill braced me again today about your roles. And he's right. Steve, you need to go back to Washington. Deuce, you need to focus on your columns. Mr. Ryland, Ms. Regan, you need to accept the unpleasant reality that if you don't pull these two away and leave this investigation to the experts, you're very likely to wind up short two very good reporters. This crowd killed a federal investigator. They've already made one attempt on Deuce. None of them will think twice about taking out two good reporters, and the country doesn't have enough of those to spare right now."

On the Skype screen I saw Talcott's face scrunch up into a frown that expressed the horror of the warning he had heard and understood. But it was my editor who gave voice to the implications.

"We understand your concerns, Ron," Eric said. "I don't know about Steve and the *Chronicle*, but this isn't the first time Deuce has been warned to back off a story to avoid a catastrophe. It's never worked before."

Colter looked at me and raised an eyebrow. "I seem to recall that," he said.

"They'll get armed protection, both of them," Eric said. "I've already called the security company we used back during the Vinnie Colangelo thing. They're good. The owner is supposed to call me with a schedule tomorrow."

Eric smiled at me. "Actually, Deuce, your boyfriend didn't give me much choice. He called after he heard about the Explorer fire. When he heard we hadn't hired security for you, he said he was making reservations to fly back here and do it himself. The only way I could stop him was to promise the paper would take care of it."

"He told me he raised the issue," I said. "I didn't know threats were involved."

I was grateful at the prospect of armed backup but dubious about its effectiveness.

"You think Joey Santoro didn't know he was in danger, Eric? He didn't get to be a capo for the Tricolettos by being stupid. You said yourself two of the men with him were bodyguards. Yet somebody slipped past them, put a hand under Joey's jacket, and stuck him. I won't fight a protection plan, but I doubt it will work. Security pros have never faced anything like murder-by-injection. What are they supposed to watch for?"

Another fifteen minutes of mindless arguing produced nothing new for me except a headache and a short temper. When I walked out of the newsroom, Steve followed me.

"You know," he said, "Colter's probably right."

"About what?" I asked, sounding as short as I felt.

"About us dropping the investigation. I'm too old for this, Deuce, and you're too young to die. Maybe we should leave the Mafia to the pros."

"Fine," I said. "You go ahead and trundle on home. You're gonna be retirement age in a few months. Enjoy yourself. I can take it from here."

"Deuce!..."

"Don't start with me, Steve. I didn't invite you here, and frankly I don't give a damn whether you stay or go. I sure as hell don't want you to stay if you have reservations. You're liable to make a mistake and get both of us killed. I've brought major stories to publication alone before. I have no qualms about doing it again."

"You wouldn't be here to try if it wasn't for me," Steve snapped. "You'd be charcoal inside a burned out Explorer."

That cut deep, and I saw the look of regret cover Steve's face as soon as the words were out of his mouth.

He stammered. "I… I'm sorry, Deuce. Really. I'm so sorry. That was uncalled for."

I stared at him for a moment then turned my back and walked away.

"Deuce, please. I'm sorry."

I stopped but kept my back to him.

"I know," I said. "Don' worry about it. We're all on edge." Then I turned around. "Look, the decision on whether you stay or go is between you and your editor. But I know you saved my life. I'm eternally grateful. If you decide to stay, I'll be fine with it."

"What about the idea of police protection?"

"I already agreed to it. You have to decide for yourself if you want it, too. I wasn't exaggerating my doubts about how effective it can be."

We walked in silence for a few moments. I realized he was still behind me.

"Your car's over that way," I said, pointing off to my left.

"I'm going to walk you to your car first to be sure you get there safe."

"You're not my mother," I said.

"No, but I'm your friend."

I stopped again and faced him.

"The Explorer fire was a quirk of timing," I said. "As a general truth, you can't protect me any more than I can protect you. That's why I said I'd accept police protection. But not tonight. Tonight I'm going home to bed. Thanks for dinner. It was… interesting."

27

An hour earlier the group meeting in the mayor's private conference room had ended. It had been smaller than the previous one. FBI AD Ron Colter wasn't available. Federal prosecutor Jerry Alvarez hadn't been invited. That left Mayor Marsha Mendes, Governor Tyler Walston, Vice Mayor John Fasso, and Cab Hill, superintendent of the Chicago Police.

The downsizing was fine with the Mayor. She understood that her job required meetings, but she had no tolerance for sessions that dragged on while everyone made their points several times. She learned early in her career in public service that any time you get more than one politician in a room for a discussion, the debate will be interminable unless a strong hand is in control. She was that hand, though she didn't expect this session to be much more than a briefing. It was, after all, very late on a Friday evening, and nobody wanted to be working at that hour.

"Tony Donato has identified the causes of death in four of the five cases we've piled up so far," Cab Hill told the group. "It's quite odd. I've never heard of anything like it before. The victims, other than the one we found in the river with two bullets in his head, were killed with a drug called..." He consulted his notes. "...Succinylcholine, called 'sux' for short."

"Really?" Walston asked. "How'd they ever get their hands on that?"

"What is it?" the mayor demanded.

Walston explained. "It's a paralyzing agent. It's used to incapacitate critical patients who are fighting medical personnel trying to intubate them so they can breathe."

The police superintendent told his colleagues why it was so hard to detect. "As

119

to how they got it, I imagine the outfit can get their hands on anything if they want it bad enough. Every lab, distributor, and medical facility in the greater Chicago area has inventoried their supplies at the request of the FBI, and none found any sux missing."

John Fasso caught the governor's eye. "You're a surgeon, Tyler. How would you get some of that stuff, off the books?"

Walston looked stricken. "Christ, I have no idea. I've worked on patients who've been given sux, but I don't recall any cases where I administered it myself. If I'm called in on a patient who needs intubation, it's always done before I get there because it's too urgent to wait for the attending to arrive. As to where I'd get it, there's always some on refrigeration in the ERs and ICUs, and it's kept stocked by hospital pharmacies. But it's tightly controlled."

Mendes asked, "Are drug inventories always accurate? Could there be any of the drug missing that's simply overlooked?"

"Oh, I wouldn't think so," Walston said. "Any time medication is ordered it's logged in on the computer systems. It's mostly a way to keep supplies at established levels. Not so much for discovering theft, though it would certainly help control that, too."

"Why are the bad guys going to all that trouble, Cab?" Fasso asked. "There are lots of easier ways to kill somebody."

Hill flashed Fasso a wry smile. "Killed a lot of people, have you?" he asked.

Mendes stepped in. "Tony Toes is one of your constituents, John," she said to Fasso. "You've known him forever. Why don't you ask him if his guys did this and, if so, where they got that 'sux' stuff?"

"First of all," the vice mayor said, "I don't know Anthony Senior that well. I grew up friends with his younger son, Jimmy, but I only met the father once or twice. We weren't allowed to play at the family home. No kids were allowed to play there. The father was afraid if somebody tried to shoot him, or blow him up, or whatever, kids would get caught in the mess and get hurt or killed, too."

"How incredibly sad," Mendes said.

"Yeah, I remember a time—I guess I was maybe seven or eight—I got an invitation to Jimmy's birthday party. My mother and I picked out a present, and I got all dressed up. At the appointed time our doorbell rang. It was Jimmy and his mom. They were visiting the homes of all the kids invited to the party, pick-

ing up presents, and dropping off cake and balloons. Then they left. I could tell Jimmy was mortified by the whole thing, and I felt bad for him. But that's the way Jimmy and Tony Junior lived their childhoods. Always away from home."

"So where do we go from here?" Mendes asked.

Hill replied, "The FBI has taken over the case, and they're calling in the DEA since regulated drugs probably were stolen and used to commit the murder of a federal investigator two federal witnesses. From here on, Ron Colter will do these updates."

"So where's Ron tonight?" she asked.

"Not sure," Hill said.

"Are they going to interview Anthony Tricoletto and Albano Callisi?"

"I wouldn't be surprised," Hill said.

"I guess we're done here," the mayor said.

Hill held up a hand. "Just one more question to satisfy my curiosity, if I may. Since I'm relatively new to Chicago, I'm not fully up-to-date on gangster lore. How did Tony Toes Tricoletto get his nickname?"

"One more sad story in the sad tale of the family," Fasso said. "Back when Tony Sr. was about six, he did something that infuriated his father. As punishment, his father threw him out of the house into a raging February snowstorm and told him to fend for himself. He didn't even give the boy time to pull on a pair of boots. By the time the cops found him wandering around the neighborhood, his shoes were soaking wet and frozen on his feet. Three toes had frozen, too, and had to be amputated. He always walked a little funny after that."

Hill looked horrified. "A father doing that to his son? Jesus. Was he prosecuted?"

"No," Fasso said. "The prosecutors wrote it off as private family business."

"Bullshit," Hill said. "It's child abuse, straight up."

"Those were different times, Cab," Fasso said. "Different times."

28

I was in the newsroom early on Monday morning reporting a column and trying to put more effort into it than other recent pieces I'd done. I felt ashamed by the thought that I'd been "mailing it in" on the job. That had to stop, and today was the day.

Eric was sitting in my side chair. "Did the security detail show up this morning?"

"They were waiting for me when I left the house. Same two as last time. I've got their phone numbers so I can let them know where I'm going before I leave."

"Good," Eric said. "Steve's detail should have been waiting for him at the hotel."

"I guess that means he decided to stay."

"We can't force him to leave," Eric said. "Do you want him to stay?"

"No, not especially. Well, I don't know why I say that. I don't really care one way or the other what he does."

Eric watched my face for a few moments. I don't know what he was trying to see there, but it made me nervous.

"What?" I asked, finally overcome with curiosity and irritation. "If you've got something to say, just say it."

"I wondered if you were telling me the whole truth. You sound uncertain."

"I don't honestly care if he stays or not," I said, my irritation rising. "I mean it. I'm not working on the Cribben story. If he wants to, he can. But I won't help him."

"Then what's bothering you?" he asked. I thought I might have heard compassion in his voice, but it was probably a bagel crumb caught in his throat. I debated whether to tell him what was on my mind. I decided I should.

"If I tell you something in absolute confidence, will you keep it that way?"

Eric nodded. "As if I were your priest hearing your confession."

"I'm not a Roman Catholic, but I'll accept the analogy. Steve and I had just gotten a pre-dinner drink at Smith & Wollensky when he asked me something out of the blue that hit me really hard. He asked me what it felt like to kill a man."

I paused and waited for Eric's response. It was way less animated than I expected.

"What did you say?"

"I was floored. My first reaction was defensive, like, 'Why in hell are you asking me that?' He told me he felt responsible for the death of a man back in, I think he said 1993. Somebody he suspected of helping cover up a horrendous crime. He pursued the man relentlessly, until the guy dropped dead. As it turned out, the man wasn't guilty of what Steve suspected. For the last quarter century he's been blaming himself for the man's death. He never got past it. I knew why he was asking me, of course, but I didn't know how to deal with him. I told him he should have gotten professional help."

Eric nodded. "I know the story. He had a drinking problem that he worked hard to beat. He was doing well. But the Dulles crash story pushed him out of journalism for a while, broke up his marriage, and sent him into a major tailspin that led him back to the bottle. It's a wonder the *Chronicle* hired him back. But he finally got himself straight."

"He told me he didn't get any help."

"Nope. He managed to overcome the drinking problem by himself, but not the guilt."

"He had two drinks with me at dinner that night," I recalled. "Both doubles."

"Liking to drink, or leaning on alcohol for support, doesn't necessarily mean he's an alcoholic. If he can control when and how much he drinks, he probably isn't. He could still be a drunk, though he doesn't have that look. He looks pretty healthy."

I paused and thought about it. I felt guilty that I hadn't taken it more seriously when he asked me the question. He was hoping for whatever insights I could offer. I wasn't sure I had any. But I should have tried harder.

Eric's next observation confirmed it.

He said, "Obviously, Steve never got over the man's death. He asked you what it was like for you because he thought discussing the matter with a fellow reporter who'd been through something similar might help him deal better. Did you talk to him at all?"

"Not beyond what I just mentioned, that he should have gotten some help. Looking back on it, it must have sounded like a brushoff. I wish we'd had a deeper conversation. It might have helped me, too."

"You did get help."

"After Mark pushed me into it. And it did help me gain some perspective. But killing that man still isn't far from my thoughts. I still wake up at night hearing the hollow thunk of his head against the sidewalk."

"Anyway," Eric said, about to change the subject, "about whether Steve stays or goes. You're right that it's between him and his editor. But you know, he's a pretty good reporter. And two of you together might be safer than one of you alone."

"What's his scoop gonna be?" I demanded. "Who killed Carl, and how? We know that. Who killed the mob guys and how? We know that, too. End of story. Let him have it."

"Ah," Eric said with a small smile. "We know the how, and we're pretty sure it's mob guys killing mob guys. We think it's to get rid of witnesses who might testify in the federal investigation, along with the leader of the investigation. We don't know if that's all. The sux is at the heart of what we don't know. It would have been easier to shoot them all, weigh them down, and throw them into the middle of the lake. It could have been years until the bodies were found, if they were ever found. There was a reason they chose succinylcholine. And therein, I think, lies a much better story. There's more to it than we're seeing. And when it becomes obvious, I want us to be the first ones to see it."

"In other words, you want me to get involved in the coverage."

I started to answer when Eric's secretary interrupted.

"Sorry to intrude," she said. "Security called. There's somebody named Steve Pace in the lobby asking to see Deuce. I didn't know how important it might be."

I looked to Eric. "Go," he said. "We'll talk more later, after you finish your column."

I got up and caught his eye. "How did you know Steve's backstory?"

"Well, I researched him when he first showed up here. Then I had a conversation with his current editor, Bryanna Regan. She filled in the rest. If you talk to him again about the subject of responsibility for unfortunate events, let him spin out the story for you. Pretend it's the first time you heard it."

"And then come back and tell you if I want to get involved in the Cribben story?"

"Yeah, something like that."

29

"Hi," I said to Steve in the lobby. "I presume you didn't come to say good-bye?"

He grinned. "No, I actually have several things on my agenda. Can you take time to go back to our coffee place and talk?"

"No, today is column day. But I can take a half hour to go upstairs and get coffee in our lounge. It isn't bad."

There were three other people in the lounge, but since it was a rather large space it wasn't difficult to find a nook away from prying ears. One of the three looked familiar, but I didn't recall ever having seen the other two. As we passed on the way to the coffee urns, I heard them discussing display ad rates, which pretty much pegged what department they inhabited. We got coffee. Steve added a bagel and cream cheese to his tray. He tried to pay again, and I declined, protesting that while newspaper finances were in the Dumpster, they still paid me enough to foot the bill for my own coffee.

When we were seated Steve said, "I'm not leaving. You might not want to work with me, and I understand that, so I'll do what I can on my own. I don't want you to feel any pressure to share your sources, especially since your main source made it clear last night he's pretty disgusted with both of us."

"That's Ron's default position when he doesn't get his way. But he should be over it because now we've got protection. And, where sources are concerned, he's not the only person I know in Chicago."

"Care to share?"

"No," I said. I felt confident that Ron would work with me again, eventually. Meanwhile, I still had the federal prosecutor, Jerry Alvarez, and the medical examiner, Tony Donato. But Steve didn't need to know that.

"Well, I'll be around if you change your mind," Steve said. "Meanwhile, we have some other unfinished business. Have you turned in your rental car yet?"

"No, and I've got to do that, but I can't do it until I buy a new car."

"How long is it going to take you to finish your column?"

"Today? Probably early this afternoon. Why?"

"Do you know which models you want to test drive again?"

"I've been doing some research, *Consumer Reports* among the references. I've pretty much narrowed the choices to another Explorer or a Subaru, the Forester or the Outback. I really liked the Outback when I drove it."

"Okay. I have a few things to check out while you're opining. Call me when you finish the column. I'll pick you up. We'll hit a Ford dealer and a Subaru dealer, you pick out your new ride, then we'll return the rental, and that chapter of your life will be closed."

That seemed a good idea. And it led into something I wanted to plan.

"Then let's have dinner in my 'hood? My treat this time. I'll put the new car in my garage while you find a place to park, and we'll go back to Bacchanalia for a feast. I still say it's the best neighborhood Italian in Chicago."

* * *

We didn't get to Bacchanalia until 7:30, and we never did get to the Ford dealership. I test drove and fell in love with both Subaru models and settled on the Outback in a lovely shade of green with a beige leather interior. With my insurance check in the bank along with a payoff from the newspaper because the Explorer was destroyed on the job, I was able to add some funds of my own and pay cash. So there wasn't much paperwork. But there was traffic. The only Subaru dealership in the city was way up on the North Side. Getting there and back and returning the rental Jeep took more time than picking out and paying for the new car.

We were followed the entire afternoon by one of our protective units.

Since we were going to be together for the rest of the day, we didn't need both.

We settled at the bar in the front of the restaurant, near the massive window that contained the largest slider I'd ever seen. It was cracked open about two inches, admitting a cool flow of air that smelled like spring. At the moment there were only two others sitting at the bar, down at the other end by the cash register. One was a former state legislator. The other was his driver-slash-bodyguard. Two of the four tables against the wall opposite the bar were occupied by people I didn't know, but they were at the tables farthest from us. I couldn't tell how many people were in the main dining room in back.

I introduced Steve to those I knew in the room. Paula, who owned the place with her brother, was behind the bar making drinks, supervising the kitchen, and making everyone within the sound of her voice feel welcome like she meant it, which she did.

She was new to Steve. She hadn't been working the day we were in for lunch.

"How are you?" she asked me immediately. "When we heard about the car fire it scared us all to death. I didn't know where you were, so I called the paper a few times and asked to talk to someone who could tell me how you were. Nobody would say much since they didn't know me. They were able to say you weren't hurt too bad, but it sounded horrible. You were in your car when it burned up?"

"No, I was in the car when it caught fire." I cocked my head toward Steve. "This is the guy who pulled me out before the car exploded. I'm fine, thanks."

Steve's left hand was resting on the bar. Paula covered it with her own. "We love Deuce," she said. "Thank you. Your drinks are on the house tonight."

"Thank you," he said with a smile. Neither of us mentioned that I was buying.

She slid a place setting in front of us and glasses of ice water, flashed her big smile, and asked what she could get us.

"I'd like a glass of the house red," I said. Steve ordered the same.

It was a good wine, and Bacchanalia didn't skimp on the servings. If I had to guess I'd say the goblets were at least ten ounces, and Paula filled them to just short of the rim. Not a connoisseur's way of drinking wine, but it was Bacchanalia's policy. I never heard anyone complain. When she put the wine in front of us, Steve's eyes went wide.

Paula gave us menus and a separate list of the specials and disappeared into the kitchen to make sure everything was going as smoothly as she and her brother demanded, even though their chef had been with them for years. She called over her shoulder that she would be right back.

I told Steve there was nothing on the menu that wasn't good but mentioned a few things I especially liked.

"If you really love garlic, the Chicken Vesuvio is outstanding. The lasagna's the best anywhere. To start, I'd suggest the calamari or the baked clams, maybe a Caprese salad. They make Italian fried chicken to die for. All the veal. I don't know. Pick anything."

In the end, I ordered the salmon Italiano, and Steve ordered the lasagna after seeing it served to a nearby table. We both got a small Caprese salad to start and split an order of the baked clams. That wasn't good enough for Paula. She brought out a few pieces of calamari (a few in her book being about a dozen) and a plate of focaccia for us to nibble on.

"On the house," she said again.

"Is it always like this?" Steve asked me in utter amazement.

"Pretty much," I said.

I didn't bring up the subject of how it feels to kill someone while we were eating. Steve was enjoying his food too much for me to spoil it. I did notice, however, that about two-thirds of the way through the meal, when Paula moved to pour some more wine into his glass, he declined with thanks.

"That first one was about half a bottle," he said. "And I still have to drive tonight."

I felt relieved. He did appear to have his drinking under control, which made me a little more comfortable about working with him, if it came to that.

Somehow, Steve managed to finish everything, though the lasagna serving was large enough to feed a family of four, another standard practice at Bacchanalia and at most other restaurants in the city. I chomped through everything, too, though the fish serving, while substantial, was easier to pack away than all that pasta. Since I knew what my dinner plate would hold, I let Steve down most of the clams and calamari.

We both declined dessert, but Paula brought us some swell cannoli covered in chopped pistachios that were not to be resisted. On the house, of course.

As we picked at the sweet, Steve said, "There's something I want to talk to you about. Is this a good time?"

"There's something I want to talk to you about, too," I said. "You first."

He put down his fork and swiveled his bar chair to face me.

"I was out of line at the restaurant the other night," he said. "I never should have brought up the subject of killing people. I'm old enough to deal with my own problems, and I have, including the reality that I used to drink way, way too much. I gave it up completely for a while, even joined AA for a bit. My sponsor took me out for coffee one day and asked me a couple of weird questions. Like, 'What do you do if you're out with friends and one of them leaves half a glass of wine on the table?' I answered honestly, 'Nothing.' Then he asked, 'Do you keep liquor in your house?' The answer was yes. Question: 'When do you drink it?' Answer: 'I don't anymore. I keep it for friends who come over.' Then he told me I wasn't an alcoholic. I remember his words vividly. 'If you were an alcoholic, you'd pick up the abandoned wine and drink it yourself. If you were an alcoholic, you couldn't keep alcohol in your home without drinking it.' Then he added, 'You're just a drunk.'"

Despite the seriousness of the subject, I laughed. "In a way, that's worse. It eliminates your excuse. You're not an alcoholic, you're irresponsible."

"Yep, and that realization turned me around. Then came an unnecessary death I felt responsible for, and I backslid. Eventually I was able to regain control of the alcohol. But I never managed to gain control of the guilt. When I learned about you, I thought it would give me a chance to deal with my self-loathing if I could work through it with someone who'd experienced the same thing. But that's your private story, and even if you were willing to share, I didn't know you—don't know you—well enough to invade your privacy. That's it. I wanted to apologize."

Suddenly Paula was there, as she had been throughout dinner.

"Anything else I can get you kids?" she asked. "Are you going to finish your cannoli, or should I pack it for you to take with you?"

"We're going to finish," I said. "We're kind of in the middle of something here."

"Yeah, yeah, yeah, yeah, yeah, take all the time you need," she said in her machine-gun style. She moved to the other end of the bar, picked up a carafe of the house red, and returned to us. "Just to keep you lubricated while you talk," she said as she poured a normal sized portion of wine into each of our empty glasses. We didn't argue this time.

After she disappeared back into the kitchen, I told Steve, "There's no reason to apologize. In fact, my editor chewed me out for not trying more to help. He thinks I still need counseling, professional or from someone like you with a shared experience."

"Your experience is more recent," he said. "Do you have trouble sleeping?"

"Not getting to sleep so much as staying asleep," I said.

"What do you do when that happens?"

"I don't stay in bed because it gets worse in the dark. I usually get up, go into my office, and watch something fun on Netflix. It relaxes me, and eventually I can crawl back to bed and fall asleep. A couple of times I fell asleep at my desk."

"Maybe these experiences will be a part of us for the rest of our lives," he said.

"I would have thought after a quarter century it would have faded some for you."

"I think it has," Steve said. "I don't get down about it nearly as often. But it's always lurking, ready to rise up and slap me upside the head when I least expect it and for no apparent reason. I don't have much hope anymore that I'll ever be rid of it."

"There's always a trigger, I think. Maybe sometimes we just don't see what it is."

"Thanks, Deuce," he said. He stood up and gave me a light kiss on the forehead. "I'll drive you down to your house. Then I need to get back to the hotel."

"We can talk more about this another time," I suggested.

"We can," he agreed.

I paid the bill and left a healthy tip. Paula gave us a big thank you, told Steve how much she'd enjoyed meeting him, and hoped he would return.

"I don't think," he said, "that I'll be going back to D.C. until I have a chance to enjoy every single thing on the menu. Thank you, Paula."

When I got up to go, I noticed that Steve had left his second glass of wine on the bar, barely touched.

* * *

We stood outside for a few minutes enjoying the night air and watching the denizens of the neighborhood milling about, laughing, and generally doing what they always do when spring begins to elbow winter aside. The largest group was gathered in front of a private club across the street where the drinks were small and cheap, and the bartenders were volunteer members who got to drink for free as payment for serving others.

There were some real hard-core alcoholics over there, but they were good and nice people. A few of them called me to come over, but I told them I had to get home because I had an early day of work tomorrow. They accepted that.

"My car's about half a block up that way," Steve said.

"You don't have to drive me," I said. My house is only a couple of blocks from here, and the security detail's still around."

"Under the circumstances, I'd feel better," he said.

"You mean the guys across the street? They're harmless. At least one of 'em's a cop. And they're all friends of mine."

"Not them. Others, who might not be so friendly."

I was about to tell Steve he was getting paranoid when I caught motion out of the corner of my eye. I turned to see if it was someone I knew, and my blood turned to ice.

30

There was nothing friendly about the face coming at me. I only got a very quick glimpse because the man reached up to what I thought was a knit watch cap. It turned out to be a ski mask, which he pulled down over his face. I could still see his eyes: hard, resolute, and mean. I ripped my eyes away from his face and down to his hands. The right was encased in a latex glove, and it held something that looked very much like a syringe.

I am not the kind of woman you see in horror movies, the one—usually blonde because B-movie casting directors love stereotypes—who is trying to escape a gruesome death at the hands of a chain saw mass murderer who dismembers his victims while they're still alive. She's the one who forgets there's an unlocked, fully gassed car with the motor running sitting three feet away from her and opts instead to race, shrieking, into a barn with chain saws hanging on every wall and the killer sitting on a blood-smeared table waiting for her. I wasn't like that. For one thing, I wasn't blonde.

Instead I said to my companion, "Trouble, Steve."

"I see him," he replied calmly.

I didn't see the security crew. Perhaps they were parked where they hadn't yet spotted the threat. So I yelled as loud as I could to the off-duty cop across the street.

"Roach, we need some help over here. This man's trying to kill us." Then Steve and I stepped apart, separating from each other by several feet. He might get one of us, but not both. "We need help over here."

And it came quickly, from across the street and from inside the restaurant. The former state legislator, who also was a former cop, and his bodyguard, who was an active-duty cop, heard me through the open window and burst through Bacchanalia's front door. If they had guns, I didn't see them. Roach, backed up by six or seven drunken civilians, was also stumbling to the rescue. They were stumbling in part because they were being knocked aside by our security detail racing from whatever shadows had been providing cover. Roach and the security men had guns drawn. There were so many bystanders around, I didn't think anyone would fire and risk hitting innocent people.

"He's got a syringe full of poison," I yelled, not being able to think of a better term to describe sux in the heat of the moment.

"Drop it," the former legislator said. "I see it in your hand, and if I don't see it on the sidewalk in two seconds, I'll put you down there." He was reaching for his weapon as he spoke. So was his bodyguard.

The would-be assailant lunged at me across the four-foot space separating us. I sidestepped to his left-hand side, away from the hand holding the syringe. Something brushed the sleeve of my jacket, but I didn't feel the prick of a needle.

One of our security men took a shot at the attacker and just missed, his bullet shattering a flowerpot behind the man. The minder was standing six feet from the would-be killer in a classic shooter's stance, the muzzle of his Glock pointed at the man's chest.

"Drop it, motherfucker," he shouted. "I'm a cop, and I will kill you if I have to."

The assassin turned and melded instantly into the crowd of bystanders, producing a screen of civilians between him and the gawkers in front of Bacchanalia. The cops lost any chance to use their weapons.

Meanwhile, Roach cut behind the group of onlookers and got a better angle on the killer. Running as hard as he could in his condition, he got almost close enough to tackle the man, but not quite. The two security guards and the legislator's body man ran hard to catch up, but Roach and the killer were almost half a block ahead of them. The legislator himself didn't follow. He was past the age for that sort of exertion. He moved toward me, instead.

"You two okay?" he asked. "Why would anybody want to kill you, Deuce?"

"Oh let me count the reasons," I said. "I need to call 9-1-1."

"Done that already," said a man I didn't know who had come out of the restaurant, too. "Gave 'em a description of the thug as best I could with the mask and all, and told them which direction he ran."

"Thank you," Steve said.

Now the men who'd given chase were drifting back. Roach told us the assailant had gotten away in a vehicle that had appeared to be waiting for him.

One of our private security men stepped up. "I called it in," he said, "a Buick Enclave, late model, dark blue or black, probably black. Roach got some of the license plate. They went west on twenty-fifth then turned south on Western. Blew right through a red light." He looked at me, eyes narrow. "You okay? Did you know the punk?"

"No," I said. "I didn't get a good look at him. Thanks for rushing over."

Roach displayed his badge. "Don't nobody leave," he said. "Detectives are on their way, and they'll want to talk to alla you."

I glanced over at Steve. "So much," I said, "for a good night's sleep."

* * *

Within minutes the streets were awash with police who hadn't been partying off-duty. They began sorting everyone out: fellow cops, witnesses, potential victims, private security, and bystanders, most of them Oakley Avenue residents.

It was 10 p.m., past Bacchanalia's normal closing time on a Monday. Paula said she would shut down the kitchen but would leave the bar area open for as long as the police needed it as a place to interview witnesses. And she said she would keep the coffee fresh.

Detectives escorted Steve and me back inside and slid the big window closed for privacy. It was also getting pretty chilly. While the two men were distracted I whispered to Steve, "Just tell them what you saw. Don't mention the sux cases."

"Hey, you two," one detective said, "no talking to anyone but us."

He came and sat at a table with me; the other sat with Steve at the bar.

Paula brought coffee for everyone and then made herself scarce in the kitchen to help with the post-closing cleanup.

I related every detail I could remember. I could have put it in the context of the sux murders, but that would have required assumptions on my part. The detective only cared about facts. That's all I gave him.

And then Ron Colter showed up. I saw him talking to the two security men outside. He left them standing watch on the sidewalk when he came in.

He flashed his credentials and introduced himself, an unnecessary move since there probably weren't a half dozen police officers in the city who didn't know him on sight.

"Thank you, detectives," he said. "I'll take over now. This is an FBI matter."

"Okay," said the detective with Steve. "All yours. We just started talking to them. You want a briefing?"

"Thanks," Colter said. "I need to start at the beginning. Where's this syringe now?"

"Witnesses said the masked guy still had it when he ran," one replied. "We've started a search between the sidewalk out front where the incident occurred and the path the attacker took to the waiting car. So far, nothing."

"Your guys know not to touch it if they find it?"

"Yes, sir."

"The Buick went south on Western?"

One of the detectives nodded.

"If the guy threw it out on the street, somebody could pick it up and die," Colter said. "You're going to have to set up a rolling blockade along Western and search the street, the sidewalks, the gutters, garbage receptacles, and the shrubbery until you find it or exhaust the possibilities. I'll mobilize a couple of squads of agents to help. If it shows up, put a couple of cops with it and tell them not to touch it."

The detectives weren't happy but left to relay Colter's orders to their superiors.

Colter sat with me and motioned Steve over. "No need to interview you separately," he said. He eyed my cup. "You suppose they still have coffee?"

I got up and leaned over the bar and called toward the kitchen door for

Paula. When she appeared, I asked, "Think you could scrape up another cup of coffee? A new guy just wandered in."

Paula looked around me at Colter. "I'm brewing a new pot," she said. "You want what's left of the old or wait for the new?"

"Both," Colter said, and Paula laughed.

When I sat down I said to Colter, "I see you met our protection. Is your snit over?"

I saw a flash of anger fire in Colter's eyes.

"Deuce, you suppose you'll ever be able to open your mouth without pissing me off? Or is that not a skill set you own?"

"I'm working on it, Ron, but it's tough."

The anger flashed again.

"I'll be good for the rest of the night," I promised, "if for no other reason than I'd really like to get home to bed before dawn."

So we went through the whole thing again, the narrative passing between Steve and me as smoothly as if we'd rehearsed it.

"Why did you step away from Steve when the guy came at you?" Colter asked me.

I shrugged. "It wasn't like there was a complex train of thought," I replied. "I saw the syringe and figured it was filled with sux. I thought there might be enough for both of us. I wanted to make it tougher for him. I thought there was a good chance Roach would take him down before he got both of us if I put some distance between us."

"You think you were his primary target?"

I nodded. "He seemed to be intent on me."

Steve said, "That's what I saw, too. He glanced at me every few seconds, very quickly. I got the impression he was making sure I stayed put. Deuce was definitely his target."

Colter nodded. "And he did finally lunge at you?" Colter asked me.

I nodded. "I felt something brush my sleeve, but he didn't inject me."

"Which arm?" Colter asked.

"Which arm did he brush? My left."

"And you're sure he didn't inject you?"

"If he had, I'd be dead by now. Why?"

Colter pointed at my left jacket sleeve. There was a circle of liquid about the size of a quarter that had soaked into the fabric.

Colter said, "He didn't miss by much."

31

So I went home without my jacket, which went somewhere with Colter packed in an evidence bag. The security detail walked me to my house and cleared it before they'd let me stay alone. Two police officers walked Steve to his car.

I was just crawling into bed when my phone rang. It was Colter.

"For someone who's not speaking to me you sure do talk to me a lot," I said.

"I thought you were going to be nice."

"I said I would try. I did. Trial's over."

Colter ignored my sarcasm. "Everything okay there?"

"So far as I know."

"The private cops Eric Ryland hired will work twenty-four-hour details in shifts," he said.

"That's what they told me when they walked me home."

"When's Mark getting back?"

"Sometime in May," I said. "Probably the end of the month. Why?"

"Do you have a key to his condo?"

"Yes."

"How would you feel about moving in there for a while? You'd be a lot less vulnerable than you are in your house, especially walking between the garage and the house after dark."

Funny, I'd been thinking the same thing and said so.

"I have a bunch of reporting to do for a column," I said. "But I can pack some stuff in the morning and take it to his place on my way to work. I might even do it tonight. I doubt that I'll get much sleep."

"Call me when the move is done," he said. "We're officially speaking again."

It was three hours earlier on the West Coast, so Mark was still up when I called him.

I told him about the attack in front of Bacch's, and he was truly alarmed.

"Honey, you can't stay alone at the house," he said. "There are too many ways the bad guys could neutralize the security detail and get to you."

I explained that I'd called to see if it was okay for the cats and me to move into his condo for a while.

"It is perfectly all right," he said. "In fact, I insist on it. For that matter, you can move in permanently."

"Well, that's not what I..."

He plowed on. "Andre should be on the front desk tonight. I'll call him and tell him to expect you and to brief the head of security before he leaves in the morning. You still have the garage opener, right?" He knew I did. "Use my second spot. I'll tell Andre to make sure nobody's squatting there and have them towed if they are. Did you get a new car?"

He went on like that for another minute, and I knew better than to try to stop him. I waited until he drew a breath and asked, "You want me to answer any of those questions?"

After I promised Mark no fewer than six times that I would be careful, I decided to start packing. I already had some clothes and personal items at Mark's condo. It was a beautiful space south of Grant Park and separated from Lake Michigan only by what's known as the Museum Campus holding the famed Field Museum, Adler Planetarium, and the Shedd Aquarium. Below that green space was Soldier Field, home of the NFL Chicago Bears. Mark had a panoramic view to the north from the living room's window walls. The spectacle encompassed downtown and the lakefront and was breathtaking.

When I finished, I had three bags of my clothes, a bag of toiletries, and a big bag for all the cats' paraphernalia. That should hold us for a while.

At 4:10, I finally went to bed, a little sad at the prospect of leaving my home, but relieved to be leaving my home. Hard to explain, but true.

32

The ordeal of packing for a long stay away from home took my mind off of the events outside Bacchanalia, but as soon as I crawled between the sheets and turned out the lights, they came thundering back. Even with two armed security officers standing guard outside, every little creak and tick around me made my muscles tense. Even Cleo vaulting onto the bed and settling between my knees, her usual nighttime nest, worried me. She immobilized me. Would I be able to move quickly if I had to?

I dozed off and on through the next four hours. I gave up a little after eight, showered, dressed, and loaded my new car for the trip to Mark's condo. The security men helped me. In fairly short order I had my car in Mark's second garage space, my stuff and my cats in his unit—a second home they knew well—and was sitting with a cup of coffee looking out his windows at a gray and rainy day.

I debated whether to take my new car to work. Those responsible for the assault the night before might not know for the moment where I was, but they could watch the office garage where I parked, make the Outback, and follow me back to the condo. I thought it might be a good idea to use Uber for a few days. Of course, one of the murderers could pose as an Uber driver, and then where would I be? But that concern was too paranoid, even for me. The cats were secure where they were. The Outback was secure in the garage. And if I had to flee an Uber car to save my life, I could outrun almost any would-be killer because my legs were so long. So Uber it was.

I called the security company and gave them the morning itinerary.

I was about to pour another cup of coffee when my phone rang. Colter again.

"Did I wake you?" he asked. "Not that I care."

"Thank you for your concern," I said. "No. I'm moved into Mark's condo and was enjoying the view with a fine cup of coffee."

"I have some news that's going to rock your day."

"I think I was rocked all I need to be last night."

"Be quiet and listen. Your security team got part of the license plate of the vehicle that whisked the would-be killer out of your neighborhood. Pieced together with their description of the vehicle as a dark blue or black Buick Enclave, we were able to narrow the choices to only two in the vehicle registry."

I was a bit surprised at the low number. "Only two?"

"There are lots of Enclaves that fit the description, but only two dark-colored ones that share the same partial series on the plates."

"Oh, okay."

"One belongs to a man who took his family on vacation to Disney World last week and isn't back yet. We confirmed he's in Orlando and that his car's parked in a remote lot at Midway. Manager of the lot says the car hasn't been moved since the owner left it there. They inventory every night."

I said, "I don't feel any rocking yet." But Colter was plunging on.

"The second one is a black 2019 Enclave that belongs to Alderman John Fasso, the perhaps-not-so-honorable vice mayor of Chicago."

Now I was rocked. I put the coffee mug down on the table harder than I intended and was surprised when it didn't break.

"Are you speechless, Deuce?" Colter asked. "If so, I want to write the date on my calendar. I called Cab Hill to let him know what we found. I figured Chicago's police superintendent should know. He told me that during Mayor Mendes's last crime meeting, Fasso was telling stories about growing up with Anthony Tricoletto's younger son, Jimmy. They were tight. Tony Toes's home and base are in Fasso's Little Italy district. I've called in that cop, Roach, and your security team from last night to look at mug shots, to see if they can identify the guy who assaulted you or the driver of the Enclave. I need you and Steve to do the same. Today. Eric is making arrangements with the security company to spell your team and Steve's while you're at FBI headquarters. The teams on duty now will follow you over. When you're done, the fresh teams will pick up."

I had known the Tricoletto family lived in Little Italy. I hadn't known Fasso was so close to one of the sons.

I didn't mention that, but I did remind Colter that the hitman pulled a ski mask over his face before I got a good look at him.

"Your security guys both say the guy pulled the mask off during the foot chase. We're hoping they saw something they'll remember when they look at the mug files. Maybe you and Steve will, too."

"You know where Steve is?" I asked.

"The Congress Plaza. I already called him. He's on his way down here now."

"The field office?"

"Yeah. When you're both here, I'll get you set up."

* * *

I cut through traffic to the north side of Roosevelt and caught a westbound cab. In the minutes it took to find one the rain thoroughly soaked me. The driver kept looking at me with disdain in his rearview mirror, aware I was leaking water all over his back seat.

The trip was a straight shot across Roosevelt to the FBI field office at Ogden. Steve was waiting in Colter's outer office. He was dry. Meanwhile, I stood dripping rainwater on the federal carpet. I took an umbrella when I moved to the condo. Unfortunately, it was in my new car, which was in Mark's garage, which did me no good at all.

Colter emerged, threw me a quick double-take—I assumed at my bedraggled appearance—and introduced us to Special Agent Alicia Vincent, who looked nothing like a stereotypical federal cop. She looked more like Sandy Duncan, the petite, pixie-ish actress who used to play Peter Pan on Broadway. Colter said Vincent would supervise our mug shot examinations, and please go with her.

He turned back into his office but left the door open. He came out a few seconds later and tossed me a beautiful small, black Davek umbrella, turned and walked back into his cave. Then he turned back to me.

"It's expensive," he said, "so please return it when you're finished." I was too embarrassed to mention that I knew it was expensive because I had two, just not with me.

Vincent took us down two floors to a cubicle where there were two computer terminals displaying the first page of what might have been thousands filled with the scowling faces of men who didn't look happy about posing for their glam shots.

"Is this every mug shot ever taken in Chicago?" I asked.

The woman didn't smile, but she answered. "We eliminated women since eyewitnesses said there were two men in the car. We also cut out anyone who didn't have a history with organized crime and those in prison. And the dead ones."

She showed us how to move the pages forward and backward in case we didn't know what left/right arrows were for. Then she added, "If either of you thinks someone looks familiar, call me. I'll be right outside. Don't compare notes. A defense lawyer might argue in court that your cooperation tainted the evidence against his or her client. Just show me, I'll make a note of it, and you can move on. Any questions?"

There being none, she left us to punish our brains on the faces of some of the worst humanity had to offer.

* * *

Toward the end of the second hour, Steve picked up his pen and jotted something on a Post-it note. He went to the opening in the cubicle wall and called softly to Vincent. He handed her the yellow paper square. She thanked him, and he sat down again. He didn't violate her admonition not to share his information. So I asked an oblique question.

"A maybe?"

"Better than maybe, but something short of positive."

Vincent heard us and wasn't happy. "Cut out the chit-chat, you two."

Steve raised his brows, and rolled his eyes, and we went back to work.

At that moment I'd have given a week's pay to know who, and what, Steve found.

33

The same two men were back at their regular table at the no-name club that the members referred to as Twenty-One because it was on the twenty-first floor of its building high above the shore of Lake Michigan. It wasn't yet ten in the morning, and the hall was virtually empty. Still, the five other members present spoke in hushed voices. The atmosphere of the place seemed to command that occupants keep their voices down.

"I heard the assignment last night failed," the younger man said to the same older man who had been with him the last time. "I told you not to go after the reporter, so you went after two? That's a fool's errand, old friend."

The older man sipped his coffee and his face wrinkled at the strength of the double-double espresso in his cup. Even the frothed milk could not hide the punch that lay beneath the foam layer. His look was not one of distaste but of the shock to his system. It was just what he needed. He had been up most of the night assessing the operation the night before.

"I will not explain what I am about to tell you," he said. "Suffice it to say that what happened last night was not the outcome we planned. Nor was it the disaster you suppose."

"I don't understand."

"I don't mean you to."

The younger man looked exasperated. "Look, I'm supplying the drugs for this operation at significant risk. I have a right to know what your plans and intentions are. I want details when things go according to plan, and I demand explanations when things go wrong."

"Calm down and lower your voice," his companion said. "I told you, so far

149

as I know nothing went wrong, at least not horribly so, and I know everything. That's a fact you should have accepted by now. You are providing the material to drive this endeavor because you owe us, because at one time we funded you, and now we need to protect our very large investment in you. But that does not entitle you to anything except our best efforts. If you can't understand that, then everything will come to a bad end, including you and me."

The older man sat in silence for quite some time, letting the four pulls of espresso wake up his nervous system and his brain. It was too early for his first cigar, but he had brought his pipe. He made a project of scouring it meticulously with a high-quality cotton-wrapped stem cleaner then carefully scraping leftover ash from the bowl. It was a ritual for the old man, a routine he thought worthy of the highly polished Rinaldo Traide that had cost him nearly $500 and was the most prized smoking pipe in his collection.

His thoughts, however, focused entirely on the man sitting beside him. They had known one another for many years, since the younger man had been in high school and performed a great service to the older man's family. The older man's gratitude knew no bounds. Over time, he came to recognize something special in the kid and set out to help mold a great future for him. With financial help and encouragement, the young, one-time neighborhood ruffian made a huge success of his life, greater than he ever dreamed as a teen. One thing led to another, and the two men, who were separated by a generation in age, forged a plan that would carry them together into the future, one to great wealth, the other to great power.

For years the feds had focused only minimal attention on the mob based in La Cosa Nostra. They were too busy with the Russian mobs, the Asian mobs, the alarming treachery and brutal enforcement tactics of the Mexican drug cartels, gangs associated with human trafficking, local ethnic street gangs—all more immediate problems than a few old Italian men still getting rich on drugs, prostitution, and protection rackets. In that small seam in law enforcement's attention span, the old man saw the opportunity to come through an unlocked back door and begin to amass huge political capital, both the influence kind and the kind that pays for lavish retirement on the Amalfi Coast of the home country.

To safeguard what he had worked so hard to build, the old man had to keep his protégé in check. If the younger man panicked, he could ruin everything. And so, the old man worried. Those within his own organization who knew too much and showed signs of breaking under the pressure of this new federal investigation were being eliminated. Those in other families showing the same cracks had to die, as well. And it all had to be orchestrated so it never appeared to be what it really was.

Another step in the process was underway even as these troubling thoughts rippled across the folds of his brain.

It would be all right. It would work out. If only everyone stayed calm. If anyone involved showed signs of breaking, he would have to die.

Anyone.

34

As Steve and I prepared to leave the FBI field office I noticed that it had stopped raining. I decided to return Colter's high-end umbrella before I forgot or worse, lost it. We were standing at his secretary's desk when he opened his door and called us in.

"Which one of you identified the mug shot?" he asked, leading us to a cluster of upholstered chairs across from his desk.

"Steve did," I said, cocking my head sideways in his direction. "We kept our promise to Special Agent Vincent not to talk about the mug shots while we were searching the files. Can you tell us what Steve found and whether it's of any value? Or are you going back to not talking to us?"

"I don't want to involve you two any farther in the investigation, Deuce, but I have no choice," Colter said. "The man you identified, Steve, is Virgil "Sonny" Barone, a Tricoletto soldier. Are you certain he was the one who came at you outside Bacchanalia?"

"Certain? No," Steve said. "He bears a resemblance to the man who charged us with a syringe. That's as far as I can go. The guy pulled his ski mask down too fast for me to be certain of anything. I definitely didn't get a good enough look to be able to testify against him in court."

Colter paused and examined a file on his desk before continuing. "We found his body this morning in the black Enclave, which had left the southbound lanes of Western, crossed the northbound lanes, cut through the grass in Gage Park, and smashed into the iron support for a basketball hoop."

"His body?" Steve said. "So he's dead?"

"Very, and he wasn't killed in the crash. He wasn't wearing a seatbelt, but

Tony Donato says the injuries caused by the wreck were all post-mortem. The cause of death was obvious. He was garroted with something like piano wire, probably by someone sitting in the back seat or hiding on the back floor so Barone wouldn't see him. Probably hiding since the cops chasing Barone last night only saw him and the driver in the Enclave."

Steve grunted. "Reminds me of an episode of *The Sopranos*," he said. "Soprano did that to a snitch while he was on a college visitation tour with his daughter. I think the character's name was Meadow. It was gross."

"Yeah," Colter said. "It's never pretty, even when it's stage makeup."

I asked, "You think he was killed to keep him quiet or because he failed to kill us?"

"No way to know," Colter began when he was interrupted by his secretary coming through the door.

"Cab Hill is on two," she said. "He says it's urgent."

I could hear the hint of a voice through the receiver pressed to Colter's ear. I couldn't come close to making out what was being said, but I could read Colter's face. His expression plus the glances he gave me said the subject was, indeed, the murders, and the news was something serious.

When he hung up, he looked from Steve to me and back again.

"Another body," he said.

"Good lord," I said in amazement. "At the rate they're going the Tricoletto family's gonna be wiped out by their own people."

"This wasn't a Tricoletto," Colter said. "It was Bobby Callisi, one of Albano Callisi's nephews and a capo in the family. Two in the head again. Body dumped in South Pond in Lincoln Park. Looks like he was thrown off the wooden bridge that crosses the pond at its waist. The ME's crew found a blood smear on the handrail."

"The city's getting littered with bodies," I said.

"That's nothing new," Colter said. "It's just a different ethnicity than usual. Cab Hill said last week we might be building up to mob warfare. I kind of waved off the idea. Now I'm not so sure."

"Mob warfare?" Steve asked. "Those days ended almost a century ago."

"Apparently not," Colter said. He got up, shrugged into his topcoat, and reached out for the umbrella I'd returned to him. It slid neatly into his pocket.

"Wherever you're going, we'd like to come," I said.

"No," he said. "I'm not going to the new crime scene. I'm going to talk to the man whose car was used at another one last night. And I'm not taking either of you."

* * *

When Steve and I got to the street, it looked as if the weather might be breaking. Scraps of blue sky appeared above a handful of breaks in the clouds, and the sun was able to hurl a few rays through the gaps.

"Where to now?" Steve asked.

I held up my cell phone. "Excuse me a minute, would you?"

When he walked away, I called Jerry Alvarez. He wasn't in. I left a message.

I caught up with Steve. "Foiled again," I said.

"I'm hungry," he said. "Any place around here to get a quick lunch?"

"There must be," I said. "FBI agents have to eat somewhere. Plus, there are hospitals all over the area north of here."

He nodded in the general direction of Ogden. "I saw a Billy Goat's Tavern up there. Is it any better than the one downtown?"

"I've never risked it," I said. "We could go up to Taylor Street and drive over to Potbelly. It's a pretty good soup and sandwich place, usually very busy, but the lunch hour's over, so it shouldn't be a problem."

We climbed into Steve's rental, notified the security company of our destination, and found a parking spot almost at Potbelly's front door, a luck-out in case the rain returned. My phone rang. It was Jerry Alvarez. He'd just gotten back from court. He wouldn't let me start the conversation until he asked me when I was going to consider staying out of trouble so I could live long enough to marry Mark, have children and grandchildren, and die in my own bed.

As soon as I had an answer to that, I told him, he would be the first to know. I asked for an appointment.

"I know what you want to talk about, and I'll tell you what little I know because you've earned the right to hear it. But completely off the record, not over the phone, and not anywhere around the office where I might be recognized or overheard."

"Tell us where and when," I said.

"Us?"

I explained. He wasn't happy.

"It's okay with Ron Colter, Jerry. It should be okay with you. I'll vouch for Steve."

"I'll make up my own mind, thanks," he said.

"Where do you want to meet, Jerry?" I asked, hoping to cut off debate.

"How about Dylan's on Clinton? West side of the street between Monroe and Adams. Six o'clock or so?"

"See you then."

"Oh, Deuce," Jerry added, "if you get there first, grab a table inside. Even if it's not raining. The more privacy, the better."

I hung up. Steve and I went about the business of ordering lunch.

"We're eating lunch at nearly two o'clock and meeting somebody at a tavern in four hours?" Steve said. "Do people in Chicago do anything besides eat?"

"Yeah, of course," I said. "We kill one another every once in a while. Go to the theater occasionally. Scream at our professional sports teams. Bask on the beach. Drink. Give directions to tourists. When we have time, of course. The five minutes between meals."

I ordered the vegetable soup and a chicken salad sandwich. He ordered chili and a sandwich called, "A Wreck." I had no idea where it got its name, but I knew it contained every meat under the sun and came with a side of cardiologist.

There were people around, so we talked about our lives and work instead of what it felt like to take a human life and what all the mob murders were geared to accomplish.

Afterward, with some time to kill, I got behind the wheel of Steve's rental car and took him on a tour of the city. We had to cut it short because the traffic started to build toward the rush hour. We got to Dylan's a little after 5:30. As Jerry requested, we snagged the most isolated inside table available and waited for our third. To pass the time, Steve scanned the beer offerings and ordered a Guinness. I ordered a Goose Island IPA.

I made introductions when Jerry arrived and watched him as he assessed Steve the way a squirrel might assess a hungry hawk. After a few moments Jerry decided it was safe to sit at the table with us. He ordered a Michelob Ultra, an alleged light beer with only a few more calories than plain water and not nearly as much taste.

He also asked for two servings of hummus for the table to nibble on while we talked. The waiter checked the beer levels in front of Steve and me, decided we were fine for the time being, and left.

"Aren't there a lot of calories in hummus?" I asked Jerry.

"It's mostly chickpeas," he said.

"Still a lot of calories."

"Chickpeas are a vegetable."

"Calories are calories, Jerry."

"Shut up," he said.

"So what do you know?" I asked.

"First, let's get something clear. What we say here at this table doesn't leave with us. It stays right here to be swept away by the clean-up crew after closing tonight. And neither of you writes anything."

"That restriction's getting kind of old," Steve said.

Jerry scowled at him. "*Al diablo con eso,*" he said. "The hell with it. I'm going to drink my beer in silence, eat more than my share of the hummus, and leave without saying another word."

"Come on, Jerry," I said. "We've given Ron our word. You have our word." As I said this, I gave Steve the proverbial kick under the table. "We're reporters. It's our job to report. We're not being allowed to do our jobs. It's frustrating."

"And if we let you make every piece of evidence public, we wouldn't be doing our jobs," he said. "Look, right now what you know isn't knowledge at all. It's speculation, a parade of maybes and possibilities. It could all turn out wrong, and the two of you would be up crap creek because you published it as truth."

My brain opened a review of the facts. There were, by my count, six dead mobsters, four from the Tricoletto family, two from the Callisi family. Those were facts. Three of the four Tricolettos were killed with succinylcholine. The other was garroted. Both Callisi soldiers were shot. The seventh victim, Carl Cribben, was killed with sux and his body hung out a window. More facts. What did they all add up to? I hadn't a clue. Jerry was right.

"What're you thinkin' about?" Jerry asked.

"Trying to sort out what we know and what we don't. Right now I guess the only thing we could write would be that there are seven people dead, the first two with solid ties to Carl Cribben, who's also dead."

"Right," Jerry said. "Of the other four, only two are from the same family as the first ones to go down, the family that was the focus of Carl's Chicago investigation. So far as we know, the two Callisis have no ties at all to the rest except proximate dates of death. There's your big scoop, kids. Nuthin'. You've got *nada.*"

Satisfied that Steve and I would keep things under wraps, he continued. "Here's what's new. The liquid in the syringe that squirted onto Deuce's jacket? It was sux. The lab estimated there was enough on your sleeve, Deuce, to kill a tyrannosaurus rex. I suspect the guy loaded a massive overdose in the hope of taking both of you out."

"We pretty much guessed that already," Steve said. "And the clumsy hitman was butchered because he failed."

Jerry shrugged. "That's as good as any speculation, I suppose."

The hummus arrived. The waiter set the chickpea, tahini, and horseradish mixture on the table with a basket of toasted pita triangles and a plate of cucumber slices. He asked if we needed another round. Steve and I did. Jerry was still working on his first Ultra.

"So," Steve said, "what else did you bring to the table beyond a taste for chickpeas, a review of what we don't know, and word that we have prices on our heads?"

Jerry nodded. "Colter and two of his agents interviewed John Fasso this afternoon. You recall it was his car that carried Sonny Barone to Bacchanalia last night."

I said, "I presume the car was stolen."

"So did the cops," Jerry said. "But it wasn't reported as stolen. That's why

Colter wanted to see Fasso. Fasso said he didn't know the car was missing until the police told him it was wrecked in Gage Park with a dead body inside and the fob in a cup holder."

"How could he not know his car was gone?" Steve asked.

"Fasso's district office is in the 2600 block of West Jackson, about a block west of Western Avenue. He lives on West Jackson, in the 1500 block just east of Ashland…"

That rocked me a little. I grew up in the 1500 block of West Jackson. I didn't remember a Fasso family, but they probably came long after I left.

"…His office and home are about a mile and a half apart," Jerry continued. "He told Colter he likes to walk for the exercise unless he has a meeting first thing in the day, then his official car and driver pick him up at home, and he uses them the rest of the day. He said he'll go a week and never take his Enclave out of the garage. He didn't know it was gone."

Steve asked, "Did anybody confirm this with his driver?"

"That right there's the thing," Jerry said. "*El esta desaparecido*. Nobody can find him."

35

"So," Steve asked a moment after Jerry left to meet his fiancé, "have any idea where we go from here?"

"I know where I'm going," I said. "I'm going back to the condo, tend to my cats, and curl up with them in Mark's big bed. Then I'll sleep for at least ten hours. I got maybe one hour last night, and I don't go very long on an hour's rest. I'll think about my next move tomorrow. Right now Costa Rica sounds pretty good."

Steve laughed. "It does, but I wasn't talking about that kind of move."

I nodded and tried unsuccessfully to stifle a yawn. Talking about being tired made me sleepy. "I know," I replied. "But my brain has turned to wet cement. It is picketing in opposition to being used again before tomorrow."

Steve drove me back to the condo. He pulled into the half-circle drive as close to the front door as he could get. He was still looking out for my safety. It was instinct with him.

He glanced in the rear-view mirror and put a hand on my arm.

"A black van just pulled in behind us."

I glanced in the side mirror and saw a burly man get out of the passenger side. He took off his cap so I could see his face and smiled at me.

"Oh, no sweat," I said. "It's the security team. I know the one walking this way."

"You sure?" he asked. "My crew was driving a white van."

I assured him it was all good.

We both got out of Steve's rental and talked to the security guys. As it turned out, I knew them both from the last time. I introduced Steve, and the four of us discussed plans for the rest of the evening and the next morning. Since I was headed to Mark's condo for the night, they decided to tail Steve.

When I got to the condo I wanted to go right to bed, but it wasn't even eight o'clock yet. So after I took care of the cats, I curled up on the couch with a glass of red wine, played fetch with the cats for a while with one of their dozens of catnip-stuffed mice, and watched the city as the final few minutes of dusk slipped into full-blown night.

My bladder woke me up at 2:13 a.m. I had dozed off and fallen into a fetal position on the sofa. There still was half a glass of wine on the coffee table. I poured it out—a shame—and stumbled into the bedroom. I stripped and let my clothes stay where they fell. I folded myself into the bed and fell asleep almost immediately. My last sensation was the feeling of two cats snuggling in close to me. One of them kneaded my abdomen. When I put my hand out to pet him, he enveloped it with all four paws and pulled it into his stomach where it stayed until I woke up again in the morning.

* * *

I was thinking about John Fasso's missing driver while I was in the shower. If he wasn't off on a spring vacation somewhere to escape the last frigid days of the long winter, then he might be dead, too.

I wondered how Fasso had screened and chosen his driver. More than a dozen public officials in Chicago traditionally had security details made up of members of the city police force. But some of those details had been eliminated and a few others cut back as a way of getting more police on the streets. Even the mayor's detail had been downsized. Fasso had city-paid security at one time, but if the mayor had lost some of her detail, the vice mayor would have lost some or all of his, as well. Fasso probably hired a new guy he paid out of his pocket to be his driver. I needed to get his name.

It seemed unlikely—though not impossible—that Fasso's driver was an off-duty police officer. It was even conceivable that a cop would play a role in an attempt on my life. They're not all choir boys. That would mean a police officer sat behind the wheel of Fasso's Enclave and did nothing as Barone was murdered in the passenger seat beside him. If the driver hadn't been murdered too, he might have gone into hiding.

I was thinking too much, chancing the exhaustion of my brain again. I'd also been standing under the hot water long enough for my skin to prune.

Both cats were sitting on the bathmat waiting for me, their heads cocked as if to ask if I'd forgotten that I owed them breakfast. I left dry food down for them all day, but in the morning and evening each got a tablespoon of a good wet food as a treat. Heaven help me if I forgot or was late with these coveted morsels. They would follow me around mewling at me until I complied with their wishes. If for some reason the mewling didn't work, I might find my favorite sweater shredded on the closet floor.

With the cats happily munching away, taking time out every once in a while to give me an "it-took-you-long-enough" look, I made coffee. While sipping my morning elixir, I focused on answering the questions I had about Fasso's missing driver. I made a call.

Sgt. Pete Rizzo, the top-ranking spokesman for the Chicago Police Department, had been at his desk for an hour when I reached him. And it was only 8 a.m.

"Whatcha want?" he asked. "Please don't ruin my day."

"I'd like to come by and see you," I said. "I have some easy questions."

His laughter sounded genuine. "I believe that to such a small degree it can't even be measured. I'll be around all morning so far's I know. The coffee's still bad, but this early it will still be hot. Gimme a time."

I said I'd be there in about an hour.

He replied, "Good. That'll give me enough time to lock up all the secret stuff I've got spread around my desk."

* * *

When I walked into Pete's office his desk didn't look like he'd filed a piece of paper since the turn of the century. The nineteenth century. He knew exactly why I was smiling.

"There's a method to this madness," he said. "All the junk you see here camouflages the cool stuff I have to keep away from nosy scribblers such as yourself."

I picked up a sheet of paper at random. "Here's one you missed," I said.

"Oh, yeah? What is it?"

"The secretarial pool rotation for your office for next week."

"Damn it. It was careless of me to leave it lyin' around." He snatched the paper back from me. "If you publish this, you'll cost me my job."

"What job? I hadn't noticed you doing any work."

He cocked his head toward his credenza. "Pour yourself a cup of coffee, sit down, and tell me what, if anything, is on your devious little mind."

I did as I was told and got right to the point.

"I know the city's squeezing some of the protective details around town," I said. "Is Alderman Fasso's one of them?"

"I believe that was one we eliminated," Rizzo said, now all serious business. "No, wait a second. We didn't eliminate it. Cut it some, but not completely. Fasso eliminated it himself. Said he wanted to pick his own detail. He took on a couple of private guys he paid out of his own pocket. I guess that got too expensive, and he cut back to one, a driver."

"Do you know who the driver is?"

"Not off the top of my head. I probably have it on the computer. But since they're not city guys, I'm not at liberty to make their names public. That information would have to come from the alderman's district office. It's over on…"

"I know where it is, Pete."

I moved on. "You know about the attack on me and another reporter by a guy named Barone, a soldier for the Tricoletto family. Afterward, somebody garroted him in a car that belonged to Fasso. Fasso says the car was stolen, and he didn't know it until one of your guys told him the car had crashed with a dead body inside, who turned out to be Barone."

Rizzo was nodding. "Yeah, yeah, I know all that."

"The driver is missing. The fob was still with the car."

"I also know the only prints belonged to Fasso and his driver."

"Who is? Or was?"

"I already told you. That will have to come from Fasso."

"You know my role in this story is totally in the background. I'm not writing anything or passing any information to our cops reporters. I won't screw you."

"Well, that's disappointing to hear." Rizzo heaved a huge sigh and turned to his computer. He scrolled and clicked around for a few seconds. "Did I offend you?"

"Probably. Now ask me if I care."

"Michael D'Amato. He was Fasso's regular driver. His mother was Gisella D'Amato. You might have heard-a her. She died last year."

"I can't say the name's familiar," I said.

"How about her full name? Gisella Tricoletto D'Amato."

I sat up straighter. "Really? What was her relationship?…"

"With old man Toes? She was his sister."

"So the missing driver is Tony Toes' nephew?"

"Yep."

"Was or is the nephew connected?"

"Don't know. He doesn't have a rap sheet."

"But he worked for Fasso? And Fasso paid his salary?"

"Seems so. Fasso grew up palling around with Tony's younger son, Jimmy. Michael D'Amato was about the same age. Makes sense he might have been part of that boys' fraternity. You know about Fasso's grandfather?"

The look on Rizzo's face said it was something serious.

"Apparently not," I said.

"He ran with Capone."

"That's not so surprising. So did most of the made guys on the South Side in the day."

"The grandfather was high up. A consigliere—counselor—at some point."

"What about Fasso's father?"

"No indication he was connected. But that doesn't mean he wasn't. Maybe he never got caught."

"So from appearances, at least, one might suspect that John Fasso, Chicago alderman and vice mayor, is on the Tricoletto pad and might be taking orders and relaying reports through the nephew."

"Speculation, Deuce. Pure conjecture. We don't have a shred of evidence."

"But I gather from your lack of surprise that you have checked out the possibility."

"No comment. But for the record, hiring a boyhood friend isn't a crime."

"But if I'm right?"

"Let's hope you're not."

36

I had grown weary of conducting newspaper business over meals, so when I met up with Steve later in the day I suggested we drive up to one of my favorite thinking spots in the city, Montrose Harbor. It sat next to the Uptown neighborhood north of the Miracle Mile. The park had a beautiful beach, marina, and a bird sanctuary where we could sit and talk in private and watch dozens of species of birds, some that spent the full year in the city, some that came only for the summer, and others that stopped along their migration routes as they moved with the seasons. Currently, migration was in full swing. We probably would encounter a few avid bird watchers, but they would be more interested in the feathered visitors than in us. It was still too cool to be crowded, a plus for me. I brought a jacket and suggested Steve bring one, too.

I let my security team know where we were going. They said they would be right behind us, and they were. They stayed close enough to be able to react quickly if we needed help but not so close that the bad guys would make them, assuming the bad guys were looking for them. When we exited Lake Shore Drive the ramp took us right to Montrose Drive, the entrance to the park complex. Just beyond Cricket Hill we found the parking lot almost empty. We took a first-row spot that made for a short, easy stroll into the sanctuary.

We stayed in our vehicle until we saw the security team pull into the same lot. Their vehicle of choice this day was a white GMC Yukon, which made it a bit less conspicuous than if it had been black.

Steve and I walked toward the sanctuary leaving our watchdogs behind for the moment. I assumed they might follow later.

The first birds we encountered were a flock of about 100 Canada geese. They paid no attention to us. They focused totally on chomping whatever Canada geese chomp on among the blades of newly greening grass.

"They don't seem to care that we're invading their turf," Steve said.

"They don't. There are probably tens of thousands of them in the city, all used to sharing ground with humans. In fact, humans are the reason they're here. They came to get away from hunters. They thrive here, though they didn't escape hunters completely. In the last few years there's been an uptick in the numbers of coyotes and red foxes around. You remember the pedestrian bridge over Lake Shore Drive a few miles back?"

Steve thought for a moment, "Oh, yeah," he said. "It's very pretty."

"Wildlife officials live-trapped a coyote crossing the bridge a few years ago. They were fairly certain it was anticipating a goose dinner."

Steve had skepticism all over his face. "There are literally tens of thousands of geese living inside Chicago's city limits?"

"Yep. Chicago has something like 570 parks that cover almost 10 percent of the land in the city. A lot of them have small lakes or ponds or creeks running through them. Then of course there's Lake Michigan over here, a fresh-water inland sea with green spaces and parks running all the way up and down Lake Shore Drive. This area's a huge goose resort."

When we got deeper into the sanctuary, we sat down where we could get a panoramic view of the day's goings on. When I started telling Steve what I'd learned from Pete Rizzo just hours earlier, he lost interest in birds and focused on me.

"So is Fasso involved in all the murders?" he asked.

"I don't know that he's involved in any of them."

"Why would he be?"

"I don't know that, either. I worked on a story a while back where a public official was beholden to the Mob for a string of things too complicated to go into now. If it's true, it could be the same sort of thing. My source tells me Fasso's grandfather was a consigliere with Capone. I don't know if Fasso's father was connected."

"Your source doesn't know?"

"No," I said. "The father's got no record. Maybe he got lucky."

"You know," Steve added, "maybe the alderman isn't tied to the Tricoletto family, but they've got something on him that opens him up to blackmail."

"That's possible, too," I said. "The family lives in Fasso's district, but I'm not sure what he could do for them that'd require blackmail. Part of an alderman's job is to boost the interests of constituents."

"Not if their interests are illegal."

I laughed. "I haven't heard Fasso promoting drugs and prostitution recently. Ever."

"So maybe," Steve suggested, "the car really was stolen and Fasso really didn't know until the police told him."

I got up and stretched. "Come on, Pancho. Let's go find some birds and then get out of here. All the fresh air and confusion are making my head hurt."

* * *

It wasn't the best time of day for birdwatching.

Migrating birds, some of which fly between South America and the Arctic twice a year, get very tired and hungry. They pause when they find a good spot to eat and rest. The Montrose Bird Sanctuary is on a hook of land that juts out into Lake Michigan, a prime spot for many species to pause their journey. It's easiest to spot them out in the open when they're chowing down early in the morning. We had arrived during prime sleeping time. But even so, we didn't do badly.

When my Explorer burned, I lost the pair of birding binoculars and my bird identification book that I kept in the front console so I would be equipped for unexpected birding experiences while traveling. I replaced the glasses and the book in two days with an order to Amazon. They were in my messenger bag, still unused. We'd share if we saw anything worth watching.

After less than half an hour of wandering the sanctuary we had seen black-bellied and American golden plovers, dunlin, semi-palmated sandpipers, and a red-throated loon. There's an area of the sanctuary—a line of trees, understory, brush, and ground cover—that attracts birds like kids to Popsicles. The foliage is carefully managed so something is blooming through the whole growing season and going to seed from late summer to the first freeze. The area attracts so many varieties of sparrows and songbirds it's known as "The Magic Hedge."

It didn't hold Steve's interest very long. He was far more fascinated by the boats that had begun to reappear in the adjacent Montrose Marina after a winter in drydock. It was all he could do to keep from drooling. I had to admit there was something compelling about white yachts on clean blue water beneath a cloud-studded cobalt sky.

When I turned back toward Steve I saw one of our minders standing maybe twenty-five feet away toward the marina. Like Steve, he seemed to be admiring the yachts. I had no idea where his partner was.

Steve said, "We need to find out more about Fasso's routine and his associates," he said. "I could follow him for a week and shoot photos, but I'd need help identifying his friends since my knowledge of Chicago denizens is pretty sparse. You have any cop friends who might help with the ID part? Or maybe you know enough of them to help."

"Maybe," I said. "It's fine with me if you want to do that. But two things: First, do not step onto anyone's private property. Shoot photos from your car parked on a public street, or standing on a public sidewalk, or in a public alley. Second, if you suspect for a moment you've been spotted, give it up. The cost of being too persistent is too high."

* * *

We walked in silence for a few minutes, the bird book and binoculars stowed back in my bag. Our thoughts were fully focused now on our story, whatever that story was.

So it took us a few moments to notice the danger.

We had emerged from the sanctuary and were next to a small bait-and-tackle shop that appeared to be closed. That was where the road that accessed the bird sanctuary ended in a T intersection with the main road through the park. And it was where the main road changed names. To our left it was W.

Montrose Avenue, which led back to Lake Shore Drive the way we'd come in. To our right it became N. Simonds Avenue and curved around to the north, running parallel to the shoreline. The sanctuary was behind us.

Two men were walking down Simonds toward us. They looked ordinary but didn't act it. Their eyes fixed on us, and their expressions were decidedly unfriendly. I glanced to my left and saw two additional men, who could have been clones of the first two, coming at us along Montrose. A glance over my shoulder confirmed that two more had followed us out of the sanctuary. Our minder on the ground had seen them, too, and was talking to someone, perhaps his partner, on a setup like the U.S. Secret Service uses: a small hand mic and a tiny earphone, both attached to a transmitter hooked on the back of the belt.

I leaned toward Steve and said in a stage whisper, "It appears, old man, that we are in some serious trouble."

37

Steve's rental car was parked directly across Montrose from us in the front row of the lot. The two of us running hard could have reached it in twenty seconds. But I didn't know if we had twenty seconds. All six men approaching us had their jackets open, despite the chill breeze coming off the lake. We were all out in the open now where the trees and understory of the sanctuary didn't provide a wind break. If all six men had guns, it's doubtful they all would have missed us, even as moving targets.

For a moment I considered trying to make the park office that was between the bait shop and the harbor. But assuming we could dodge bullets long enough to arrive alive, and assuming the office was open and staffed, it would just give the six men more witnesses to shoot and kill.

Then it crossed my mind to run for the harbor and jump in the water. But Lake Michigan was still partially frozen from the long, hard winter. Even in the relative shallows that no longer supported ice the water temperature hadn't yet climbed out of the thirties. We wouldn't survive hypothermia for five minutes.

We could have run back into the sanctuary, bowling over the two men behind us if they didn't shoot us first, and try to find cover long enough for our minders to handle the situation, assuming two men could take out six. That's when I saw a scene that made my heart sink. One of the gunmen was standing beside the white Yukon with his gun hanging at his side, a cylinder I recognized as a silencer attached to the barrel. The minder who had stayed with the SUV lay crumpled on the ground beside the driver's door. As I watched for a few seconds, the attacker put bullets into the two driver's side tires, immobilizing the Yukon. Leaving his gun visible, he joined his own partner in advancing toward us. The second minder was nowhere to be seen, but I heard people screaming behind me in the sanctuary. All the evidence told me that Steve and I were on our own.

I caught motion to my right. Steve had his cell phone partially out of his pocket.

"Calling 9-1-1," he said.

The operator asked the nature of our emergency. Steve handed the phone to me.

"Tell her where we are," Steve said.

I did. And about the six armed men. And the fact that we were trapped and in imminent danger. I said the attackers had already shot one man and possibly two. I also identified myself and explained I couldn't talk any more, that we were going to have to make a run for our lives. The operator tried to tell me something, but my focus was back on a possible escape route.

I kept the phone so I could maintain contact with the emergency operator. The police would need its GPS signal to track us.

Our only course was straight ahead to the parking lot, running a zig-zag route and praying none of the six guys was an expert shot, likely an erroneous assumption. They were all still thirty yards from us, however, and handguns at that distance aren't reliably accurate in bringing down moving targets—movie chase scenes notwithstanding.

The downside of the plan was this: While the men were thirty yards from us, the two on Montrose and the two on Simonds now were flanking Steve's car. Running straight to the car would put us between them, and we could get caught in a crossfire.

Now I saw Steve holding the fob that would unlock the car, his thumb on the unlock button. "I'm ready," he said. I decided not to mention my fears.

"Stay low and run a crooked route," I said. "No sense making this easier for them."

We sprinted across the main road when the first shots came, all sounding like dull thuds as the silencers did their jobs. I thought I heard one shot buzz past my head. I saw another blow up the asphalt at Steve's feet. The gunmen would get the range soon enough.

We ran like hell.

When we hit the grass between the road and the parking lot my feet slipped and went out from under me. I was down on one knee in the wet grass, and the thought flashed through my mind that if I let my body fall and remain still in the grass, perhaps the gunmen would think they killed me and ignore me. But Steve wasn't about to abandon me. I saw him turn to help.

"Keep going," I yelled and stumbled to my feet.

We gave up on the zigging and zagging. It was slowing our progress, and the gunmen were closing fast as a result. We made a beeline for the car, and I heard the lock chirp. The problem was, the fob only unlocked the driver's door. Steve would have to unlock the passenger door manually. Precious more seconds gone.

I slammed into the passenger side and tried to take the best cover possible. Steve's car was on the east side of me, and a motorcycle was parked in the spot to the west. I crouched down. As cover goes it wasn't much. A bullet hit the window beside my head and brought back some grim memories. I felt rather than heard my door unlock and leaped inside. Steve already had the engine running. He squealed backward out of the space and hit a concrete wheel block on the parking row behind us. I hoped he hadn't flattened a tire.

There were two exits from the parking lot. Steve started to turn toward the one we entered, the one that emptied onto Montrose Avenue, the route to Lake Shore Drive. I saw two of the gunmen get into their car and move off in the same direction. They were anticipating our move.

"No, no," I screamed. "Turn the other way. Trust me."

Steve nodded and swung the car left, heading east toward the Simonds Drive exit.

"Turn left," I said as we got out of the lot. I saw that all three vehicles were now behind us pointed west on Montrose toward Lake Shore Drive, opposite the direction we were going. They were on both sides of the road. They guessed they could catch us in a crossfire as we tried to go between them. They guessed wrong.

Simonds turned north, and Steve followed it.

"Next left," I told him. I glanced back at our attackers. Now they weren't bothering with streets. They were blowing through the grass, a shortcut to us. While their detour cut the distance between us, the uneven nature of the ground forced them to slow down.

Steve turned onto West Wilson Drive, and there in the near distance, past another parking lot, was another entrance to Lake Shore Drive.

"Take the first ramp up to the right," I said. "Northbound."

"That'll take us away from the city," he protested.

"We can't take a chance getting caught in traffic trying to make a left turn."

When we were back on Lake Shore I told Steve to take the exit toward Lawrence.

"When you get to Lawrence, take a left away from the water and floor it."

"You're trying to lose 'em," he said.

"Trying is the right word," I said. I turned in the seat and tried to spot their cars. But everything had happened so fast, I wasn't sure I'd have known them if I saw them.

There weren't many vehicles that followed us off Lake Shore and onto Lawrence. None of those I saw looked familiar. But I did see two police cruisers screaming in the opposite direction. I pulled out Steve's cell phone. The 9-1-1 operator was still on the line. I told her the two police cars were going in the wrong direction.

I gave her an update, told her where we were and where we were going.

She told me to stay on the line and keep her informed on the location of every turn we made and what direction we were going. Several cruisers, she said, were moving in our direction and would intercept us. It was unlikely our attackers would move against multiple police officers.

Mentally I crossed my fingers.

I continued to hold out hope until I heard a slug break the rear window and felt it slam into the back of my headrest. I was about to be thankful it didn't come all the way through when it fell onto my shoulder and into my lap. I knew it would be searing hot, so instead of picking it up I flicked it onto the floor. It left a burn mark on my sweater.

Steve glanced over at me. "You okay?" he asked.

I took a deep breath. "Just dandy," I said.

"Tell the dispatcher I'm headed north on Sheridan, passing Hollywood Avenue."

And I did, just as Steve ran a red light.

Chicagoans don't honk their horns often, but the cacophony that erupted around us could have damaged my hearing.

Steve grinned. "The guys with the guns have slipped back. All the cars around them stopped for the light. For the moment we're clear. As soon as we're out of their sight, I want to get off this street. Too much traffic."

"We'll turn left on Granville and then south on Clark a few blocks later," I said. "Stay on southbound Clark."

I knew that once we got to Graceland Cemetery, we should be right in the middle of Wrigley Field traffic. The Cubs were playing an afternoon game today. From the looks of all the 'Cubs' and 'W' flags on the cars up here, the game is over and the Cubs won. Traffic would be horrendous with way too many people around for the gunmen to risk anything.

"Tell me when the turns are coming up."

Graceland Cemetery had nothing to do with Elvis Presley. It was the scenic burial ground for lots of famous Chicagoans. I had no desire to join them.

I was updating the police on our plans when we crossed a street called Glenlake. I pointed ahead and told Steve, "Next left." Then I finished telling the police the rest of the plan so they could anticipate where we were going instead of trying to play catchup.

We never got to Graceland or to Wrigley Field. The police set up a roadblock north of both sites. We ran into them at Clark and West Lawrence, at the southwest corner of St. Boniface Catholic Cemetery. As soon as the cops heard Steve honk his horn and saw him flash his lights, they motioned him to stop. One officer approached us and made a motion for Steve to put his window down. He asked for IDs. But as soon as he saw the broken windows and bullet holes he told Steve to move in behind two squad cars.

"Follow me, and I'll run interference for you," he said.

After waiting for more than ten minutes with no sign of the gunmen, the cops partially opened both Clark and Lawrence. The opening was wide enough to allow the increasingly impatient post-baseball fans to leak through one lane at a time and slow enough for the officers to get a good look at the occupants of each vehicle.

We had given the cops only sketchy descriptions of the men who attacked us. We were running too hard for our lives to stop for close looks. But the one thing that struck both Steve and me is that all six were similarly dressed in khaki pants that could have been Dockers, dark Polo style shirts, and Italian style leather jackets. To me the jackets looked like they came from Georgio Armani. Supple leather with turned down collars, ribbed cuffs and hem, and distinct arrangements of front zipper pockets. Mark had considered buying one a few months earlier. Eventually he rejected the price tag.

None of the passing vehicles had men dressed like that. So most vehicles, especially those carrying people wearing Cubs gear and groups that included children, were allowed to pass quickly. I saw only two cars pulled over for closer looks.

Steve and I sat still in the back of a squad car, both of us breathing heavily as if we hadn't drawn in air since we first encountered the six men at the bird sanctuary. The air conditioning was blowing, but I could feel perspiration trickling down my spine and pooling beneath my shoulders against the car seat. The sweat was pouring off Steve's face.

He said, "At least the day can't get any worse."

But it could, and did. The sergeant directing the blockade came back to talk to us. The private cop I'd last seen on the ground beside his Yukon was dead. His partner was found, also dead, back near the Magic Hedge. Witnesses said two men in black leather jackets walked up to him and put four bullets in his chest.

I felt sick to my stomach.

38

The mayor's eyes flashed fire as they flicked back and forth between the police superintendent, Cab Hill, and Ron Colter. Both men knew when Marsha Mendes called this meeting they were in for a beating. Cab Hill kept his job largely at the mayor's discretion. He wouldn't like the thrashing he knew was coming, but he also knew he would take it calmly. Ron Colter wasn't so tolerant. As he had told the mayor at least twice, he didn't work for her and was not subject to her orders or her wrath. Still, he had some sympathy for her position. A rolling shootout on the North Side following the murders of two security guards was not to be taken lightly. A Come-to-Jesus meeting with Deuce Mora and her editor was in order.

Hill and Colter filled in those present on the murders and the attempted murders at Montrose Harbor Park and the brief continuation of the gunfire on Lawrence Avenue near the Aragon Ballroom. It truly was miraculous that no bystanders were hurt. But that was of little comfort to Mendes.

"What is this?" she demanded. "A resurrection of Bugs Moran and Al Capone? Only things lacking are tommy guns, and a St. Valentine's Day almost a century ago."

Her reference was to the storied St. Valentine's Day Massacre of 1929 when the warring North Side Gang led by Bugs Moran was virtually wiped out by killers from Capone's South Side Chicago Outfit. The seven victims, two of whom were Moran's most reliable killers, were herded into a garage, lined up against a brick wall, and executed. Moran, who was the primary target of Capone's men, would have been among the dead but for a twist of fate. Two of Capone's men dressed that day as police officers. When Moran showed up at the garage late for his meeting and saw two men he presumed to be cops, he didn't go inside.

The mass murder eventually spelled the end of both gangs. Capone went to prison two years later for tax evasion. Moran, who lost his gang, went to Leavenworth federal prison in 1946 and died there of lung cancer eleven years later.

The brick wall that served as the backdrop for the shootings still stood on North Clark Street at West Dickens Avenue in the Lincoln Park neighborhood, though most of the garage itself had long since been torn down.

Ron Colter knew the story all too well. It crossed his mind that the site was only a few blocks west of the wooden bridge that crossed the South Pond in Lincoln Park where Bobby Callisi was murdered and thrown into the water not so many days before.

It had been a tough period for mob nephews. First Bobby Callisi, nephew of the boss of the Callisi crime family, takes a double tap to the head. Then Michael d'Amato, nephew of the boss of the Tricoletto crime family and driver for John Fasso disappears. It wouldn't surprise Colter to learn that he was dead, too. Such are the risks of those life choices.

Mendes's sharp voice interrupted Colter's thoughts.

"Are you listening to me Agent Colter?" she demanded, probably demoting Colter's title on purpose as an insult. He chose not to rise to the bait.

"Yes, Ma'am," he said. "I was thinking about the irony of your first question. But it's not important. Please continue."

"You're damned straight I will," she snapped. "I want the entire Tricoletto family off the streets and behind bars, preferably within the week."

Jerry Alvarez, the deputy U.S. attorney, cleared his throat. "On what charges?" he asked. "We suspect they're responsible for several murders that have become federal cases, but we have no proof. One eye-witness account implicates one person who was a member of the Tricoletto family, Virgil Barone. He was likely the thug who attacked Deuce Mora on Oakley Avenue. But Barone was murdered, which puts him out of the reach of all federal law I'm familiar with."

"What about the person who killed Barone?" Mendes demanded. "Or the driver of the car where the murder happened?" She turned to John Fasso. "He was your driver, right, John?"

"My driver, my car," Fasso said. "But he couldn't have driven and garroted a man at the same time. I'm sure the police would ask him about it if they could find him."

She turned to Colter. *"Any progress there."*

"None," Colter replied.

"They're not only endangering citizens of Chicago, they're making fools of us," the mayor said. *"Have you interrogated Anthony Tricoletto?"*

"I did, with two other agents," Colter said. *"He denied any involvement and asked for privacy because he was in mourning for the close friends who recently died."*

"Oh, horseshit," the mayor said.

Fasso jumped in. *"I talked to him, as well,"* he said. *"As you know, he's one of my constituents. So I had a responsibility there. I want to know what happened to my driver. He said he had no idea."*

"Remind me, what's the driver's name?" Hill asked.

"I gave it to the cops who came over to tell me my car'd been stolen."

"If I read it in the report, I've forgotten it," Hill said.

"Michael d'Amato," Fasso replied.

"Oh, yeah," Hill said. *"Tony Toes' nephew."*

Fasso looked like a man who knew he was being goaded.

"Yes, but he didn't have mob ties. He was a Navy Seal. Did three tours, mostly in Middle East war zones, I imagine. Honorable discharge. Awarded the Navy Cross, The Navy Commendation Medal. Purple Heart."

"Sounds like a good choice," Colter said. *"What'd he get the medals for?"*

"He wouldn't tell me. Said it was all still classified."

"Still," Colter said, *"he doesn't sound the sort who'd take part in the attempted murder of a reporter. And he wouldn't sit still and watch a man nearly decapitated with piano wire while he drove down Western Avenue."*

"Usted no sabe. You don't know," Jerry Alvarez said. *"Some of those high-pressure, high-violence service guys see so much blood and killing they get inured to it. Some even have a violence habit seething in their brains when they become civilians again. It's post-traumatic stress disorder."*

"I never saw any sign of PTSD in Michael d'Amato," Fasso said. *"If anything, he seemed to be strong but low-key. I never even saw him flip a bird in traffic."*

Gov. Tyler Walston had been silent up to this point. Now he had a question.

"*So why'd you go see Tony Tricoletto in the first place without telling anyone?*" he asked Fasso.

"*I visit constituents all the time,*" the alderman said. "*I've known some members of the Tricoletto family for thirty years. Why shouldn't I visit with them?*"

Colter was as curious as the governor. "*The old man's not just any constituent,*" the FBI boss told Fasso. "*There might have been things we didn't want him to know, things we didn't want you to mention. I could have briefed you.*"

Fasso looked irritated. "*I didn't give away any of your precious secrets,*" he snapped. "*I don't even know any precious secrets.*"

"*Maybe you don't know what you know,*" the mayor said. "*We are completely open in these meetings, and we don't expect our discussions to leave this room.*"

"*Oh, for God's sake, Marsha, leave it alone.*" Fasso was flustered now. Colter and Alvarez exchanged glances.

"*Back to the matter at hand,*" Mendes said to Hill and Colter. "*Find a way to get the Tricoletto family off the streets. The Callisis, too, if you can. The killing has got to stop.*"

The meeting ended and everyone got up to leave. Mendes asked Colter to hang back.

"*You think we should cut Fasso out of these meetings?*" she asked when it was down to the two of them. "*He's a little too tight with the Tricoletto family for my comfort. He tried to get Jimmy Tricoletto, his boyhood buddy, a job with my administration.*"

"*Doing what?*" Colter asked.

"*As an advisor of some sort, maybe a deputy department head. We never got to specifics. I cut off the idea at the knees. Fasso was pissed already over losing the election. My rejection of his boyhood friend made it worse. I have no reason to think he's over it.*"

"*What are you thinking?*" Colter asked.

"*That he wouldn't be upset if he could help his old friends make my administration, and me, look bad. The Tribune has already written two bad editorials about our lack of action on these killings. The second one contained a thinly veiled suggestion that at some point a recall petition on me might be worth consideration. If I'm forced into early retirement, John Fasso becomes mayor until there's a new election. The mayor's office is John's wet dream.*"

"*And you think he'd help start a shooting war on the streets of Chicago to get there?*" Colter asked. "*On the other hand, would the voters even notice, given all the other shooting wars going on in this city?*"

"*Not funny, Ron,*" she said. "*These are white guys killing white guys, Mafia or not. Chicago's a very liberal city, but there's still an undercurrent of racism that lets influential white voters and wealthy white donors think deaths on the streets aren't quite as important when the bodies are people of color.*"

"*I don't even like to hear that,*" Colter said. "*You think Fasso's on Tony Toes' pad?*"

"*I'm beginning to wonder. He grew up in those surroundings. Jimmy Tricoletto's got a juvie record, but it's sealed, of course. I wouldn't be surprised if Jimmy and John did a few bad things together. Shoplifting, maybe. A little B-and-E. Who knows? Maybe the family's got something on John that would squash his rise through the political ranks, and they're using it to pressure him. Or maybe he's doing willing favors for old friends. Don't get me wrong. I don't have any proof of any of this. But if Tricoletto's got somebody on the inside, I don't see a better candidate than John Fasso.*"

39

I was sitting at my desk in the newsroom typing away furiously on a column I really hated. It would catch readers up on the mob violence that had broken out all over the city and culminated (so far, at least) in the shootout in Lincoln Park with Steve Pace and me as the targets. Details of the shootings that began at Montrose Harbor and spilled onto crowded city streets were public record now, including the identities of the two security agents who died trying to keep Steve and me alive. Those two agents, who started out as Steve's detail, had been replaced. That detail was not public. But everything else was on the police blotter where every reporter who covered the Cop Shop could find it.

I had already fielded dozens of questions and expressions of sympathy and concern from colleagues, plus six calls from local media outlets wanting grim details. I was grateful to my colleagues. I told the outside media in the most pleasant way possible that I had nothing to say. If they wanted comment, they should talk to my supervisor, Eric Ryland.

Ryland walked up to my cubicle at that moment and slammed his hand onto the wood slat that ran along the top of the partition. It made me jump.

"My office, now!" he said. Then he turned on his heel with me following. We didn't go to his office. We went to his conference room. Steve Pace was already there. His editor, Bryanna Regan, waited on a Skype connection to learn what was happening.

I knew this wouldn't be good when I saw Ron Colter and the Chicago police superintendent, Cab Hill, already sitting at the conference table. Hill's face was tight with fury.

"Who the hell do you two think you are?" he shouted at Steve and me loud enough that Eric got up and closed the door. Hill hardly paused. "You're out on my streets speeding, driving like maniacs, running lights, and drawing gunfire on roadways packed with innocent people trying to get home from work or from a baseball game. Shots are flying all over the place. Two men are dead. It's a miracle nobody else was hurt or killed. I won't tolerate it. The mayor wants you cited and jailed for every traffic violation I can dream up, and I'm tempted to do it." He was shouting louder now. "You have no right. No right!"

"We didn't start it," I insisted. "They killed two people who were detailed to protect Steve and me, and then they tried to kill us. We weren't shooting. We didn't even have weapons. We were running to try to save our own lives."

Now Colter jumped in. "You egged it on," he said. "If you'd let your police and city hall reporters handle this using normal news-gathering procedures, you wouldn't have needed security, you wouldn't have needed to run from anything. But no. You tried to justify your persistence with some cockamamie idea that you weren't really working on the Cribben story so you weren't in any danger."

Eric intervened. "Gentlemen," he said, "could you tone this down just a little? Could we have a civil discussion about where we go from here?"

Cab Hill shot out of his chair so fast the medals on his chest rattled.

"There is nothing to discuss," he said, his tone modulating only a little. "I am laying down the law. Leave this to the professionals or there will be serious consequences."

He stormed out of the room not even waiting to see if Colter followed.

I glared at the FBI's AD. "Thanks for throwing me under the bus," I said. "When I had questions for you, you didn't exactly push me away."

"I know, and I'm sorry," he said. "But it would have inflamed tensions even more for me to leap to your defense and make Cab look foolish. I need the cooperation of this city's officials. If I have to pound my shoe on your conference table to keep it, I will. Besides, when all else is said and done, I think Cab is right. It's not my place to order you to stand down, but it certainly would be my strong recommendation before we have dead bodies all up and down Lake Shore Drive."

Ron Colter had released us from our pledges to keep official fears of a possible new Mob war out of our newspapers. He gave us permission to publish what we knew about who had died. But he barred speculation about the identities of the killers beyond saying the violence seemed to be concentrated within the Tricoletto and Callisi organizations, the two largest and oldest mob syndicates in the city.

Colter also didn't want any mention of succinylcholine in our stories. The how and why of that substance becoming a weapon of murder were still bizarre unknowns. We settled on some vague language, that preliminary autopsy findings suggested the dead who weren't garroted or shot died from the administration of an as-yet-unidentified "poison." For the time being Eric let two of our police reporters handle the news accounts of the killings. I wasn't sure what Steve wrote for the Washington *Chronicle*. Our research library was watching for his story to pop up on the *Chronicle* website and would forward it to me as soon as it showed itself.

I returned to my column.

I didn't want my column to focus on what it felt like to have bullets whizzing by my head and thumping into the car in which I was a passenger. I was more fascinated by the similarities between the warfare between Al Capone's Southside Chicago Outfit and George "Bugs" Moran's North Side Gang, two of the Prohibition-era mobsters who left dead bodies and pools of blood all over town. Italian vs. Irish. Classic movie stuff.

Because of the enactment of Prohibition, a constitutional amendment making alcohol for human consumption illegal, and because there was so much dirty money passing hands in the process of filling the public's insatiable appetite for booze, there was also a whole lot of murder going on in the Windy City. It began 100 years earlier, in 1920, and hung on until the amendment was repealed in 1933. It was the era of Elliot Ness and his Untouchables, Capone, Moran, Dean O'Banion, Meyer Lansky, Lucky Luciano, Johnny Torrio, Frank Nitti, Bugsy Segal, and dozens more. I wanted my column to lift those men out of the history books and remind people they weren't just characters in Brian De Palma movies starring Kevin Costner, Sean Connery, and Robert De Niro.

Eric Ryland was so intrigued by the column idea that he allocated more column inches than I usually got. He also asked the photo department to send somebody up to Lincoln Park to make pictures of the infamous brick wall that served as a backdrop for the St. Valentine's Day Massacre and any other infamous sites from the Capone/Moran era.

That included the old Biograph Theater on Lincoln Avenue just north of Fullerton Street. The building, now home to the acclaimed Victory Gardens drama stages, still sat beside the alley from which notorious bank robber John Dillinger emerged on the night he was gunned down by the FBI. Dillinger had nothing to do with bootlegging, but he was still a part of Chicago's crime lore.

Eric also wanted photos of what remained of the Schoenhofen Brewery in the South Loop at the three-way intersection of Canal, Canalport, and West 18th Streets. Capone stole the place from the family of its original owner, Peter Schoenhofen. Peter came to Chicago as a penniless immigrant from Prussia, learned the brewing trade, and built his brewery in 1861. Of the fifteen or so original buildings, only five remained. They retained their original spectacular stonework, through most of the century they served as warehouses. Now they were being renovated. The original massive piece of real estate that housed the brewery had been given "historic district" status decades earlier.

Among the notable aspects of the main building was stonework displaying what appears to be a Star of David. Many mistake it for Schoenhofen's message of pride in his Jewish heritage. Far from it. The star is a brewer's symbol of purity. Nothing more. In fact, lore says federal agents believed members of the Schoenhofen family used their famous Edelweiss brewery tower to transmit intelligence to German agents during World War I. If there is evidence of truth in this allegation, my research didn't unearth it.

My research had taken much of the morning, and I was about to polish off the first draft of the column when my desk phone rang. I ignored it, and it stopped. Then it started again. I cursed and picked up the receiver. It was George, one of the guards at the reception desk in the lobby. He told me Ron Colter of the FBI wanted to come up to see me, but he said he didn't have an appointment. So George called to confirm it was okay.

I said it was.

Ron knew where my cubicle was, so I went back to writing for the few minutes I had before he arrived.

"Sorry to barge in," he said when he showed up.

"I'm surprised to see you at all after this morning," I said. I saved my column and invited him to come in and sit down.

"Could we talk some place private," he said. "I don't want to be overheard by someone who might report my whereabouts to Chicago's excitable top cop."

I stood up and looked around. Everyone whose desk was near mine was gone. Several people had invited me to come along with them for lunch, but I wanted to stay with the column and declined.

"They're all out eating," I said. "We've got maybe an hour before we get company."

"You writing about the shootings?"

"Yeah. I thought it would be interesting to do a column about the Mob history in that part of town. It's fascinating, and writing history won't get me in any trouble."

"I was thinking about that same subject the other day," he said. "History, not trouble. It was during a meeting in the mayor's office."

"Oh, how'd she feel about your mind wandering?"

"Not pleased. But she's rarely pleased with me. That meeting is why I'm here. It's a subject where I'll have to reimpose the restriction on you writing about it."

"After I hear what you have to say will I be sorry for agreeing not to write it, or for listening to you at all?"

Colter shook his head. "I hope not, on either count. If my line of thinking is wrong, and you wrote about it, you'd be libeling a very powerful man, and I'd probably be fired."

"Oh," I said. "Wouldn't want that to happen. So yes, I'll agree."

"The mayor thinks one of us who has been inside her super-secret meetings is leaking stuff to the Tricolettos. And she thinks it's John Fasso."

"Yikes," I said. "Can you tell me why she thinks so?"

Colter reviewed for me all the factors that went into the mayor's thinking.

"That's all pretty circumstantial," I said when he finished.

"It is. That's why I said you probably wouldn't write it even if I gave the okay."

"You were right." I thought a moment about what I'd just heard. "So Mendes's whole supposition is based on her belief that Fasso is ticked off at her for not giving his childhood buddy, Jimmy Tricoletto, a patronage job in her administration?"

"Well, that and the fact that he was also running for mayor in the brutal election she won. His hurt feelings haven't subsided, and he hasn't lost his passion for power. If anything, the election loss made him even more eager to gain control of City Hall."

I was thinking out loud. "If Mendes was forced to step down, Fasso would move up, which would give him a chance to build a record for the next election. As acting mayor he would have a lot of patronage to spread around, favors he could call in later."

"If that's true," Colter said, "Fasso's helping spill an awful lot of blood because he's not willing to wait a few years to make another run at the office."

"Maybe he's under duress from his old buddies."

"Like blackmail?" Colter asked. "For what?"

"I don't know."

"That's why I'm here," he said. "You know as much about the power structure of this city as any reporter in town. Can you think of anything Fasso has done, or is alleged to have done, or favors he's granted, or misdeeds he's done or enabled, that would open him up to blackmail by the Tricolettos or the Callisis?"

"Wow," I said. "Can you be a successful Chicago politician and not have done something that leaves you beholden to the wrong people?"

"That's an interesting and troubling question," he replied. "I would say that tryin' to strongarm Mendes to get a good city job for his boyhood friend treads pretty close to the line, especially if Fasso was rewarded in any way for his effort. At best it was a stupid thing to do. At worst, it could have been illegal."

"So what do you think? Thirst for power and money can be powerful motives for murder. So can blackmail."

"There are a lot of things that don't add up," Colter said.

I waited in expectant silence until Colter was ready to continue.

"For one thing," he said, "I don't remember discussing anything in those meetings that would be of real use to the Tricolettos. I guess Fasso could tell them we discovered what the so-called poison is. He could report that the mayor has given orders to her police super and me to get the Tricoletto and the Callisi families off the streets and behind bars, charged with murder, conspiracy, and excessive ear wax. Even though we have no evidence to support any of those charges."

"Nothing there that couldn't have been predicted," I said. "Except the ear wax."

"Think about it," Colter said. "What could make Fasso vulnerable to leverage?"

"I will. Meanwhile, any notion yet where the sux came from?"

"Not a clue. We're still working on it."

"And how's Emily Goodsill doing? Still in protective custody?"

"Yeah, but I don't know how much longer. She's working from our safe house. But she's pushing hard to be allowed to go back to Walnut. She perceives it as her safe place."

My colleagues were beginning to drift back in from lunch. A few recognized Colter, and he saw them watching us. I think it made him nervous. He stood.

"Keep in touch," he said.

"You, too."

He turned and left. I had a nagging feeling that our conversation had gotten us close to something important. But I couldn't for the life of me figure out what it was.

40

I finished my column and waited until Eric had read it. He loved it. Even as a native Chicagoan and a student of the city's crime history, there were some story details I wrote about that he said he hadn't known before. He called it a fun trip back in time.

I didn't know how much fun bootlegging and murder could be, but if my editor liked it, that was all that mattered.

I called Steve Pace and asked him if he wanted to get a drink and catch up on the day. He asked if there was some place fun we could go, some place where nobody was likely to get whacked at the valet stand. I knew just the place. He said he'd pick me up in front of the *Journal* building in twenty minutes.

We wound up in the River North neighborhood at a dive called the Green Door Tavern. It fit in perfectly with the story we were working on. I told Steve about its history on the drive over the Chicago River and north on Orleans Street.

The two-story building was erected in 1872, a year after the storied Chicago Fire. A year later the city banned wood-framed structures in the general downtown area to avoid a repeat of the blazing catastrophe. The Green Door was allowed to remain, though it leans to this day due to a settling problem, called racking, that occurred shortly after the structure was completed. Even the front door is tilted. And not on purpose. Its first life was as a grocery store. In 1921, a year after Prohibition was enacted, a new owner named Vito Giacomo converted the main floor into an Italian restaurant and opened a small speakeasy hidden away in the basement. It was one of Al Capone's favorite haunts, though going from his South Side headquarters up to Orleans Street took Capone outside his comfort zone and into the North Side territory of arch-rival Dean O'Banion. The speakeasy at the Green Door was one of O'Banion's biggest booze clients.

The establishment did have a green door, as did all speakeasys in Chicago during Prohibition. The doors were signals to patrons that alcohol was available inside. I never found out how, if patrons knew what the green doors meant, the feds never found out.

Once inside the tavern patrons had to be privy to the secret location of the speakeasy; it wasn't something you stumbled into. The tavern still has a green street door. In fact, the entire exterior front of the first floor has a façade of rich green. And inside, in addition to walls full of mementos of that memorable era of the twenties and thirties, many of the fixtures date back 100 years, too.

"I can't wait to see it," Steve said.

"It's fascinating," I said, "though it will never win any Michelin stars for its food."

After Steve and I took a self-guided tour of the place along with about half the people who were in at the same time, most of them tourists, we got a table where we would have some privacy. We ordered drinks—some especially funky-sounding draft and craft brews that turned out to be delicious—mine from the Off-Color Brewing Co., of Chicago and Steve's a selection from the Mac Fannybaw Brewery in Kentucky. Steve's selection had been brewed in barrels used initially to age a bourbon called Angels Envy.

Before we took our first sips, we toasted the two agents who gave their lives for us.

"May flights of angels sing thee to thy rest," Steve said, and we touched glasses.

After a few swallows of our beers, we turned the subject to our story.

As planned, Steve had followed Fasso through his day and reported that he went nowhere you wouldn't expect of his job and met with no one who appeared suspicious.

"He spent a lot of the day in his office," he said, "and I couldn't identify the people who came and went from the building. While I was waiting outside for him, I did some extensive computer research on his background. I didn't find anything that seemed like infractions anyone could use for blackmail."

"Did he go anywhere in a car?" I asked.

"You mean like with a driver? No, though he did drive himself a couple of times. He went to a restaurant called Rosebud Prime on Dearborn for lunch and valet parked his car. He went in and came out alone. Then he drove to City Hall, where he spent most of the afternoon. Then he went home. There was never anyone in the vehicle with him. It was a black Chevy Tahoe. Looked like a rental, a temporary replacement for his Enclave."

"What makes you think the Tahoe was rented?"

Steve shrugged. "Maybe the Alamo sticker on the back window."

I filled him in on my conversation with Colter. Steve didn't buy the idea that Fasso was working with the Tricoletto family to discredit the mayor and chase her out of office so he could move in.

"That's a little too Machiavellian for me," he said.

"I know. It's a stretch. But this is Chicago, and all politics in Chicago is at least a little Machiavellian. It's part of the city's cachet."

"I still don't buy it," he said. "I keep coming back to the succinylcholine. Why was it being used in the first place, and where did it come from?"

"I can't answer the second part, who supplied it. I assume it was used in the first place to hide the fact that the deaths were murders. That cat's out of the bag now, and everyone is speculating on an unidentified poison. My guess would be that they're still using it because they think the police don't know what the substance is and therefore can't track it back to the source."

"I guess."

"If it can't be traced back to a source, we'll never know who supplied it or how the supplier got his or her hands on the stuff. And the FBI won't have anybody to arrest."

Steve reached into the chair beside him, where he had rested his briefcase, and pulled it into his lap. He extracted a carefully folded newspaper page.

"I saw this while I was reading one of your competing newspapers over breakfast," he said. "It's from the section that covers news in the western suburbs."

He handed the paper to me and pointed to the story he wanted me to read. It was short and devoid of many facts. It had an Oak Park Village dateline. The headline read: "Shooting Vic Dies as EMTs Fight to Save Him." The story did little to elaborate on the headline except to note the shooting occurred in front of a chicken place in the 500 block of Madison Street. There was an anonymous quote from one of the EMTs who responded to the shooting. "If we could have gotten him on a breathing tube, he'd be alive."

"Well, that's weird," I said. "And given your suspicious mind…"

"I want to talk to the EMT. If we can find him. He obviously didn't want his name in the newspaper. Why couldn't they get the guy on a breathing tube?"

"I'd say the place to start is the facility where the victim died. Just say we're doing a follow-up and have some questions. They'll invoke privacy laws to keep from answering, but it might be worth a trip out there."

"You sound like you're chasing your tail."

"That's the way I feel," I said. "Almost all the time. I also get cravings for dog bones."

41

Oak Park's central fire station was an attractive building, as fire stations go. A mottled beige brick façade with a dark brown metal roof over the reception area and offices in front, and a line of bays behind for the big equipment. There probably were more offices, sleeping quarters, a community bath and shower room, a kitchen and dining area, too. Unlike many fire houses it had nice landscaping. The big open concrete pad where fire trucks and ambulances were serviced and cleaned was on the side, not in front, a more attractive arrangement.

Steve and I went in and asked to see the person who was in command two days earlier when the 9-1-1 call on the shooting on Madison Street came in. We promised not to ask personal questions about the victim. While we were sorry he died, he wasn't our story.

"That would be Lieutenant Sansenheimer," an attractive young woman told us. She was dressed in a well-ironed department uniform. The creases on her pants and shirt were so sharp it might have been dangerous to hug her. Her badge said her last name was Pratt. "She just took a phone call, but when she's off I'll ask her if she can see you. Do you have business cards? She likes to get cards from people she doesn't know."

We both did and offered them up. Pratt disappeared into the back of the building. Steve and I hadn't been offered seats so we stayed on our feet and spent the next few minutes looking over the walls where there must have been sixty or seventy photos of firefighters posing with their equipment and in action at some pretty horrific-looking blazes. The house fires, at least those I could identify as houses through the smoke and flames and water and snow, were particularly heartbreaking. In a few of the winter photos the fire fighters had so much ice hanging off them it was hard to tell there were humans under all the frozen water. These were not jobs for the faint of heart.

A department ambulance pulled into the facility, possibly back from a lunch run or an emergency. Pratt, who had reappeared while our backs were turned, said, "That's the team that took the call you're interested in. I probably shouldn't have told you that, so you didn't hear it from me, please." She looked embarrassed.

I said, "Didn't hear what from you?"

She smiled sheepishly.

An attractive woman who probably was in her early fifties but looked to be in her late thirties came in from the back. She had a similarly starched uniform, but there were more stripes and other decorations attached to the blouse. Somehow, whoever made the badges for this department had the skill to get the name "Sansenheimer" on the same size nameplate as "Pratt." Everyone seemed to have skills I didn't possess.

Although she was holding our cards, we introduced ourselves.

"What can I do for you?" she asked. "Wait. Before you answer that come on back to my office. It's more comfortable." She turned to Pratt. "You can interrupt if necessary."

Pratt nodded and replied, "Yes, Sir." I wanted to ask when the military and paramilitary organizations in the United States would drop the "Sir" now that there were so many women serving in high ranks, but that was a question for another time.

The lieutenant pointed Steve and me at two chairs in front of her desk in an office that looked as I suspected it might. Well-painted block walls with more photos and a half dozen commendations mounted within easy view, family photos on a credenza, and assorted politicians standing with Sansenheimer on ceremonial occasions, the nature of which didn't interest me at all.

"What can I do for you?" she asked again. "Pratt said you were asking about an EMT call we made on a shooting victim. I can't give you an ID. The Cook County Sheriff's Office is still trying to contact next of kin, last I heard."

"We're more interested," I said, "in the circumstances surrounding the death. We stopped by the police station on the way here to look at the report. All we learned was that the victim was a Hispanic male, twenty-eight, who died of a gunshot wound to the chest en route to a hospital. The hospital wasn't identified, either."

She nodded but said nothing.

Steve jumped in. "A short story in the *Sun-Times* quoted somebody as saying the man would be alive if the EMTs had been able to get him hooked to a respirator."

"I don't know who they were quoting, but it was inappropriate," Sansenheimer said.

"To quote him?" Steve asked.

"No, for him to comment."

I said, "Let's take this away from the personal. Do your emergency vehicles carry a drug called succinylcholine for patients who need to be intubated?"

She looked from me to Steve and back again. "Perhaps you should tell me why you're interested. It sounds as if there might be a liability question here, and I won't be able to answer you without permission from my superiors."

I told her we also were somewhat circumscribed in what we were allowed to say.

"This would probably be a lot easier if we trusted each other," I said. "We're working with the FBI, and they gave us permission to say some things but withhold others."

"I saw your column about the Mob killings," the lieutenant said. "I'm going to put two and two together here and come up with the suspicion that the so-called poison you wrote about was sux."

"Well, I didn't write about any poison," I said. "Our police reporters have, based on information the police released."

"Does this have anything to do with the inventory we were asked to take recently to determine if any of our sux supplies were missing?"

"Off the record?"

"Yes, absolutely. I should definitely not be talking about this. For now, the whole conversation should be off-the-record, please."

"Good enough," I said. "Under those terms, yes, we're talking about sux."

She frowned as if in pain. "My God, you mean there are killers using sux as a murder weapon? That's inhuman."

"The Mafia isn't exactly renowned for its humanity."

"Yes. Okay. My EMTs tried to use a unit of sux from the fridge in the bus," she said. "It apparently didn't work. We can't figure out why. I've never heard of anyone being resistant to it, though I suppose it's possible."

Steve asked, "Is there any chance that syringe is still aboard the ambulance?"

"We can check, but I doubt it. The buses are cleaned and restocked after each run, especially when there's medical waste, or blood, or other bodily fluids involved. And on this run, there was no shortage of blood."

I asked, "Is the crew that made that run yesterday working today?"

"Yes," Sansenheimer said. "They're on the same bus. I think they just came back from picking up lunch for the house."

"Could we talk to them?" I asked. "Still off the record, and only about the sux failure."

"Let me talk to them first," she said. "I want to be sure they understand the rules of the discussion. I'll bring them in here in a few minutes."

The EMTs told the same story. The two men, one a middle-aged black man and the other a younger Hispanic, said when they got to the victim he already had lost a lot of blood. They hooked him up to a saline IV and began trying to stop the bleeding. He kept going into cardiac arrest. They used CPR and paddles to bring him back twice. The third time they tried to put him on a respirator. Although he was near death, he put up a fight against the machine, which is why they tried the sux. It had no effect on him at all. He went down a third time, and nothing would revive him, though one of the men straddled him and administered CPR and heart stimulation for the entire trip to the hospital, where he was pronounced dead in the emergency room."

"You think you could have saved him," I said, "if you'd been able to use intubation?"

"You never know," the older man said. "Maybe. By the way, that wasn't either of us quoted in the paper. We didn't even see a reporter all day."

"We're not interested in that," I said. "What happened to the syringe you used?"

"We sealed it up and threw it in the medical waste bin," the younger man said.

Lieutenant Sansenheimer was thinking out loud. "That's standard procedure, but in retrospect I wish you'd held onto it so it could have been sent to a lab. Tested for purity. If it was adulterated somehow, the substance might have left a residue."

"That occurred to me later, too," the older EMT said. "But we'd already cleaned out the bus, and the medical waste had been picked up for disposal."

"Do you have any more in the ambulance?" I asked.

The younger man spoke up. "Yeah, I replaced the unit myself. As junior guy, most of the cleanup and restocking falls to me. You'd be amazed how much stuff winds up in a soggy mess on the bus floor."

I said, "I probably wouldn't be surprised at all." I turned to Sansenheimer. "Could we take a look at the bus, especially the sux that's in there now?"

She nodded. "I'll take you out there. But don't touch anything. All the supplies are sterile. I'll put on gloves to handle them."

We walked outside, and I felt grateful the ambulance was parked in the shade. The day had turned prematurely hot for the season. The sun blazed unrelenting from a cobalt blue sky as the thermometer reached for ninety.

The two EMTs and the supervisor put on latex gloves. Sansenheimer crawled inside.

She looked back at me. "Is the sux the only thing you want to check?"

"For now," I said.

She pulled open a small refrigerator filled with vials and syringes full of drugs. "There are supposed to be two units of sux on each run," she said. "We get it in pre-filled syringes so the crew doesn't have to waste time breaking into tough packaging."

"Yes, ma'am," the younger one said. "When we need it, we need it fast. We don't have time to be messing around. On the shooting run we only used one syringe, so I replaced it with one. We use them in order of the expiration dates, first in, first out."

She took both syringes out of the refrigerator and held them in her hands. She looked at one, then at the other, then back at the first. She bent for a closer look at the first. She touched the cap over the needle and groaned.

"Gentlemen," she said to her EMTs, "I think we have a problem."

42

The first to arrive at the firehouse was Richard Romero, the Oak Park fire chief and Sansenheimer's boss. She had called him immediately. Minutes behind Romero came Louis Runnels, Oak Park's chief of police. Romero had called him. Within a few minutes Ron Colter arrived, though how he got there from downtown Chicago so fast befuddled me. There were no light bars on his vehicle. He probably had one of those blue gumball flashers held to the roof with magnets. I knew he had a siren. I heard it die as he approached the small crowd waiting for him.

Romero looked somewhat peeved when he heard that a reporter had called the FBI and not left that decision and subsequent action to him. I didn't feel the need to explain myself. If he brought it up, Colter could tell him what he wanted local authorities to know.

"What's going on?" Colter asked.

"I'm not sure you needed to be called right away..." Romero started, but Colter stopped him with a raised hand.

"If Deuce says it's urgent, I take her at her word," he told the fire chief. The use of my first name and the vote of confidence appeared to set Romero's self-assurance back a few paces. He looked from Colter to me and back again, unsure now what he faced.

"I'll let Lieutenant Sansenheimer explain," he said. Then his arrogance returned. "For my part, I'd also like to know how two reporters found out about this before I did, and why this matter is of any interest to a Washington, D.C. newspaper."

Colter shook his head in a subtle way that said he wasn't happy about dealing with a suburban ego subtext. Then he asked, "Would somebody please tell me what's going on here before I charge the lot of you with obstruction of justice?"

That quieted Romero, though I suspected it wouldn't be permanent.

Sansenheimer started with what was known already about the shooting death. Then she related the conversation she had with Steve and me and moved on to relate what she'd found in the ambulance, which is what really interested everyone.

"I put on gloves and removed both syringes of sux from the cooler," she started, then noticed the police chief giving her a questioning look. "The succinylcholine," she said quickly. "Sux is medical shorthand and easier to remember than the full name." Runnels nodded, apparently satisfied, and signaled for her to continue.

"At first I saw nothing amiss with either unit. They both appeared clean and filled to the standard 200-milligram line. Both needles were capped. Then I noticed that one of the caps looked odd, a little crooked. I turned it a little. It moved with no resistance, and there should have been some resistance unless the cap had been removed earlier. The second syringe was normal. No tampering that I could detect. I returned both to the cooler and called the chief."

"Are they single-dose vials?" Colter asked.

"They're prefilled ten milliliter syringes, all with 200 milligrams of the drug," Sansenheimer said. "How much we administer depends on the patient's weight. It's a formula. We only administer what the formula calls for. The 200 milligrams will cover almost any adult patient. There are a variety of syringes with different doses, but we only stock the one size to prevent accidents. Our people know that any sux unit they grab will contain 200 milligrams of the drug. Knowing that can help prevent overdosing a child or underdosing an adult."

"And what happens," Colter asked, "if you use less than a full syringe? What do you do with the rest?"

"We empty the syringe and dispose of it and the drug in medical waste. We'd never risk reusing a needle."

Romero turned to his EMTs. "Which one of you picked the unit for the shooting vic?"

"I did," the younger man said. "Rudy was getting the intubation device ready."

"And you didn't notice any tampering?"

"No, sir," he replied. "Everything was happening so fast I didn't notice anything. I just glanced at the unit to make sure I had the right drug and handed it to my partner."

"I took the cap off," the senior EMT said, "but I didn't notice anything wrong, either."

"Any chance the medical waste from yesterday is still around?" Colter asked. "I could have a lab team here in under an hour."

Sansenheimer shook her head. "The guys checked already. The medical waste is picked up every night."

Colter turned to the older EMT, the one named Rudy. "You injected the vic?"

"I did. Yes."

"And what happened?"

"Nothing," Rudy replied. "Absolutely nothing."

"What should have happened?"

"I put it right in a vein," Rudy said. "I should have seen paralysis setting in within seconds. But I got nothing."

"Where do you get your supplies?" he asked the group.

Sansenheimer replied, "We have a contract with Village Hospital. They have a rep who comes once a week, checks all our medical supplies, and replenishes what's low."

"Well," Colter said, "they're going to need to make a special trip. I need to log in the two units of sux aboard your bus and all the syringes in your stock as evidence. Our lab people will pick them up."

The police chief, Runnels, jumped in with a cop question, but it was a good one.

"Who would have access to the sux supplies we get?"

"I can't give you a confident reply on the whole chain of possession," Romero said. "But when it arrives here at the house, it's put on refrigeration under lock and key in the dispensary. The watch commander has the only key, and when he or she leaves shift, there is a check made to ensure that our bus has the required supplies, including drugs. If anything needs to be replaced at shift change or during the ensuing watch, the incoming watch commander supervises every step."

"But there are no checks to be sure there's been no tampering?" I asked.

"No," Romero said with a deep sigh. "There's been no reason. Until now."

43

My phone started ringing at six a.m. two mornings later, waking me from a lovely dream about Mark and a beach and some wonderful, if gritty, sexual activity. I woke up aroused, angry that someone burst my fantasy bubble, and feeling the need for a shower.

All the lovely memories evaporated when Eric Ryland started speaking. He was never happy during his early morning calls to me, and he didn't start to get happy until he made me unhappy. It didn't take him long this morning.

"Have you seen the *Beacon-Herald* yet today?"

"No," I said. "I was still asleep when the phone started ringing."

He didn't apologize. He didn't even pause to think about apologizing.

"Call it up on your computer," he said. "You'll know the story I'm referring to. It's a column teased in maybe seventy-two point type off the front page."

"Who wrote it?" I asked.

"Get out of bed and read it. Then call me on my cell." He hung up.

I excused myself as I pulled my numb feet out from under the two cats that had been sleeping on top of them most of the night. I didn't know what the story would be, but it wouldn't be good.

I figured I would need some support for this, so I pulled a triple large espresso on Mark's machine and took it to the dining room table where I had my laptop. I set the twelve ounces of powerful caffeine on a coaster and opened the lid of the MacBookPro. Though I didn't read the *Beacon-Herald* every day, I did have it bookmarked for easy access in case the staff someday tripped over a real story. Normally, the tabloid more resembled the gossipy, unreliable rags found in racks along grocery store checkout aisles. When the front page came up on my screen, I immediately saw the piece that had my editor steamed.

The headline read: "Exclusive! Vice Mayor Probed in Mob Killings." I wasn't sure if John Fasso was being investigated or getting a prostate exam.

I smiled at the thought and turned to page three, which is page one in a tabloid. I actually laughed out loud when I saw the byline. Harry Conklin, a man who spent at least half his professional life trying to scoop me or destroy my reputation. His last effort had been an attempt to convince Chicagoans that I was getting inside tips on a major arson investigation by sleeping with the city's top FBI official, Ron Colter. I was furious. Colter simply waved it off. "At best it's worth a good laugh," he said. "At worst it's a nuisance. The story and the author are best left ignored."

I wondered if Colter would feel equally dismissive of this.

Conklin was normally a gossip on a second-tier TV station in Chicago, but occasionally he freelanced pieces to the *B-H,* a second-tier print outlet.

I read the article quickly at first. It was as I expected. A lot of speculation and innuendo with a few facts I knew to be true thrown in to give the story a bit of cachet. I read it a second time, more slowly, to be sure I'd missed nothing. I wouldn't have wanted to write a story like this. Eric Ryland wouldn't have published it.

In a nutshell, Conklin said he had reliable sources who suspected that the deaths of six connected guys and one federal investigator were tied to a congressional examination of organized crime activity in the United States in general and in Chicago in particular. The sources, Conklin wrote, had told him "exclusively" that a high-level panel of local and federal officials, organized by Mayor Marsha Mendes, suspected Deputy Mayor John Fasso of leaking details of the work being done by Mendes's committee to crime boss Anthony Tricoletto. It was well-known in political circles, Conklin wrote, that Fasso had a long history with the Tricoletto family. Fasso, the story said, had pressured the newly elected Mayor Mendes to award a lucrative post in her new administration to Tricoletto's younger son, Jimmy, a boyhood friend of Fasso's.

Suspicion, supposition, and mysterious tales "well-known in political circles" did not a valid story make. But it had a ring of truth, and there were just enough facts sprinkled about that Conklin's exclusive would be the talk around every water cooler in the city.

I called Eric Ryland. "It's trash," I said when he picked up. "You know that. And I know if I'd turned in that same story to you it would have wound up in your scrap pile."

"It's not all garbage," Eric replied.

"The true parts, few and far between though they are, we've already published, Eric. The deaths and the stink of an oncoming mob war have been in our paper two or three times. The only thing that bothers me is how Conklin found out about the group Mendes put together to deal with the violence. That was being held very close. Ron Colter hadn't even given me permission to write about it."

"Perhaps it was a lucky guess on Conklin's part," my editor said. "A task force of combined law enforcement to deal with something like this could be anticipated."

"Apparently after the group's last meeting, Mendes asked Colter to stay after everyone else left. She told him that after the mayoral election results were certified, Fasso came to her. He did ask her to give Jimmy Tricoletto a top patronage job. She refused. According to Her Honor, Fasso was furious and still is. It's her theory that Fasso is helping Tricoletto perpetuate the killings to make her look bad. As in, her city's going to hell, and she doesn't have the wherewithal to shut down the warfare. Her theory, according to Colter, is that Fasso hopes the pressure will cause her to step down, or possibly be recalled. As Deputy Mayor, he would step into the top spot."

"And if she doesn't step down, and if she's not recalled, what?"

"He can use it all to kick the stuffing out of her in the next election."

"So what do we do about Conklin's story?" Ryland asked.

"I think we ignore that little twerp and keep on keepin' on. I don't want to follow Conklin on a bad story. The task force is off-limits. The appeal for a patronage job for Jimmy might be part of a larger story one of these days, but it's not news right now. It's just a lingering echo of an old election."

44

Eric went with my instinct on the matter of Harry Conklin's story. But by noon I was having second thoughts. The noon broadcast news programs led with Conklin's so-called scoop. Conklin would never win the title of Most-Trusted Newsie in Chicago. News editors throughout the city and all over the Upper Midwest knew him to be unreliable and careless. But still, a story deemed worth publishing, even by the *Beacon-Herald,* and worth public discussion on Conklin's morning TV talk show from ten to noon, couldn't be ignored completely. If it didn't lead regular local news programming, it got at least a couple of minutes before the first commercial cutaway.

I told Eric I'd had a change of heart.

"How are we going to ignore it?" I asked. "It's out there getting way more attention than I expected. We have to notice, don't we? We'll look petulant if we don't."

"I've got the cops reporters working on it," Eric said. "Call your sources and see what they have to say, then we'll talk."

Pete Rizzo, the police spokesman, said he had already given a no-comment to one of our police reporters and wouldn't expand on that. Jerry Alvarez wouldn't even pick up the phone. He told his secretary to give me a no-comment. Ron Colter was more expansive.

"There is a task force, yes," he said. "I told you about it already. You can go ahead and write that and attribute that to a source. The rest of this is for your ears only. I have a strong sense that Mayor Mendes is talking to Conklin. She thinks Fasso's trying to sabotage her administration. But other than

211

the thin rationale that Fasso wants her out of office, she didn't offer me a single shred of evidence that Fasso is up to no good."

"What gives you the sense that she might be Conklin's source?"

"Again, there's no evidence. But I have no doubt about it. She thinks Fasso's out to get her, and she wants to eliminate him first. Harry Conklin doesn't strike me as the kind of journalist who demands hard evidence of wrongdoing before writing things given to him anonymously by sources with an axe to grind. The mayor knows that, so she chose Conklin to write her story."

"Can we say with any surety that the mayor's suspicions aren't true?"

"Nope," Colter said. "Conklin might be a jerk and an ass wipe, but he's clever in the way of words. He didn't say any of the allegations in his story were true. He said officials told him they suspected certain things. And that's exactly what the mayor told me. Source the task force confirmation. Write that I wouldn't comment at all beyond saying I have no idea what Harry Conklin is talking about. That should mess with his mind a bit."

"Thanks, Ron," I said. I sent all my meager notes to Eric so he could send them on to whoever was writing the story.

He sent back a message saying Fasso had given Mary Edmonds, one of our City Hall reporters, a five-minute interview that would be the basis for a decent follow up. "And FYI, he denies abetting any crimes in any way. Surprise."

* * *

Over the next few days, Harry Conklin kept up his assault on Fasso. It became increasingly clear to me that Colter was right in pointing to Marsha Mendes as the source of his stories, and clearer still that if there was any hard evidence against Fasso, it was not being passed to Conklin. His work continued to be tantalizing and voyeuristic, but almost baseless, bordering on libel. Nevertheless, the drumbeat of public demands for a plausible explanation quickly reached the level of a firestorm.

And then the roof fell in.

45

"I'm getting very nervous about all of this," the younger man said as he set down his glass of Martell Creation Grand Extra, deemed by some aficionados the finest cognac in the world. The man might have been drinking Boone's Farm Strawberry Hill or Mad Dog 20/20 for all the attention he paid it.

"Will you relax and keep your voice down," the older man said. "I told you we have this completely under control. What about it concerns you?"

"The TV reporter, for one. He has a reputation as a screw-up and a blowhard, and if this path he's following washes out from under him, we could all get thrown off the bridge."

"Interesting metaphor, my friend. But there have been no slipups yet. The worst is behind us. John Fasso can deny the facts until it snows in July, and people will continue to believe the news reports. Even the legitimate media outlets are reporting that Fasso's approval ratings are in the tank. This is a scandal he cannot outrun."

"This is Chicago, remember," the younger man said. "Snow in July is not impossible."

"Not this year. Trust me. The final shoe will fall tonight. Stay positive. Do your job. And wait for the final act. Take it all in stride. You are covered."

"I'll hold you to that."

The older man took a long pull on his fine cigar, held the smoke for a moment, letting it out in increments, dragging out and deepening the tension.

"Do not threaten me," he said in a low, calm voice. "I created this opportunity for you. I gave you a great future. And I can take it all away. Do not push me. That never ends well, no matter who tries."

*The younger man leaned forward in his chair, his elbows on his knees.
He stared between his feet at the carpet and nodded.*

* * *

*It was a blustery, chilly evening, this second week in May. Dominic Tufino had
been looking forward to a baseball game between his beloved Chicago Cubs and
arch-rival St. Louis Cardinals at historic Wrigley Field. But the cold, spitting
rain, which had been falling all day, delayed the first pitch. It was forecast to stop
in about an hour, but Tufino wouldn't have bet money on it. Even if the rain
ceased, the outfield would be dangerously slick.*

*Not wanting to sit in the stands and freeze their asses off waiting, and not
particularly interested in eating stadium food—though much of it at Wrigley was
good—Tufino and his driver, Stefano Cappa, had walked across the intersection
of Clark and Addison and sat at a round high-top in the nearly deserted Cubby
Bear bar. They sipped Anti-Hero IPAs from Chicago's own Revolution Brewery, a
craft operation a couple of miles away on the other side of the North Branch of the
Chicago River. A waiter brought them a double order of chicken nachos, which
the Cubby Bear did well.*

*It was quiet in the place now. Once the game ended the joint would come
alive with Cubs fans drinking and dancing until the early hours, even though it
was a weeknight. If the game was postponed, the levity would begin a little early.*

*But Dominic Tufino was not a patient man. One had only to look at him to
know that. He wore a perpetual scowl. When annoyed or kept waiting he had a
habit of turning over his right hand, curling his middle finger, and knocking the
second knuckle softly on the nearest hard surface, which tonight was the round
high-top.*

*He carried his bulk elegantly. At three inches over six feet tall, with broad
shoulders, a barrel chest, and a hint of a paunch, there were no off-the-rack suits
that fit him right, at least in his opinion. Not even Armani, Ralph Lauren, or
Brioni. So, his suits were all custom-made at about $4,000 per. He wore his thick
dark hair curly, always had a stubble of dark beard, and didn't mind wearing
Ferragamo leather shoes out in the weather. Their quality was so high that, with
proper care, a little water wouldn't hurt them. If they were damaged, well, Dom-*

inic had a source in the company's headquarters in Florence, Italy, who could get him more at half the normal $700 price tag.

He and Cappa had come to Wrigleyville to watch a baseball game, and if there wasn't going to be a baseball game, he wanted to go home. The middle finger of his right hand sent a very clear signal of his feelings.

"Wadda ya say, Stefano?" Tufino asked. "Wanna bag it and try again, maybe in July?"

"Whatever you want, Boss. Hate to see you waste the tickets tonight, but this shit ain't gonna stop any time soon."

Cappa was a head shorter than Tufino, but even under his suit (Armani was fine with Stefano), you could see his body-builder's physique and the bulge of his Browning 1911-380. It was a flashy semi-automatic handgun, well-suited as a concealed carry weapon. With a barrel of less than four inches and weighing just a pound, it was easy to draw and light enough to maneuver and aim quickly. Cappa's jaw was square, his eyes dark, hard, and always moving. He was a product of Chicago's original Italian neighborhood, centered on South Oakley Avenue around Twenty-Fourth Street. It was Deuce's neighborhood, an area where many Italian immigrant families with roots in Tuscany had settled during the last century. Though "driver" was Cappa's title, "bodyguard" described the true nature of his job.

Tufino threw four twenties on the table and anchored them under salt and pepper shakers. He stood up and shrugged into his topcoat.

"You wait here, Boss," Cappa said. "I'll bring the car."

"I'll walk with you," Tufino said. "Car's two blocks away. Ain't either of us gonna melt."

They left the bar, crossed Addison, and walked north on Clark, surprisingly unhurried by the weather. Neither noticed the men who followed them out of the Cubby Bear, though Cappa should have. It was his job to notice. If someone could have asked him later, Cappa would have said he saw them in the bar, one young, the other approaching middle age. Cappa would have recognized the older one immediately had he seen his face, but the man wore a Cubs cap pulled low and studiously kept his back to Cappa and Tufino, so Cappa never got a good look.

The weather had washed most people off the street. Once Tufino and Cappa crossed Waveland, at the north end of the Wrigley campus, the pedestrian traffic dwindled to nothing.

That's when the two men closed ranks with Tufino and Cappa. The younger man crept up behind Cappa and brushed him. When Cappa turned to see who it was, the kid apologized. Cappa didn't like the look in the kid's eyes, but it was too late to do anything about it. The man raised a hand holding a revolver and shot Cappa twice in the forehead. As Cappa fell, the shooter tossed the gun under him.

Tufino gaped at his driver's body falling to the sidewalk like a sack of lost laundry. While Tufino was distracted, the older man stuck him in the neck with a syringe, got lucky, and hit a vein. Tufino's eyes went wide. He tried to run, made two steps, and joined Cappa on the sidewalk. But unlike Cappa, Tufino wasn't yet dead. He was beginning to feel the first shock of the succinylcholine in his system: the loss of control of his limbs and his lungs, the loss of any sense of his body, the slow motion in which things began happening around him.

He knew he was dying, which didn't frighten him as much as knowing how he was dying. He couldn't breathe. He couldn't cry out. His body demanded oxygen it couldn't get. He was in agony. Suffocation had always been his most nightmarish end.

The pain and terror lasted for little more than thirty seconds, and Tufino lost all contact with the world around him. Minutes later, his heart stopped.

By then the two killers were at the intersection of Clark and Racine. One continued north on Clark; the other angled south on Racine. If there were any witnesses telling cops the murders were committed by two men, these two men would not be found together.

Back on Clark, where two bodies lay splayed on the concrete, the cold mist washing Cappa's blood down the sidewalk, people gathered to gawk. Sirens shrieked a short distance away, an ambulance and two police units responding to frantic 9-1-1 calls.

When they arrived at the scene, the first responders realized there was nothing they could do, either to help the two dead men or to identify the person or persons who killed them. They couldn't move the bodies until the medical examiner released them, and they couldn't cover them because they might contaminate evidence. The EMTs stood down. The cops busied themselves interviewing those *still hanging around. Nobody saw anything. Nobody knew anything. But the questions still had to be asked.*

The cops knew what they were dealing with. Stefano Cappa was small potatoes, a Goodfellas wannabe. But the other body had been Dominic Tufino, the underboss of the Callisi crime family, and one of the most powerful men in the city.

46

I was sitting in my office cubicle the next morning with Steve Pace, who had taken my side chair and was using my waste basket as a footrest. I was fine with that because he'd also brought me coffee from Peet's.

"You really need a recliner," he told me. "Makes things more homey for visitors and gives you a more comfortable place to sit and read long, boring government reports."

"You have a recliner by your desk in Washington?" I asked.

"No, which is why I try not to go to the office any more than necessary. I work from home most days, where I have a recliner built for two." He waggled his eyebrows like Groucho Marx reincarnate.

"And your editor approves?"

"Of what? My working from home or having sex in a very big recliner? If it's the working-at-home thing, I never hang around long enough to hear her opinion on it."

"Can we get to the point?" I asked. To his blank stare I said, "Last night?"

He nodded. "That's why I'm here. Hard to believe somebody would take down the underboss of a major Chicago crime family and his bodyguard out in the open at Wrigley Field. During a game, no less. In a less PC world, I would say that's really ballsy."

"There wasn't a game," I said. "It was postponed by the rain. But it was ballsy, and it could very well start a new mob war in the city."

"Seems to me that's already well underway. But explain something, if you can. Let's assume this is a mob war we're watching. The bodyguard was shot twice in the face. The underboss was hit with sux. What if the underboss,

Tufino, had been armed? He might-a shot the guy comin' for him before the sux could get injected. Why would the killers take that chance? Why didn't they just shoot both guys?"

"I don't know," I said. "Maybe to put the fear factor in play. According to the ME, the look frozen on Tufino's face when he died was one of agony and terror. If you recall, that's the same look we saw on Joey Santoro's face when they hit him outside the steakhouse."

"Yeah, I guess word of shit like that gets around," Steve said. "Anybody who doesn't want to die a horrible death better not be thinking about flipping on Tony Toes."

"Didn't that message get sent," I asked, "when they killed the first two made guys who were going to flip for Carl Cribben and then killed Carl?"

"You'd think," Steve said. "But they kept on killing." He shook his head. "Seems to me there's something bigger going on here that we're just not seeing."

My phone rang and put an end to useless speculation.

It was Ron Colter, and he sounded exhausted.

"Steve's here," I told him. "Can I put you on speaker?"

"Sure," he said. There was no enthusiasm in his voice, just resignation. "But for the time being, we're still off the record."

Both of us agreed.

He continued, "We won't stay off the record long on this. It could blow up quickly. We found a gun under Stefano Cappa's body. The shooter must have dropped it or planted it there. It's a North American Arms 22-caliber short-barrel five-shot revolver. Bought legally, it'll run you a bit over $200. But it's no Saturday night special. It's a decent weapon. And it belonged to John Fasso."

Steve sat up so fast he nearly knocked over the trash can. I felt an adrenaline rush.

"You think a Chicago alderman and the vice mayor is a murderer?" I asked.

"I don't know him that well, and being in charge of the investigation, I don't want to come to any conclusions prematurely. We're questioning him now."

"What's he saying?" Steve asked.

"Well, he's denying that he had anything to do with the killings," Colter said. "For any more, you should talk to his lawyer later. He's busy right now."

I challenged him. "We're not writing anything. Tell us what you know."

"When did I start taking orders from you, Ms. Mora? You and Mayor Mendes. You're both pushy broads. You know sometimes you make it hard to be your friend."

"I'll forgive the gender slur," I said, "if you tell us what Fasso's saying."

"Big surprise. He says he's innocent."

"You said that already. He explains the gun how?"

"He makes a pretty good argument, and a jury might even buy it. He says the gun was in the console of his car when the car was stolen."

"That is a pretty good defense," Steve said.

I asked, "Not that it means anything, but did he have a concealed carry permit? He'd have to or carrying the gun in his car console would be illegal."

"He didn't, and that's a definite violation of federal law," Colter said. "He does have a FOID card, but that doesn't mitigate the concealed-carry violation."

Illinois doesn't issue gun licenses. Instead, gun buyers must apply for a Firearm Owner's Identification Card, which triggers a background check. Until the check is completed, the purchase goes on hold, and the gun stays in the store. The FOID is not a permit to carry the weapon concealed. That's a whole different process.

"So," I said, "he's arguing that somebody involved in the attack on me stole the gun from his car and used it to kill Stefano Cappa, while somebody else stuck a syringe full of sux into Dominic Tufino."

"But you don't buy it," Steve said.

"I don't *not* buy it," Colter replied. "The investigation is ongoing. We got some vague descriptions of the killers from a couple of eyewitnesses, and one of them does fit Fasso. The witness even picked Fasso out of a photo lineup. But he could have recognized him from him bein' on the news a lot."

I asked, "When the alderman was told his car had been stolen, did he report there was a gun in the console? That's something the police would want to know, I think."

"He did not report it."

"Did you ask him why?"

"We did. He said it was because he didn't have a concealed carry permit. He didn't want to admit to a federal gun violation."

"You going to charge him?" I asked.

"Getting a murderer on a gun technicality is sort of like getting Capone on unpaid parking tickets, don't you think?" Colter said. "At most, Deuce, it's ninety days in jail."

When we hung up Steve said, "I don't buy it. It's too convenient."

"How so?" I asked.

"Why did the guy who made the move against us outside Bacchanalia have to steal Fasso's car, his gun, and maybe his driver? Is the Mafia in Chicago that hard up for weapons and transportation? It feels like a setup, and a twofer at that. They get a shot at killing us and set up Fasso at the same time for a killing later."

"I don't know," I said.

Steve pressed on. "Did you ever wonder about the ID of Fasso's car and the partial license plate? Roach got there first, even though he'd been drinking. Presumably the would-be killer hadn't been drinking. There's no way the sober killer couldn't have outrun a blitzed Roach to the Enclave and made a clean getaway. It's like the killer and the driver deliberately waited long enough for Roach to catch up and get a look at the car and its plate. They waited so long that even our two security guys had time to catch up and get close enough to ID the make and model. The attackers did it to implicate Fasso. Getting his gun was a bonus, maybe."

"Why go to all that trouble?"

Steve said, "Because they like misdirection. What's the whole purpose of the sux? They expected that nobody'd be able to identify it as a weapon of murder, so the crimes would never be solved. Same with the whole locked-office thing the night they killed Carl. It sent investigators off on all kinds of tangents, just like the gun theft has. There are three options on the gun. First, it was never stolen, and Fasso used it on Cappa. Problem. Did Fasso then drop the gun under Cappa? And implicate himself? Not likely. Did he drop it accidentally? If so, why didn't he reach down and pick it up? Second possibility: Somebody broke into Fasso's garage and his car, stole his gun, eventually killed Cappa with it, and threw it down to frame Fasso. Third possibility: The car was stolen and wrecked, some gangbanger happened by Gage Park, saw the car wrapped around a post, viewed it as an invitation to poke around, and found the gun in the console. Maybe he used it on Cappa or sold it to someone who did. Who knows? The three choices not only complicate the police investigation, they give the real killer good reasonable doubt defenses if he's caught."

I nodded. It made sense. "Maybe. But tell me this. Why didn't they kill both guys the same way? Shoot them both or inject them both?"

"We already talked about why they used sux on Tufino," Steve said, "to leave a message of terror. Even an underboss isn't safe from a horrible death. As for Cappa, they were closing the trap tighter on Fasso, leaving his gun at the scene with its bullets in Cappa's head."

For the first time in a good long while, I was speechless.

47

I began to wonder if the lab analysis was back on the succinylcholine confiscated from the Oak Park firehouse. I was debating who to call, Ron Colter, Tony Donato, or Jerry Alvarez. I hadn't talked to Jerry in a while, so I tried him first. He was in a grand jury and would be at least until mid-afternoon. I started to call Colter when Steve called me.

"I just scored for us," he said. "I haven't been able to get past the impression that while the FBI insists the investigation of John Fasso is open and no conclusions have been reached about his guilt, they think he's the killer. So I've been trying to figure out people who might be able to provide some insight into Fasso or anybody else involved in this tangled spider-web we weave."

"And you came up with?..."

"Frank Chapin, the building contractor who was headed straight for the governor's mansion until he was headed straight for prison."

"He's not in prison yet," I said. "The guilty verdict is under appeal."

"Yeah, whatever. It was a nice turn of phrase. Anyhow, since he's looking at a lot of years in prison for embezzlement, conspiracy, extortion, mail fraud, and tax evasion, he might be willing to talk to us a little about Fasso."

"There's never been any speculation that Fasso was involved in Chapin's shoddy building practices and phony invoicing schemes. Talking to us could only make Chapin's problems worse."

"Maybe not," Steve said. "I called his lawyer yesterday and requested an interview. He just called me back. Chapin has agreed. We're meeting him and his lawyer at three this afternoon in the lawyer's office."

"You think he can give us anything new?"

"I guess we'll find out this afternoon."

* * *

The law offices of Coates, Richardson, Gonzalez & Freed were on a tastefully redecorated high floor of Tribune Tower at the foot of that portion of Michigan Avenue known as the "Miracle Mile." I've never been sure why it's called that. Maybe it's a miracle that so many high-end stores could be packed shoulder-to-glass-shoulder in a length of street I could walk in half an hour or so. Okay, maybe forty minutes to leave a little time for window shopping and wiping the drool off my chin.

As the name suggests, the building is the home of one of my arch-competitors in Chicago, the Chicago *Tribune*. The *Trib*, as everyone calls it, had fallen on financial times sufficiently dire that it was forced to lease or sell off large parts of its building, much as my own paper had. I knew and liked many members of the *Trib's* staff, but still, as you might imagine, it felt weird to walk through the front doors of the enemy camp.

The offices of Coates, Richardson, Gonzalez & Freed were lavish, as befits an old-money Chicago law firm. Evan Freed headed the criminal division, but there were no murderers hanging around the reception area. The firm dealt only in white-collar crime, exactly what Frank Chapin had been charged with. Another firm was handling the willful negligence lawsuits brought against him by the families of the men who died in the building collapse that precipitated the collapse of Chapin's construction firm.

We were shown into a conference room large enough to handle a meeting of the entire Chicago Symphony, including staff and all their families. The two of us took seats at a conference table that was finished in a way that highlighted the wood grain by not burying it in layers of high-gloss polish. We contemplated the breathtaking views through two walls of windows that took in the Navy Pier and its heart-stopping Ferris wheel, a grand panorama of Lake Michigan, and the northern half of the city of Chicago to its northern border and beyond.

"My office," Steve said, "is a little bigger than this, but this will do."

On that note a door behind us opened, and two men walked through, one of them in his fifties, I would judge, and clothed as if he just stepped off the pages of *GQ*'s annual best-dressed issue. I guessed that he was Freed.

The other man, also well-dressed but not as spectacularly, looked to be in his fifties or early sixties. He might have been younger than he looked, though, because the lines of his pale face appeared to have been drawn by stress, and he wasn't standing as erect as his companion. This had to be Chapin.

Steve and I rose and shook hands with them. Introductions were made all around.

The conference table was wide enough that two chairs occupied places at its head. Freed and Chapin took them. Steve and I sat in the chairs we'd claimed when we came in.

"My client's case has been fully covered in court and in the media," Freed said. "What more do you want to hear?"

"As you know," Steve said, "I work for a newspaper in Washington, D.C., so I wasn't here to follow your client's case. Though to be sure it did get a bit of national attention. I'd like to hear the story from Mr. Chapin's point of view, without prosecutors and lawyers and judges objecting and ruling and squabbling and smoothing the edges of the evidence."

"I'd like to know why your paper is interested at this point, Mr. Pace," Freed said.

"I'm not sure my paper is that interested," Steve said, "but I am. I've been trying to cover the organized crime investigation Carl Cribben was running when he was killed. Deuce and I have been doing a lot of reporting, and we think Mr. Cribben's murder and several more might tie in with the accusations against Mr. Chapin. What we're doing is called 'tugging on threads to see what unravels.'"

"Interesting," Freed said. "I presume you aren't accusing my client of murder."

"No," Steve said. "Absolutely not."

Freed then proceeded to tell Chapin's story himself, allowing his client to interject thoughts only occasionally. It was a good way for the lawyer to control the conversation and protect his client, if not very gratifying for us. He covered what we already knew, adding very little helpful detail, fully earning his fee. I decided to interrupt his monologue.

"Mr. Chapin," I said pointedly to his client, "didn't you have invoices detailing exactly what products you ordered for your projects and proving you bought the correct material?"

"I didn't do the ordering," Chapin replied. "I worked with the project supervisors and specified to them what I wanted. They did the ordering. So the invoices in the files work against me. I have my original notes, but the prosecutors alleged that I created those after the fact, which isn't true."

"How well do you know your supervisors?"

"Real well. All-a them, with one exception, have been with me more than ten years. Two of them more than twenty years."

"The one exception," I asked, "was he in charge of one of the projects found to be sub-standard?"

"Yes," Chapin said. "He was indicted, as well as two guys who'd been with me eleven and thirteen years, and one who'd been with the company for twenty-two. And the city inspectors. I knew them, too."

"How about the supervisors who weren't dragged into this? Did authorities talk to them? And if so, what did they say?"

Freed decided to field that one. "They were questioned by the grand jury, and since we weren't permitted in the grand jury room, we can't give you first-hand information on what they testified. But they told us later they vouched for my client, his honesty and his integrity. They supposedly said they'd never known him to cut corners."

"I never have," Chapin said.

I asked, "Have you ever had any contact or dealings with members of the Tricoletto or Callisi families?"

Freed nearly cut me off. "We're not going to answer that," he said sharply.

Chapin faced his lawyer with a deep frown. "Why not, Evan?" he demanded. "I've got nothing to hide. You can't be in the construction business in any big city in America and not have some contact with organized crime. I want to be completely open here."

The lawyer sighed and tried to stare down his client. Chapin wasn't having any of it. He turned back to us.

"I've met both Tony Toes and Albano Callisi dozens of times," he said. "Mostly at charity functions and social events around town. When either of them had beefs with the way I was handling issues with trade unionists, I wasn't above sitting down with them and trying to work things out. That's the way you gotta operate in this town. It's give and take. I always held these meetings myself to make sure they didn't try to take too much. They both understood I wouldn't break the law for them. We weren't bosom buddies, but we got along good enough to make me and my people nice livings, and their trade unionists got square deals in safe environments. Until now."

Steve asked, "If what you say is true, why did some of your guys order substandard material? Were there ways they could engineer things so some of the money saved went into their pockets?"

"I don't know about none-a that, and I don't believe it. Not my guys."

"Do you know John Fasso?"

"I met him. I don't live in his district, and his first priority is furtherin' his career, not my construction problems. So I didn't run into him very often. I do know he and Jimmy Tricoletto been tight since grade school."

"Did he ever strike you as the type who could commit murder?"

"Frank," Evan Freed cautioned. His tone conveyed his message.

"Ms. Mora, I don't know the answer to that. I ain't a shrink. But I can tell you one thing. You push a man hard enough, he'll reach the point where he can kill. Believe me, it's somethin' I know for true."

48

"Honest to God," Steve said as we walked out of the *Tribune* building, "I think he might be innocent."

I barely heard him. I was occupied looking out for *Tribune* staffers who would recognize me and wonder what I was doing on their turf.

"Deuce?" Steve said.

"Uh, I don't know. He doesn't have a whole lot falling in his favor." I turned to face him. "What's with you? First you think Fasso's innocent. Now Chapin."

He put an arm out and stopped me in the middle of the scenic DuSable Bridge over the Chicago River. "It's possible," he said.

I put my forearms on the railing and looked east at the lake, letting the breeze fly in my face. It carried a chill off the water, which had only begun to warm. But it also carried the fragrance of clean air and spring flowers. Steve leaned in beside me.

"Look," he said, "what kind of fool puts invoices proving his culpability in all sorts of crimes in his own office files? If something goes wrong, as it did, that's the first place investigators look. Even the dumbest crooks keep two sets of books."

"Yeah, I have a feeling Ron Colter is asking himself the same thing."

"I wish we could talk to Fasso," he said. "I only got to follow him for one full day and parts of two more. He didn't do anything or meet with anyone suspicious. But that's not a very good sampling of his time or his friends."

"A meeting with him isn't going to happen, not while the state's attorney's investigating him on a murder charge, and the U.S. attorney's investigating

him for possible RICO violations. If they find out he was using his city
council seat to benefit elements of organized crime, he'll go away for as long
as Frank Chapin."

My phone rang. I almost didn't hear it in the din of the vehicles rattling
over the drawbridge and along Wacker Drive. It was Colter.

"It was water," he said without preamble.

"I'm standing on the DuSable Bridge looking down at the Chicago River
and out at Lake Michigan," I said. "What water have you got to beat that?"

"A much smaller amount," he said. "The syringes we took from the Oak
Park ambulance? One was fine. It contained a full measure of full-strength
sux, and the plastic cap was tight. The other contained water. The needle cap
was so loose it might have worked itself off eventually. Somebody removed
it, drained the sux, and replaced the drug with tap water. We can't prove it,
but I'd be willing to bet the missing sux was drawn up into a generic syringe,
the kind you can order in bulk from Amazon, and used in one of the murders. Filling syringes with water and putting them back in their proper places
would explain why every inventory of sux in the county came up with the
right numbers. The inventories had the correct number of real sux syringes,
but an unknown number of the syringes had the wrong contents. That would
also explain why the drug used on the shooting victim in the ambulance
didn't work."

"Wow," I said. "I think we should wander out to the Village Hospital and
ask the director of pharmacy who would have had sufficient access to their
sux stores to do that."

"By 'we,' you mean?..."

"Steve and me."

Even over the ambient noise I heard Colter's laugh.

"I think your friendly neighborhood FBI is going to take over from
here," he said. "But I can be magnanimous. Cross over Wacker and stand on
the southeast corner. Traffic permitting, I'll pick you up in twenty minutes."

* * *

On the drive to Oak Park, speeded immeasurably by Colter's blue gumball roof light and siren, he told us the Village Hospital had checked their sux syringes and found no additional units that had obvious signs of tampering. But the manufacturer was going to replace all of them to be on the safe side. Before the recalls were destroyed, each would be tested for purity. If any more were found to be adulterated, the syringes would be checked for other ways their contents could have been stolen and replaced.

"I doubt they'll find any additional methods of tampering," Colter said. "The bad guys only need one."

I asked, "So why are we going out there if the syringes have all been checked?"

"Because the hospital is Ground Zero," Colter said. "I know what a tampered unit looks like. Nobody on the hospital staff has actually seen one. I want to look myself."

"The city's got a population of nearly three million," I said. "The county is over five million. How are you going to find every tampered vial of sux at every supply house, every lab, every clinic and hospital in an area serving that many people?"

"Same answer," Colter said. "The killers only need one method to steal the sux. Why would they need more than one source of supply? It's not as if they're stealing syringes by the gross. They're taking one or two at a time. We found their source, the hospital."

"There could be more than one thief," I suggested, "each working a different place."

"That's possible, but I don't think it's likely," Colter said. "Every thief you add to the equation increases the chance for slipups that could bring the conspiracy crashing down. On the off-chance that there is more than one thief working more than one site, we've sent an order to all sites that stock sux to check for tampering. Again, the manufacturer has volunteered to assign staff to help get the survey done faster. Personally, I don't think we'll find any additional crime scenes. The killers only need a limited supply of sux, unless they plan on waging war on all of Wisconsin."

* * *

Howard Levy, the director of pharmacy at Village Hospital in Oak Park, was waiting for Colter but was shocked to have him dragging two newspaper reporters behind him.

"Just ignore them, Doctor," Colter said. "They're harmless."

Levy wasn't going to be put off so easily.

"Why are two reporters, one who's not even from Chicago, getting such deep access to an FBI investigation?"

Colter caved. "Because they're working together, and Deuce is the one who discovered the succinylcholine connection to all these murders."

Levy looked disgusted. "So you think you owe her? That's a damned lame excuse. But it isn't my call. Whatever."

He had put every syringe of sux in his pharmacy on a cart beside his desk.

"What are we looking for now?" he asked, a distinct tone of annoyance in his voice.

"Any vial where the needle cap is loose," Colter said.

"My staff has already done that," Levy snapped. "They found nothing."

"I want to doublecheck," Colter said. "No disrespect for your staff. Just a precaution."

Steve had been looking down at the tops of the syringes. As they had been at the firehouse, all were all 200 milligram doses in ten milliliter syringes.

Levy's assistant came in with a second, empty cart to hold undamaged syringes so they could be put back on refrigeration as quickly as possible.

Steve and I had to sit out. We weren't trained to handle lethal drugs and had no legal status beyond amateur sleuths. So we watched the others don latex gloves and set to work examining every unit of sux in the hospital except those already out on the airways carts near the resuscitation bays. Levy said he had checked each of those personally and found none that had been tampered with. All the caps were firmly in place.

"Maybe," Levy said, "it's over."

He was wrong.

49

Toward the end of the examination, Colter found one syringe with a slightly loose needle cap. It was the only one. He set it aside for lab analysis.

Levy got defensive. "Maybe it came loose when my people checked it," he said.

"Maybe," Colter said. "But I'm taking it anyway. And I'm going to recheck the units out on the airways carts just to be safe. I presume you're not willing to take a chance with somebody's life."

Levy looked like a chastised child. When asked he quickly supplied Colter with the chain of possession for the hospital's sux supplies, from the manufacturer to his lab. There were only three points of possession, the middle one being the distributor. Colter called his office and sent a group of agents out to check all the sux at the distribution warehouse and on the company's trucks. If they found nothing, it would pretty much guarantee that the thefts and substitutions all occurred at the hospital itself.

"Who here has access?" I asked.

"To the pharmacy?" Levy asked. "Only the pharmacy staff. Somebody is here twenty-four/seven and holidays. We can get whatever doctors need faster than they could find it for themselves, and we don't want meds getting pushed around and mixed up."

"Does that rule out a member of the staff from being the thief?"

"Unfortunately, no," Levy said. "I would be shocked if the thief was someone who works here in the pharmacy, but it's not out of the realm of possibility. The more likely point of theft, I think, would be down in the resuscitation bays. Doctors have access. Nurses. EMTs. Orderlies. Even maintenance and janitorial staffs."

"You don't keep the dangerous stuff locked up?" I asked.

"Oh, sure we do, but anyone who might need immediate access has a key to the refrigerators. And keys occasionally go missing. Maybe lost. Even stolen and copied."

"This doesn't add up," I said. "You have a specific number of syringes in the building." I glanced at the cart by his desk. "Let's say fifty. Somebody steals one from a refrigerator near an airways cart. Somebody else notices the bay or the refrigerator is one unit short, notifies your department, and you replace the unit. Meanwhile, the thief withdraws the sux and replaces it with water. Now the thief has to get the adulterated syringe back into the hospital so the inventory numbers are right. How does he, or she, make that happen? Just stick it back where it came from and hope nobody will notice there's an extra?"

"That's a totally legitimate question," Levy said. "It needs an answer, and right now I don't have one for you. But one possibility is that somebody does notice the extra unit near an airways cart and calls us to put the extra back into inventory up here. That would explain how the adulterated units got into the pharmacy."

Colter was examining the walls and ceiling of the pharmacy.

"You have video cameras," he said. "Surveillance, I assume?"

"Oh, yeah," Levy said. "We have to with so many controlled substances around."

"I'll need the tapes for the last month," Colter told him.

Levy pointed to a cardboard box by the lab door. "Already done," he said. "But we'll need them back when you finish."

Colter nodded his agreement.

"One other thing and I'm done," I promised. "Do you ever have patients who successfully fight through the sux so it doesn't take effect, even though they got the real drug and not water?"

"I've never heard of that happening," Levy said after a moment's thought. "But I can't say with positive certainty that it couldn't happen. As I said earlier, proper doses of sux are determined by the patient's weight. If somebody calculated a dose with the wrong weight—something substantially low—the sux might have a significantly reduced impact. I'll have to ask around. I'm not a doctor, and I don't know if a low dose would be totally ineffective or simply produce a shorter period of paralysis."

There were a few more questions from Colter and one from Steve before the session started to adjourn. As we were leaving, I asked if we could stop in the executive director's office for a minute. Colter was in a hurry to get back to the city, but he humored me.

When the exec director came out to meet us, I asked if he could supply me with a list of every member of the hospital staff, including all the doctors who were not on staff but had privileges at the hospital. He was reluctant until Colter stepped in and said, "Consider this a request from the FBI."

"She's not FBI," the director said.

"Then consider it a request from me, through Deuce, and get it together by the end of the day. Please."

"Do you want me to deliver it to you personally?" the director asked me with a maximum amount of sarcasm.

"Email's fine," I said and handed him my card. "The address is right there in the bottom left corner."

As we left Colter asked, "What do you plan to do with the list?"

I replied honestly, "I haven't the vaguest idea."

* * *

The list popped into my mailbox just before I left the office for home. I took a quick look at it, saw nothing especially revealing, and decided to print out a copy and take it with me. I could run over it as I ate dinner, whenever and whatever that was going to be.

Meanwhile, Steve had gone off to find and shadow John Fasso again. Apparently, Fasso hadn't yet been charged with a crime and was free to roam about where Steve could keep track of his whereabouts and meetings. I wasn't sure what he hoped to learn, but I wasn't his editor and had no authority to question his choices.

Perhaps I should have.

I was halfway through dinner when the phone rang. I was going to let it go to voicemail until I heard the caller ID say, "Pete Rizzo," or some close Siri approximation of the name of the spokesman for the Chicago PD.

"Hey, what's up?" I said when I accepted the call.

"Your partner almost took a bullet tonight," he told me without preamble. My mind immediately flew to Mark.

"What?" I demanded. "What happened? Is Mark okay?"

"Not Mark. The guy from Washington. Steve Pace."

I felt a flood of relief, and I felt guilty about it. Was Steve's life worth any less than Mark's? Well, to me, yes.

"What happened?" I asked again.

"He was sitting in a car in front of John Fasso's office. A white panel truck pulled to the curb behind him. Two guys inside. The passenger got out and was walking around to the driver's side of Pace's car when Pace noticed him and saw in his side mirror that the guy had an automatic in his hand. Fortunately, Pace had left the motor running. He floored it out of there, apparently brushing the gunman as he went by. The thug got off two shots. One smashed through the side window and sprayed a lot of pebbled glass around, but the bullet missed Pace. The second shot wound up in the pavement."

"Thank God," I said. "Was Steve hurt?"

"Some pebbled glass in the left side of his face is all. The guys in his security detail transported him to the ER at Stroger to get patched up. You remember what that's like."

Unfortunately, I did. "Are they admitting him?"

"I don't know, but I'd doubt it. The wounds are superficial. He'll walk around for a day or two with little pieces of toilet paper stuck to his face."

"I'm going to run over there and see if I can catch him," I told Rizzo. "Thanks for the heads up, Pete."

I caught up with Steve as he was working with a hospital staffer on all the insurance paperwork that goes with a hospital visit. The two minders were standing watch nearby. The senior man took my elbow and moved me a few feet farther away.

"Sorry about this," he said. "We assumed the van was a service company vehicle. We would have chased them, but we had to make sure Steve was okay and get him here."

I patted his shoulder and told him not to worry.

Instead of announcing my presence to Steve, I reached around from behind him and shoved my iPhone in front of his face. I had pulled up a photo of me after getting pelted by pebbled auto glass in a shooting a while back. I had little surgical strips all over my face when Mark took the picture in the hospital. I had been admitted because I also had a bullet hole in my arm. Steve glanced at the photo and burst out laughing. Then he said, "Ouch," and stopped laughing. "That hurt."

"I'll wait for you over here," I said, motioning to some chairs set out for people waiting for something or other.

When Steve joined me, I asked, "You okay?"

"Good enough," he said. "I'm not especially impressed by this hospital building, but the staff and the docs were great."

"Unfortunately, they have a lot of experience here with the results of gun shots. I think half the shooting victims in the city are brought here."

He sat down next to me and told me what had happened.

"Did you get a good look at either guy?"

"Not the driver at all," he said. "The man with the gun, sort of. Not good enough, I don't think, to pick out of a lineup, though the cops want me to look at mug shots again. I only got a vague impression of him. I don't think I've ever seen him before."

Steve dropped his head into his hands. "That's the closest I've ever come to getting killed," he said. "Let's get out of here. Maybe you could drive me back to my car."

"Be happy to, but you need to talk to the police first. Make a report. They're on their way over now."

Once the report was filed, I asked Steve, "You want to stop for dinner somewhere? Or let me buy you a couple of drinks?"

"No, thanks," he said. "I want to go back to the hotel, order room service, and go to bed. Or maybe I'll skip room service and go straight for the minibar."

I followed Steve to his hotel, trailed by his detail and mine, and watched as he handed his car key to the valet, who was frowning at the broken window. I don't know what Steve said to him, but the guy nodded and took the car. Steve waved to me and went inside. In addition to the guilt he brought with him from Washington for the role he played in the death of an innocent man, he now had a new experience for his brain to gnaw on. He was worried about being able to sleep this night after the attempt on his life. I could have told him it's not a one-night thing. He had acquired a recurring nightmare that could still be chasing him years from now.

I knew this because I had been there.

50

The Fasso story broke on Monday. The alderman/vice mayor of Chicago was arrested and charged by the state with first degree murder. Federal RICO charges were expected to follow when a grand jury impaneled by Jerry Alvarez finished its work.

Once all the legal boilerplate was stripped from it, the murder indictment charged that Fasso had killed Stefano Cappa with two shots to the head from a North American Arms 22-caliber short-barrel five-shot revolver while an accomplice injected Dominic Tufino in the neck with a poison as yet to be identified. The charges against Fasso included abetting Tufino's murder, and conspiracy to commit murder. The gun, the indictment said, was owned by Fasso and had only Fasso's prints on it.

The cops forced Fasso to make the perp walk, as it's called, where the accused and his lawyer must walk a gamut of media between the police car transporting them and the courthouse where the accused would be arraigned. Reporters shouted questions at Fasso. Neither he nor his counsel answered any of them. Photographers made pictures of a powerful man in handcuffs, and everyone knew he was in handcuffs even though his jacket hung over them like a towel tossed sloppily onto the back of a chair. Nobody walks with his hands clasped in front of him unless he's a prisoner in restraints or a priest about to say mass. Trust me when I say Fasso was no priest.

On the other hand, Steve Pace continued to believe he wasn't a killer, either.

* * *

I had an appointment at Ron Colter's office the next afternoon. His agents had finished reviewing all the documents sent from Washington pertaining to the organized crime investigation headed by Carl Cribben. Ron said he would have to withhold most of the files from me because confidential sources and investigative methods were not in the public domain and never would be. However, if I wanted to see the rest, I could, but I couldn't take the files from his office or copy them.

I was going to be doing the review alone while Steve followed up other leads. He thought that would be more productive because of his lack of knowledge of Chicago crime families. I agreed. When I reached Colter's office, his secretary showed me into a conference room where folders fat with paper were stacked in nine piles of eight to ten folders each.

"AD Colter will be right in," she said. "Please don't touch the folders until he arrives."

She almost bumped into Ron on her way out.

I waved a hand across the formidable assemblage of paperwork. "Are you telling me that most of the files aren't here?" I asked. "This looks like a whole investigation's worth."

He nodded. "There are almost eighty files that aren't on that table. That's why it took so long for my agents to get through them."

"Is there any significance to the arrangement of the piles?" I asked.

He frowned and showed me half a smile. "Because they'd fall over if they were all in one stack? Instead of reading you'd be picking up paper until midnight."

"That works," I said. "I know I can't copy these, but may I at least take notes?"

Colter hesitated. "Maybe. Well, go ahead, but I might need to review what you've written before you leave."

I spent nearly three hours with the files before I took a break. Ron's secretary kept coffee, hot and fresh, coming in for me, and I needed a bathroom break and a stretch. I made notes on my iPadPro. Scrawling things on a yellow legal pad had gone extinct. It was slower and much harder to read later.

The paperwork was expertly redacted where the feds didn't want me to see tidbits of information. Amateur censors will simply draw a black Magic Marker line through material they want to conceal. What they don't realize is that the material can still be read through the back of each sheet of paper. All the text is backwards, but it can be deciphered without much effort. Expert censors—and the feds were experts—use the Magic Marker and then make copies of the redacted pages so there is no bleed. I checked the back of each page, anyway, to catch it if they missed something.

I wrote down every name I found and made copious notes on the context in which the names appeared. Eventually I would dump the whole load on the *Journal's* researchers for background checks. There were a few names I recognized but not many. None of them rang any loud alerts.

When Ron came in at 6 p.m. to tell me they were closing up, I had gotten through only half the files. "Can I come back in the morning?" I asked him.

"Sure," he said. "But before you go, I'll have to take a look at your notes."

He sat down next to me and scanned my iPad. Either he was a speed reader, or he was looking for something specific because he went through the notes quickly.

"Okay," he said when he finished. "They look fine." He waved at the table. "Any of these files you're done with?"

"I think I've finished with the ones in front of you, but I'd like to have them tomorrow in case I need to refer back."

"We'll leave everything as is and lock the door. Come back at eight."

I had a feeling he was expecting me to find something, but I had no idea what it was.

* * *

I didn't have to wait long the next morning to figure it out. I was an hour into my reading when I found redactions on a page that had not been copied after being censored. The blacked-out text was quite legible, if backwards, on the back of the page. It took me only about ten minutes to decipher the whole visible text.

What I read was an enticing excerpt from a deposition taken from an individual identified as Matteo Messina. The name was familiar, not only because he shared a last name with a Hall of Fame baseball player for the Baltimore Orioles and the New York Yankees. I had vacationed in Sicily several years earlier, and it seemed as if every other person I met was named Messina. In a country where many surnames were regional, Messina had jumped from the province of Messina, on the northeast corner of Sicily, across the narrow Strait of Messina to the toe of the boot of Italy, to the region called Calabria. There, too, I encountered residents named Messina, though fewer than in Sicily.

I'm not sure why I remembered that. It wasn't important except for the fact that this Messina, the Matteo Messina left unredacted in the FBI file, was familiar to me, too.

Why?

Then I remembered.

I lurched across the table and grabbed my metro bag. I snatched my wallet and dug out the piece of paper that, according to Steve Pace, fell out of my jacket when we got knocked down by the exploding Explorer. My hands trembled as I unfolded the paper.

My memory was correct. Matteo Messina was the name on the slip of paper. The accompanying phone number carried the 3-1-2 area code, one of several assigned to Chicago. As I sat at the table and stared at the note, a memory formed in my mind that brought moisture to my eyes.

The last time I had seen Carl Cribben alive we were walking north on Wabash Avenue. We stopped for a light at Congress. He enveloped me in a hug—not a gesture we had ever shared before. When we broke, he had run his hands down my sides, stopping at my waist, the exact location of the pockets in my jacket.

Now I realized the hug wasn't an act of affection. It was Carl's way of delivering a message. Perhaps he had a premonition of his own impending doom. Perhaps it was his way of passing on classified information he didn't want to offer openly. Whatever his rationale for the somewhat melodramatic message delivery, he wanted me to interview Matteo Messina.

I would, for two reasons. First, he might have evidence that could finally resolve this case. And second, the note was Carl's way of asking for help. I intended to do as he asked.

* * *

I finished up the files late the same afternoon. It had been a slog. My mind kept drifting back to Matteo Messina, who he might be, and why he was important. I had no idea in either case. I'd found no other instances of the same redaction error that occurred on the page revealing Messina's name. Just in case Colter chose to edit that material out of my iPad notes, I transcribed the whole page by hand and hid the written notes in a zippered compartment of my bag. Even as I did so, I marveled at how paranoid I'd become.

Ron went through my notes again. I saw him crack the slightest smile at one point. I almost asked him what the smile was about but thought better of it.

When he was finished, he handed me my iPad, its contents intact.

"Find anything interesting?" he asked.

"Hard to tell without some digging," I said.

"Because sometimes you run across things you don't expect."

"And what do you do when that happens?"

"Follow it as far as it leads me," he said.

"Are we talking in circles about anything specific?" I asked.

"Just chatting," he replied. "Go. Follow your instincts."

It hit me as I walked out of the building.

The unredacted page had been left on purpose. Ron wanted me to find the name. He smiled when he ran across it in my notes and knew I had discovered the redaction "error." Or perhaps he knew Carl had slipped the name into my pocket and wanted to confirm for me that it was important. It didn't really matter which scenario was true. Only that I was carrying around a major new lead.

Now if only I knew what to do with it.

51

I stopped by the office to take a fresh look at a column I'd written over the weekend before turning it in. While I was there, I stopped in to talk to Eric. I had to tell him about Matteo Messina and the strange note. Before I could begin, he told me about his day.

"I got a call this morning," he said, "from Steve's editor, Bryanna Regan, wanting an update on how her wounded reporter was faring. She had talked to him directly, but apparently wasn't sure whether to believe it when he said he was fine."

"It's true," I said. "Though I suspect he's going to have nightmares for a while."

"What's he doing?"

"I'm not sure," I said. "But let me tell you what I'm doing."

As I gave him a report on what I'd found in the FBI files and the saga of the strange note, his eyebrows shot up and seemed to get stuck part way up his forehead. I told him I wanted to track down Matteo Messina and see what he had to say.

"Then what?"

"I'll go see him and hope he'll talk to me. Maybe Carl told him to trust me."

"You know," Eric said, "for somebody who didn't want to get involved in this story, you look to be in it about chest high. Be careful it doesn't rise above your head."

As I approached my desk, I saw my favorite *Journal* researcher, Lucy Sandoval, waving at me from the library.

"What's up?" I asked her.

"You asked me to see if I could run down Matteo Messina, and I found him with the same phone number you have," she told me. "The number's unlisted, but I got the address."

"How, if the number's not listed?"

"There are some things in this life you can't do without revealing your address and phone number. One of those things is opening an electric utility account. I have access, and I won't tell you how, to ComEd's customer data base."

"Is this going to get us in trouble?"

"Nope, not with ComEd, at least. I only look. I never tamper. And I don't use any phones or computers that belong to the *Journal*. I have a friend on the inside who goes into the database after me and cleans out any record of my intrusion. And even if ComEd found a trace of me, it wouldn't be worth the time and money to track me down since I don't do anything mischievous or illegal."

"Just breaking in is illegal, I think."

"No breaking in involved," Lucy insisted. "I know the passwords."

"Oh crap," I said. "I don't want to hear any more. Let's see the results."

* * *

An hour later I found myself in Cicero, an independent city west of Chicago but inside Cook County, the same place Emily Goodsill lived until she moved in with the FBI. Matteo Messina lived on South Forty-Ninth Avenue in a small, single-family tan sandstone brick house of the variety ubiquitous around Cicero. The home was modest but neat, with a tiny, well-maintained front yard and a block of eight concrete steps mounting to the front door. The house had no garage and no driveway. Parking was first-come-first-served on the street. I parked two doors up from the address, walked back, and rang the doorbell.

It was answered by a woman who could have been anywhere from fifty to seventy. She stood very proud and erect, her gray hair pulled back in a long pony tail she must have spent most of her life growing. I liked it. She wore little, if any, makeup on a face lined with age, and judging from its tone, sunshine. She was dressed in blue jeans that fit her form and a black, V-neck, zip-front top that draped loosely over her hips. Her feet were bare, her toenails recently manicured and polished in bright red.

I smiled at her, and she asked, "May I help you?"

"I understand Matteo Messina lives here," I said. "A mutual friend sent me."

Good grief, I thought, did that ever sound hokey.

"And who would this mutual friend be?" she asked.

I went all in. "Carl Cribben."

Her eyes went wide, and she stepped back. I thought she was going to slam the door. I couldn't let her do that. But she was stepping back to call out to someone.

She spoke in Italian, which I couldn't translate. But I was all but certain I knew the meaning of the word, "*pistola*." She was telling someone to bring a gun.

I wasn't wearing a jacket. All I could do to indicate I wasn't armed was to raise my hands to shoulder level, palms open and facing the woman. "I mean no harm," I said.

An older man appeared at the door, his right hand hidden behind it. His thick, dark hair was going to gray. His eyes and the set of his mouth were hard. I suspected he was holding a *pistola* and hoped he didn't feel the need to use it.

"Mr. Messina?" I asked.

"Who wants to know?"

I held up a business card and told him what was on it.

"I'm Deuce Mora, a columnist for the Chicago *Journal.* The column runs on the front page of the Metro Section three times a week. I also was a good friend of Carl Cribben."

The woman left the door abruptly. I continued, bending the truth a little.

"Shortly before Carl was murdered, we had lunch together, and he gave me a slip of paper with your name and phone number. He asked me to get in touch with you if anything bad happened to him. That's why I'm here. Did you know Carl?"

The woman reappeared with a newspaper in hand. She held it up for the man to see and pointed at something on the page. I suspected it was my column with my mug shot.

"And what do you want?" he asked, the edge gone from his voice. "I don't never talk to the newspapers."

"This isn't for a story," I said. "I won't print anything we talk about. I need some help. And I'm here because Carl asked me to come."

He relaxed his right arm so that now his hand, wrapped around a Glock-style weapon, hung loosely at his side. He looked past me and scanned the immediate area, most likely looking for other sources of trouble.

Then he opened the door.

52

"Carl told me I might hear from you if anything happened to him," Messina said when we were settled into their comfortable living room with steaming cups of freshly pulled espresso and plates of cantucci, which are Italian almond biscotti.

There is no delicate way to eat properly made biscotti. It's hard and brittle and produces prodigious numbers of crumbs when broken into pieces. Mrs. Messina—she told me to call her Adriana—laughed as she watched my polite struggle.

"There are two ways to deal with biscotti," she told me. "You can dip it in your coffee to soften it up, or you can simply ignore the crumbs. Either is acceptable."

I tried the former and settled on the latter.

That matter resolved, I turned to her husband.

"So Carl expected to be attacked?" I asked.

"Expected's too strong," Messina said. "More like he recognized the possibility."

"What did he tell you about me?"

"Said I could trust you."

"I hope you will," I said. "Carl didn't tell me anything about you. Just the note with your name and phone number."

"I was sad when he died. Too bad. He was a good man."

"Mr. Messina, since he didn't tell me anything about you or your role in his investigation, would you fill me in?"

"I can, and I will. But first you need-a know that Adriana and I will be leavin' here tomorrow, maybe for good, maybe only 'til all this murder stuff gets resolved. The phone number you have will be disconnected forever. Before you go, I'll give you the number of my satellite phone in case you need-a reach me again. It's expensive, but it's secure. We're goin' back to Italy. I ain't gonna tell you where we are goin', but it's nowhere near the Sicilian places we grew up."

"I completely understand," I said. "I'd probably be doing the same thing in your place. But you still must be careful. Even satellite phones are not foolproof. Skilled hackers can break down the encryption."

"I doubt the guys who might want-a find me have those skills. But I'll remember your warning. Now, let me tell you a story."

I took out my digital voice recorder and showed it to Messina. He agreed that I could use it to record our conversation. This is the story he told me:

He lived as a child on what is now called Chicago's Near North Side, near the intersection of Division and Larrabee. "In those days it was the Sicilians' 'hood," he said. His family later moved to my neighborhood, now called The Heart of Italy, and then up to today's Little Italy territory running along both sides of Taylor Street west of the campus of the University of Illinois/ Chicago. It was here, when he was in middle school, that he met John Fasso and Jimmy Tricoletto. Messina became part of their clique, "which really was a junior division of the Tricoletto crime family."

"We did lotsa stupid stuff, like kids that age will try," he said. "Nothin' really bad until high school. Then came the summer after my junior year. There was maybe six or seven of us hangin' out on a corner. Jimmy pointed out a guy comin' out of a restaurant on Taylor Street. He said the guy had cheated his father, then dissed him when confronted about it. There was, Jimmy said, a price on his head."

"You were how old then?" I asked.

"Sixteen. Don't interrupt."

I sat back, properly chastised.

"I said I could kill him. Jimmy and John and the other guys laughed. I asked how much it paid. Jimmy told me ten Gs. I'd never even thought about having that much money. I found out later the price was really twenty Gs. Jimmy kept half for himself. I asked where I could get a gun. All of a sudden there was one in my hand. I don't know who put it there. Jimmy told me, 'Go. Do it. Put two in the backa his head. You'll be a made guy, in the family forever. Fuhgeddaboud college. You won't need it.'

"I was a crappy student and probably wouldn'ta got into college, anyway. So it all sounded too good to be true. I ran after the guy, and before I could think twice about it, I'd put two in his head. Then I ran like hell. Next day, Jimmy gave me my money. I was in."

He said he remembered only three more murders he committed in the following years, mostly because he found himself working the somewhat less-violent protection rackets. He was well-suited to that because he was big, strong, and intimidating. He beat up guys, broke a few limbs, but wasn't asked to kill again until he was about twenty-six.

"I kinda retired last year," Messina said. "Tell you the trut', protection isn't much of a thing anymore, and I was really tired of all the violence and blood. But sittin' around the house and tryin' to sleep at night, I couldn't get the faces of the guys I made dead and the guys I sent to the hospital out of my thoughts and dreams. There wasn't much about my life I was proud of. So when Carl Cribben came to talk to me, I listened. First time I ordered him outta the house. I yelled at him so anybody in the neighborhood who might be listenin' in would hear me tell him in no uncertain terms to leave me an' my family alone. I did it to keep us safe, an' I think Carl unnerstood that."

But Cribben had given him a card, Messina said, and wrote his private phone number on it. A week later, Messina called him.

"The wife and me, we made a big deal outta takin' a vacation to Hawaii," Messina said. "That's where Cribben and I met up, at a beach resort near Kona on the Big Island. He'd changed his hair color, grown a mustache, and had a beard stubble. I almost didn't recognize him. That's when I told him everything, including how Tricoletto framed that building contractor, Frank Chapin, so he'd lose the election for governor. Chapin was running on an anti-corruption platform, and he had the clout in the legislature to get most of the stuff he wanted. Tony Toes couldn't have that."

I had to interrupt. "All those code violations…"

"Yeah, and the building that came down. All part of a big frame."

I waited for the kicker.

"That Chapin guy didn't know nothin' about any of it. All his plans, his materials, all his orders were clean and legal. Tony Toes had his guys inside change 'em all, put the phony invoices in Chapin's files, and sabotage that building that collapsed. Chapin mighta done a few shady things that all contractors do, but he never did nothin' to risk lives. He was totally framed, and he could spend the rest of his time in prison for shit he never done."

* * *

At this point Messina had to excuse himself to use the bathroom. Too much coffee. I was feeling the need, as well, and so we adjourned while Adriana made even more espresso and replenished the biscotti basket.

When we resumed, I took over with questions.

"Mr. Messina, have you told anyone else about this?"

"No," he said. "I got a call from a fellow said he was FBI, but I'd had enough. I told him I didn't know nothin' and to leave me alone. He called again a couple-a days later. I hung up on him. He never called again."

"Is John Fasso a 'made guy?'"

"Fast Johnny? Nah. He don't have the stomach for killin'. That's why I was so surprised when he got arrested for that thing in Wrigleyville."

"If he doesn't have the stomach for killing," I asked, "why did he own a gun?"

"Protection, maybe. I know lotsa people who own guns who haven't got the moxie to point them at anybody. Johnny likes to shoot at targets on a range, long as they ain't alive. Least wise, that's how it was years ago. I don't know much about how he turned out as he got older. He pretty much drifted away from us when he got into politics. Guess it don't work to be too close to a crime family when you're running for office. Though I think him and Jimmy T. are still pretty good friends. But they don't do no business together."

"So you don't see him shooting Stefano Cappa?"

"Who? Oh, Tufino's body man? No, I don't. He's too soft."

"Mr. Messina, if what you say about Frank Chapin is true, there must have been somebody in his office who switched out the invoices in his files."

"There was. Like I told Carl, I can't name names 'cause I never knew 'em.

But there was a woman who I heard was havin' a hard time, financial-wise. Three kids, a husband who ran away and was never heard from again, bills out the wazoo, I don't know what-all. She had a regular full-time job but needed to make more. Somebody got her a part-time job as a file clerk in Chapin's office. If I needed somebody inside an operation to do some dirty work, my target would be somebody who needed cash. They're the vulnerable ones. All's she had to do was take delivery of the bad papers and swap 'em out for the real McCoys when there wasn't nobody around to see."

"Do you know who might be able to put a name with this woman?"

Messina shook his head. "I really don't. But I'll tell you something I only found out a couple-a days ago. This woman, the one who switched Chapin's paperwork, her full-time job was with the some federal agency, if that helps."

Suddenly my pulse jumped.

"What kind of job?" I asked.

"I don't know," Messina replied. "But it was her office in the federal building where Carl got himself offed."

53

Messina and his wife wandered off again, leaving me to sit quietly in the living room for a few minutes and gather myself. I knew there were several calls I should make, but I had more questions to ask Messina, since I probably wouldn't get another chance.

Messina had to have been talking about Emily Goodsill. If he was right, then Emily's whole story was a carefully constructed lie with just enough hints of truth to make the lies believable. She probably did start her career with the ag extension service back near her home in Walnut, Iowa. But she never mentioned a runaway husband or kids. Where were the children? Perhaps living with their grandmother back home. That would help explain why Emily was so eager to leave protective custody and get back to Iowa's corn country. It would also explain why she desperately needed money. Her mother couldn't be earning enough from her farm and antique selling to provide food, clothes, medical care, and likely some measure of day care for three young children.

Emily probably left her ag extension job and came to the big city to try to earn more, to develop a real career, and maybe bring the children here to live with her.

She had to know the case against Frank Chapin had been built on falsified evidence she planted. That made her an accessory to local, state and federal crimes. She had conspired to break city building codes, helped commit manslaughter, all in support of a crime family attempting to duck a federal investigation. She had lied to the FBI. And if she had lied when she said her Medeco office key had never been out of her possession—if she had loaned the key to the men who killed Carl Cribben—she was complicit in a conspiracy to commit a heinous first-degree murder. Was she capable of that? When all this settled out, Emily would be lucky ever to see her children again until they were grown and married with children of their own.

How much of this did Ron Colter know? He obviously knew Matteo Messina was a key figure in Carl's investigation. Colter likely knew that Carl had given me Messina's name and number. He likely knew that Messina trusted Carl. So if he trusted Carl, he might trust me and retell his story to me. Colter's sloppy redaction wasn't sloppy at all. He wanted to remind me that Carl had left me a big pointer to Messina and prod me to make the call.

Well, it seemed to have worked.

And better yet, I had it all on my voice recorder.

But I needed answers to one more question.

* * *

"Mr. Messina," I said when we were settled again, "Do you know who's actually committing all the killings?"

He thought for a minute. Then he said, "I probly don't know any more than you. I heard one of the needle men was Tricoletto Junior, Tony Toes's older son, but that's only hearsay. The rest, I don't know. I'm outta the business and outta the loop."

He paused, and I knew there was something else on his mind. "I'll tell you one other thing. On this I got first-hand knowledge. But before you tell anybody else, even Colter, give us a couple hours to clear outta the house and get someplace we can be safe tonight. We'll be on a plane outta the country by 8 a.m. Then you can tell anybody you want."

"I promise," I said.

"When I retired from the family, I didn't wanna just lie around the house all day. I don't play golf or fish. A little bocci—that's like Italian bowling—with the boys once in a while. But I didn't have no hobbies. I talked to Tricoletto Junior about getting some part-time work somewhere. He got me on as a bartender at a club on the Gold Coast that don't have no regular name.

But the members call it Twenty-One cause it's on the twenty-first floor of its building. It's a real elegant place, and very private an' exclusive."

He paused and inhaled deeply. "I really ain't supposed to talk about what I see while I'm workin', but what the hell. I won't be goin' back there."

"Not if you're leaving the country tomorrow," I said.

He continued as though he hadn't heard me. "Once or twice a week, Tony Toes would come in an' meet somebody, I assumed it was bidness."

"Who?" I asked.

"It was a variety-a people, mostly people I didn't recognize. But lately he's been meetin' one guy in particular about once or twice a month, maybe more than that. I can't hear what they're sayin', but sometimes I can tell from their expressions and gestures that the conversation's gotten pretty intense. About half the time this guy passes somethin' to Tony Toes at the end of their meetin'. Once it was a briefcase. Most of the time it's a small zippered pouch. Leather, I think."

"You have any idea who the other man is, or what he's passing?"

"I couldn't tell you what he's passin'. But who he is, that I know. Name's Tyler Walston. The governor of the state of Illinois."

* * *

During my drive back to the city, my mind was racing, but it wasn't going anywhere. I suffered a case of information overload, and I didn't know what to make of any of it. On one hand, the governor might have a perfectly legitimate reason to meet with Tony Toes. Lots of legitimate people in Chicago had a passing acquaintance with members of the mob. I could also make a case that the governor would naturally not want to be seen with the Tricoletto boss in public.

Still, it smelled bad.

I wasn't going to risk doing anything with this new bombshell until I told Eric Ryland about it. Making decisions about the handling of incredibly sensitive material was what he got paid the big bucks to do. I knew what I thought should be done with it. In any other circumstance I would fight like bloody hell to get it published under my byline. But this was nothing like other circumstances. We had guaranteed Ron Colter he could trust us not to go to print without his okay. I was fairly certain now would not be the most opportune time from his point of view to end the restriction. Plus, I had promised to give the Messinas some time to vacate their home and until morning to get out of the country.

After I had filled Eric in completely, he agreed.

"Have you told Steve about this yet?" he asked.

"No. I came straight back here from Cicero. Ron Colter called me once, and I let that go to voice mail until I had a chance to talk to you."

My editor, normally the bane of my existence, nodded in approval. "I think you're beginning to grow up," he said.

"That's the meanest thing you've ever said to me." I pretended to pout. "I didn't plan on growing up much before 2040 or so."

"I need to fill in Jonathan Bruckner," Eric said. "He'll probably want to hear the whole story from you. Hang around 'til he gets here. When we're done, go home. Don't return Colter's call or say anything to Steve until tomorrow morning. Give the Messinas time to get on their plane."

"I don't know about Steve, but Ron's going to be pissed," I said.

"I don't care. I don't want the FBI staking out O'Hare and taking the Messinas into custody where the whole world can see it happen. It'd be like signing their death warrants."

"Yeah, okay," I said.

"Meanwhile, don't lose that digital recorder."

* * *

I was sitting at my desk awaiting the arrival of the newspaper's lawyer. While I waited I picked up a thin sheaf of papers sitting on my desk. It was the list of staff from the Oak Park Village Hospital that I had printed out and run through once. Nothing stood out in the relatively long list that ranged from members of the maintenance and janitorial crews to the doctors and administrative staff and the board of directors. Any of them could walk through the corridors of the hospital and not seem out of place. Any one of them could duck into a resuscitation bay and steal a syringe full of succinylcholine if he or she had a key to the refrigerator, whether officially issued or lost or stolen. I had scanned the entire list with nothing to show for it.

I thought.

I realized there was a final page I hadn't seen. A list of doctors who, while not on the hospital staff, did have privileges there. These were mostly doctors with specialties that weren't required on a daily basis and had privileges at several hospitals so they could choose the most convenient for their patients and surgical teams.

My eyes drifted down the list. I expected nothing.

I was wrong.

Had I seen this particular name prior to my conversation earlier with Matteo Messina, I might have thought it an interesting coincidence. Now I sat, dumbfounded, looking at a single name that explained everything.

54

When I finished up with the lawyer I returned to my desk to find Steve waiting and my phone ringing. Caller ID read, "Ron Colter."

I accepted the call and, without preamble, I said, "I've got to see you. Right now."

"Hello to you, too," he said. "Come on over."

"One thing first," I said. "Is Emily Goodsill still in protective custody?"

"I'd prefer to call it 'protective care,' but yes, she is.'"

"You'd better up it to custody," I said. "I mean it. And call Jerry Alvarez. What I've got to tell you he needs to hear, too."

I hung up.

"What's up?" Steve asked, easing himself down in my side chair.

"Don't get comfortable," I said. "We're leaving. I'll fill you in on the way. I think I've found all the answers. What I don't know is whether we can use them."

* * *

By the time we reached the FBI building, Steve knew everything I knew—except the part about the incomplete redaction in the FBI files that led me to Messina. I figured Colter wouldn't want anyone else to know. I hit only the highlights of my conversation with Messina because Steve would be in Colter's office with me to hear the recording for himself.

"Jesus," was all he could bring himself to say.

When we got to Colter's office, he saw us right away.

"Jerry's on his way," he told us. "You want to get started or wait for him?"

"If you don't mind, I'd rather wait," I said. "We can go sit in your reception area if you have things you want to do before he gets here."

"I'm editing a couple of briefs from staff," he said. "Sorry for getting my back."

He had to turn away from us to use his computer. I looked over the material on his desk, a natural instinct for a journalist, but I was sitting too far away to see anything.

"Stop prying," Colter said.

How did he know? He hadn't even turned around.

"Sorry," I said. "Habit."

Jerry arrived ten minutes later.

"I broke every traffic law in the city getting over here," he said. "If I get any nastygrams from the meter police, Deuce, I'll hold you responsible for paying them. Now *¿Que esta pasando?* What's going on?"

I told them about the final meeting I'd had with Carl and my assumption about the note that fell out of my jacket pocket when the Explorer's destruction blew me into the side of a building. I explained that in the crush of developments I had forgotten the note, and only recently rediscovered it in my wallet.

Then I placed my digital voice recorder on Colter's desk and hit 'Play.' When the recording ended, Jerry's mouth was hanging open, and I thought I saw the slightest hint of a smile on Colter's face. Steve had his elbows on his knees and held his face in his hands. I couldn't see his expression.

"You've done a day's work and tossed a month's worth in my lap," Jerry said.

"Sorry," I said. "But you wouldn't want to send an innocent man to prison."

Jerry shook his head. "The trouble is, it's all hearsay."

"It's pretty obvious to me the woman who helped frame Chapin is Emily Goodsill," I said. "Ron still has her under wraps. If you confront her with her lies, she might give you the first-hand information you need."

Jerry asked, "Did Messina tell you where he got his information?"

"You just listened to everything he told me. But I'm not quite finished."

Everyone turned to me expectantly, even Steve. I had not told him what I found on the hospital staff list.

"AD Colter used his powers of persuasion to get the head of the Oak Park Village Hospital to release to me their entire staff list. I wanted to see if there were any clues as to who might have been stealing sux. I don't know why, but the first time I went over the list I stopped one page before the end. I don't remember if something interrupted me, or whether I didn't see it, or what. But while I was sitting in my office earlier today, I picked up the list again. This time I got all the way through it. Note the name I've circled."

I handed the papers to Colter, whose eyes went wide. Then Jerry, who whispered, *"Dios mio,"* and handed the papers across to Steve.

Steve looked at me, frowning. "I guess it could be a coincidence," he said.

"Ask anybody who knows me, and they'll all tell you I don't believe in coincidence."

* * *

"I don't want to speculate about this," Colter said. "We need more information."

"Means, motive, and opportunity," Alvarez said. "That's what we need to prove guilt in a criminal investigation, and we're almost there. Walston has access to the sux and the expertise to make the switch. Motive is the tricky one. My spider sense tells me the Mob has something on him that it used for leverage. The *quid pro quo* was the sabotage of Chapin's campaign, clearing the way to the governor's mansion for Walston and dooming the tough new anti-crime legislation Chapin was pushing."

I asked, "You don't think Walston actually committed the murders, do you?"

"No," Jerry said. "Even if he were so inclined, which I doubt, he'd be too readily recognizable on the street. Besides, the Tricolettos don't need his help. They needed his skills to get the sux and maybe train the real killers so they didn't off themselves."

"They did everything," Colter said, "to throw us off. The mysterious locked office, the way they tried to make it appear that Carl was hanged and possibly committed suicide, the vanishing murder weapon, the dubious appearance of a burgeoning mob war. As long as nothing fit right, they could duck responsibility."

Steve asked the biggest question remaining on the table. "Why would Walston agree to be a part of something like that? Did he owe Tony Toes a really big favor?"

"That's a major hole we have to fill," Colter said. "If it comes down to it, we'll confront Walston with the evidence. If that doesn't break him, we can always offer him a deal. If Tony Toes has dirt on him, maybe he thought he had no choice but to help. The Tricolettos could have ruined him. So he suggested sux as a weapon that couldn't be identified or traced and procured it for them. Since he didn't have time for many patients after the election, but he was still doing some surgeries. So nobody would have questioned his presence in the hospital from time to time. Finally, he's the governor of the freaking state. He had reason to feel comfortable that his culpability would never occur to anyone."

I said, "What I need to do right now is to talk to Emily Goodsill. Maybe I can break her down and get her to corroborate Messina's story."

"I'll need to be there," Colter said as he picked up his phone. "We'll have to offer her a lawyer, maybe even immunity. We'll be asking her to confess to a string of criminal acts."

While Colter was getting through to the agents guarding Emily, the rest of us had a quiet conversation in the background. Colter's shout silenced us.

"She what?" he yelled. "How did that happen?"

We glanced at each other with apprehension. Colter's face was growing flushed with fury over what he was hearing.

"Keep everybody there," he said. "I'm on my way. And call a forensics team."

"Deuce, Steve, you're with me," he said. "Jerry, I'll call you later. Let's go."

"Where *are* we going?" I asked.

"To the safe house. Emily Goodsill has disappeared."

55

The safehouse sat on West Walton Street in a neighborhood commonly known as Ukranian Village. Though the population of the old North Side district had long since ceased being dominated by homeowners and shopkeepers of Ukranian descent, there still was enough of the old blood around to provide some interesting and tasty Ukranian food, religion, culture, and texture.

Our destination looked similar to many of the homes along Walton: brick, two-story, with flights of eight to ten steps up to the front porches. Almost all had third, lower floors that were half below street level and accessed through a door under the main front steps. The spaces often served as rental apartments or homes for extended family members. Nothing suggested the FBI structure was used in any way inconsistent with other homes on the street. Until you got up close.

Then you might notice an unusual number of cameras all but hidden by the ivy climbing the exterior walls. Their only giveaway were the small, irregular openings cut into the ivy to clear the cameras' views. Sensors had been embedded in the low brick walls sandwiching the main steps to alert occupants of the building to possible intruders. There might have been alarms on all the windows, too, but I couldn't see them as I trudged up the stairs behind Ron Colter. Overall, the home gave the impression of security-conscious occupants, nothing more.

The door opened for us even before we got to it. The young agent standing at the entry looked as if he expected a beheading at any moment. But Colter kept his cool.

"They're with me," he said, cocking his head toward Steve and me. He didn't introduce us. There were two additional agents in the dining room. Ron didn't introduce us to them, either. The room had been converted to a surveillance center where agents could keep close watch on all parts of this property and parts of the grounds of adjacent properties. At the moment, there was nothing to see.

"Where's the forensics team?" Colter demanded.

"They're finishing up something down in Englewood," said the man who looked to be the oldest of the three agents charged with maintaining Emily's safety.

"Screw Englewood," Colter said. "Tell them I want them here yesterday, and they should park around the corner and come up the alley. I don't want to expose this place any more than it has been." He sighed and looked around him at nothing in particular. He seemed to be gathering his thoughts. "You said on the phone there was an alarm from her back window. I want to see her room."

"You don't want to go in until…"

"I didn't say I wanted to search it," Colter snapped. "I want to stand in the hall and have a look inside."

"Are they coming, too?" the agent asked, pointing his chin in the general direction of Steve and me.

"No," Colter said, turning toward us. "The two of you stay here and don't touch anything. I'm leaving two agents with you who won't let you get into anything you shouldn't. They're in enough trouble already."

With that he turned on his heel and followed the third agent out of the room.

I addressed the two agents who stayed behind.

"I'm Deuce Mora, and this is Steve Pace."

"We know," one of the agents said. They didn't seem to want to make introductions, either. So I moved on.

"Can you tell me what you're watching?" I asked.

"Nothing at the moment," one of them replied.

"Do you know when Emily disappeared?" Steve asked.

"If we did, we wouldn't tell you," the agent said.

"Do you know how she got out?"

"Same answer."

"Did she leave on her own, or was she forced?"

"Same answer."

I summed up, "So it wouldn't be worth our while to make nice with you in the hope we could become friends?"

"Not worth even two minutes of your time, or ours," he replied.

"Okay then," I said. "Got any good magazines?"

"Guns or girl stuff?" the other agent asked with a small smile. I let it pass.

I walked to the bay windows that overlooked the front and side yards. All was quiet, though I did notice substantial shrubbery under all the windows that showed wicked-looking thorns. No one could get through them without some serious puncture damage.

"I wouldn't want to try to get past these plants," I said.

"Then don't," one of the agents replied to my back.

It was hopeless.

I pulled a chair from its spot at the table, sat down, and shut up.

* * *

Colter reappeared a few minutes later, walked past the dining room without a word or a glance toward any of us, and banged out the front door. The older agent stayed behind. He paced in silence. I took a chance.

"How'd she get out?" I asked. I was surprised when I got an answer.

"The alarm she triggered was on the window," he said. "And since it's open, it's a pretty good bet she went out that way."

"If you've got the same landscaping outside her room that you've got here," I said, "she musta got cut up pretty bad."

"That's what the AD's gone to look for now, blood on the shrubbery."

"Why would she run away?" Steve asked.

The agent replied, somewhat curtly, "Not for us to speculate."

It was a good twenty minutes before Colter returned. He was trailed by two other people, a man and a woman, who were dressed in jumpsuits and carried large black crime scene supply kits. The man also carried something

that looked like a futuristic camera. They nodded to the other agents and
followed Colter back toward what had been Emily Goodsill's bedroom.

"What was the man carrying?" I asked more out of curiosity than snoop-
ing.

"A forensics supply kit and a Leica RTC 360."

"Am I supposed to know what a Leica whatchamacallit is? Sounds like a
camera."

"See," the older agent said, "you're not so dumb after all. It is a camera,
and it costs about $80,000. They take three dimensional, high-resolution
photos of a crime scene. Looking at the photos back in the lab is like being
right here. Every detail the eye can see in Emily's room, it will be able to see
in the lab. It's a real time-saver. It's amazing what they sometimes catch in the
lab that they didn't notice at a scene."

Colter came back, presumably leaving the lab people to their work. He
sat down at the dining room table.

"So tell me what happened," he said to the three agents, ignoring Steve
and me.

"The alarm system was triggered at 4:34 p.m.," the oldest agent said. "It's
not the first time it's happened. Emily has been miserable and lonesome. She
quit her job with the USDA and spent all her time reading. And she slept a
lot. Day and night. She liked to sleep with the window open. It triggers the
alarm every time. We've begged her not to do that, but she does it, anyway.
Says she's claustrophobic and has panic attacks if she tries to sleep with the
windows closed. So when we went down today and saw the window partially open and a form we believed to be Emily under the covers, we made
an assumption we shouldn't have made. We didn't realize she was gone until
Quinn went down to ask her what she wanted for dinner and discovered the
ruse."

"Old, old trick," Colter said. "A line of pillows under the covers fluffed
up to look like a body. I'm surprised you fell for it."

"I know," the lead agent said. "I'm not making excuses. If the window
had been open wider, with enough room for her to crawl out, I might have
found it suspicious. She usually doesn't open it more than maybe four inches.
She must have crawled out and found something to stand on so she could

raise herself up enough to reach back and close the window most of the way. There's an old plastic milk crate in the bushes she could have used. It probably wouldn't have happened if there were bars on the windows."

"Washington won't appropriate the funds for upgrades to safe houses," Colter said.

He scrubbed his eyes, perhaps in frustration, perhaps in exhaustion, perhaps in both. "You searched the neighborhood?" he asked.

The senior agent nodded. "Agent Marteen and I drove it three times. No sign of her. Except the blood on the bushes. The thorns seem to have torn her up pretty good. I called in four agents from the office to canvass the neighborhood on foot, out at least a dozen blocks in every direction. Maybe somebody saw something."

"Can we do anything to help?" Steve asked. "We don't have our cars here, but we could get them quick enough and get back."

"The best thing you two can do is stay out of the way," Colter said.

The senior agent's phone rang. He listened for maybe two minutes then said, "Keep after it." He hung up and looked at Colter.

"A shop keeper over on Hoyne saw a woman matching Emily's description," he said. "She was running, and her arms, legs, and face were bloodied. He said he was going to ask her if she needed help. But a black Tahoe pulled up and two men got out and put her in the vehicle. He said it appeared she didn't go willingly. They pulled away so fast he didn't have time to get a license plate."

Colter looked stricken. "She could be almost anywhere by now," he said. "You'd better hope to God she's alive now and still in that condition when we find her. She knows the truth about what's been going on in this city. Without Emily Goodsill, a lot of very bad people are going to get away with murder, extortion, and blackmail, not to mention election fraud and conspiracy. She's the only witness we have."

56

"It's all coming apart," the governor said, swallowing a slug of fine Scotch as if it came from a glass of water. He winced as the amber liquid scorched its way down his throat and through his esophagus. His eyes never strayed from their lock on Tony Toes's face. "The mayor just told us the woman has escaped from the FBI, and no one knows where she is. Who knows what she told the FBI while she was in their custody? Who knows what they plan to do? I don't know how I ever got mixed up in this, but I want out."

"The only way you'll get out is feet first," Tricoletto said, apparently not embarrassed by the cliché. "I wouldn't trust you for a cocaine heartbeat. When you stop doing what we tell you to do, that's when you stop living. Do I make myself clear?"

"Of course," Walston said. "But I don't want to spend the rest of my life in prison, and that's where I'll be if this situation crumbles."

"In the first place," Tricoletto told him, "the woman isn't on the loose, and she hasn't talked to anyone. My boys picked her up not thirty minutes after she got away from the feds. She's locked up where we can keep watch on her. And I seriously doubt she said anything to the FBI because she knows her family's lives are at stake."

"How did your people know where she was?"

"We know a lot of things," Tricoletto said. "And none of it's your business."

"What about the reporters?"

"We're gonna take care-a them first chance we get."

Tony Toes took a pull on his cigar and ashed it in a grooved silver dish on his small table. He took a sip from the glass beside his ashtray. He wasn't drinking alcohol this time. His glass was filled with club soda and fresh lime.

"More killing?" Walston asked, his dejected tone suggesting he already knew what the answer would be.

"I do what I have to do. I'll do it to the reporters, to the woman and her family, to meddlesome FBI agents, if need be. And if you don't stop driving me crazy with your constant questions and doubts, I'll do it to you, too."

What the older man didn't say was that all those plans, with the possible exception of the death of the man who sat next to him, were already in preparation. The governor was potentially too valuable to the family to waste, which is why the lives of the others became necessarily expendable. Walston had to be protected. Unless his jittery nerves became a detriment, he would remain alive.

But that outcome was increasingly in jeopardy.

* * *

Steve and I were sitting in the back seat of Ron Colter's work car, a black Chevy sedan, headed east back into the city as fast as traffic would allow. I wondered idly why Colter didn't use his blue flashing gumball and his siren. Mostly my thoughts were with Emily Goodsill, wherever she was. She had been coerced into cooperating with the thugs who framed the contractor, Frank Chapin. Emily understood why the Tricolettos wanted Chapin gone from the gubernatorial election. Refusing to do what was demanded of her would have gotten her killed along with her entire family. She lived in a world of lies and terror with no idea how to extricate herself from the conspiracy. I hoped there was something we could do to save her.

I would have preferred sitting in the front seat of Colter's car, but it was filled with electronic equipment and would have been a tight fit. Besides, Colter made it clear he wanted us in back. It made me feel like a criminal under transport. The two rear doors had been built without interior handles to open them—a common law enforcement alteration to prevent suspects from escaping. Steve and I weren't suspects, but we were trapped.

Perhaps it was the configuration of the car that caused my strong sense of unease. I kept wondering how I would save myself if somebody came driving by and sprayed us with an assault rifle. The rounds would penetrate the car's sheet metal as if it were soft butter and turn everyone inside into bloody mounds of Spam. Steve and I had no escape route.

The tension began to subside as we approached The Circle. The term described the perpetually under-construction confluence of Interstate 290, which we were traveling, and Interstate 90, the main north-south thoroughfare through the twenty-two-mile length of Chicago. It was a complex tangle of lanes and ramps that looked from the air like a snarl of last year's Christmas lights. I would feel even better once we got to the Loop, though assault rifles work as well on local streets as an interstate.

I was so deep in thought that it wasn't until I heard Steve yell, "Look out!" that I saw the monster semi veering across two lanes heading directly for us. Drivers in Chicago don't use their horns often, but a cacophony of blaring suddenly enveloped us, joined by the sick thunk of crunching sheet metal. The semi smacked a half dozen smaller vehicles. The damaged cars and trucks hit other cars and trucks. The semi never slowed or veered away. It simply pushed wreckage aside as the determined driver raced toward us.

Colter's vehicle was in the right lane because he had been preparing to exit to the local roads below us. The right shoulder was consumed by a massive concrete construction barrier. There was a long line of traffic in front of us. The semi roared in from the left. We had no route of escape.

The right side of the truck cab hit us first, directly next to Colter's door. I saw a spray of deep red and smelled the coppery odor of blood before I got knocked sideways by the devastating impact of the trailer. It hit my door a second after the cab hit Colter's. Glass shattered. I had a fleeting glance of open space beyond my door as it buckled inward. I heard the jagged metal rip through my seatbelt.

Our tires scraped sideways over the rough pavement. I heard one explode.

I got a momentary glimpse of Steve, turned away from me, staring agape at the concrete barrier coming up to meet us. I thought briefly that we would be sandwiched between the semi and the concrete, squashed like bugs on a windshield.

It was worse. We hit the concrete barrier so hard we went right through it. The impact blasted one of the barrier sections free, and it tumbled toward the roadway below. We followed it down.

I felt a sharp pain in my neck, and my vision pixilated.
I said a brief prayer for the people below us.
Then the world winked out.

57

I survived.

It was one of the few instances where the failure of a seat belt saved a life. There were long stretches of time when I wished it hadn't.

I suffered through the night and into the following morning before anybody would tell me how Ron Colter and Steve Pace were doing. I began to suspect after a few hours of medical obfuscation that the news was unthinkable and likely unbearable.

I became disconsolate bordering on hysterical. I screamed so hard at my doctors and thrashed so violently in the bed that I threatened to do additional damage to my fractured wrist and wrenched knee. All that prevented me from banging my head against the metal bed frame was a neck brace I wore for an injury the doctors assured me was a muscle strain and bruised nerves that would heal without permanent damage.

I didn't care about any of it. All I wanted to know was how my friends fared. No one would tell me. Not even Eric. Not even Jerry Alvarez. But I could read their faces.

It was Mark who finally broke the news. He had taken a redeye back from California after Eric Ryland called him about the smashup. He had seen video of the aftermath on CNN, but he hadn't known immediately that I was involved.

The concrete barrier section and Ron's car both landed—in a cruel irony— on top of a semi-trailer on the street below the interstate. The empty metal box caved in from the force of the twin impacts. Ron had died instantly when the truck cab hit him. The car's left front quarter was flattened, and he was crushed under the mashed frame and sheet metal. Steve died from blunt-force trauma to his head and a broken neck. His area of the car hit bottom first, hurling him through the side window head-first into a chunk of the concrete.

I tried to remember if he'd been wearing a seatbelt and couldn't. Apparently, the side-impact air bags didn't help him, or at least not enough.

Thankfully, no one rammed by the semi was seriously hurt as it plowed through interstate traffic hell-bent to head-butt us into oblivion.

"It wasn't a survivable accident," Mark told me. "You were spared because you got thrown into Steve's body. It cushioned you. As he was dying, he saved you."

"Twice," I said in a voice I couldn't raise much above a whisper. My throat was raw from screaming and crying, and the tears threatened again. "He saved me twice. He's the one who pulled me out of the Explorer. You know what makes this really sad, Mark? He wanted to meet me because he'd been carrying around more than twenty-five years of guilt over the death of an innocent man he investigated for a horrible crime. Steve felt that the pressure he put on the man created the stress that killed him. He never got over it. He came to Chicago to work on the story of Carl's murder. He also wanted to talk to me about how I coped with the fact that I had killed another human being." I felt my eyes begin to sting again. "I couldn't help him. I didn't know what to say. He saved my life twice, and I didn't know how to make his life more bearable. I was never able to help him." I was choking up. "How am I going to live with that?"

Mark leaned over my bed and hugged me as gently as he could to avoid causing pain in my battered body. He kissed me just below the jaw line.

"We'll get through it together," he said. "I promise you. In the meantime, let yourself grieve. I've called Simon Richey and told him you might need to talk to him again."

I was still groggy, and it took me a second to remember the shrink I'd seen a dozen times after my experience in causing a man's death. The incident had pushed me into a black funk, much as Steve's had punished him so many years ago. Mark encouraged me to see Richey, who was under contract with the city to treat first responders for post-traumatic stress syndrome. I resisted, but Mark persisted. In the end I think Richey helped me. This time, I didn't know if I would ever regain a sense of equilibrium or normalcy.

I hoped, wherever he was, that Steve Pace had found peace at last.

<u>58</u>

I left the hospital the next day and went right to the office. I saw pain in my colleagues' faces and sorrow in their voices as they commiserated with me.

My body looked like a crazy quilt of blue-black islands on a cream-colored ocean. I had a black eye and a bruised cheek. A long, heavy plaster cast encased my wrist, which I had to keep raised. Sitting or lying down I could accomplish that with pillows. While standing up I had to use a sling that kept my forearm nearly vertical. A brace encased my neck. The doctors told me I probably wouldn't be able to go from the wrist cast to a brace in six weeks. I could lose the neck brace in maybe ten days. At that, I was lucky. I had avoided another concussion. The human brain can't stand too many of those before it begins to fold in on itself permanently.

Beneath my clothes, bruises splotched my chest, back, and legs. Fortunately, no one in the newsroom asked me to undress.

Eric Ryland was encouraging but couldn't tell me much more than Mark had.

"The doctors can only speculate on how you came away alive and without much more serious injuries," he said. "They think maybe after your seat belt ripped you slid across and grabbed onto Steve. His body cushioned your fall—your landing, more accurately—and kept you from pinballing around the car. Whatever the explanation, I'm very thankful that you're okay. And, oh, by the way, you're off the story. This time I refuse to cave in to your resistance. Security obviously isn't enough to protect you. We're going to let law enforcement work it without you and let it play out however the facts fall.

It would be a smart move if you take a couple of weeks' vacation, way out of town. Hawaii, maybe."

"I'm not on the story, Eric," I reminded him. "I haven't had or shared a byline with anyone on any news story."

"Let's not split hairs," he said. "I'm done buying that nonsense. I don't want you anywhere near the story or anyone connected to the story again."

"There aren't that many left alive," I said as tears began their slide down my face.

There was no use arguing with him. His mind was made up, and I was too emotionally exhausted to make the effort. I tried to do some work on a column. But I couldn't type with one hand, and the voice-recognition software in my computer was more erratic than the effort was worth. So I left the office with the intent to go back to Mark's condo and lie down for the rest of the day. When I got to the lobby, I was surprised to find Nancy Cribben, Carl's widow, waiting for me.

We exchanged light hugs.

"I'd like to say you're looking well, Deuce, but you aren't," she said candidly.

I smiled. "If you'd said I look good I'd have known you were lying. How are you?"

"Can we go somewhere and talk, over coffee or a glass of wine, or something? Can you have a glass of wine, or are you on meds that aren't compatible?"

"I only take a couple of Tylenol before I go to bed. Wine's not a problem."

"Then let's drive up to the Wyndham Grand. It should be quiet at this hour."

We said almost nothing until we had found a place to sit where we had a wonderful view of the east end of the Chicago River and Lake Michigan beyond.

"How are you holding up?" I asked Nancy, not really wanting to get to the part of the conversation that would deal with me.

"Incredibly sad most of the time," she said. "Lost, occasionally. Lonely. Disbelieving. Empty. Mostly, I'm angry. Furious. I'm furious with the people who killed Carl, and God help me, sometimes I'm even angry with Carl for dying. How unfair is that?"

"How are you dealing?" I asked, since much of what Nancy described fit me, too.

"I got a call a few days after Carl died from your significant other," she said. I must have looked shocked.

"I was surprised, too," Nancy said. "He gave me the name of a psychologist who works with traumatized first responders to help them with PTSD. He urged me to call him. He'd apparently notified the man already that he might hear from me."

"Simon Richey?" I asked. "Small world." I didn't explain. Nancy didn't ask me to. "Did you see him, or am I prying?"

"Not at all," Nancy said. "I brought it up. I didn't want to see him, no, but my kids insisted. When he started in with the God stuff it put me off. Carl had all the religion in the family, and I don't even believe in God— especially not right now. When I mentioned that to Dr. Richey, he adjusted his approach to better fit me. When I finally got past my initial resistance, his therapy protocol began to make sense. I appreciated that he was brutally candid. He said there was no way to stop the pain or the grief. As time passes there's more distance between attacks, but they always come back eventually. You have to embrace them, let yourself cry, scream, curl up in the fetal position with the covers over your head. And don't ever feel that you're acting weak. It's not healthy to keep it in. So I don't, and that alone makes me feel better."

Our drinks came, a chardonnay for Nancy, a pinot noir for me. I looked at Nancy over the rim of my glass, wondering if she was telling me about her therapy or trying to practice Simon Richey's therapy on me. I decided to let the conversation play out.

"Anyway," she continued, "I know how devastated you were by Carl's murder and the lengths you traveled to prove it wasn't suicide. I'll always be grateful for that. And now you have the deaths of two more friends to deal with. I hope you can find someone to help you the way Simon Richey helped me. Have you heard of him?"

I decided there was no sense holding back.

"I actually saw him at Mark's behest for a while," I said and told her the whole story. "I still haven't come to terms with taking a life, but Simon did help. I don't know if his magic will work this time, though. I feel as if all my positive emotions have died and been replaced by total fury. I'm always on edge, lashing out at everybody, even Mark. Everywhere I look I see crime and unspeakable corruption, and nobody seems to want or know how to do anything about it. I could expose bad acts by bad actors until hell freezes over, and it wouldn't do any good. In the end, the bad guys always win. Everything seems so hopeless."

I sagged back in my chair and took a deep breath.

"Three good men," I said. "Two of them dear friends and the third on the same track. And what did they die for? The corrupt politicians are still in office. Two innocent men could be on their way to prison. And the mob leaders likely have replaced their lost hitmen already. Life will go on unchanged. It would be one thing if all this left the world a better place. But no one can make that claim with even a morsel of credibility. No one."

We tried to make happier talk as we drank our wine. It didn't work for either of us. So Nancy drove me back to the office where my car was parked.

"Thank you for this," I said. "Given your own situation, it means even more to me."

She slipped her hand onto mine and squeezed gently. "If you don't remember anything else, remember this. Grief never ends. But it changes. It's a passage, not a place to stay. Grief is not a sign of weakness, nor a lack of faith. It's the price of love."

I felt my breath catch. I had to get out of the car and get some air.

I smiled at her and walked toward the garage where my SUV was parked.

Had I known what was waiting for me at home, I might have gone elsewhere.

59

For more than a year I had made it a habit to alter the final segment of my drive home to make me more unpredictable, even if I was only returning from a trip to the grocery store. The obsession began after I was assaulted in my yard as I walked from my garage to the back door of my house. My sadness deepened when I remembered that Ron Colter played a big role that night in saving my life.

The alley that accessed my garage ran maybe a tenth of a mile from Oakley Avenue on the east to Western Avenue on the west and was cut by several cross streets. I tried to vary my points of entry to the alley each time. But whatever entry point I chose, I always drove slowly by the front of my house first, looking for trouble that might be lurking in the landscaping or on the front porch. I had installed floodlights that came on at dusk and stayed on all night. So did the lights behind the house that illuminated the back yard and the alley. My neighbors didn't mind. The illumination crossing our property lines gave them an added measure of security, too.

On this particular night the lights hadn't come on yet. Since we'd switched to Daylight Savings Time, the natural light remained sufficient longer. Still, in the gloom that was moving in as I did my drive-by, I saw the figure of a man sitting on my front porch.

At first, I thought it might be Mark. But I was only stopping at my house long enough to pick up a few things, and then I planned to return to his condo. I didn't want to be home alone until the killings were resolved. So I wasn't sure why Mark would be waiting here for me. Besides, he wouldn't be sitting out in the chill. He had a key. My concern notched up when I didn't see his truck on the street.

I pulled over next to the vehicles parked at the curb and thumbed my window down.

"Who's there?" I yelled.

I saw the man's head turn toward me.

"If you're askin' whether I'm friend or foe, Ms. Mora, the answer is friend."

I didn't recognize the voice and said so.

"It's John Fasso," he called back. "I'm alone."

I was stunned. The city alderman who was the prime suspect in a mob-connected murder was sitting on my front porch identifying himself as a friend. Really?

"Stay right there," I told him. "I'll be out in a minute."

As I drove around to the garage, I called Mark and told him what was happening. He first suggested that I call the police. I told him there didn't seem to be a need for that, but if he could swing by I would feel a little better having company. He said he'd be there as fast as he could drive and to keep Fasso outside until he got there.

Fasso was still sitting on the porch, waiting for me, when I came out the front door.

* * *

He didn't offer to shake hands, nor did he stand up when I appeared. There were two Adirondack rocking chairs on the porch. He had one. I took the other, lowering my aching body slowly. I focused on his eyes. The muscles around them appeared relaxed. He appeared relaxed. He didn't seem threatening.

I said, "It probably won't shock you when I say I'm surprised to find you here."

He smiled. It seemed genuine. "No, not at all." His eyes examined my face and my neck brace, then dropped to the hard cast on my wrist and then to the wrap supporting my knee. "You got pretty beat up. I'm sorry to hear about Ron Colter an' the other reporter. He was from Washington, right? What was his interest in this story?"

"It's not my place to tell you," I said sounding snappish. I felt snappish. It was becoming chronic. "Why are you sitting on my porch?"

"Cause you haven't invited me inside?" he said with a light laugh. Then he put up a hand. "A joke," he added. "I presume we're waitin' on the police. You probly called them while you were parkin'. I don't blame you."

"I didn't call the police," I said. "I called my partner, who's an arson investigator and usually travels with a weapon. I'm a little edgy right now."

"So I noticed," Fasso said.

He leaned forward and settled his elbows into his knees. His hands fell loose between them. He had a full head of dark hair going a little gray at the temples but full and thick at the crown where male-pattern baldness usually sets in. His face, like most everyone else's in Chicago at the end of a long winter, was devoid of any tan but did have a tinge of the olive complexions common among people of Mediterranean heritage.

"I'm sorry," he said. "I really am. I didn't call before I came 'cause I was afraid you'd tell me to stay away. I'm here to help."

"With what?" I asked.

"Resolving this mess before we have a full-on mob war on the streets. It hasn't even been 100 years since the last one."

I waited for him to explain how he planned to do that.

"Look," he said, "the reporter from Washington tried to reach out to me through my office. He left a message that he thought I might be innocent and wanted to talk to me. Normally, I wudda made an up or down decision on my own. But given that I'd never laid eyes on the guy, hadn't even heard of him, I consulted my attorney. She hated the idea of me talkin' to anybody in the media. She wouldn't like knowin' I'm here now."

"Are you here to give me the interview that Steve Pace asked for?"

"In a way, yeah, I guess I am. If he thought I might be innocent, maybe you do, too."

"Actually," I said, shifting to a more comfortable position in my chair, "I wasn't convinced one way or the other. The evidence against you is pretty damning."

"And circumstantial."

"That, too," I said. "But that's all it has to be."

"Reasonable doubt," he said. "My car was stolen. The gun was in the car. Whoever took the car took the gun."

"Which could have been you. You could have set up the whole thing. Yours were the only prints on the gun."

"So the shooter wore latex gloves." He started to stand up, saw the surprise on my face, and sat down again. "You wanna hear my story or not?"

A voice came from behind me. "I do."

The voice made me jump, though I knew immediately who it belonged to. Mark was standing behind the screen door. He opened it and walked out and introduced himself.

I saw the bulge under his jacket at his waist. I knew he'd brought his Glock.

Again, Fasso started to stand, as if to offer Mark his seat. Mark put up his hand.

"I'm fine," he said, and took a position against the porch railing, giving him a tactical advantage if Fasso presented a threat.

"May I start from the beginning?" Fasso asked. "I'll try to be brief as possible."

"May I record this?" I asked.

He nodded, and I took another of my little digital voice recorders from my metro bag, laid it on the big flat arm of the Adirondack rocker pointed at Fasso, and turned it on.

This is the story he told us:

John Fasso had been born in Pilsen, my neighborhood, which is also known as The Heart of Italy. Years earlier, the center of Chicago's Italian world had begun to shift north to Taylor Street, an area now known as Little Italy. As clearly as he could remember, his family moved up there when he was four. He met Jimmy Tricoletto later, when they got into the kind of schoolyard altercation common to six-year-old boys—a lot of pushing and slapping, a couple of scratches, minor bloody noses, and crying. After a reprimand from the head nun, Jimmy and John morphed into best friends.

"I got no recollection how that evolved," he said. "We became inseparable, except I was never allowed to go to his house to play. It wasn't my parents' choice. It was an iron-clad rule put down by Jimmy's father. To this day I don't think I've met Tony Toes more than a half dozen times, and I been friends with Jimmy more than forty years."

There were some troubles during their teen years. A little shoplifting, a few lunch-money shakedowns, a joyride that ended quietly, some pot smoking. What you'd expect from kids left too often to their own devices.

"I was in high school when I first found out about the business Jimmy's family ran," Fasso said. "It was years 'til Jimmy and I talked about it. It wasn't the sort of thing you discussed back in the day, not unless you wanted a put-down beatin.' The first time Jimmy mentioned it openly to me we were juniors in high school. He recruited me for his crew."

Mark interrupted. "He had a crew at the age of seventeen? Isn't that a little young, even for the boss's son?"

"He was a member of a crew, not the top guy," Fasso corrected. "A capo in training."

I asked, "What did he want you to do?"

"Help him stand lookout while two-a the older guys killed a snitch. They were gonna walk up behind him inna a bar in another neighborhood an' put two in his head. Jimmy was sposed to stand at the front door and look out for cops. The shooters thought maybe the bartender had one-a those panic buttons you push that triggers a call to the police. They wanted some warning if the cops showed up without sirens or lights. Jimmy asked me to stand with him."

"Did you?" I asked.

"I was tempted. Sounded exciting, an' if anything in my life needed excitement, it was my junior year in high school. But in the end, I was too scared. I kept thinkin' about cops on the sidewalk, blazin', and the shooters firing back, and me an' Jimmy caught in the crossfire. So I said no."

Fasso's rejection of Jimmy put a strain on their friendship, but both got over it.

I asked, "Just out of curiosity, did Jimmy do it?"

Fasso shook his head. "I don't know. We never talked about it again. I suspect he did. Jimmy wanted to be a "made guy" as soon as he could. He used to talk about it alla time."

Mark asked, "Did he ever tell you he killed anybody?"

"Not that I recall," Fasso said. "And I think I'd remember. Jimmy compartmentalized his life. He kept the business side separate from our friendship, especially after I went off to college and law school and got hired as a prosecutor in the state's attorney's office. You don't sit down with an assistant state's attorney, even if he is a long-time best friend, and confess to a string of felonies that might or might not include murder. After I became a city councilman, if the family wanted anything from me, the message was always carried by Anthony Junior, Jimmy's older brother—the godfather in waiting."

I said, "What sorts of things did Tony Junior ask for?"

"Nothin' huge," he replied. "Nothin' criminal. Mostly the favors had to do with a vote on one city code or another. The things I remember were pretty small stuff. I do know I never cast a vote I didn't believe in, and I'd-a had to think real hard on a vote the Tricolettos came out and asked me for. That isn't me. Over the years, as I said, me and Jimmy's friendship rarely touched on business, his or mine. An' lately, we hadn't been seein' that much of each other."

Fasso's eyes actually teared up.

"I believed in Jimmy. I let myself think he was different from his brother and his father. I didn't believe he would let himself sink into their cesspool."

He sighed and added, "Least not 'til this thing came along."

<u>60</u>

It felt as if something big was coming. I checked my recorder. It was chugging along, the battery indicator reading full.

"What," I asked, "is 'this thing'?"

Fasso eyed the little recorder as if realizing it held the potential for getting him into deeper trouble. But then he seemed to remember that telling the truth might also get him out of the trouble in which he was already embroiled. It doesn't get much worse than a charge of premeditated murder.

"The first time Jimmy called and asked to see me was a couple months before the election," he said. "The date's on my calendar. I can find it if it's important. I remember he sounded nervous. Said he had to talk to me in secret, where he could be sure nobody but me and him would know what was said. I assured him my private law office wasn't bugged. I told him to come over after hours so there'd be nobody there but the two of us."

Jimmy showed up, Fasso recalled, with a large pizza from Phil's in Bridgeport.

"Doesn't get any better than that, and I was starving," he said. I sympathized. Phil's was one of my favorites. "He brought a six-pack, too. We talked until two in the morning."

That was the night, Fasso said, that Jimmy Tricoletto told him of his father's and older brother's plan to manipulate the outcome of the gubernatorial election by implicating the frontrunner, Frank Chapin, in a series of building code violations. They would steal the paperwork in Chapin's office that proved he ordered the quality materials he billed his clients for, including the city and the feds. Those legitimate invoices would be replaced with invoices for the substandard material delivered to his building sites without his knowledge. So, in addition to code violations, Chapin would appear guilty of a series of major frauds. Their planned sabotage, Fasso said, would lead to several of Chapin's most important projects being condemned. One building, the federal project, would be rigged for a partial collapse. If anyone was injured or killed, Chapin also would be charged with murder or manslaughter and face a string of personal injury lawsuits. All in all, it would kill his campaign and his business and ruin him financially.

Chapin's exit from the race would lead to Tyler Walston's election as governor.

It was much the same story I heard from Matteo Messina, though I didn't mention that to Fasso. Instead, I expressed disbelief at the audacity of the plan.

I said, "Those are extraordinary lengths to go to fix an election. I mean, killing innocent people? Workers? People walking along the street? Come on. What did you tell Jimmy? Did you even try to talk him out of it?"

"I did," Fasso said. "But he said the paperwork in Chapin's office was already being exchanged by a woman who worked there."

"Emily," I said.

Fasso looked surprised at my mention of the name.

"I think that was her name, yes. She was from some place in Iowa. Tony's crew had found her family's home, and she was told her mother and children would be killed if she didn't cooperate and take a job as a clerk in Chapin's office. Once she settled in there, she would be expected to do what Tricoletto Junior told her."

Mark glanced at me and frowned. "I thought she worked for the USDA," he said.

"She did," Fasso said. "The job with Chapin was part-time. When Junior got her the job, she was looking for a way to earn extra money to take home to Iowa. She was in her USDA office until after ten the night the crew took Carl Cribben up there to kill him. She had to make up the time she spent in Chapin's office durin' the day. I also suspect she put the extra locks on her doors because she was there late so many nights, and she didn't want Anthony Junior or his crew bustin' in on her when she was alone. From what Jimmy told me, they terrorized her family. They'd go to Iowa and break into her house down there and move things around, so her mother would know someone had been inside. She begged them to stop. She told them her mother was nearing a nervous collapse. She agreed to cooperate."

Then he laughed in a rueful way. "Weird thing. Jimmy said Junior was sweet on Emily. His first wife, Maria, died in a skiin' accident six or seven years ago. Jimmy said Junior was real lonesome and was falling for Emily. Trouble was, she didn't show any signs of returning the feelings."

"And that surprised you?" I asked in disbelief. "He ordered Emily around, threatened her, terrorized her family. I don't know a whole lot of women who'd respond positively to Junior's courting ritual."

I had to get up and move a little. I was stiffening up.

"Why did Jimmy tell you all this? You weren't involved. Were you?"

"Not then. Not at all. Never. I didn't have a hint what was goin' on. I asked Jimmy why he was comin' clean to me. He said his family had concerns that I knew too much from all the years Jimmy and I were friends. I think they were afraid I'd flip on them, too."

I asked, "Had you ever talked to the feds about them?"

"No. It never occurred to me that I knew anything that important. And what I knew I couldn't prove. It was just shit Jimmy told me. I didn't even know if any of it was true."

"Then what," Mark asked, "made them suspicious now?"

"I don't think they were suspicious so much as they wanted to put me in a box."

"Like how?" Mark asked.

"I'm on the mayor's select committee on crime. Carl Cribben used to give us regular briefings on the progress of his congressional investigation, none of which did I ever pass on to any Tricoletto family members, even though Junior asked. My loyalty was to the city and the county, not to the family. But somebody talked, somebody who was in the meetings. The fact that it wasn't me made Tony Toes worry that maybe I wasn't so loyal to my old friends. He worried about what I might tell Cribben. So they came up with this plan. If they let me in on the truth about the murders and the whole Chapin frame, it made me an accessory after the fact to all the crimes. My only way out would be to tell the feds. But then me and my family would get killed. No matter which way I turned I was toast. My only choice was to sit quiet and hope the feds didn't find out what I knew. Same sort of set-up they used on Emily. It worked."

Mark asked, "Did Jimmy tell you specifically that the family was setting you up?"

"Didn't have to," Fasso said. "I know Jimmy well enough to understand him."

"Do you know," I asked, "who made up the phony supply orders and rigged the building to collapse? Whose plan was it? Who carried it out?"

"I honestly don't know. One or more friends of the family in the trades, I'd guess. But I don't have a name or even a guess."

"Who were the actual killers?" Mark asked. "Who's been injecting people with sux and .22 slugs?"

Fasso averted his eyes and shook his head. He wasn't going to tell us.

I asked, "How did they get their hands on the succinylcholine, the sux? You can't walk into Wal-Mart and buy that stuff."

"I can't tell you that, either."

"Can't, or won't?"

"Both, actually. I don't have first-hand knowledge and wouldn't tell you if I did. I meant it when I said I'm terrified of those guys. But you're a smart lady. You should be able to figure it out. Who had the most to gain?"

"Tony Toes and Anthony Junior," Mark said. "They donated heavily to city council candidates who came out against the anti-crime initiatives the mayor's been pressing for."

"But the Tricoletto's have no obvious source for the sux," I said. "No doctors or other medical personnel in their family tree that I could find."

Fasso just stared at me. I got his message.

"So what does Tyler Walston, medical doctor, owe the Tricolettos? What did the improbable new governor of Illinois offer in return for an election victory? An endless supply of sux so the family could kill its enemies? What did he sell his soul for?"

Fasso looked away in silence.

"Come on, John," I insisted. "You came to see me. Tell me what Walston wanted."

"Money and power," Fasso replied. "What does anybody sell their souls for?"

61

"I'm not tracking this," I said. "Walston's a very successful surgeon. He already has money's ancestors. He doesn't need to practice medicine any more. And if he's not performing surgeries, how does he get away with prowling a hospital stealing sux?"

"The hospital in Oak Park?" Fasso asked. I nodded. "He still does surgeries there if the clients are wealthy enough to buy him. Maybe it's his cover. Maybe he's stockpiling money to make a run for president someday. I hear that's what he wants. He'll need a lot of connections to make that happen, and they don't all have to be above board. It's happened before. The Kennedys had major ties to the mob in Chicago. They were hooked into the Giancanas through Frank Sinatra during the 1960 elections."

"That was like sixty years ago," Mark said.

"Some things change," Fasso said. "Some don't."

He turned and glanced around at the street, apparently seeing nothing suspicious.

"I could get killed for telling you this stuff," he said. "I'm not kidding. I think Jimmy'd kill me to protect his family. If not him, then Anthony Junior, for sure. With the blessing of the father. These are not nice people."

"And at the risk of repeating myself," I replied, "you came to me, Alderman. I won't settle for half the story."

"An' who's gonna protect me?"

"I'll take you to the assistant U.S. attorney who's working all these cases. You'll tell him your story. If he believes you, he'll be able to arrange federal protection for you and your family, for the rest of your lives, if necessary."

"I hate the idea of witness protection."

"Look, you've got decisions to make here, and I don't have all night. I'm exhausted, and I hurt. I need to go to bed. So make up your mind. Tell me everything or leave now."

I was taking a risk. If he opted to leave, I might never learn the whole truth. My heart dropped when he stood up. But I had misinterpreted his intent. He moved to the porch railing and stood beside Mark, his back to the street, perhaps so no one driving by would recognize him. My porch and yard lights had all come on. Fasso was well-known in Chicago, and his council district was only a few blocks north of my house. A lot of people from Little Italy came to Oakley Street to eat cooking from the old country. That Fasso might be recognized from a passing car wasn't an impossibility.

"Years ago," Fasso said, "when Tyler Walston was starting out in his medical practice, he made a horrible mistake during a relatively simple procedure, and the patient died. I never knew the details, but Jimmy told me years later the state medical board was leaning toward jerkin' his ticket to practice. I don't know who got paid off, but Walston's hearing disappeared from the board's agenda. The family of the dead person filed a wrongful death suit, but that disappeared, too. Walston kept his practice and his insurance. Old man Tricoletto arranged the payoffs, and Walston's been in his pocket ever since."

"Why would Tricoletto do that?" Mark asked.

"'Cause years ago the doc saved Tony Toes' little nephew, his sister Gisella's son. Not Mike d'Amato, the guy who drove for me. It was his baby brother. I don't remember his name. The boy fell off a bluff over Lake Michigan up around Wilmette, or Winnetka, or somewhere and was floatin' in the water unconscious and drowning. Walston jumped off the bluff after him, pulled him out, and did CPR until the kid started breathin' again. Tony Toes wound up payin' off all Walston's medical school bills, underwriting the cost of opening his practice and, like I said, made some serious professional and financial troubles go away. When Tony Toes told Walston he'd help him become governor if he'd battle the new mayor of Chicago over her crime package, I guess Walston thought he had no option but to say yes. Tony Toes could-a ruined him if he didn't cooperate. That's how the mob does business. Extortion-'r'-Us."

I blew out a deep breath. "I'm going to need a wall mural to keep all this straight."

Mark asked me, "How are you going to prove the alderman's allegations?"

"Good question," I said. "No offense, Mr. Fasso, but what you've told us is mostly hearsay. You weren't a witness to most of it. I don't think it will be admissible in court, even from the vice mayor of Chicago."

"Yeah," Fasso said. "I thought of that even before my talk with Jimmy." He shifted uneasily. "I told Jimmy my office wasn't bugged, and technically that was true. Nobody ever sneaked in and planted listening devices under the furniture. But I have a system on my phone that will record my land-line conversations as well as any face-to-face conversations in the room. I had it running that night. All night."

"Holy crap," Mark said.

I wasn't so enthusiastic. "Did Jimmy agree to the recording?" I asked.

"No. He didn't know about it."

"For both reasons, it might not be admissible, either."

We all fell silent. Then I said, "Not all is lost yet. Emily Goodsill is a first-hand witness. If she can substantiate enough of what's on this recording we could be good to go. We're going to have to find her and hope she's still alive when we do." I turned back to Fasso. "Do you have any idea where the family might stash her?"

"If I hadda guess, I'd say she's already dead," he replied. "They don't like leavin' loose ends that could trip 'em up."

Ironically, it was at that point that Fasso asked for some water, just as Emily had when she was pouring out her story to Ron Colter and me in my living room. Mark went in and returned with a bottle from the refrigerator. Fasso cracked it open and drank half.

"When we were kids," he said, "Jimmy told me once they had a secret spot in the lake where they dumped dead bodies. Said it was real deep so nobody'd find it, an' the bodies had weights on 'em so they wouldn't pop to the surface when they got bloated with gas. I believed him back then. Now I think he might-a been gaslightin' me. He wasn't involved in family business, not at that age. So he might-a been tryin' to impress me and scare the crap outta me at the same time. We were kids, an' kids do that stuff."

"But if it's true," Mark said, "and if they've killed Emily, they could have dumped her and your missing driver at the same time in the same place."

"Michael d'Amato, yeah," Fasso said. "Man, I hope that's not true."

"So do I," I said. "But I have a bad feeling about this."

62

I was in Jerry Alvarez's office first thing the next morning. I had called him after Mark left with Fasso to drive the alderman to the "L". The nearest train stop was a pink line station eight or nine long blocks north up Western Avenue, and Mark wanted to be sure Fasso got there safe.

I didn't want to go into any details with Jerry over an unencrypted cell phone—that's how paranoid I was getting—so I just told him how urgent I considered it that we meet face-to-face as quickly as possible. I told him I had information that could only be defined as explosive. Jerry asked me if he should include Maeve MacAuliffe, who had been named the acting special agent in charge of the Chicago Division of the FBI, succeeding Ron Colter. I didn't know her and told Jerry so.

"She's good," the assistant U.S. attorney told me. "I've known her since she got here in 2011. Very professional and personable. She's an admirer of yours."

I thought about it for a moment. If Jerry vouched for her, I assumed I could trust her.

"Sure, fine," I said. "What time?"

* * *

As I drove with Mark back to his condo, I gave serious thought to calling my editor.

I was about to explicitly ignore his direct order to stay as far away as possible from anything related, even distantly, to the city's mob-related murder

301

epidemic. There was nothing distant about John Fasso's experience. It went right to the core of the story. At least my confession could wait until after I delivered Fasso to Jerry and the FBI.

I shared my thoughts with Mark.

"Eric's going to soil his pants," Mark said. "He told me he was making arrangements to get you a new protection team today unless I could convince you to take a vacation for a while, a long way from Chicago."

"Not right now you can't," I said. "Maybe when this is over. I can't turn my back on all the killing now."

Mark reached over his console and wrapped my left hand in his right. He squeezed gently and said nothing. I snapped.

"What?" I demanded. "You trying to mollycoddle me: Let's fly off to paradise and leave this ugly world behind? That's beneath you, Mark." I jerked my hand away.

He stomped on the brake and rolled to the curb. He undid his seatbelt and turned to face me. The look on his face was neutral, but his eyes flashed.

"The hell, Deuce?" he said. "I was trying to be supportive, trying to send you a signal that I'll be with you no matter what you decide. Will you please stop biting my head off every time you turn around? If you don't, you'll turn around one day, and I won't be there."

There it was, a fulsome warning that I was wrecking the best thing I'd ever had.

And Mark was right.

I couldn't let that happen. I had to make an appointment to start seeing Simon Richey again for some counseling and therapy first chance I got.

* * *

I walked into Jerry's office the next morning on the stroke of 10 a.m.

There was a striking woman sitting in Jerry's outer office. I figured it was either his girlfriend, whom I'd yet to meet, or Maeve MacAuliffe. The woman stood and held out her hand, glanced at my cast encrusted right wrist and dropped her arm. "Sorry," she said. Then she added, "I'm Maeve MacAuliffe." Her brown eyes sparkled and her dark hair bounced as she walked across the room. She was almost as tall as me. "I'm so sorry for what you've been through. How are you feeling?"

"Sore," I said. "It will pass. My condolences on Ron Colter's death. He was a man the Bureau should be proud of. We didn't get off on the best of terms, but over time we came to respect, and even like, one another. Chicago will miss him. I'll miss him."

"Thank you," she said and changed the subject. "Jerry says you have some information that you described as explosive. I'm eager to hear it."

She agreed to wait until we were in Jerry's office, so I only had to tell the story once. That location change occurred about thirty seconds later.

We were settled at the conference table tucked into a corner of Jerry's space with coffee from the Nespresso machine Jerry had given himself as a gift when he was promoted. It wasn't as good as the espresso pulled from Mark's more professional Breville model that ground its own fresh beans, but it was good and strong and hot.

I put my little digital voice recorder on the table. I checked it the night before to be certain it had worked properly. Satisfied that it had, I topped off the battery charge to prepare it, and me, for this meeting.

"I'm not going to tell you yet who the informant is," I said. "The two people asking questions are me, of course, and Mark Hearst, an arson investigator for the state."

MacAuliffe smiled. "And your partner," she said.

"Yes," I said. "He was there because when I found the informant on my front porch last night, I wasn't sure of his intentions. So I asked Mark to come by. He's generally armed, and he's quite proficient with his weapon."

"Not a problem," MacAuliffe said. "I know him by reputation."

I pushed the play button. Both of my companions leaned forward to listen. They didn't need to. The recording was quite clear.

A minute in Jerry held up his hand, and I hit pause.

"Just so you know," he said, "I recognize the informant's voice. But I won't tell Maeve yet. I'd like her to listen to the whole thing without his identity prejudicing her reaction."

MacAuliffe nodded.

I hit play again. They both took notes at various points in the playback, but their only overt reactions came when Fasso told the story of the frame worked on Frank Chapin, and again when he recounted the long, slow corruption of Tyler Walston.

When the recording ended, Jerry said, "We're going to need that recorder."

I felt my shoulders tense and sat back in my chair to try to relax them. Instinctively, I placed my hand over the small recorder and dragged it back toward me.

"Let me tell you about the arrangement I had with Ron Colter," I said. "I gave him my word, as did Steve Pace, that whatever we learned we would share with him and not publish. There was a condition. At such time as publication would not impede his investigation, we would get first crack at the story. Under those same conditions, I would be willing to play the recording again and let you use your own equipment to pick it up. But you cannot have my original. That is not negotiable."

"I could arrest you as a material witness," MacAuliffe said.

I turned to Jerry. "Tell her how that worked out for Ron when he tried it."

"I already know," she said.

* * *

In the end, we did things the way I wanted them done. And I disclosed to them, under pledges of confidentiality, who the informant was.

Jerry nodded. MacAuliffe said, "Really? Interesting."

"I hate to listen and run," MacAuliffe said peering at her cell phone, "but I just got a text I have to attend to. We have a line on where Emily Goodsill might be. A police patrolman who pays attention to BOLO alerts spotted a woman fitting her description coming out of a building in Bridgeport, near the White Sox stadium, flanked by two tough-looking thugs. They took her to a little restaurant about a block away. The cop noticed her at first because she looked scared, and he didn't like the looks of the two guys with her. He checked the BOLO sheet and confirmed it was Emily. There's a SWAT team ready to converge on the area. They're hidden in several places nearby. They don't want to storm the restaurant and risk bystanders. They're going to move on the building where Emily's being kept as soon as she's returned there."

"What if they don't take her back there?" I asked.

"Then plans will shift accordingly," MacAuliffe said. "There's always a Plan B."

"Wouldn't it be safer to take them on the street, where it'd be two bad guys against all you good guys?" I asked.

"Not with so many pedestrians and traffic around," she said. "Too much danger to innocent bystanders if there's shooting. On the other hand, that's probably Plan B."

She pushed her chair back, and so did I.

"Where are you going?" she asked.

I said, "With you, and don't even try to argue. Please."

"Me, too," Jerry said. "It's my case."

* * *

We sat in the back of MacAuliffe's SUV, which brought back terrifying images of the day Ron and Steve were killed. Same absence of door handles. Same cop-car smell. MacAuliffe used her lights and siren until she was three blocks from the target building then killed both and approached in silence.

"It's that yellow brick house," she said. "Second from the corner. I'm going to walk back a block and talk to the SWAT commander. The two of you stay here. I can't do my job and be responsible for you at the same time."

She cracked all the windows to give us some fresh air, got out, slammed her door, and locked the car. She forgot to close and lock the wire door in the plexiglass barrier between the back seat and the front.

Jerry and I looked at one another. I said, "I think I can get the top half of me through the opening far enough to reach the front passenger door and open it. But how do we get the rest of our bodies past the barrier to get out of the car?"

Jerry undid his seatbelt and looked behind my head.

"All we have to do is release the seats and pull them down, then crawl into the cargo compartment. After that, all we have to figure out is how to open the back hatch."

"There should be an emergency release back there," I said. "It's probably behind a latched door to prevent kids from releasing it by accident. How hard can it be to find?"

We contorted our bodies in ways I never would have dreamed possible in order to get out of our own way and make room to lower the two sections of the back seat. My battered parts let their objections be known. I slipped my right arm out of its sling to improve my balance, but I kept my encased wrist out of the action as much as I could.

Once the seat backs were flat, I slid over them and into the cargo area. Except for getting my right ankle tangled up in a seat belt shoulder strap, the maneuver worked. The cargo space was filled with gadgets and gizmos I didn't recognize, basic medical kits and a defib unit, and boxes of things that held no interest for me. I pushed and shoved things around, looking for the release but not finding it. I worked up a good sweat.

"Maybe it's in the spare tire compartment under the floor," Jerry suggested.

"And how exactly am I supposed to get down to that with all the crap back here?"

He pulled whatever he could over the collapsed back seat and out of my way.

"Man, Maeve's gonna be pissed," he said.

We were running out of room to move things forward when I spotted a small compartment on the side wall of the cargo bay but down at floor level. It had been hidden behind boxes of gear. I pulled it open. A red button with "EMERG" stamped into it stared back at me. I pressed it. The tailgate released and it beeped its way open.

I looked at Jerry and grinned. "Easier than tunneling our way out of prison," I said. "Can you climb over the seat okay?"

"It's for this very occasion that I've been losing all the weight," he said.

"Hand my bag over first," I told him. If Maeve MacAuliffe abandoned us in Bridgeport after this was all over, I'd need my wallet to pay to get us back downtown.

Once we were both out, I closed the hatch and heard it lock.

Jerry wiped sweat from his face with his handkerchief and asked, "Okay, Houdini, now that you got us out, where do we want to go?"

"Let's mosey on over toward the yellow house," I said, affecting a drawl.

"Not too close," Jerry cautioned. "I'm almost a married man who doesn't want to get any critical parts shot off. And there might be someone inside who could recognize you."

We never got that far. Maeve appeared as we neared the cross street.

"How the hell did you two get out?" She demanded. She wasn't happy.

"You'll probably figure it out," I said, "when you see your SUV."

"Well, if you're going to stay with me," she replied, "you're going to have to do exactly what I tell you. From now on. And I don't have time to argue."

"Don't you have to be up at the house with your troops?" I asked.

"This is a Chicago PD operation initially," she replied, "but my agents are ready. They'll go in once the yellow house is cleared. Maybe we can recover Emily Goodsill unharmed. But we'll have to be quick, or they might kill her on the spot."

MacAuliffe heard something on her headset and peeked around a wall that was hiding us. She nodded. "They're coming back," she said. "We have surveillance on all possible exits. As soon as the three are inside the streets will be blockaded. The go-order will come momentarily. The three of us will stay right here for now."

She touched the bud in her ear again and nodded again. It had started.

63

I heard the muffled crashes of what I thought must be battering rams hitting doors. The now-vacant red brick building on the corner blocked my sensory access to the yellow house. I couldn't see the action and couldn't be certain what I was hearing.

Until the shooting started.

I heard a fusillade of gunfire, undoubtedly from automatic weapons. I saw Jerry cringe beside me. No doubt I'd had the same reaction. Only MacAuliffe seemed unaffected, though I could see tension in her face. People inside were trying to kill cops. That will make any law-enforcement commander tense.

I heard glass shatter, wood splinter, explosions so loud they made my ears hurt even at a distance and muffled by the target building. Although it was broad daylight, I saw intense flashes of light reflected off structures surrounding the yellow house and what looked like white smoke convulsing on the breeze around us. When I got a stinging whiff of it, I knew it wasn't smoke.

From past experience, I guessed the police were trying to disable their opponents with tear gas and flashbangs, also called stun grenades. They produce light so brilliant and explosions so loud that those unprepared to deal with them are left temporarily blind, deaf, and disoriented. While the enemy was disabled, law enforcement could gain control.

Other flashing lights joined the fray from at least two dozen CPD squad cars and FBI vans that squealed in and spun to stops sideways on streets and sidewalks. They cut off the yellow house completely. The newly arrived officers took up positions behind their vehicles and the vehicle doors with guns drawn.

MacAuliffe turned to us. "I'm going to work my way around to my agents in the alley. You two stay right here and stay low. I mean it."

As if on cue, the neighborhood grew quiet.

"Stay here," she yelled at us again as she sprinted off toward the mouth of the alley. It seemed an inappropriate time for me to notice such a thing, but I couldn't help but admire how well MacAuliffe ran in shoes with two-inch heels.

No sooner had she turned the corner than the shooting started again.

"Oh, crap," Jerry said. He didn't elaborate. He didn't have to.

"Emily's probably more terrified than she was before," I said.

"*Bueno.* Good," Jerry replied. "That would mean she's still alive."

Beside me the windshield of MacAuliffe's SUV exploded. I don't mean it developed a small hole with rays of disassembled glass pebbles radiating outward, damage a stone might have caused. It literally exploded, torn in half by the type of ammunition specifically manufactured to tear people and objects to shreds.

Jerry hauled me to the ground at the curb by the SUV's right front tire. The driver's side would have offered more protection, but we couldn't risk exposing ourselves by running around to the street.

I raised my head a little to see if I could tell where the shot came from. The house on the corner across from us, the red brick one, should have absorbed gunfire coming at us from the yellow house, but it hadn't. A moment later I understood why. The bullet that hit the SUV came from that red house, one of the buildings MacAuliffe said the cops had evacuated. This was confirmed when I saw the edge of a second-floor curtain move and the barrel of what looked like an assault weapon poke through.

"Move, now," I ordered Jerry. "Follow me."

He looked at me in surprise, not understanding. So, I got up and sprinted for the rear of the SUV, trying to pull him along. A bullet blew a baseball-sized hole in the sidewalk next to us, and that's when Jerry got my urgency. We made it to the rear of the SUV before another shot came through the broken windshield and the lower part of the tailgate. From the chunk blown out of the asphalt street behind us, I judged the slug had sailed right between us. We moved again, this time to the street-side rear tire. I made a small wish that the next shot didn't puncture the gas tank. I'd come close enough to burning to death once this year. I didn't want to go there again.

"I thought the red house was evacuated," Jerry said when I told him where the shots were coming from.

"They must have sussed out the operation and moved Emily over after they got back from lunch," I said. "They probably broke in before the cops sealed off the yellow house."

I caught motion in my peripheral vision. I saw Jerry's head turn toward it, too. We saw a man drag a staggering woman away from the red house and across the street toward us. He was a big guy and looked as strong as a team of oxen. He had a bear-paw hand wrapped around Emily's arm and an automatic rifle in his right hand, roughly aimed at us.

Jerry had ducked down by the driver's door and put a finger to his lips in the universal sign to be quiet. He drew a Glock from under his jacket. The shooter and Emily continued to walk toward us. I didn't know what to do. I couldn't let him get past us, or we'd never rescue Emily. I also didn't want him to kill us but had no idea how to prevent it. If we got lucky, Jerry might get off a good shot. He remained crouched by the left front tire of the SUV.

Now the gunman and Emily were on our side of the street. I recognized him this time. It was Anthony J. Tricoletto Jr., heir to Chicago's most ruthless crime family.

He yelled at me. "Where's the dude wit' ya?"

I forced myself not to glance down at Jerry.

"He ran away," I said. "He ran up the street." I was counting on the likelihood that Tricoletto Junior lost sight of us when he dragged Emily from the second floor to the street. "I don't know where he is now," I added, wishing we'd both taken that opportunity to run. But that wouldn't have helped Emily.

The gunman, who must have been double my weight, mostly in muscle, moved his eyes around, trying to find some sign of my partner. He was now only three feet from me near the rear of the smashed SUV. I could think of only one thing to try.

The odds were heavily weighted against my survival.

64

"Run, Emily," I screamed as loud as I could. I pushed off the side of the SUV and made a projectile of myself aimed straight at Tricoletto. Shocked by my audacity, he let go of Emily and turned back toward me, the muzzle of his deadly weapon coming to bear on the center of my chest.

I had launched myself at the hand holding the rifle and hit the man so hard I knocked him off his feet. He pulled the trigger, but the force of my body against his chest and arm forced the muzzle upward. His short salvo of shots probably did no damage on the way up. I hoped they didn't hit anyone on the way down.

He landed hard in the grass, on his back. and I landed harder on his chest. The huge exhale he blew in my face told me the twin blows had knocked the wind out of him.

What happened next covered maybe ten seconds of elapsed time, but it seemed like an hour. As I stared down into the face of the gunman struggling to get his breath, my rage grew exponentially, expanding faster than I could control it.

I pushed my left knee into Tricoletto's groin and put as much weight on it as I could. If I crushed him, that would be fine with me. His body tried to lurch against the pressure, but that only increased the pain. I could see it in his face, and I might have smiled. I put my left hand around his throat and squeezed, leaning into that pressure, too, adding to his difficulty breathing. He grabbed my arms and tried to launch me off his chest. I refused to be moved, knowing each second I could sustain the agony in his groin and the pressure around his throat was a second he grew weaker.

"It was you, wasn't it?" I screamed. "You were driving that semi. Weren't you?"

I squeezed his throat harder. I knew if I had been able to use my right hand instead of my left, I'd have crushed his larynx by now.

He couldn't move his head much. But his faced morphed into a sneer, and he nodded enough for me to understand.

I had nothing more to give. My left hand began to cramp. I couldn't maintain the pressure on his throat, and he had begun to recover. He reached over his head and got a grip on the assault rifle. He didn't have enough maneuvering room to bring it around and shoot me. So he wrapped both hands around the muzzle. He could swing the heavy weapon down into my head, using it as a hammer to cave in my skull.

I took a moment to wonder what happened to Jerry and his gun. I realized my body was probably blocking his shot.

I had one chance left. I raised my right arm as high as I could and slammed six pounds of steel-re-enforced plaster cast into the side of Junior's head with all the power I could muster. I saw his eyes glaze.

I raised my arm and hit him again. And again. Five or six times in all. After the fourth blow his arms went limp and the rifle fell from his grasp. Yet I kept hitting him until his body collapsed under me like a balloon doll stuck by a pin.

The strength and life ebbed from Anthony Tricoletto Jr.

Just as the rage and fury drained from me.

* * *

I don't know how long I lay on top of Junior. I knew I didn't have the physical or emotional strength to move. It wasn't long before several pairs of strong hands were lifting me and rolling me onto my back in the grass, everybody asking at once if I was okay. When I looked up, the first person I saw was Jerry Alvarez standing over me with a pistol in his hand hanging at his side.

"You gonna shoot me?" I asked.

He looked startled, as though he'd forgotten he had the weapon. He quickly slid it into the holster on his belt at the small of his back and crouched down beside me, smoothing hair off my sweating face.

"I was about to shoot him when you jumped him," Jerry said. "You blocked my shot."

"Is he dead?" I tried to sit up. Jerry put a hand on my shoulder and pressed me back.

"Quite," Jerry said. "You need to wait for the EMTs. I'm pretty sure they're going to want to take you to the hospital to check out your wrist and replace the cast."

"Replace?..." I raised my right arm, which had gone numb, and saw that the cast had cracked from the fingers to my elbow. And it was covered in blood.

"Mine or his?" I asked Jerry.

"His, thank God. The third blow's the one that broke it. But that didn't stop you."

"I didn't know."

"You didn't care. I have a feeling you were seeing the faces of dead friends."

I nodded. "I kept thinking, *this one's for Ron Colter.* And again. *For Steve Pace.* And again. *For Carl Cribben.* And again. *For the security agents.* And finally, *for me.*"

"I'm so sorry, Deuce," Jerry said. "I wanted to take the shot. I really did."

"I guess this time I'll face some charges, huh?"

"Well, it would be a state case, not federal. But since Junior was intent on killing all of us, I don't think you've got anything to worry about. I'll make a pretty good witness for you." He looked up. "There's somebody else here who wants to have a word with you."

Jerry got up and walked a little way toward Maeve MacAuliffe. Emily Goodsill walked over and took his place beside me.

"You okay?" she asked.

"Unless they decide to amputate my arm, I think so."

Emily looked horrified. I quickly added, "I'm joking." I thought she breathed a sigh of relief. I decided to change the subject.

"Tell me something. Why did you leave the FBI's safe house? That was a huge risk."

"I know that now. But I was so homesick. I miss my mother. I really miss my kids. They were all in danger, too, and I wanted to get a rental car, drive home, and take them all away somewhere that nobody could find us."

"Please, don't run away again. We can't straighten out this mess without you. Let the FBI or federal marshals protect you until this is over. As long as it takes. I'm sure once you're safe they can arrange for you to see your family."

She chewed on her lower lip. Tears welled in her eyes.

"How're you doing now?"

She shook her head. "I caused all this. I'm probably going to prison."

"Look," I said. "I know the whole story. I know why you came to Chicago. I know how you were recruited to work for the Tricoletto family. I know what you did to Frank Chapin. I know you lied about what happened in your office the night Carl Cribben died. I know almost everything. I'm not a lawyer. But if I had to bet, I'd lay a lot of money that after the authorities ask you a whole bunch of questions they'll decide you were in fear for your life, and you were coerced. You're going to be able to head back to Walnut to your family."

"Really?" She asked the question as though she wanted to believe me but didn't.

"Really," I assured her. "You'll see. Relax and enjoy that it's over."

"I'll try. I need to call my Momma."

"Can I ask you a few questions first? They might be hard to talk about, but I need to know the answers."

"Go ahead," she said.

"Why didn't these thugs kill you? I was scared to death that if we ever found you it would be too late."

Now she sat down beside me in the grass and crossed her legs, like a schoolgirl about to play a game of jacks.

"They talked about it a lot," she said, "especially after they caught me when I ran away from the FBI. She pointed toward Junior's body but couldn't bring herself to look at it. "He told me nobody was going to die. He told me he had never killed a woman in his life, never struck a woman in his life. And he wasn't gonna start with me. He said he was brought up in the old Italian way, learning respect for women, for his own mother especially. I'm a mother, too. He said it would be a sin to kill me."

"Somebody told me he was falling in love with you."

"Love is too strong," she said. "I think he had some feelings for me that might have made him hesitate to kill me. But mostly it was his upbringing. The Tricolettos are bad people. They'll search out men they consider enemies and kill them all day and all night. They won't give any of it a second thought. But their respect for women was a powerful and enduring attitude that saved my life."

"Interesting," I said. "But I'm not sure I believe it. I'm a woman. That didn't stop them from trying to kill me. Several times."

Emily regarded me with curiosity for a moment. "I don't know," she said. "I only know what Junior told me. Maybe they didn't care about you because you're not a mother."

I didn't believe that, either.

I had one more question, and it was a big one.

"Emily, do you know how the people who killed Carl Cribben got into your office, past the Medeco lock, and how they relocked the door when they left? Were you there?"

She shook her head vehemently.

"No, no, no, I wasn't there. And I didn't give 'em my key. I didn't even know it was gonna happen."

"Then how?..."

"It started one afternoon, about a week before the hanging, I think. Tony took me to his house to watch a baseball game on TV with some of his friends. One guy was named Joey something. I don't think I ever knew his last name. Tony called him 'Gimp.' At one point, I went into the kitchen with one of the other women to make us all some lunch. I didn't know anything was goin' on in the living room except for the game. But a couple of weeks after the killing, I asked Tony the same question you're asking me. I suspected he'd done the killing or at least set it up. He said while I was in his kitchen makin' sandwiches, this other guy, Joey, took my key ring out of my backpack and memorized the cut of the Medeco. He put the keys back, and later that afternoon he made a duplicate on his own key-cutting machine.

I wasn't sure I believed it. Who can just look at a key and remember it well enough to copy it later? I think he must-a taken a picture of it with his phone."

"Probably not," I said. "Too many witnesses around to see him if he did that."

"So somebody could memorize the key?"

"Someone with an eidetic memory, yes," I said.

"A what?" Emily asked.

I didn't feel like explaining it right then.

* * *

The commotion we caused drew cops—more than a dozen of them with guns drawn—and a couple of EMTs who pronounced Junior. The body was still lying on the lawn. Moving the dead man, even to drag the rifle out of everyone's reach, was off limits until the medical examiner finished with him. But the EMTs did cover him with a sheet. Since the whole world knew how he died and who killed him, preserving evidence of death-by-plaster-cast wasn't a priority.

Maeve MacAuliffe led Emily to her SUV, but when she saw that she had no windshield and the inside of the vehicle had been trashed, she turned the Iowa woman over to another agent, probably with detailed instructions on not letting her get away again. Somehow, I thought Emily was done running.

Pete Rizzo, the spokesman for the Chicago Police Department, bent over Junior, lifted a corner of the sheet, and peered at what was left of Junior's head.

"Good thing there were a lot of witnesses so we know who the guy is," Pete said to me. "Otherwise we'd be waiting on DNA."

He moved over onto one knee next to me. "You cold?" he asked. I realized I was shivering. I nodded. "Maybe shock," he said. He told an officer nearby to get some EMTs and a bus over to us on the double.

Within minutes I had several blankets over me. They didn't stop the cold from the ground from seeping through the back of my clothes and permeating my body. But I heard the rattle of gurney wheels approaching and figured relief was on the way. Hands lifted me up but didn't strap me in. Instead, somebody put a small heating fan under the covers where it blew much-appreciated warm air over me and quickly devoured the chill. The straps came later, after the warmed air had a chance to do its job.

But I wasn't aware of all that. I had closed my eyes and fallen into a shock-induced half sleep.

65

Five weeks later...

The whole sordid mess was a tangled web that wouldn't be resolved for nearly a year, when some kids playing in Dan Ryan Woods way down on the South Side found human remains at the bottom of a steep ravine. It took Tony Donato the better part of a month to positively identify what was left as Michael d'Amato, John Fasso's missing driver. Birds, coyotes, and other woodland creatures had used him as a handy food source until the body decomposed to the point where even the scavengers couldn't tolerate it. The two smallish holes in the back of the skull told the story of how he died. Why he was killed would remain a mystery for the ages. Whether he was part of the crime family who wasn't trusted, or a witness to some events he shouldn't have seen we would never know.

No trace was ever found of the missing security guard from the federal building. Perhaps his remains were at the bottom of Lake Michigan. But since his wife disappeared several months after he did, most speculation focused on the likelihood that they were together on an extended, mob-paid vacation in some remote corner of the globe.

Matteo and Adriana Messina apparently made a clean getaway. Interpol conducted an international search for them to no avail.

As for me, X-rays disclosed that I'd miraculously done no additional damage to my wrist despite the excruciating new pain that dogged me for three days. I was fitted with a new plaster cast and a new sling and told, once again, to take it easy.

Back in the yellow brick house on Thirty-Fifth Street, police and FBI agents had managed to arrest two capos in the Tricoletto family and nine of their crews. That so many were there led the FBI to conclude that they either had information or a hunch about trouble in the offing. Where such information could have come from no one knew. John Fasso, Jimmy Tricoletto's old friend, was an obvious suspect, except that Fasso had no prior knowledge of the raid. Another mystery that would go unsolved.

Speaking of Jimmy Tricoletto, two SWAT officers swore that Jimmy had been in the house when they went in, and both said they saw him draw down on an officer, who shot him. Tricoletto fell, but when FBI agents searched the house after the shooting ended, they found no sign of him. They did find some blood where he had fallen. When the DNA in the blood sample was compared to the older brother, Anthony Junior, the results indicated the samples had come from siblings.

As for Anthony Tricoletto Sr.—"Tony Toes"—he stripped all of his bank accounts and disappeared. FAA records showed that two days after the Bridgeport raid, his private Falcon 900LX had filed a flight plan from O'Hare International Airport to JFK in New York, and on to Le Bourget in Paris. French aviation authorities determined that a day later, the plane flew to Dubai. From there it disappeared. Popular conjecture had it that while in Dubai the plane was repainted and given a registration designation quite different from the one it came with. Then it could have gone anywhere without being recognized, even to Italy, the home country.

There was nothing for Tony Toes to remain in Chicago for. His family had been decimated. His older son was dead, his younger son wounded and in the wind, his criminal infrastructure stripped of much of its manpower and firepower. If he had decided to retire to some remote part of Italy, he might well have taken Jimmy with him to recuperate. If Jimmy survived, he might decide to return to Chicago some day and try to rebuild his father's criminal enterprise, though John Fasso said he didn't think Jimmy had the spine for it. And why risk it? He and his sister were the only heirs to Tony Toes' considerable fortune, wherever it had been stashed. Once you're set for life, why push for more? Especially if it means an all-out war with the Albano

Callisi crime family, which surely was moving swiftly to pick up whatever pieces remained of the Tricoletto empire?

Several of the murders that populated this story were resolved. While it was Virgil Barone who tried to kill me, it was Anthony Junior who garroted Barone while Michael d'Amato drove the Buick. Anthony Junior killed Dominic Tufino, and Jimmy killed Stafano Cappa outside Wrigley field. Other members of the Tricoletto and Callisi families were killed by the two brothers abetted by members of their crews. And, we confirmed later what Anthony Junior seemed to confess as he was dying. It was he who drove the semi into Ron Colter's car and drove us off the interstate. That one hurt.

The murder charges against John Fasso were dropped. When a few of the details of how Fasso helped the police incriminate the governor, Tyler Walston, and clear Frank Chapin, Fasso became something of a hero in the city. The early line on the next mayoral race said he would have a good shot at unseating Marsha Mendes if he chose to take it.

Walston denied every whichway that he played any part in the theft of succinylcholine from the Oak Park Village Hospital. But when two syringes were found in his refrigerator tucked into a head of cauliflower, he gave up everything. He was indicted by the state's attorney for first degree murder and every federal charge Jerry could think of.

Emily Goodsill was not charged with any crime since her participation in the frame of Chapin had been coerced, and because she agreed to testify truthfully to everything she knew. With her cooperation, the Cook County State's Attorney and the U.S. attorney for the northern district of Illinois were able to dismiss all charges against Frank Chapin. Chapin vowed to reopen his construction business and to repair or replace every building that had been put up in violation of building codes. Although the wrongful-death suits that had been filed against him were thrown out of court, he paid the families of each of the victims of the building collapse a half-million dollars to help them defray their expenses and get on with their lives. He, too, was hailed a hero. There was serious talk of him running for governor again in the next election; the lieutenant governor who rose to succession with the demise of Tyler Walston should be easy to beat. But for the time being, at least, Chapin wanted nothing more to do with politics.

Mark cancelled the rest of his trip to California. He set up several webi-
nars to wrap up the obligation via computer lectures, and that worked out
well. I agreed to take that long vacation Eric Ryland had forced on me. Mark
and I would spend two weeks of it in Tahiti.

"Two weeks?" I asked him.

"Might as well," he said. "That's a long time to hang in the sky if you're
only going for a week."

I couldn't argue.

* * *

Two days before we flew out we finished up our vacation shopping along the
Miracle Mile, stashed our packages in Mark's truck, and made it to Spiaggia
for our 7 p.m. reservation. Spiaggia was one of the best high-end Italian
restaurants in Chicago, the sort of place Tony "Toes" Tricoletto would have
called "a rug joint."

We had decided Spiggia would be a good place to begin our vacation,
even though we hadn't left Chicago yet, so we started dinner with a couple
of rounds of Hendricks gin martinis with cucumber garnish. Steve Pace had
taught me to love them. Now we were sharing a Charcuterie appetizer of
soppressata and a beef salami made with American wagyu, eating slowly and
savoring every bite. We were laughing a lot.

"It's really good to see you happy again," Mark said. "The sessions with
Simon must be working out."

"I haven't seen Simon in three weeks," I said.

"You quit?"

"He discharged me."

"You didn't tell me that. Is it something you don't want to talk about?"

"No, actually, I'm pretty okay with it. You wanna hear?"

"Uh, yeah."

"As I was pounding on Junior, very strange things were going on in my
head. With every blow, I felt my anger seep out of me. I saw the faces of
the people he killed, one at a time, one with each fall of my arm. It was like
a colon cleanse for my brain." We both laughed at the distasteful analogy.

"When it was over, when I was lying in the hospital being fitted for a new cast, I realized I actually felt liberated. That's why I was so eager to talk to Simon again. I needed to understand."

"And do you?"

We had to pause as a waiter came by and cleared our empty plates, and another replaced used flatware. A sommelier brought an excellent bottle of cabernet to the table, poured a sip into the cellarman's cup that hung from a chain around his neck, and nodded. He poured a little into each of our glasses. He bowed slightly, said, "Salute," and retreated.

The next course was a gnocchi filled with a ragu of wild boar. Outstanding.

"So, do you?" Mark asked.

"Do I what?"

"Understand why ridding the world of Junior helped you so much?"

"I think I do. I can't explain all the psychological jargon for it, but it forced me to face my demons and helped me beat them back. Last year, when I killed the Saudi who was trying to kill me, it was an accident. I was just trying to get away from him. I hit him in the throat, but it wasn't a killing blow. It wasn't meant to be. He died because he fell straight back and hit his head on the concrete sidewalk. I didn't want that to happen. I had no clear certitude that he deserved to die. So I created a boatload of guilt about it."

"But you were sure with Junior?"

"Absolutely certain. I wasn't trying to play prosecutor, judge, and jury. But I knew without question that if he ever got up from that patch of lawn, more people would die who didn't deserve to die. The crime and corruption that infest this city would continue and grow. I look around me, and don't see anyone prepared to step up and face it down. I'm not a vigilante. Junior came for me, not the other way around. I have no misconceptions that I just stepped out of the pages of a Marvel comic book. I'm an average person who's faced certain death and survived because I did what I had to do when I had to do it."

"I think I get it," Mark said.

"It was me or Junior that afternoon, Mark. I didn't let evil win then. I'm not letting guilt win now."

The staff member who cleared our plates told us, "Your dinners will be right out."

"That's fine," Mark said. He had ordered Italian pork sausages with polenta and rapini. I had ordered lamb tenderloin with root vegetables.

"I'm sorry I brought this up, Deuce," Mark said. "We should be enjoying dinner. It's really quite extraordinary."

"I think it's good to talk about it, especially in a quiet, pleasant atmosphere surrounded by pleasurable things. I hope you understand that I have no intention of prowling the streets after midnight looking for evil to smite. I don't ever want to take another life; I don't want to find myself in a position where I even have to consider it."

"I do understand," Mark said. "And I have a question I want to ask you."

"What's that?" I asked as our dinner plates were set before us.

"You know how we've been sort of planning our itinerary for Tahiti, making reservations where we'll need them but leaving a lot of open time for doing spontaneous things? Well, I'd like to fill one of those spontaneous holes with a plan."

"Sounds intriguing. What is it?"

"While we're in Tahiti," he said, "let's get married."

Acknowledgments

If anyone out there thinks I keep scraps of weird knowledge tucked in the recesses of my brain so I'll have them handy if Deuce Mora ever needs them—like the phenomenon of eidetic memory or the possible murderous uses for succinylcholine (which I can actually spell now without looking it up)—think again.

The "sux" idea was provided by one of the directors of pharmacy at St. Joseph's Hospital in Tampa years ago when I thought I might use it in another book but didn't. As I recall, the good doctor did not want me to disclose his name. I wonder why. And the notion for the eidetic locksmith came from a lock wizard in Raleigh, who actually knew his eidetic counterpart who pulled off the armored car trick. I don't have permission to name him, either, but he knows how grateful I am.

Among those I can name, my eternal thanks to David Ehrman, who made so many brilliant suggestions I lost count. David, a veteran television writer/ producer in Hollywood, is the best "story" person I've ever known. Ever.

Thanks also to Dr. Kathaleen Porter, who endured a year of questions about the medical uses for sux and the effects of the drug. She claims she's never used it for murder, and I tend to believe her.

A tip of the green eyeshade to my therapist/author/painter friend Deborah Dunn for her help in defining grief and dealing with it.

Also, my thanks to Julie Smith and Mittie Staininger of booksBnimble, and Kimberly Hitchens of Booknook, without whom the Deuce Mora series wouldn't exist. Also to crack copy editor Jessica Tastert who expunged all my typos and other errors.

Finally, a tip of the hat to my Sarasota, Florida buddy, Howard Hickok. He knows why.

About the Author

JEAN HELLER

My mother once confronted my husband and me, put her hands on her hips, and asked,

"Can't one of you hold onto a job?"

She was joking – sort of. Both of us were journalists, and we kept getting better jobs, which required moving. A lot. Moving frequently is, I have discovered, a good way to avoid having to clean out the closets, the garage, and the cabinets under the kitchen sink.

Through it all, I have been one thing above all else, a writer, a journalist for most of my career.

I started my first novel when I was in the third grade, the story of people living at the center of the earth. I liked the concept, but I really didn't have a good plot point, and when I discovered what it's really like at the center of the earth, the project went up in flames, so to speak.

My first complete novel, a thriller called "Maximum Impact," was published by Forge, an imprint of St. Martin's Press, in 1993. It was nominated for a Pulitzer Prize. My second, "Handyman," came two years later. Both received great reviews from critics and readers.

My current series features Deuce Mora, lead columnist for the Chicago *Journal.* Deuce normally writes about politics, but every once in a while her search for a good story brings her face to face with more trouble than she can handle.

The first Deuce mystery, "The Someday File," won wide reader and critical acclaim. The second, "The Hunting Ground," was hailed as even better, and won a national award.

The series is set in Chicago, a city I have loved since I was in college and which I called home for years. I set the stories here because Chicago is such a great character in its own right. The stories I can build on these bones – quite literally in the case of "The Hunting Ground" – have infinite possibilities.

* * *

Jean's news career included serving as an investigative and projects reporter and editor for The Associated Press in New York City and Washington, D.C., *The Cox Newspapers* and *New York Newsday* in Washington, D.C. and the *St. Petersburg Times* in Washington, D.C. and Florida. Jean has won multiple awards, including the Worth Bingham Prize, the Polk Award, and is an eight-time Pulitzer Prize nominee and twice a Pulitzer finalist.

**Want to learn more about the mystery
that changed Steve Pace's life?**

Check out **MAXIMUM IMPACT**, *a chilling Pulitzer Prize-
nominated thriller of aviation tragedy, political exploitation, and
corporate corruption.*
*Airline engines are designed for dependability, and the new Converse
engines are as good as airplane engines get. But when one self-
destructs it destroys the plane and kills more than 300 people.*
*The initial explanation doesn't wash with Steve Pace, Pulitzer Prize-
winning reporter for the Washington Chronicle. When several sources
die mysteriously, it seems to be undeniable evidence that someone
will go to any extreme to cover up the truth.*
*Pace must race a lethal deadline before another Converse-powered
plane meets the same fate and hundreds more die.*

*Read this riveting thriller and the rest of the Deuce Mora mystery
series on Amazon Kindle or in print editions.*

Printed in the USA
CPSIA information can be obtained
at www.ICGtesting.com
LVHW090730020724
784417LV00033B/257